PRAISE FOR *MEETING TWILIGHT*

*"Don't miss this gripping first book in Aria's
story as the adventure begins!"*

—Early Reader Review

*"Meeting Twilight is the roguish adventure of Percy
Jackson blended with the whimsical world-building
of Harry Potter! I absolutely adored the characters and
fell in love with the fantastic magical world they are
woven into. This is absolutely a book that will cause
you to become a book dragon and devour it all!"*

—Cheyenne Nielsen, Editor

*"Magic, summer camps, enchantments, and creepy old
mansions. Aaralynn keeps you reading until the very last page!"*

—Early Reader Review

*"…Characters and friendships you'll be
sad you have to leave behind."*

—Early Reader Review

Meeting Twilight

For information contact:
Sunflower Petals Press, LLC
sunflowerpetalspress.com

Hardcover: 978-1-7347736-2-0
Paperback: 978-1-7347736-3-7
Ebook: 978-1-7347736-4-4

First edition September 2023

Edited by Cheyenne Nielsen
Cover Design by Damonza

MEETING TWILIGHT

THE GREAT DIVINER SERIES
· BOOK 1 ·

AARALYNN KARMAN

Sunflower
Petals Press

"There is a light and there is a way through every darkness and down every path. You just have to find it and keep going. Don't give up."

—A note from the author

Pronunciation Guide

Characters
Alaric: a-lar-ic
Malus: mah-lus
Malamone: mal-uh-MONE
Celaena: suh-LAY-nuh
Avi: AEY-VYE
Ciaus: KAI-us
Viola: VYE-OLE-uh

Places
Vezchia: vez-CHEE-uh
Tungsinn: Tongue-sin
Viden: VYE-den
Hora: HOR-uh

Other
Nevidit: NEE-VEE-DEET

A Legendary Blast

IT ALL BEGAN with one tragic event in the Vezchia Realm that changed everything. What happened that day of August 2, 1713, all started with the leader of the Dark Forces—a group of malicious and harmful people—Alaric Malamone, and his eighteen-year-old son, Malus.

It was in the gloomy countryside of Tungsinn where there is now only one house—the Malamone Mansion—that the famous blast was sent out across the Vezchia Realm. There used to be a town of kind people that surrounded the mansion. All the people of the Tungsinnian town had avoided the contemptible house of the Malamones'. However, the town mysteriously disappeared in the late 1700s with only a few people knowing what had happened to it. The Tungsinnian language died out and there was almost no trace that they had ever existed.

In the Malamone Mansion, on the dense, fog-filled day of August 1, 1713, sat Malus and Alaric Malamone at their supper. The chefs had prepared a massive, elegant meal of pot roast, potatoes, chipock, tarts, roasted vegetables, rolls, and soups for them. But Alaric's head hung low and pale, and he wasn't eating anything.

"What is it, Father?" Malus' menacing bright green eyes noticed the glum look upon his father's face. The fine white dress shirt, black pants, and frilly collar Malus wore matched the proper decor of the room. His long blond hair tied with a white ribbon cascaded down his back. He sat on the other side of the long wooden table that had many empty chairs situated around it, across from his father.

"My son, I have discovered how to make two stones," Alaric said, looking down at his plate with a tightened jaw.

Malus couldn't restrain a gasp. Every day since he was eight, he'd walk past the study as his father flipped through books, old scrolls, and maps. He'd been easily drawn towards the room, wanting to see what his father was up to, but he was always pushed away. Rumors had spread through the mansion that Alaric was researching dark, unthinkable magic. Despite Malus' efforts, he never could find a way to figure out what his father's ambitious plans were.

"One will make me immortal and the other will allow me to draw power from whoever I wish," Alaric continued. "Not only that, but one will curse the Diviner so she can no longer use her full power. Once she is weaker, we can kill her. The Forces of Light will be weakened without her on their side." He didn't finish as happily as Malus thought he would. His father seemed to blend into his chair with a black cloak on, but a gold dagger embroidered on the right shoulder and his lowered hood that revealed his thin face easily gave him away. It was this that the Dark Forces wore most of the time, the dagger representing them.

Malus' eyes widened and his mouth hung open. *How could such magic be possible?*

"That's great, Father!" Malus dropped his fork to the table

with a clunk, and a surprised smile lit his face. "We can finally rid the realms of the great Diviner!"

"It is not that easy, my son, for to forge the Stones, I must spill the blood of that which I love." At those words, a single tear filled Alaric's eye, but he blinked it away and looked down at his tightened fist resting on the table.

Malus' stomach tightened, his lip trembled, and he took in a quick breath as he immediately understood the words that had come out of his father's mouth. "Do you mean me, Father?"

"I am afraid so." Alaric glanced up at his son with a sternness flickering in his eyes.

"Then we cannot forge them…" Malus looked down at his roast and potatoes with a frown. A sigh escaped his lips and his heart felt like it was sinking into the pit of his stomach.

"I will still make the Stones. The Forces of Light are far too powerful with the Diviner and I am far too weak to stop them. I am growing old, son, and I will not let myself die." Alaric couldn't meet Malus' eyes.

"But father!" Malus shouted, his voice cracking on the words, and stood up quickly from his seat, banging his fists on the table. His heart was suddenly hammering against his ribs and he felt a pain swelling in his heart. "You can't! I'm your son!"

Alaric's hooded guards approached Malus from their posts at the door and seized his arms, their faces concealed behind their large hoods.

"Throw him in the cellar!" Alaric's face looked heated and thin, a single tear sliding down his cheek. He wiped the tear away with a sudden ire and furrowed his eyebrows.

Malus tried to fight back, screaming, but one of the hooded men hit him with an Immobile Enchantment, causing every one of his limbs to grow weak and limp. The enchantment took over and he was dragged down to the wine cellar with ease.

Malus was locked in the cellar all night, the cold night air wiggling through the bricks of the mansion. When the enchantment wore off, he got up off the frigid concrete ground and tried to pry open the sealed door. No matter how much he pulled, it stayed stuck and made his skin turn white around his knuckles. He grabbed every wine bottle off the shelves and threw them against the walls, shattering them across the floor.

After his mother passed, he'd been shoved away—from love, from fighting, even from his own father. His father had stopped teaching him to practice magic, so he and his only friend, Viola Hunts, snuck into the backyard to teach themselves. Viola had taught him everything she knew, and when they ran out of things to learn, they snuck into the old library of the mansion and took books to learn from. He could still recall the very moment they'd met on the steps of Tungsinn's orphanage at eight years old. He had tried to sneak his way past the guards standing outside his father's study, but as soon as he'd made it past the door, his father had stood up and yelled at him to leave. So, he did; not bothering to pay attention as he came to the lower end of town. A tugging on his arm had snapped him out of his tears, then he saw Viola standing there next to him with a look of understanding. They'd been inseparable since. Because the orphanage had taught her all the basics of magic, she'd taught him what his father wouldn't. It wasn't until now that he understood why his father tried to keep him from practicing it.

He sat on the rough concrete floor of the wine cellar, trying to keep the cold draft from seeping through his clothes. How could his own father sacrifice him? *This is the Diviner's fault! She killed my mother and now because she is too powerful, my father is betraying me,* Malus concluded, his hands balled up into tight fists. He had wanted the Diviner to pay for his mother's death. Now he wished she would pay for his father's betrayal as well. He wanted to punch his shaking fists into the stone wall to distract him from the lump in his throat or the aching feeling building in his chest. His father's words echoed inside his head, *'I must spill the blood of that which I love.'* The one thing Alaric didn't get, though, was love. He would never be able to understand it. Alaric may say he loves something…but even if he did, it wasn't very much because Alaric always put himself first.

The morning of August 2nd approached, and Malus woke to a cold breakfast waiting for him on the floor of the cellar. Lunch came and went, and soon it was nearing supper. The door burst open and Alaric grabbed Malus by the arm, dragging him into the next room over where he did his weapon-making.

The room was empty of people, with a metal table in the middle. Shelves and shelves of weapons and tools covered the red brick walls. Malus' boots scuffed across the rough concrete flooring as he was shoved forward. Bowls bubbled with scalding crimson liquids on the table, glowing in the low light. A necklace chain and golden ring were perched beside them. Two molds for the stones sat askew beside various other deadly materials of illegal and dark magic origin. The smell of the musty room stung his nostrils as he breathed in poison-laced air.

"Moltens were here last night to help me." Alaric let go of Malus. "I have done almost everything I needed to do," he continued, but Malus wasn't listening.

Malus charged towards the door, but it slammed in his face. Despite his best efforts, he couldn't pry it open. He had two options: he could attack his father and force him to free him, or he could try to reason with him. Maybe, just maybe, there was some mercy in him.

"I need your arm, son." A dagger glinted in Alaric's hand as he took it down off a shelf.

"Please! Father, don't do this!" Malus pleaded, his voice cracking, and held his trembling hands in front of his chest as if to use magic against Alaric. "There has to be another way! I am your son!"

Alaric looked at him through solemn eyes, his lips carved into a frown. "There is no other way. Son, I was hoping one day you would learn that there are only two options in life: rule or be ruled. There is no love or mercy. There are just people too weak to do what must be done."

Malus received a piercing stare from his father and his face fell, suddenly feeling that maybe he *was* weak. His father's words were getting to him. He felt that maybe he could change his father's mind still…That maybe there was still a bit of care in him.

Malus hurried to think, his mind running to a memory that took place right before his mother had been killed. Flickering sparks of magic had appeared in his palms and his parents had applauded, Malus' young face beaming up at them. If he could just remind his father of the love they'd once shared…

"Father, do you not remember when I did my first enchantment? You said you were so proud of me, and Mother did, too. But after the Diviner killed her in that fight—"

"Don't you dare speak of her!" Alaric's voice rose over the quiet of the room and his face seemed to turn as flushed as the red-hot liquids on the table.

"I was just four! And you abandoned me—" Pain swelled up across his skin and Malus fell to the floor, grabbing the side of his face where his father had hit him. His head hit against the cement, knocking him unconscious.

Alaric didn't bother to check his pulse as he sliced Malus'

arm open and spilled his blood into the two solutions. Believing his only son was gone, he left him on the floor of the room and went to finish making the Stones.

A blast burst from the mansion the moment the stones were completed, rampaging across the Vezchia Realm. Malus flew against the wall and the impact knocked him back into reality. Pain lanced through his arm, and he clutched it tightly to stop the bleeding. In the shadows of the room, he dragged himself to a pile of cleaning cloths and rags having been used to clean Alaric's workspace. He tied the rags around his arm as tightly as he could, drawing the wound closed.

Alaric left the chamber, his heart beating like a ferocious fire as the white Life Stone hung around his neck. He wrapped his fingers around the empty, black Death Stone to be hidden until he was ready to use it. On a piece of parchment, he wrote a riddle with the information on how to find and destroy the Death Stone, but it's said that it's unable to be understood by anyone else.

He left the mansion to hide the Death stone, abandoning Malus on the rough, icy floor of the dark room. As Malus tended to his wound, drawn up against the wall, he heard footsteps and the calling of his name in the main part of the house. The second he heard the strong, confident, female voice, his heart lifted. He knew Viola's voice anywhere. The clacking of her shoes echoed just above the staircase leading down to the cellar.

He tried to push up from the ground, but his muscles gave out, and he yelled, "Help!"

The sound of her footsteps grew louder in the darkness. The door flew open and Viola stood there, flicking her hands in the air to illuminate all the candles in the room. Her long obsidian-black dress with purple lace ruffled around her leather boots as they clacked against the floor. She fell to her knees at his side, her black, wavy hair falling like a waterfall from her messy bun, and her chocolate brown eyes flickered with horror.

"Malus, what happened to you?" Viola asked, her voice cracking.

His voice was rough like sandpaper scraping against his throat, so he lowered it to explain everything as she helped him to his feet. Pain shot through his arm and a headache pounded in his head. The more he told her, the more her eyes narrowed to slits and red-hot anger blazed beneath her skin. It seemed impossible to both of them that he was even alive, but that made him question if the Stones would even work.

"Your father will pay," she growled.

Upstairs in the lounge, Viola applied medicine to the slice in his arm, then tied it shut again. Malus gritted his teeth against the pain, tears threatening to escape his eyes. He blinked them away. *No, I will not be weak.* It was no longer bleeding, but dry blood covered his arm and his face was lost of color.

"I need to get you to a Healer." Viola secured the new piece of cloth on his arm with a knot.

"No, not yet," Malus said through clenched teeth.

"But Malus—"

"I have to take care of something first." Malus' face turned scarlet, and a mercilessness set into his eyes.

Later that night, Alaric Malamone finally returned to his house. He went up the curved staircase in the dark, an eerie silence filling the air. The lighting throughout the mansion was dim, allowing shadows to form. He turned in the direction of his office and out of the corner of his eye, he caught movement. Malus stepped out from the room behind Alaric. Alaric's heart nearly leapt out of his chest as shock crackled through his veins. Malus had been waiting, and behind him,

Viola helped to hold him up. An Immobile Enchantment shot from Malus' hand and hit his father in the chest, making him fall to the floor. He bent over and snatched the Life Stone from around his father's neck, then hung it around his own. Malus used the Life Stone on his own father that day, giving himself life and reviving the strength that had been stolen from him. The last expression Malus saw before Alaric's eyes glazed over with his last breath was utter disbelief. And so, the Life Stone did actually work even if Malus hadn't died, but that had him questioning everything his father had believed.

The years turned into decades, and then into centuries. Malus could have turned out okay if his father had not put himself first. Malus could have been innocent, but instead, Malus Malamone became the new leader of the Dark Forces. The Diviner had disappeared and though the Dark Forces looked, she was unable to be found. Malus took life after life so he would continue to live, looking young as the years went by, Viola always by his side.

Malus had everything that was his father's…except the Death Stone. For the next two centuries, he searched everywhere for it, but it was nowhere to be found. He watched the ways of people change as time moved on, himself changing along with them. The Dark Forces were no longer the biggest thing people feared. The Dark Days were over. At times, people could forget they were lurking around in the shadows of the Vezchia Realm. Schools and camps made by the Forces of Light had been put up in the Mundane Realm in the beginning of the Dark Days so that children fleeing with their families could still learn magic. As the Dark Forces influence faded away, the schools started accepting enchanters and enchantresses who didn't yet know about magic and might never find out. Many people wanted to leave the world of magic far behind them, thinking it was a dangerous thing. There were those that feared Malus and his Life Stone, but many people no longer believed self-protection was a first priority. The Diviner became a legend, a debate, and a fairy tale to tell children so that they could have a sliver of hope that one day the Dark Forces would be gone for good.

In the late 1900s, Malus fell in love for the first time. He married a woman, and he shared the life he'd collected from the Life Stone with her. She bore a child named Seth Malamone, and they were happy for a time. But his wife got sick soon after the child's birth and the Life Stone was unable to save her. He fell into a depressed, merciless, heart-wrenching fury. He made no progress in taking over the world like he wanted, he couldn't find the Death Stone, and he had to raise a child by himself. After his wife died, he added to his plans. He wanted to find the next Diviner and draw power from them once he had the Death Stone. Drawing power from the Diviner would make him even more powerful than drawing power from an ordinary enchanter or enchantress, even if the Diviner had lost their powers. The powers run in the veins, locked away, just out of reach.

Chapter One

T HE WALLS WERE painted a hideous mustard yellow, which she'd hated the whole year she had lived there. She was never allowed to repaint the walls. All that was left in the room was the bed that had been stripped of the sheets, pillows, and blankets. Boxes stuffed as much as they would allow were pushed against the wall of the room. There were only a couple of boxes, as most of it had already been taken out to the moving truck.

Aria stood there, her light blue eyes staring at the emptiness of everything. Her wavy brown hair swung behind her back as she turned, rubbing her hand over her freckled face in exhaustion. She was quite speechless, a weird feeling bubbling in the pit of her stomach. Was it the annoyance of going to a new school? The frustration of moving *again*? She had no clue what to expect or what to feel. Her parents always said they moved because of their jobs. Aria understood, but she didn't even know what their jobs exactly were; they never elaborated and always got distracted. Her fists clenched at the thought, a strange pulsing like the beat of a heart forming in her palms, and she blew out an irritated sigh.

A knock sounded on the door behind her, startling her out of her trance-like state. She turned towards the door, her eyes settling on her father. He waltzed into the room, his graying brown hair causing a halo of silver. His smile made the edges of his dark eyes twinkle. He was always smiling, especially when Aria was around, which usually brightened Aria's spirits, but not at this moment.

"Oh…hey, Dad," she said in a bored tone, sounding almost dazed.

He continued to look happy as a crew of men and women appeared behind him to grab the rest of the stuff from her room.

"Is something wrong, sweetie?" he asked, dropping his wide smile and looking at her kindly.

"Oh, nothing…I—I just don't like that we have to keep moving all the time." She stared down at her fidgeting hands.

"Oh…well…you know, your mother and I have…jobs that…keep us on the move." His gaze abruptly changed to the window, his feet tapping anxiously on the floor.

That was what he had said last time, but still, it made Aria's jaw clench. She forced herself to keep her mouth shut despite the desire to ask for the truth. Her fists grew tighter, the throbbing of her palms growing stronger. Of course, she knew they were not doing anything shady despite how secretive they were about it. Aria knew and trusted them too well to think that; they were her parents, after all. If they didn't want to tell her things, they didn't have to. Everyone has their own secrets. Even if Aria wanted to know what they were.

"Yeah, I understand that." Aria breathed in deeply, pushing down her irritation. She glanced back at the room again, stepping out of the way as the crew of men and women carried things past them.

"Well…what would happen if we moved into an igloo and

some friends threw us a *housewarming* party?" He changed the subject, drawing Aria's attention back to him.

She raised her eyebrow, trying to hold back the smile that was already threatening to show. "I don't know. We're not moving into an igloo this time, right?" She joked.

"We'd be homeless," he finished with a silly smile on his face. "You know, because it would melt from the party."

Aria shook her head and rolled her eyes, but her wide grin was showing now. "That was horrible." She laughed.

"Really? I found it on a website. It said it was a really good joke. Anyway, we should get this stuff out to the moving truck."

They picked up a few boxes and exited the room. Aria's mother gazed at the empty walls of the living room that would soon become condemned with dust until someone bought the house. Her brown hair fell off her shoulders as she turned her freckled face to look at Aria and her father with soft blue eyes. Aria and her father walked outside, the air nipping at their skin. The leaves on trees were just beginning to bloom. After such a long winter, it was nice for the weather to finally be brighter.

They loaded the last of the things into the moving truck and shut it up tightly. Most of the crew headed into a separate small business van and drove out of sight now that they had done their job. A few movers got into the moving truck to take it to the new house. Aria looked at the house one last time, her heart clenching with the fact that they were abandoning another home. Her eyes settled on the gardens overrun by weeds; nobody had ever had the chance to fill them with flowers. Her mother came out of the door and locked it behind her.

"Well, off we go." Aria's mother cheerfully walked down the path that led up to the front door.

Aria took a deep breath of the fresh countryside air before she got into the back seat of the small maroon vehicle. Her parents clattered into the car and pulled the doors shut with a bang. The old vehicle roared to life, her father turning the key in the ignition. He looked back at Aria, who stared at the floor of the vehicle. She appeared like a dismal, rain cloud. Wrapped up in a cocoon of her own worries about moving, filled with the uneasiness of going to some new school, she didn't even hear her parents whisper to each other under their breaths, "She'll be fine. It's for the best."

The car stumbled over the bumpy swaths of empty road like a cloak spread out into the horizon. Aria barely watched out the window, fidgeting with her golden sunflower necklace that sparkled when the sun hit it. As her fingers found the grooves of each petal, thoughts of school entered her mind. She didn't like school in the slightest. Strange occurrences always happened around her that made her look foolish, and then people turned her into a gag. Sometimes she could still hear people chanting *'Aria's a weirdo'* over and over. Seven years ago, the bullying had started, and it had crushed her like a rock against a fly. She'd been seven, pretending to be a fairy princess with flowers in her hair, when the school bullies had walked up to her at recess. Her heartbeat had fluttered into her palms as they tore her flower crown off her head and stomped it to pieces on the ground, calling her weird. Sorrow had filled her, overflowing like a glass cup, then shattering to pieces as the nearby tree's branches began to break off. The sticks were large, barely missing her and the bullies as they scattered. From that moment on, the strangeness only continued and followed her from one school to the next. She ignored them, but that did not mean that it didn't hurt her. Every time she moved, she usually joined a school in the middle of the year, which was the worst. This year, she'd be joining in the middle of March.

Seven years ago, Aria had told her parents about how

horrible school was, but when they contacted the school, the bullies just came back even harder. Ever since then, her parents never knew what went on at school. Aria wanted to stick up for herself. She didn't want to put any worries on her parents, and she definitely didn't want any more trouble for telling them.

As for the new house, she really didn't care what it was like because they were sure to move again within the next year. For as long as she could remember, she'd never had any neighbors close enough to truly call them neighbors because they always lived in the countryside. The countryside life was nice though; it meant less people, more fresh air, trees, and glorious fields of flowers and vegetables.

The car suddenly pulled to a halt under the coral sky after what felt like days of boredom. She opened the door and stepped out into the nipping air. She clutched her arms and pulled her sage green sweatshirt tighter on her as an evening breeze swept past her. Her eyes fell on the small, old house and her heart sank. Overall, the house was not the prettiest sight to see. The paint was wearing away, the wind made the old windows rattle, and the pavement was cracked. Dense cornfields were growing on both sides of the house and a silhouette of thick forest grew off in the distance. The sunset on the horizon highlighted the distant farms with gold. Aria blew out an exasperated puff of air as her father went to open the light blue door of the house.

Her mother appeared beside her with a soft smile. "Darling, go have a look inside and then we will start taking some things in." She gave Aria a gentle rub on the back.

Aria shoved her hands into the pockets of her sweatshirt and walked slowly up to the house. The front door was now wide open. Inside, her father was taking a look at the empty, dusty living room. Aria frowned at the banana yellow walls, recalling the mustard ones in the old house as her feet dragged over the gray carpet.

"Nice, isn't it?" Her father turned to her with a grin, his hands on his hips.

Nodding, she glanced around the room. "Yeah. Where's my room?"

"To the left at the end of the hall."

She followed the hall to the end, where there was a small room with lively purple walls. Her feet shuffled over the gray carpet as she stared out the wide window overlooking the front yard drenched in fading light. A golden glow shone through the window and onto an abandoned dresser up against the wall. She gave a quick nod of approval and went back to help her parents unload.

As Aria stepped onto the path leading to the driveway, the moving truck rolled to a stop in front of the house. The doors opened and boxes began to be taken inside. Her father stood behind in the living room, his voice floating to her ears from him ordering pizza.

Aria plopped down on the floor beside her parents and the movers, surrounded by random boxes and furniture. She sank her teeth into the pizza with a crunch, the fluffy crust caving in her mouth and flooding her senses with warm butter and parmesan. Aria's parents were kind enough to share the pizza with the movers and Aria's mother tried to include them in conversation so they wouldn't feel awkward.

"What are you if you can't choose what kind of pizza you want?" her father suddenly asked, a silly smile spreading across his face.

"Oh no!" Aria laughed, nearly choking on her pizza when she saw the movers' faces.

They raised their eyebrows in confusion, turning their gaze to Aria and her father, their eyes switching back between the two of them.

"Here come the dad jokes." A smile swept across Aria's face.

"You're inde-*slice*-ive." He gave himself a round of applause and Aria snorted.

"That was so cringy," she told him, but laughed in spite of herself.

"No, I would say it was *cheesy.*" He held up his cheese pizza, smiling so wide that the edges of his eyes crinkled, before he scrunched up his face to look like a fish.

Aria tossed her head back and laughed. The movers were grinning a little too. Honestly, the joke wasn't even that funny, but whenever her father made fish lips, he looked ridiculous. It always made Aria laugh, which brought him the greatest joy.

"Oliver, we have guests over," her mother teased with a grin. "At least don't do the fish lips. You'll make Aria laugh so hard she'll choke on her pizza."

"All right, fine," he replied, dropping his fish lips.

Aria stood, trying to calm her breathing back down from all the laughing as she threw out her paper plate.

Under the ebony sky, Aria, her parents, and the movers passed in and out of the house. Aria's arms ached from heaving boxes back and forth. The house seemed to sigh with relief as the movers left and she kicked off her shoes. She looked about her room, at the boxes stacked against the wall, and sighed. A frown sagged at her lips, and she tried to add a mental tally to the number of homes she'd lived in. But she'd already lost count. Her teeth worried her lower lip and she tried to push her rising frustration down, a tingling starting in the palms of her hands again. She flicked off the light and sunk into her bed, clenching her eyes shut against all her thoughts.

Bright light flooded the window and Aria opened her eyes, warily looking around the new room. She sighed with relief as she realized it was Sunday. No School. But irritation bubbled in the back of her mind like an unwanted guest. Pulling her CD player from a box, she turned it on and allowed the music to drive out her thoughts while she pressed forward with work on her room. *I Won't Give Up* by Olivia Marshall came on and Aria's eyes lit with passion, the lyrics rolling off the tip of her tongue. She turned to tape up her artwork above her desk, lost in the song and rapture of beautiful flowers and fields. The CD slowed to a silence, allowing all her thoughts to crash back into her mind and the door creaked open. Her mother stood in the doorway with a slight smile adorning her face.

"Hey," Aria forced a smile onto her face.

"What's up, darling? How are you settling in?"

"Good." Aria gestured around at all that she had organized so far as her mother walked to sit on the edge of her bed.

"It looks great!" Her mother patted next to her, her eyes searching Aria's face for a moment.

Aria plopped down next to her. "What is it, Mom?"

"I just want to know how you really feel, Aria. I'm not a mind-reader, so you'll have to tell me."

"Mom, I…" Aria's words died. "I don't know. All I know is I just don't want to go to school tomorrow."

"I understand. Going to a new school is hard, but try to make friends this time. If you talk to people, they'll talk to you." She gave Aria a soft rub on the back.

That was what her parents always thought her problem with school was. That she had a hard time making friends, which was true, but not the whole story.

"Thanks, mom."

"Of course, and if you need anything, just come get me or your father." Her mother pushed to her feet.

Just as her mother reached the door, Aria dared to ask, "Mom?"

"Yes, darling?"

"What are yours and Dad's jobs?"

Her mother's eyes widened the slightest bit and she bit her lip, looking as if she was pondering something for a moment. "We help people." She smiled kindly before grabbing the doorknob and shutting the door quietly.

That was what she had said last time, and the time before that, but it was vague. Helping people could be a hundred different jobs. Aria's fists clenched and she fell backwards on her bed, blowing out an annoyed puff of air.

It felt like the day had gone by in a flash, and Aria's hands were now getting shaky and clammy. Butterflies filled her stomach, and she had a strange throbbing feeling in her hands. The pulsing felt so familiar and intense, like a calling she had felt before. There was another feeling inside her, too, like a caged animal wanting to escape. Wishing she could prolong the day somehow, but knowing she couldn't, she went to bed with her heart beating intensely.

CHAPTER TWO

THE SUN WAS just beginning to come up over the farms that dotted the horizon outside Aria's window. With a yawn, she sat up out of bed and kicked the covers off her. Her head ached from the turmoil of nightmares.

She'd been in the middle school cafeteria, sitting alone after the window in history class flew open and blew the papers all around. Before that, she'd been handed a test marked with a red F. Her first F. One of the boys behind her began to snicker, glancing over her shoulder. A lump had risen in her throat and her hands grew shaky, a pulsing beginning to tingle in her hands. She'd tried to shut it out of her head, but that same boy, Billy Jones, came up behind her in the cafeteria, sneering at her grade and claiming she had something to do with the window flying open. Everyone always linked her to the strange happenings that went on around her, like it was somehow her fault. She had no idea what it could be, only that she was easiest to blame always being the new girl. As Billy Jones continued to poke at her feelings, her tray of sloppy joe flew up from the table, her hands pulled into tight, throbbing fists. Sloppy joe dripped down her face, sticking in her hair, and everyone in the vicinity laughed.

That had not been just some nightmare, though. It had happened at her old school. That day when she'd gone home, she lied about why her clothes were stained, saying it was just a mishap in art class. She wanted to stick up for herself and not burden her parents with her problems.

Aria got out of bed as slowly as possible, hoping maybe she could miss the bus. But then it hit her like the ringing of a bell that the school she was about to go to doesn't have buses. Sighing, she went to take a shower and got dressed in simple clothes. After brushing her tangled brown hair and putting on the sunflower necklace her parents had given her for her birthday, she grabbed her gray fabric school bag she'd left on the side of her bed. Some notebooks had toppled out, so she made sure to shove them back in before grabbing her sweatshirt off her bedpost. She'd be going to a private school about a couple miles away, and as she pulled on her favorite sage green jacket, she felt relief she wouldn't be required to wear a uniform. As she walked out of the room, she slid her bag onto her shoulder.

The sound of pots clanging and the shuffling of boxes met her ears as she entered the modest kitchen. Her mother set a box on the granite countertop, underneath the white, wooden cabinets.

"Good morning, sweetie!" her father said joyfully as he stood up from the box he was unpacking.

"Good morning." She forced a dull smile.

Her mother turned away from putting the pots and pans away in the cupboard and said, "Oh, good morning! We are going to pick up donuts from the town bakery for breakfast, then we'll take you to school."

"That sounds great!" Aria said, trying to sound as enthusiastic as possible, but ended up sounding fake instead. The empty pit in her stomach seemed to grow wider and the strange pulsing feeling started in her hands again.

Her mother and father pushed the boxes to the side and disappeared down the hall. Heat crept into her cheeks at the thought of going to school and everyone seeing both her parents with her. She felt like a small child. Hopefully, donuts would lift her spirits.

Aria slipped on her shoes by the front door, clutching her sunflower necklace with shaky hands and tapping her foot on the floor. It felt like a million minutes trapped in just a few before they walked out of the house together, her mother locking the door behind them. The early spring air was brisk and moist. Dark clouds hung in the sky, waiting for the perfect time to let the rain fall. The three of them walked down the path and got into the old maroon car. Aria looked out the windows this time. A car went by every so often as they drove down the dirt road. The drive was bumpy, but Aria was used to such roads. More and more buildings popped up as they approached the town, the road changing from dirt to concrete. Small businesses were all over the place and not a piece of litter lingered, like a perfect picture you might see online.

Aria's father parked the car in a teeny tiny dirt parking lot next to another strip mall. They climbed out of the car as a drop of rain landed on Aria's jacket. Then another and another as they walked into the bakery. The smell of fresh pastries and sweet icings hit her in the face. Two small tables sat by the two, giant floor-to-ceiling windows at the front of the bakery. The display case was filled with donuts, cupcakes, lovely cakes, and all sorts of yummy desserts.

"How can I help you today?" The cashier flipped her blond hair back.

"Could I get a glazed chocolate donut with sprinkles, please?" Aria said.

The cashier opened the display case from behind the counter

and grabbed the donut, then handed it to her. While her mother and father ordered their donuts and paid, she sat at one of the tables by the windows. A few minutes later, parents walked over and sat down with her as she bit into the warm, fluffy donut. The delectable pastry did manage to lift her spirits slightly.

"Thanks for the donut." Aria grinned and it managed to reach her eyes.

"Of course, darling. We have no food in the house anyway. I'll have to head to the store while you're in school," her mother said.

"How did I know you were going to ask for a chocolate donut?" Her father smiled.

"I don't know. Maybe because I like chocolate?" Aria raised an eyebrow in question.

"Yeah, you do, like, *a lot*." Her father laughed. "But...I just thought of a joke."

"Okay, what is it?"

"Why did the donut go to the dentist?"

"Hmm..." Aria thought for a moment, wanting to beat her father at his jokes for once, as she ate her donut. "Because... because...it...needed a chocolate filling?"

"What? How did you guess that?" he asked, raising one eyebrow as he bit into his donut again.

"I'm pretty sure I've heard it from somewhere."

"Oh, I know where, Aria," her mother joined in. "In that movie you're always watching."

"Oh yeah." Aria nodded as she pointed at her mother to motion that she was right.

Aria could feel her stomach starting to churn again as they left, the thought of school coming back into her mind.

The trees that Aria had seen before were now guarding them on both sides of the long road to school. Aria felt as though she was going to retch, her face turning paler. Her fingers found her sunflower necklace and traced the grooves of it, her palms tingling. It was like something crackled through her veins, trying to release through her hands. Soon, a tall, massive, brick academy with wide, elegant windows came into view. The school building itself looked nice, but all that surrounded it was a dingy dirt lot and tons of thick forest.

"Okay, we're here." Aria's mother smiled as the car halted. "You just head into the office. They'll help you."

Aria stepped out of the car and grabbed her bag. Before she closed the door, she said, "Love you guys. See you later."

"Love you too, darling!" Her mother waved goodbye, eyes bright to match her smile.

"Bye and have a good day, sweetie," her father said.

Aria forced a smile and shut the door, knowing she surely would not have a good day at all.

As she took a quick glance around, she realized that showing up with her parents hadn't been as embarrassing as it had been last time. There were not many people outside the building. Some gathered by the doors of the school, and others were walking up the stairs into the building from the parking lot. Huge letters were mounted high on the outside walls of the building that read: *Incanting Academy*. Underneath the letters a large crescent moon with a star each at the top and bottom was engraved into the stone building. The motto underneath it read: *You are magical in your own way*, which Aria found to be a strange saying for a school. She squinted her eyes at the peculiarity of it.

The huge, dark, wooden doors of the school were wide open, revealing the immense school halls awaiting her. Her unrecognized face prompted people to glance at her as she stepped through the doors. Glancing around, an odd energy sparked inside of her, as if calling her. It was like she was having dèjá vu and she tried to shake it from her mind. She looked to her right at a shiny gold plaque next to an oak door that read: *Office.* Aria clasped the metal handle, opened the door, and walked inside. The office, which smelled of cleaning supplies, was small and empty of people other than the staff that sat behind dark wooden desks. Aria's eyes lingered over everything, taking in the strangely darkened atmosphere.

"Hello! Dear, how may I help you?" a plump woman with a curly white-blond bob asked. Her desk was covered in papers, a computer, an office telephone, and little knickknacks. A golden plaque on her desk said: *Patricia Stax, Secretary.*

"Hi, my name's Aria Chesler. I'm new to the school." Aria pushed her brown hair out her eyes.

"Wonderful! You're going to go right in there. The principal has your schedule and map." Miss Stax pointed to a door on the left.

Already, Aria thought of how different this school was from all the other schools she had been to. She walked up to the door, took a deep breath, and stepped inside. An older woman in a gray suit, with long, gray hair, and a wrinkly face, looked up from her work.

"Hello! And you are?" The principal had a light smile showing on her face, crinkling the corners of her eyes.

"Aria Chesler." Aria felt awkward standing next to a chair but felt it would be weird to sit down without being asked to.

"Hmm, the new girl! Well, Aria, I am Principal Molly Mckinney, but just call me Mrs. Mckinney." The principal shuffled together a few papers sitting on her desk. "Here is your schedule and a map of the school. Everything else that you will need—if you do not have it—is supplied by your teachers. I hope that you will have a wonderful year here, Aria." She handed the schedule and map to her, then stared at her for a moment, as if studying her.

"Thanks." Aria turned on her heel and quickly left the office.

The office door clicked shut behind her as her eyes began to wander, landing on a set of double doors to the cafeteria across the hall. Her eyes continued to glide over the glossy stone walls and finally noticed the two staircases leading to the second floor. There were no lockers, so Aria assumed she was going to carry her bag around all day. She followed the map up to the second floor, feeling other teenagers' eyes on her the whole time. They were probably very curious to find out who she was.

Aria swiftly found sanctuary in the back of the English classroom as the other students scrambled to their seats and placed her bag beside her chair. The teacher adjusted her lively purple blouse behind her desk, then went back to scrawling grades on papers. Her eyes framed by glasses sparkled with a smile, her blond bun perched atop her head. Posters about writing rules peppered the walls, a bulletin board displayed on one side of the whiteboard.

The teacher's white skirt flounced as she stood. "Good morning, students!"

"Good morning, Miss Truffle," the class—except for Aria—replied in a bored tone.

"Today we are going to start a fun writing project about animals, but first I have an announcement to make."

Aria felt the sweat starting to build up on her forehead and heat rose into her face. She knew exactly what was coming.

"We have a new student in the class!"

Everyone began looking around to identify the new student

and many eyes landed on Aria. Miss Truffle strode across the room to stand next to her.

"Please give a warm welcome to Aria Chesler!"

Aria's face was redder than hot iron. In the front of the class, a girl glowered at Aria through narrow green eyes, her straight-as-a-ruler black hair curtaining her face. The girl's black leather jacket almost seemed to blend in with the odd dark wood scenery of the school. A chain hanging from her ripped jeans tapped the leg of her desk. Aria felt a cold shiver go up her spine and she quickly looked away from the girl. The teacher walked back up to the front, babbling about something Aria wasn't paying any attention to, since it wasn't about the assignment.

She hoped there would not be that dreadful introduction for her in every class, but sure enough, there was.

Aria made her way through the bustling and noisy halls into the cafeteria. Long, wooden, rectangular tables stretched into the distance of the room, matching benches placed around them. She walked to the back of the cafeteria where a line was forming to get food, her stomach grumbling at the smell of sizzling food. As soon as she got food, she sat down at the emptiest table she could find. Only one other person sat at the table, but they were all the way down at the other end. Aria pulled out her notebook and began to jot down animals she could research for the writing project while she munched on her food. Miss Truffle had droned on about the project—and her weekend plans—for so long that Aria had barely any time to start.

She started hearing *psst, psst* sounds, so she looked up from her notebook and food to see who was being so annoying. Her eyes landed on two boys sitting at the table across from her, who were staring directly at her with curiosity flickering in their eyes. She recognized them from English class, but she didn't know their names. Aria stared for a moment as one of the boys ran his tanned hand through his mocha brown hair, freckles seeming to dance on his cheeks as he tried to fight a kindhearted grin. He watched her, his eyes the deep blue of the ocean, as she took in his sky-blue shirt and dark jeans. The boy beside him tossed his head to adjust his auburn hair, hazel eyes concentrating hard on twirling his spaghetti. As he ate, he got sauce all over his pale face and one noodle flopped onto his shirt. Aria couldn't make out the words on his shirt as the boy desperately tried to wipe off the food. He set the napkin on the table and looked back up at Aria. Both of the boys were making the obnoxious sounds and beckoning her over.

She pointed to herself and mouthed *"me?"*

Simultaneously, the boys nodded.

For a moment, Aria sat there, just staring back at them. After the last seven years of moving from one school to the next, she knew better than to talk to people. Anyone she ever talked to eventually just wanted to laugh at her as if there was something wrong with her. Her fists clenched momentarily, hoping that something odd wouldn't happen. Her heart fluttered and her palms began to throb, as if something was trying to claw its way out against her wishes. But against all her instincts, there was something about these two boys that made her think it was okay to walk over there. The pulsing of her hands began to fade away. *No, Aria, don't do it*, her inner voice scolded her as she stuffed her notebook back into her bag.

If they just want to make fun of me, I'll walk away. Easy as pie, she told herself as she got up with her bag and tray of food.

She walked over to the table the boys were at and sat down right in front of them, setting her bag on the floor next to her.

Her insides seemed to tighten as she looked at them and set her tray down. Butterflies appeared in her stomach again and her hands began to shake slightly, so she clenched them shut.

Before she could even ask what they wanted, the dark-haired boy spoke, "So, you're the new girl?" His voice was kind, and not deep, but not high like a little boy's either. As Aria took in his face up close, she couldn't help but notice how charming he appeared. His tanned face turned a tinge of pink.

"Um, yeah." She felt a sudden heat creep into her face.

"My name is Luke, and this is my friend—" the darker-haired boy started.

"I'm his friend, Avi—Avi Braxdon," the auburn-haired boy finished.

"Nice to meet you both. My name is—"

"We know your name. The whole school is talking about you." Avi's tone was not rude. It was actually quite sweet, but what he said still made Aria gulp. She had to resist the urge to grab her sunflower necklace, the water in her bottle starting to shake with her nerves.

The fact that the whole school knew her name sent shivers up her spine. What were they saying? Was it good things or bad things that they were talking about?

"They aren't saying anything mean about you, of course. Everyone here is actually really nice…except Celaena…" Luke added, clearly seeing the sickly face on Aria.

Aria's fear diminished, but she still couldn't shake the butterflies in her stomach.

"So…um, how do you like it here?" Luke changed the subject, scratching the back of his neck.

Aria took a bite of her chicken patty sandwich. "Oh… uh…" She tried to think of something to say that didn't make it seem like she wanted to flee from the school. The whole place had an odd feeling to it, the feeling that gave her déjà vu when she first walked in. It was as if the dark scenery of the school was calling out to her, *"You belong here."* It made chills creep across her skin. "Well, the teachers and staff are all nice…And—and I like choir." It was all true for the most part.

"Oh, is choir your favorite subject?"

"No, art is."

"Art is a subject? I thought it was more of a hobby." Avi squinted his eyes like he was thinking.

"It's both," Aria said. "Well…what are your favorite subjects?"

"None," Avi stated. "I mean, anything but school stuff… Unless video games count as a subject."

"I don't believe it does." Aria tried to fight back a grin.

"Unlike Avi, I actually like at least one subject: coding."

"Really? I didn't know they taught that here," Aria said, genuinely intrigued. "What's it like?"

"Oh…uh…it's cool," Luke replied, scratching the back of his neck as his face turned pink again. "I'm not really that good at it."

Avi slapped Luke on the back after putting his fork down, smiling amusedly. "Luke is undermining himself. He made a video game for us to play a couple of months ago. It's awesome."

"Wow, that's amazing!"

"I suppose so…" Luke shoved a bite of food in his mouth.

Aria felt a chill and turned to see the girl that had glared at her in English. The girl flipped her long, black hair as she strode across the cafeteria. She stood next to Aria and looked down on her with a smug face. Not many people were looking around to see what she was doing, but a tiny group of girls with decorative chains and black leather outfits were staring from across the cafeteria with the same smug faces as the girl towering over Aria.

Aria looked at her as the girl spoke with a nasty, impolite grin, "So, you're the new girl?"

Why was everybody asking her that? It was quite obvious, wasn't it?

"Yeah…" she answered like it was the most conspicuous thing in the world.

"What's your name, *new girl?*"

She really didn't see why this girl was asking her name if she was in two of Aria's classes, which both teachers had introduced her in. Her fingertips began to pulse again, her heart beating anxiously against her ribs.

"Aria." Her tone started to show her annoyance.

"*Not your first name!*" the girl shrieked, an attitude lacing her tone.

"My last name's Chesler…Why?" Aria raised her eyebrows, giving the girl a questioning face. The water in her bottle shook ferociously, as if trying to escape from its prison, and suddenly tipped over. *No, not again!* Her heart sank and she quickly picked it up with throbbing hands, holding it as tight as she could to stop its shaking.

The girl's eyes narrowed at the bottle, a smirk quirking up at the corner of her lips like she knew something Aria didn't. "Just making sure I heard the teachers right, so I know to make your life a living nightmare." She leaned in close to Aria's face, nearly touching her nose, when the secretary, Miss Stax, started walking up to them.

It took the girl only a few seconds to transition from looking smug and mean to looking kind and sweet as she straightened up.

Miss Stax looked straight at the girl and said, "Mr. Monroy would like to see you about a paper you wrote. Welcoming our new student, I see?"

"Okay, and yes, I was welcoming Aria. I think we are going to be great *friends*," the girl responded in an overly sweet way that made the hair on the back of Aria's neck stand up.

"Always accommodating, as usual." Miss Stax smiled, and the girl walked away with her.

"Who was *she*?" Aria turned back to Luke and Avi.

"*That* was Celaena Malamone," Avi answered, looking disgusted by the girl who was now walking out of the cafeteria.

"Well…I don't think she likes me very much," Aria told them.

"Don't take it personally. She hates everyone," Luke said, looking just as outraged as Avi. "I don't understand how the teachers let her get away with everything. Though, Celaena does pretend to be a perfect princess in front of the adults."

Avi, Luke, and Aria got lost in conversation, mainly about random things such as movies and songs. Apparently, both of them hated country music and liked blues and rock instead.

"Rock is way better. Have you ever listened to *Persevere* by Drake Barlo?" Avi asked.

"No," Aria admitted.

"Luke will have to show it to you sometime then." Avi glanced at Luke with a smirk twitching at his lips.

Aria grinned as the conversation carried on. It was nice to have some people other than her own shadow and her parents to talk to.

The end of lunch was nearing and a young, pale girl in lavender-colored clothes came wandering over, her frizzy, bushy blond hair bouncing against her back in a blue ribbon. Aria recognized her from choir class. She plopped down next to Aria with a bright grin that lit up her blue eyes, sitting so close their arms brushed each other's.

"Hello," the girl said. "Aria Chesler, right?"

"Uh, yeah."

"Nice to meet you, Aria. I'm Willow. I recognize your name from somewhere. I'm not sure where, but I'll come to realize where soon enough." The girl put her hand on top of Aria's gently, smiling to reveal a dimple on her cheek.

Aria moved her hand away slowly, feeling creeped out, and looked at Luke and Avi with a questioning face. They both shrugged as if they were used to this odd behavior.

Willow looked at Avi with a dreamy smile and said, "I should be going. Fourth period is starting very soon. I have advanced biology next."

With a smile, Willow got up and left the cafeteria as swiftly as she had come.

"What was that all about?" Aria asked the boys as they got up to throw out the rest of their food.

As they approached the garbage cans, Luke responded, "That is just the way Willow is…She's…weird. She makes up stories all the time that are completely unrealistic and impossible…She is just overall odd."

As they were leaving the cafeteria, Avi said under his breath, "She *is* pretty though."

Avi was a terrible whisperer, however, so Luke and Aria still heard him.

"Oh, Avi, I thought you were over her! The girl is obsessed with cats and volcanoes for Pete's sake!" Luke blurted.

"*Volcanoes?*" Aria asked with furrowed brows as they reached the steps to go up to the second floor.

Avi's face was blushing a deep scarlet.

"Yeah, she is always adding them into her stories. Like yesterday, for example, she told me that she lives in a volcano and that her cat fell out her window and into the lava, but that her cat was okay," Luke explained. "Tell me how that isn't crazy!"

Aria couldn't help but laugh a little.

"And she tells her stories to *everyone*," he added.

"I know she's…a little crazy…but…" Avi said, but he couldn't seem to find something to counter the crazy part.

Aria's stomach tightened as giggles threatened to escape and she pressed her lips together to hold them in. Luke looked like he was going to laugh, too, causing Avi to go redder in the face.

At the end of the school day, Aria was waiting at the entrance. The butterflies in her stomach and the pulsing of her hands she'd felt in the cafeteria was gone now as she stood on the steps of the school. Luke and Avi—Avi still feeling slightly embarrassed by the earlier talk about Willow—walked up to Aria.

"Hey, guys." A smile appeared on Aria's face and her heart leapt.

"Hey, Aria," they both said.

"See you tomorrow?" Luke ruffled his hair, grinning in a way that made his eyes shine even brighter.

"You bet." Her smile grew wider despite the tingling feeling in her stomach. She looked into Luke's deep blue eyes… getting lost in thought.

"Aria!" Her mother's voice broke through her trance, causing a jolt to be sent through her as she realized what she had been doing.

Why had she been staring at Luke? It's not like there was a treasure in the cerulean ocean of his eyes.

"Well, I have to go," she said and hurried down the steps, her heart thumping unusually hard.

Aria was in the car in a matter of minutes and getting questions thrown at her.

"Did you have a nice day? Who were those boys? Who's your favorite teacher? Did you make any friends?" her mother asked in a rush.

"*Boys?*" her father asked, turning around to raise an eyebrow at her.

Aria heard her father but chose to ignore him. "I had a wonderful day! I can't decide on a favorite teacher. And those boys were my…uh…friends," Aria answered as they pulled out of the parking lot.

It was an odd thing to say, like the words shouldn't be coming from her. *Friends.* After so many years of not having any friends, maybe she had actually found some. Of course, she didn't know if Luke and Avi considered her a friend, but it was the closest thing she could think of. Her parents seemed happy with her answers, especially that she had finally made friends. Her father was still questioning her about why her friends were boys, but she chose to keep ignoring him. He was always weird on the subject of boys.

That night, Aria had gone to bed ecstatic. Many things had been moved around the house and her parents had unpacked a lot, and at dinner, she couldn't stop talking about her day. She had completely forgotten that she had woken up that morning feeling glum, and instead, she felt full of glee.

Chapter Three

THE NEXT MORNING, Aria was flooded with joy as she hurried to get ready. Truly, she couldn't wait to get back to school and see Luke and Avi again. She also was excited to hear Willow's ridiculous made-up stories to get a crack out of them. The feeling inside her was one she had never felt before. It was filling her all the way up and then spilling over the edge.

The car came to a stop in the school parking lot, her mother the only other person in the car. Her father was already at work. Students were making their way up the stone steps of the school. Aria bid her mother goodbye with a smile and hurried to join everyone else inside the school. She'd easily managed to remember her classes and where they were. She hurried up the stairs leading to the second floor and zipped down the hall. Celaena and her gang of friends were right outside the door to English class, laughing viciously about something. Celaena walked in front of the doorway, blocking it when she saw Aria coming. Aria moved to the side to try and get around her, her jaw set tightly, and her eyes narrowed.

"What's the *magic word*?" Celaena asked her in a mock-baby voice.

"Celaena, get out of my way." Aria clenched her teeth before taking a deep breath.

"Nope, that is *not* the magic word." Celaena and her friends wore sly smirks as they began laughing softly.

"Are you sure you really want to be acting this way? You know, when the teacher is just on the other side of the doorway?"

"Well, lucky for me, the teacher *isn't* in there right now," Celaena said smugly.

"Just move." She really didn't want to be dealing with Celaena, a girl who would already be on her enemy list if she had one.

Footsteps came from behind Aria, and Celaena quickly hurried into the classroom to take her seat. Aria walked inside, taking another deep breath now that Celaena's shenanigans were over. Miss Truffle came into the classroom and the class began. After a little while, the class proceeded through the empty school halls to the computer lab. She could tell by the looks that Luke and Avi were giving her that they really wanted to talk to her.

In the computer lab, all three of them took seats next to each other. Miss Truffle sat in the corner at a very petite desk to grade different papers. The three of them talked to each other in hushed voices as they did their research on the computers. The lights from the computers reflected on their faces, casting a bluish glow on them.

"What did Celaena want?" Avi turned in his seat.

"She was just messing with me." Aria moved her mouse around to open a new tab.

"Already? Gosh, if she is already messing with you, things are about to get ugly between you two."

"Thanks…" Aria sighed and pinched the bridge of her nose.

Luke shot him a disapproving look and hurried to say, "Don't worry about it. She's practically harmless."

Aria was trying hard not to think of Celaena, so she quickly changed the subject. "What are you guys doing for the project?"

"Platypuses. But for the project, I'm going to prove that they aren't real."

"Um…Avi, platypuses *are* real," Aria told him, a giggle developing in her throat.

"Yeah…" Luke shook his head with a smirk. "Anyway, I'm doing Komodo dragons." He stared at the screen on the computer, the light from it reflecting in his eyes. As he opened a new tab, he ruffled his hair. "I have coding after this, which is great because I don't have to leave the room." He glanced around as if to make sure no one was watching before typing something into the browser. "But I want to quickly show you this thing I made."

Aria tore her gaze away from her own screen and stared at Luke's.

"Are you showing her the video game?" Avi asked, staring at Luke's screen as well.

"No, it's just a little something I've been learning to make in coding class."

"Wow…" Aria's eyes went a little wide and she smiled when she saw what appeared on his screen. "It's beautiful."

There was an intricate picture of a Komodo dragon filling his screen, but when Aria squinted her eyes, she saw that each little detail was a colored number overlapping others.

"Ta-da, I guess," Luke said softly. "I'm not good at any art, but I can do this. I thought you might like it since you said you like art yesterday."

"It's wonderful," Aria told him. "You like Komodo dragons, then?"

"Yeah." Luke scratched the back of his neck, and his face turned a tinge of pink in the light from the computer.

"Luke likes all lizards," Avi told Aria.

"That's very cool," Aria said. "I like rodents."

"Maybe Luke can make one of those? Like a rabbit or something?" Avi glanced at Luke with a smirk.

"Rabbits aren't rodents." Aria shook her head, a grin twitching at her lips.

The day carried on, Celaena kept at bay, but she continued to make the same smug face at Aria. At this point, the expression seemed stained to her face. When lunchtime arrived, Luke, Avi, and Aria were sitting at the same table they'd met at the day before.

"Do you guys have any classes with Willow?" Aria asked as she sat down with her lunch tray. "I have her in choir, but that's it."

"She's—she's in my—my history class." Scarlet splotches flushed Avi's face.

"I don't have a single class with her." Luke took a big bite of his food before adding, "But she's often in the computer lab when it's unoccupied. Why do you ask?"

"I was just wondering if you guys have heard anything from her?" Aria poked at her cheesy noodles with her fork before scooping some up to eat.

"W-what do you mean?" Avi suddenly blushed a deeper red that evidently made Luke fight a grin, which made Avi's face look as bright as a tomato.

"Her weird stories, you know. I'm dying to hear something funny. Seriously, after all the faces Celaena has made at me today, I need to laugh."

"No. She just keeps staring at me, which to be honest is kind of starting to creep me out…" Avi fidgeted with his fork, keeping his gaze down.

"Well, she did tell me in…uh…the computer lab right after school—I had snuck in there to work on that art I showed you earlier—that she plans to visit an active volcano over spring break. Honestly, though, who would even be thinking of spring break? It's like a month away."

"That's really odd," Aria said, accidentally snorting. "I wonder if she knows that volcano fumes are poisonous… Anyway, other than yesterday at lunch, she hasn't said a word to me. And in choir, she just kept staring at me like she was shocked to see that I exist…" She trailed off as she saw Willow making her way toward them, her ponytail bouncing behind her and her face bright with glee.

"Hello," Willow greeted as she slid onto the bench beside Aria, her elbow bumping her. "Oh, I apologize, Aria." She reached out to lightly touch Aria's arm where her elbow had hit it.

"Um…uh…I'm fine," Aria stuttered, trying to find the words.

For a moment, all of them remained silent, just staring until Avi finally spoke up. "Uh, hey."

"Hello, Avi," Willow replied, looking straight at him with a softhearted smile.

Aria shifted in her seat slightly, waiting eagerly for Willow to tell one of her strange stories. But instead, Willow just grinned. Unexpectedly, she turned to Aria, looking at her face as if trying to register something. Her smile faltered, but she quickly hid it and turned back to Avi, blushing a little and biting her lip. Aria felt awkward, so she looked down at her tray of food and fiddled with her thumbs.

The clacking of boots against the tiled floor met Aria's ears, and she spun around in her seat.

"I see you *suck* at making friends," Celaena said as she towered over Aria and scrunched up her face, gesturing to each of them. "Hanging out with the two dweebs of the school…And, oh! You're friends with Willow, the little weirdo. Is she telling you her stories? How *pathetic*…"

Before any of them had time to say something defensive, Celaena walked away with a pleased smile. Luke and Avi didn't seem fazed, but Willow's face turned a shade of pink and her eyes welled with tears. She blinked them away, looking down at her hands. Aria felt as if her heart was being squeezed, remembering all the times she'd been laughed at. She never should've laughed at Willow's stories, and the fact that she had made a knot in her chest. Whether her stories were weird or not didn't mean Willow wasn't a human with feelings.

"I don't think you guys are dweebs! Willow, don't listen to her. You are very…uh…kind. You're not weird." Aria bit her lip, not sure what else to say to make them feel better. Yes, she thought Willow's stories were odd, but she also thought Willow was a genuinely kind person. What Celaena had said didn't hold any real truth. Seven years ago, when she had told her parents that she had been bullied, her mother had told her that bullies act as a reflection of themselves. Aria believed that Celaena was intentionally targeting those who were different but kind because she lacked any genuinely nice people in her own life.

"Thank you," Willow said very quietly as she got up from the table. She bent back down to touch Aria's hand for a moment, then straightened up. It weirded Aria out that she did that, but she wasn't going to say so. Willow spoke lightly, looking directly at Aria, "You don't have to listen to the stories I tell everyone else, you know."

A pit widened in Aria's stomach as she watched Willow gracefully walk away. "What was that supposed to mean?" She hadn't meant to say it aloud.

"I don't know…But, as I've said, she's weird." Luke took another bite of food, staring at Aria as she turned her gaze back to him and Avi.

"Yeah…I know…" She was trying to find the right words. "It's just, calling someone weird is a little mean, don't you think? I used to be called weird all the time and I hated it."

Luke's face turned a shade of pink, and he hurried to reply, "You're right. It's rude."

"Anyway—" Avi changed the subject. "—You shouldn't worry about what Celaena says to you. She's just looking for a reason to bully you. Of course, she'll go for your friends, because we are awesome, unlike her…I didn't know you were friends with Willow. Are you?" His face flushed like a tomato.

"Oh, no," Aria said. "And she'll have to do better than that to provoke me. Yeah, what she said was annoying, but I know it isn't true, so what does it matter? You guys are great, not dweebs or anything like that." She still felt a knot in her chest for Willow, but wondered what Willow had meant about not listening to her stories. The thought was pushed from her mind as she grinned, realizing that Luke and Avi officially considered her a friend. "Are we allowed in the library? I have to get some books for the writing assignment."

They nodded, so she picked up her tray of mostly eaten food, threw it away, and left the cafeteria.

Pulling the fancy glass doors of the library open, she tucked her map of the school away in her pocket. At the front of the library, an older, wrinkly woman with a gray bob cut sat behind a long, wooden counter piled up with books. The woman continued to stare at the computer in front of her and didn't seem to notice Aria passing by. Other than the librarian and her, nobody else was in the library. Many rows of tall bookshelves covered with dusty books—some so worn they looked to be centuries old—filled the massive room. There was a thick scent of parchment and a floral candle burning in the drafty air. After she had found a couple books to help her with research, she walked up to the librarian and set her books on the counter.

"Hello," Aria greeted, and the woman finally noticed that there was someone in the room.

"Oh! Hello, dear." The librarian blinked her eyes a couple times, as if coming out of a daze, before she checked out the books for Aria.

Aria walked out of her last class, carrying her painting of a sunset over hills. The wet paint shimmered over the surface of the canvas. She turned the corner with a grin and met eye to eye with Celaena. A startled jolt to her stomach caused her wet painting to fling out of her hands and she felt as if an invisible force was pushing her backwards. She fell to the tiled floor and her canvas landed on her, splattering onto her face and clothes. Crimson, olive, bright yellow, coral, and mahogany paints covered her. Her hands tingled and pulsed, a crackling energy trying to escape from her. Celaena's teasing laughs floated to Aria's ears, and it grew louder as others joined in. Aria shook on the ground, tears threatening to spill, and fury began to charge through her veins. She had only felt a small jolt in her stomach when she saw Celaena, yet her painting managed to fly into the air, and something forced her to the ground. What had just happened?

"Oh, this is wonderful! Aria, you have a little something… *everywhere!*" Celaena pointed at her, a sly grin sweeping her face.

It felt as if everyone was staring at her, their laughs echoing through Aria's mind.

"Shut up, Celaena!" Aria shouted, seized her painting with shaky hands and, before Celaena could make fun of her more, she hurried away from the crowd of people.

The jeers seemed to follow her all the way outside. A crackling, throbbing beat echoed through her veins like a burning rage made of flames. She sat down on the steps of the school, trying to wipe paint out of her hair and off her face. The sound of footsteps bounding towards her met her ears, and the next second, Luke and Avi were plopping down next to her.

"What on earth happened to you?" Luke's eyes widened.

"Yeah, you look like someone tried to paint on you," Avi said.

"*Cruel*-laena is what happened." Hot tears began to well up in her eyes, but she pushed them away.

"Ha! Cruel-laena—that's a good one!" Avi said. "But what did she do?"

Aria explained exactly what had happened and the weird way her painting had been flung into the air along with the strange force that pushed her to the ground.

When she had finished, Avi asked, "So it felt like the painting was ripped from your hands?"

"Yes, that is exactly what it felt like!"

"That is very…interesting." Luke and Avi exchanged looks, but Aria didn't notice as she uselessly tried to wipe the paint off herself.

"I really don't want to come to school tomorrow. Who knows what Celaena will have in store for me." Aria wished she could just scream out in frustration. *It's like I'm cursed or something.* "Everyone is going to laugh at me again, just like they always do."

"Well, we have your back no matter what." Luke awkwardly patted Aria on the shoulder.

A voice called out and she looked up to see her mother pull to a stop in front of the steps with the window rolled down.

"Thanks, Luke," Aria said. "I've got to go."

"Bye," Luke and Avi said.

"What in the world happened to you, Aria?" her mother asked after Aria had waved goodbye and climbed inside the vehicle. Her mother spun around in her seat to look Aria up and down, her brows furrowed.

Her father wasn't in the car, which meant he was still at work…wherever that was.

"Nothing, I just spilled paint on myself in art." Aria bit her lip, avoiding eye contact.

She really didn't want to explain the bullying situation to her mom, who would then probably freak out. She'd deal with Celaena on her own, just like she always did when it came to bullies. Plus, Celaena was already looking for things to bully her for, and she could not give her any more to feed off of like a piranha. She could already hear what Celaena would say if she did tell her mother: *"Oh, running to your mommy?"* That had been the sort of things bullies had said to her seven years ago.

"You managed to spill paint *all over* yourself?"

"Yeah…"

"Well, try not to get any on the seats."

Chapter Four

SHE COULD FEEL her heart sinking lower and lower into the pit of her stomach as the car pulled into the parking lot of the school. Unable to control the urge, her hands found her sunflower necklace and traced the golden petals. The night before, she'd tried to prolong time by staying up late doing homework. But time still flew by fast, as it usually does when something dreadful is approaching.

Once the vehicle halted, she slowly climbed out of it and exchanged goodbyes with her mother. The pulsing began to flutter in her hands again and she clenched them tight, subconsciously willing it to go away. She forced herself to walk up to the steps of the school, seeing Luke and Avi waiting for her near the door, and for some reason Willow was, too.

"H-hey," Aria said, her eyes darting this way and that.

"You might want to put up your hood. Celaena is being really cruel about the painting incident," Avi told her. "She's already got her friends talking about it."

It was just as she feared. As quickly as she could, she pulled her sweatshirt's hood up and pulled the strings to make it tighten around her face. It felt like her stomach was caving in on itself, causing her head to spin and her fingertips to tingle. Willow was sitting on the steps of the school, looking out into the thick woods, but Aria knew she was listening in.

"We should get to class," Luke spoke up.

"Yeah," Aria agreed reluctantly.

The three of them walked inside with Willow trailing behind them. Aria kept her gaze down, trying not to make eye contact with anyone. Maybe people wouldn't notice her if she kept her head down, but then she saw them. Celaena and her friends were at the foot of the left stone staircase that led to the second floor. It was as if they were waiting for her to walk in, each of them wearing smug smirks.

"Oh! Guys, it's the clumsy little puke painter!" Celaena jeered, pointing her finger at Aria.

Trembling, Aria's stomach clenched as she realized that her painting did look very similar to vomit when all the paint mixed and smudged the day before. The laughing of Celaena's friends filled Aria's ears. Most of the people gathered in the hallway just stared and others moved past to get to class, not aware of the painting incident. Whether they were making fun of her or not didn't matter. People were staring, causing sweat to gather in Aria's trembling hands as she clenched them tight in her pockets. Energy crackled through her veins down to the tips of her fingers, calling her. Déjà vu hit her like it had on the first day. It was as if the very halls were now saying, *"You don't belong here."* She was frozen in place as the surrounding people stared at her, whispering and shrugging. The noise from people getting to classes and Celaena's friends jeering at her hammered in her ears, making her feel as if her lungs were blocked. Luke gave Aria a light push and she began to make her way up the stairs. Willow still trailed behind them as they walked toward English class, trying to blend in with the crowd. She didn't have the first hour with them, though, so she turned on her heel and headed back down the hallway.

Breathing in deeply to calm the adrenaline rushing through her veins, Aria asked, "Why was Willow following us?"

"I have no clue," Luke answered as they sat down. "She's been acting weirder than usual since you came here. She did tell me one of her stories though."

"She hasn't told me anything for over a week now." Avi put his bag beside his chair. "Instead, she just keeps staring at me! It's really creeping me out. Like, if she wanted to talk to me, you would think she would just say something like she does with everyone else!"

Luke smirked. "Well, she told me that when she goes to Hawaii this spring break, she's going to adopt several kittens."

"I don't think that's all that odd," Aria admitted.

"She claimed they'd be mutant kittens."

Celaena and one of her friends walked by; her friend sat down, but Celaena flipped her hair and bent down so she was eye level with Aria. "Hey, puke painter, I wanted to say that you should really watch your back. The world's a lot scarier than just my friends and I…" Celaena spoke softly, so only Aria, Luke, and Avi could hear her. Her face was scrunched up and callous-looking. "You know…" she continued. "This isn't an ordinary school…"

With a wicked smile, Celaena stood straight up and walked back to her seat. Luke and Avi gulped and eyed Aria, waiting for her to react.

Aria tried not to show it, but her cheeks became a flaming red at Celaena's words. Celaena bothered her more than any other bully had before. Usually, she could stand up for herself, tell someone to just go away, and eventually they would get bored and move on, but something about Celaena seemed like a threat. Her heart rate hadn't even slowed down until English class had finished. The pulsing of her palms didn't go away though, as if demanding to be noticed. Celaena's words kept running through her head and distracted her from her work. She felt the whole school was sure to know about her being the *'puke painter'* by lunch.

In the cafeteria, conversations reverberated off the stone walls as Aria sat down in front of Luke. Aria kept thinking that everyone was talking about her, but she hadn't heard her name, not once. Her eyes darted around to everyone until they landed on Willow at the other end of the table. She was reading an odd book titled: *Mystic Beings of the Sea*. Aria was sure she was still trying to eavesdrop but didn't care.

Celaena's friends, for once, were scattered around the cafeteria, chatting to each other about Aria. It seemed every remark, comment, and tease floated to her ears, making her heart pound against her ribs and her tingling hands clammy as she clenched them around her silverware.

"Don't listen to them, they're all just rude," Luke said reassuringly. "This is exactly what *Cruel*-laena wants…and it wouldn't be so funny to her friends if she hadn't made it into a joke. Celaena has done stuff like this in the past, and they usually get bored with it after a day and then nobody ever talks about it again."

"Thanks, it's just so irritating," Aria said, but then pounded her fist on the table, rattling Luke's opened bottle of water. "The whole 'puke painter' name calling doesn't bother me so much. I mean, a kindergartener could have come up with that, but it's everything else that annoys me. I can't stop thinking about what Celaena said in English today, what she said about this not being an ordinary school."

"Oh…uh…I'm sure she's just trying to…mess with you… or something, that's all." Avi shoved food in his mouth and looked the other way. "You know, trying to scare you into leaving or something."

"Maybe…I just really wish I knew why she hates me so much." Her feet tapped rapidly on the floor, trying to distract herself from the crackling of energy flowing through her veins.

"I think the solution to the Celaena problem is to try your best to ignore her and don't give her any reasons to make a joke out of you," Luke suggested.

"Oh, well, that's *easy*," Aria said as sarcastically as possible. "She's watching my *every* move!"

The three of them looked across the cafeteria to where Celaena and a couple of her friends were watching them with cunning smiles. Aria bit down on her lip, her nostrils flaring, as she met eyes with Celaena. She brought her fist down on the wooden table again, startling Willow, who had still been reading, and causing Luke's bottle of water to tip. Aria reached her hands out, trying to stop it, but a sudden burst of energy lit in her fingertips and water exploded from the top. The water ran under Luke's tray of food, off the table, and onto the bench next to him. He slid away from it, remaining calm.

"Oh, Luke, I'm so sorry!" She jumped to her feet. "I'll go get you napkins!"

"No, Aria, it's fine," he told her, but she was already heading for the back of the cafeteria where they kept the napkins and condiments.

She grabbed a stack of white napkins and hurried back to him, smacking them down on the water. The napkins soaked up the water easily. She handed Luke several napkins to hopefully dry off his clothes, and she wiped off the bench right next to him.

"I'm so sorry, Luke. I didn't mean to," she said again as her shaky hands cleaned up the mess and butterflies filled her stomach.

His hand was suddenly on her elbow and she looked up from the spilt water. Her already heated face turned redder as she stared into his eyes.

"Seriously, Aria, it's not a big deal. It was just an accident."

She stood straight up and he set his hand back into his lap. Avi was just staring, looking from Luke to her, then back to Luke again. She gathered all the soaking wet napkins back up.

"Well, I think that is all cleaned up," she said before quickly throwing the napkins away.

She sat back down in front of Luke and tried to calm herself back down, tried to get the butterflies in her stomach to go away. Her hands shook and all she could do was clench them tightly in her lap and take a deep breath.

"You okay?" Avi asked, staring at her.

"Uh, yes." She tapped her fingers on the table, then took another bite of her food.

They ate in silence for a moment. Aria closed her eyes, trying to calm the thoughts spinning out of control in her mind, but all it did was make it worse. She abruptly broke the silence.

"I just wish Celaena would stop. I would tell a teacher, but I don't really want to…" She trailed off, thinking of what happened seven years ago, but another thought popped into her head. "Wait, don't the teachers know what Celaena's doing? Why doesn't she get punished?"

"I highly doubt the oblivious staff know anything. Celaena keeps this kind of stuff just between her and her friends.

Everyone else ignores them and doesn't care enough to tell a teacher," Luke explained.

"The staff barely pay attention to what is going on around them and most of them don't really care." Avi shrugged.

"Well, if I did tell a teacher, that would just give Celaena another thing to laugh at me about. She'd probably call me a baby or something." Aria sighed and ate the last of her food.

Wherever Aria went the rest of the day, Celaena and her friends laughed and pointed at her, causing others to whisper behind her back. She hated being a gag. When she went home, she shut herself in her room. She hoped that, like Luke and Avi had said, the rude remarks would die out by the next day. Her mother came in to check on her before her father finally got home from work, but Aria had to head to bed. Odd dreams that she was at school crept into her mind, but the halls were empty, and Celaena's voice was whispering from somewhere, *"This isn't an ordinary school, Aria."*

They sat at a wooden table that was meant to seat six with their books and notebooks spread out, having skipped lunch to work on the writing project in the library. Luke and Avi had been right; Celaena's friends had grown bored of the joke and now only Celaena continued it. Still, Aria didn't want to hear it if she didn't have to, so she suggested going to the library instead.

As they scratched down notes, they quietly talked amongst themselves. The librarian sat at her desk, typing endlessly on her computer, and still hadn't noticed them when they had already been there for fifteen minutes.

The library doors clicked shut in the silence of the library and they looked up. Willow was coming towards them with her own large stack of thick books, one of them being *Mystic Beings of the Sea.*

"Hello. May I sit with you?" She came to a stop next to their table and grinned, showing the dimple on her cheek.

"Oh…yeah," Avi said with what Aria guessed was supposed to be a smile and his face blushed hot pink.

"Stupendous!" Willow exclaimed, plopping her books down on the table and taking a seat in front of Aria.

Luke and Avi stared at Willow's pile of books, shaking their heads disapprovingly.

"What are y'all working on?" She began to spread out her books in front of Aria.

"We're working on a project for English," Aria said.

"Oh, that is very cool. Writing is great, isn't it? Is it the animal research project? I had to do that, too, but I already finished it and turned it in the day after it was handed out. I'm just here to further my studies. This school does not teach me *everything* I want to know." Willow spoke so fast, but lightly, that what she said left Aria gaping at her. How could someone finish a project so quickly?

"Wow…" Aria was lost for words. "Um, you like to write?"

"I suppose. I've never written much other than research projects, book reports, biographies, book reviews, et cetera, but I did write a book once about a girl and her horse. I know a lot about horses, but the book didn't make any sense."

"Really?" Avi joined in. "Uh—what was it called?"

"I called it *Cowgirl and Majesty.* The horse's name was Majesty." Willow grinned. "But…I sadly lost the notebook it was written in."

"Oh…" Avi went back to scribbling down notes.

"At least you have the memory of creating it, right?" Luke looked up from the book he had been flipping through.

"Yeah. Memories truly are great things." Willow nodded.

As Aria talked to Willow, she discovered that Willow was really kind when she wasn't acting weird. Aria, Luke, and Avi jotted down more notes while Willow switched back and forth between the books she was reading. Every so often, one of them would say something to the other and then they would go back to their research.

When Aria could resist the urge no longer, she asked Willow, "What is that one book about?"

"Oh, which one?" Willow moved her books around.

"The *'Mystic Beings of the Sea.'*" Aria pointed.

Luke and Avi looked at each other with alarm before their eyes pinned to the strange-looking book.

"It is just about sea creatures, but all sorts of different kinds. It's extremely fascinating."

Luke let out a sigh of what sounded like relief.

Another half an hour passed in the library and Willow had not spouted one word of nonsense.

"Well, I'll see you around. I have a class that starts in a couple of minutes." Willow picked up her books, and with a smile, she exited the library.

"She acted…normal," Luke said in a shocked but hushed voice once Willow was out of sight.

"Yeah, she's nice." Aria began gathering up her own things.

"She seems really smart." Avi swung his backpack over his shoulder, crimson splotches on his face.

Luke gave a laugh when he saw Avi's hot, sweaty, blushing face.

"What?" Avi asked.

"Shh!" the librarian yelled from her desk.

Aria pressed her lips together to hold in her giggles, fighting back a smile. As they walked out of the library, Luke held his hand to his mouth to hold in his own laughs and even Avi grinned.

The weeks passed and spring break grew closer. In those weeks, they spent more time with Willow and learned that maybe she wasn't so weird after all. Aria had turned in her project on hamsters and received an *A*. Luke had also received an *A*, but Avi got an *F*. When Avi saw his grade, he grunted, but then said, "In this case, I believe *F* is for fantastic."

At lunch, Willow and Aria sat by themselves at what was now their usual table after Luke and Avi ran off somewhere.

"Where did Luke and Avi say they were going?" Willow asked before taking a bite of her burger.

"I think they said they were going to the computer lab." Aria scooped up her macaroni, the smell of warm cheese drifting to her nose.

"Why?"

"I'm pretty sure they were going to sneak video games." Aria shrugged.

"What?" Willow looked utterly shocked. "They could get in trouble for that."

"Luke said they have done it many times before. I'm sure they know what they're doing," Aria said before taking another bite.

"Do you know what else Avi likes?" Willow asked, reaching her hand across the table to lightly touch Aria's. "You know, other than video games?"

Aria shrugged off Willow's touchiness and resisted the urge to say *"you"*. Instead, she just responded with, "You should ask him. I know he likes superheroes and weird jokes."

"What kind of jokes? You mean like the one he said yester-day at lunch?" Willow raised her eyebrow.

The joke he told yesterday popped into Aria's head, causing her to snort. *English is weird. It can be understood with tough thorough thought, though.*

"Yes."

"That was a joke?"

"Apparently," Aria laughed.

Another week passed and it was the day before spring break began. Everything was alive, fresh, and green now; the grass had grown back, bright flowers filled the gardens, and new leaves were on every plant outside the cafeteria windows. Willow, Avi, Luke, and Aria sat down at their usual table with their trays of food, stuffing their faces and chit-chatting.

"Does anyone have any plans for spring break?" Willow asked, grinning at them.

"None for me—my life's pretty boring. Maybe I'll do a self-portrait." Aria poked at her food with her fork.

Avi pushed away the food he'd barely eaten and looked away from the group.

"What's wrong, Avi?" Willow asked, reaching out her hand to touch his.

Aria couldn't help but wonder why she was always doing that.

"Oh…uh…nothing. I just…I don't have any plans for the break," Avi replied quietly. Aria wasn't sure if she had just imag-ined it, but it looked like his lip started to tremble.

A sorrowful look appeared on Willow's face and she pulled her hand away gently, saying, "It's okay."

Luke didn't seem to know what to say, so he twiddled his thumbs.

"I'm going to…uh…go get something to drink," Avi said, and he got up from the table.

Avi, however, didn't get a drink. He left the cafeteria.

"Is he all right?" Aria had the urge to get up and follow him, but she forced herself to stay sitting and respect his privacy.

"I—I don't know." Luke looked down at his hands.

They stared at the cafeteria doors, where people were passing in and out, where Avi had just walked through. Willow's face looked full of sorrow as her eyes lingered on the exit, and she bit her lip.

"Well, for spring break, I am adopting a cat!" Willow told them abruptly, her face suddenly changing to a look of liveliness as she stared at Aria and Luke now.

"That's cool," Aria said in a very distant tone.

Luke and Willow began talking, but Aria felt removed from the rest of the chat at lunch. Looking into Luke's eyes, her mind filled with all the possibilities of what could have made Avi leave them. She hadn't even noticed that Luke's eyes had locked on her own.

"Aria?" Luke stared at her with soft eyes, cocking his head to the side.

She jolted back to reality, getting hot in the face and blinking wildly. "W-what?" she asked.

"You haven't said a word since Avi left. Are you okay?"

"Oh, yeah, I'm fine," Aria hedged.

She looked away, biting her lip. Why had she even been staring at him? Tapping her fingers on the table, she willed herself not to be creepy again—not to look into those eyes of his and get lost in thought.

"Well, we better get to class," Willow suggested.

The rest of the day went by rather quickly, and Avi was vague and distant. Aria was sitting on the steps like usual with Luke and Avi, though this time Willow had joined them.

"Hope you have a good break," Luke said to Aria, smiling in a way that made his eyes shine brighter.

"Thanks, you, too." They smiled at each other for a moment before a tingling filled her stomach, her face turned a tinge of pink, and she changed her gaze to the parking lot. Her mother was late to pick her up. "Where could she be?" she asked nobody in particular. "Your parents must be late, too."

Avi, who had been on the verge of tears all day, spun on his heel and ran back into the building, avoiding their eyes.

"Oh, Aria…we live on campus," Luke said, scratching the back of his neck.

"What? That's a thing here?" Her jaw dropped slightly, and her eyes widened. "I never saw any rooms." *How did I not notice?* Her mother always arrived early to pick her up, so she supposed she'd never had the chance to.

"The rooms…are on the…uh…third floor." Luke glanced back through the doors, running his hand through his hair.

"So, you aren't going on spring break?" Aria asked him and Willow.

"No, my parents have jobs…" Luke trailed off, scratching the back of his neck. "They study creat—animals…in a different place…far away…Anyway, it's better for me to be here with—" He talked fast and flustered, making it hard for Aria to keep track of anything he said.

"I am, my mom's been waiting for me in that car for a while," Willow interrupted, and pointed out a teal car in the parking lot.

"Uh…" Luke and Aria murmured.

"I should probably go…See y'all after the break!" Willow waved and hurried off.

Aria waved goodbye to her as she climbed into the car and drove away, then turned back to Luke. As she realized that it was now just the two of them, butterflies filled her stomach, but she couldn't place her finger on why.

"If my mom doesn't hurry up, I'll have to walk home," Aria joked as her stomach growled for food.

"Do you know the way?"

"Yeah. It's easy to see my house in the distance once I get out of the woods. It'll take forever to get there, but I can manage," Aria said, now only half joking.

Ten more minutes passed, then twenty, as she shifted her weight from one foot to the other, about ready to walk herself home.

"All right, I'm going." She hoped her mother would suddenly show up.

"Goodbye, then," he told her. "See you after spring break!"

Aria waved goodbye to him and stepped down the stone steps, starting her trek down the road leading through the tall, shaded woods. She pushed on and managed to get to the house, longing to drop her bag down somewhere. The car was still in the driveway, along with the bicycle her father always rode to work. She walked up to the front door to find it was unlocked. Her parents never left the door unlocked…

She walked into the house and threw her school bag down on the floor. It was eerily silent, but she yelled, "I'm home! Why didn't you come pick me up?"

She waited for a response, but none came.

"Hello? Mom? Dad?"

The house remained silent.

Fear swept through her, and her heart began to pound in her ears. Still calling for them, she bolted down the hall and tore every door open, but they were nowhere to be found. Her breaths became heavy, her whole body trembling. Grasping her sunflower necklace, she went into her room and found a note on her bed. It was written in her mother's handwriting.

Chapter Five

Aria, you need to run! Go back to school and see Principal Mckinney. She can help you. Tell her that your father and I have been taken into custody by the police. I know this must be a shock to you, but you are not safe outside of school and you need to get back there. We love you, darling, more than anything in the world. Pack things to take with you to school! You are the—

THE LETTER HAD not been finished and the writing was messy. Aria reread it, unable to comprehend any of it. Her parents were taken by the police? That couldn't be possible. But fear was pressing on her like a weight, clouding her thoughts and making her feel like she couldn't get enough air into her lungs. She read it for the tenth time and the words finally registered completely. Hot tears welled in her eyes and dripped down onto the paper in her hands. She fell to her knees, then sideways, and curled herself into a ball as tears blurred her vision. The letter fell out of her hands and slipped under the bed. The sound of crinkling papers filled the air as all her artwork flew from her desk and around the room like a gust of wind had blown by. Laying on the floor, she began to shake like the room was suddenly freezing. She balled her hands into pulsing fists, feeling them getting clammy, and sweat beaded up on her forehead. Her heart was beating extremely fast like a drum in her ears, but also like a song telling her to listen to what her mother wrote in the note.

Adrenaline kicked in, numbing Aria's emotions, but she sat up and searched the floor for the note. Her artwork had fallen all over the floor, some of it ripped to pieces, making it hard to tell one scrap from another. She scurried across the floor on her hands and knees, her trembling hands sliding across the mess in search of the letter. Peeking under the bed, her tear-stained eyes landed on it. She reached her hand out, pawing at the dusty floor to grab it. Once it was in her hand, she rapidly pulled herself back up, accidentally banging her head on the bed. She winced and stood, almost stumbling over onto her bed, and scanned the note again. Her eyes were drawn to the last three words: *You are the*—You are the *what?* She couldn't help but wonder what her mother was going to write, but she couldn't worry about that right now.

Frantically, she tore open all her dresser drawers. She flung clothes everywhere before she finally located her duffle bag in the bottom drawer with all her other miscellaneous things. Running across the room, she grabbed some of the clothes she'd tossed, tripping over her own feet and falling on her bed.

She could hardly think as she stuffed several mismatching outfits into the duffle bag, not bothering to fold them. Once she'd tossed some other necessities into it and zipped it up, she stuck the note in the back pocket of her jeans. Her heart hammered in her ears and she walked out into the living room. Tears ran down her face as she pulled on her shoes and took a last look at the empty, silent, and eerie house. Her parents should have been there, but silence and a note said they weren't.

She picked up her school bag from where it rested next to the gray sofa and slipped it on her shoulder, assuming that she might stay at the school if that was where her parents wanted her to go. She peeked out the door to make sure the coast was clear before stepping outside and locking the door behind her. The road was desolate other than the squirrel running across it to get to a corn field. Hurriedly, she started down the road. So many emotions filled her up, yet she was numb at the same time. Her sweaty, shaking, free hand found her sunflower necklace, tracing the petals to keep her mind off all the horrible questions popping into her head.

Why were they arrested?

Because they're criminals? A voice said in her head.

No! Mom and Dad have always been kind to people! They always said they would try to help people! They're not criminals!

But you're always moving all the time. Ever think that's the reason? The snarky voice continued to say. *And to think you thought they weren't doing anything shady…*

NO! STOP THINKING! THAT CAN'T BE TRUE! Aria wanted to scream and cry and rip apart the corn fields that were on both sides of her now. How could someone live with a ball of fear twisting inside of them like a knife? She wanted to fall to the ground and curl up into a ball to cry, but something was driving her to keep going. Something inside her was urging her to figure out why her parents were taken, what they had done to deserve it. She couldn't listen to that scathing voice in her head.

She tried to stop the thoughts, but she was in a whirlpool of them, each one just as confusing as the next. *How is the school principal supposed to help me? What does Mom mean by 'You are not safe outside of school?' What if the cops come after me too? I've got to get out of here!*

Jogging down the bumpy dirt road, the bags weighed her down and her heart thumped aggressively in her chest. She tripped abruptly over her trembling legs, but her squishy duffle bag caught her fall. She stood up, reciting the words from the note in her head, and took off down the road again. A muted pain from a scrape on her leg barely registered in her crowded mind. She felt vulnerable and unsafe out in the open. She'd never been without her parents. And she'd never been in a situation like this. What was she supposed to do if no one could help her?

As she recalled the words and formed images of her mother's handwriting in her head, she couldn't help but wonder what the last sentence was meant to be. And she couldn't help but question why her mother had written that she was not safe outside of *school*. What had she meant? Why did she not write down any other place?

Maybe because you don't go anywhere else and you have no other family, the voice returned.

She shoved that thought out of her head and focused on the last three words of the letter instead as she came to a fork in the road. One road led through the trees to the school, and the other led straight ahead and into the distance.

You are the—

You are the what? Aria wondered. *You are the best? No. You are the one the police want? Well, that makes no sense.* It really bothered her how the letter had not been finished. What if that last sentence was important? What if it was an explanation for why they were taken? She wanted to pound her fist against something as another round of tears left her eyes, almost choking on the lump in her throat.

As the school came into view, she felt sure that her heart would leap out of her chest from all its beating. That or she would collapse from the bags weighing her down. The soft sound of chit-chat grew closer as she approached the school where people were playing catch outside. The sun was just beginning to set, casting dark shadows on the school and in the thick forest. Luke and Avi's bodies put shadows behind them on the stone steps as they spoke to each other, but Aria couldn't hear what they were saying. She walked into the parking lot, and people started to stare. They were clearly curious as to what on earth she was doing back at school.

"Help! Luke! Avi!" Aria called, about to collapse from the weight of her bags.

They stood up from their conversation at the sound of her voice, their eyes searching the parking lot for her.

"Aria?" Luke bounded toward her.

Everyone had their eyes on the three of them now as they came to a stop in front of her and Avi took her school bag. Luke and Avi's eyes were wide, searching her face for a reason behind why she was back.

Luke took the duffle bag from her. "What happened? Why are you back here? Are you okay?"

"My parents, they got arrested."

Their eyebrows raised and jaws dropped.

"Let's get you inside." Luke put his hand lightly on Aria's shoulder and began to guide her inside.

The hairs on Aria's arms rose, sensing eyes on her, as they walked into the school. The halls were silent and empty except for a few students who lived on campus. Aria positioned herself so that she was leaning against the wall just outside the office.

"I need to see the principal," she said. "I will explain everything once I tell the principal what happened. My mom wrote me a note—" Aria took the letter out of her back pocket. "—That said I am to tell Principal Mckinney what happened."

She handed Luke the letter and his eyes scanned it. Avi peered over his shoulder. They handed it back to her without saying anything, their brows furrowed, and their eyes flickering with pity. Aria swung the office door open, clutching her sunflower necklace, and stepped inside.

Miss Stax looked up from her computer at the sound of the door thudding behind Aria.

"Oh, gracious me, what's wrong, miss?" The blueish glow from the computer highlighted the look of concern on her face.

Aria handed the note to her over the desk. Miss Stax's jaw dropped, her hand slowly raising to cover her mouth in horror.

"Head on in and show Principal Mckinney straight away!" Miss Stax handed the note back to her, her eyes searching Aria's face anxiously.

Aria wiped away the sweat that had built up on her forehead, then walked to the principal's office door, opened it, and stepped inside.

Principal Mckinney looked up from her desk to see who had come in, putting down her pen. Seeing the cushioned armchairs, Aria rushed to plop down in one, her legs feeling like noodles.

"Aria…" Mrs. Mckinney had a huge smile on her face, but it slowly faded into a frown as she noticed Aria's sweaty, scarlet, tear-stained face. "What's wrong?"

Aria handed her the letter.

Mrs. Mckinney read it, her frown dipped deeper, her eyes wide and starting to water. "Oh dear, oh dear." She opened her mouth to say more, but closed it again, staring at the note.

Aria breathed in deeply, gaining control over her breathing.

Her adrenaline seemed to be wearing away and she began to shake.

Mrs. Mckinney looked up. "Aria…" She couldn't seem to find the words. "There is something I need to tell you. You will find it very hard to believe me, but you must. Your parents told me that if any harm was to come to them, I should tell you. That's why they placed you in this school."

Aria squinted, trying to think through all the thoughts spinning in her mind, but she didn't say anything, so Mrs. Mckinney continued.

"There are three realms: the Vezchia Realm, the Mundane Realm, and the Space Realm. We are in the Mundane Realm right now: the realm of mundane beings. The Vezchia Realm is the opposite of this realm. It is the realm known as home to all magical beings."

Aria's brow creased, staring wide-eyed. All the thoughts in her mind ran to an abrupt halt upon hearing Mrs. Mckinney's words. She thought Mrs. Mckinney sounded like Willow. How could Mrs. Mckinney talk nonsense when Aria's parents had just been arrested?

"Aria, I know you're going to find it hard to believe me. I understand why, but just think, has there ever been anything that has happened to you that does not make sense? Something that *you* did not actually do?"

The question felt very specific, and Aria tossed it over in her mind. Yes, a great many things she hadn't caused—or at least she hadn't meant to—had happened over the years like the painting incident and the flying papers in her room. It felt as if air had ripped her painting from her hands. And she had no clue what had made her papers fly. She narrowed her eyes even after having thought about it. How would Mrs. Mckinney know about all of that? Had she found out about the painting incident?

"You have, haven't you?" Mrs. Mckinney clasped her hands together. "That happens whenever you experience a sudden surge of emotion if magic runs in your blood. That will stop happening once you learn to control your gift…Well, I'll continue…This realm is the safest of the realms. The Vezchia Realm is the realm of magical beings like unicorns, dragons, and such. Men with magical powers are called enchanters and women are called enchantresses."

Aria was still quiet with her mouth hanging open, staring into Mrs. Mckinney's eyes to find a lack of seriousness. She found none. When Aria didn't respond, Mrs. Mckinney continued.

"This may sound great to hear that magic runs in your blood, but there are dangers in the world of magic. I am afraid I have no clue why your parents were taken by the police. But they are vulnerable now and you are even more. Your parents are the leaders of the Forces of Light. There were more leaders, but they were all sought out and destroyed by Malus Malamone and his Dark Forces."

"Mrs. Mckinney, I'm sorry, but you can't be serious! Dark Forces? Forces of Light? A Space Realm? Please, my parents were just arrested! I need your help!" Aria pleaded, hot tears welling up in her eyes. She fought to keep her growing anger in check.

"Aria, I *am* being serious. I *need* you to understand what I'm saying. I am trying to help you by giving you the knowledge of our world of magic." Mrs. Mckinney paused for a moment, looking at Aria with kind eyes before continuing her story. "You asked what the Space Realm is. It's really nothing of importance. It's just an empty void of nothingness other than what we enchanters and enchantresses have built within it.

"Anyway, the Forces of Light were created centuries ago to defeat the Dark Forces, but we have been unsuccessful. Your parents are the only ones that know how to supposedly destroy the Dark Forces. We can't let Malus get a hold of that information. If he and his Forces knew, they would destroy whatever it is that will destroy them. This school here is one of the many schools built by the Forces of Light to protect the under-aged enchanters and enchantresses from the Dark Forces. The Dark Forces are led by Malus Malamone, who has been alive for hundreds of years. Malus wants all the realms under his control. Everyone and everything under his control. He wants to rule as the most powerful being in the universe forever. He is cruel and unmerciful. Malus has been after your parents for years, but because of their constant moving, he has been unable to locate them. There is no doubt that Malus will be after you as well, so you are not allowed to leave the school grounds under any circumstances. Do you understand, Aria?"

Aria sat, unable to make her body move with all the information that had just been dumped on her. Not that she believed any word of it, though. Her fingers tapped rapidly on the chair's arm as she bit her lip.

"Oh, and one more thing," Mrs. Mckinney added. "You are not allowed to tell any student this. Many people in this school are just here under protection and they know no information about magic…and they may never. You can, of course, talk to your friends, Luke, Avi, and Willow about it, though. They know all about it, and if you don't believe me, just ask them."

Aria stared blankly at her.

"Come, I will show you to a room. You will stay on campus

until the situation with your parents is sorted out." Mrs. Mckinney stood from behind her desk.

"Mrs. Mckinney, are you okay? Are you like…taking something?" Aria asked, trying not to sound offensive. "Do you need me to get someone, like Miss Stax?"

"What? Oh, Aria!" Mrs. Mckinney exclaimed, then added, as if to herself, "Mundanes always coming up with a reason behind magic."

"Huh? Mundanes?" Aria raised an eyebrow.

"People who are born without magic or don't know about it. Aha! That must have been what happened to your parents. Mundanes must have seen them use magic and assumed they were committing a crime. It's quite common, actually."

"Mrs. Mckinney, I'm not trying to be disrespectful, but magic isn't real. My parents are not enchanty people or whatever it is you called them. They are not leaders of some organization that has to do with magic and there are no other realms." Aria shook her head and squeezed her eyes shut as if that might clear her mind of the rapidly spinning thoughts.

As much as everything added up in her head, she refused to believe what she was hearing. Yes, her parents were always gone. Yes, she had no clue what their jobs were because they were secretive about it. But that didn't mean they were part of a magical organization. Yes, they were always on the move. But that didn't mean that some evil guy was out to get them. Yes, insane things always happened to her. But that was just a problem with her, right? It was simply that Mrs. Mckinney was going crazy.

"Come, you'll see," Mrs. Mckinney said as she got up from behind her desk.

Aria followed, almost stumbling over her own legs. She found it hard to think with everything that had happened, and she didn't know what else to say, so she stayed quiet and followed Mrs. Mckinney out of the office. Luke and Avi were still waiting patiently outside with her bags, leaning up against the wall. Mrs. Mckinney didn't even look at them as she started for the second floor, beckoning for Aria to follow. Aria glanced at Luke and Avi, then hurried after her. They followed close behind with her bags. They walked through the empty halls, Mrs. Mckinney's heels clacking through the silence.

"Guys, I think Mrs. Mckinney is going crazy," Aria whispered to Luke and Avi as they passed the dark classrooms.

"What?" Luke asked.

"Why would you think that?"

Before Aria could answer, they arrived at the end of a dim hallway that she had never journeyed to. Mrs. Mckinney walked right up to a stone wall at the end of it. Aria was going to yell at her to stop, but Mrs. Mckinney continued and strode right through it, disappearing. She just about jumped out of her own skin and her eyes nearly popped out.

"H-How," she stuttered, shock reflecting in her eyes.

"*Enchanting*, isn't it?" Avi said with a smirk.

He stepped in front of Aria and walked backwards toward the wall, vanishing through it as well.

"So, did Mrs. Mckinney tell you about us and this school?" Luke asked, beaming.

"Yeah, but I—I didn't believe her…" Aria stuttered, sweat slick on her palms. "I—I s-still don't believe her…"

"Well, it's all real." He turned and walked through the wall, too.

Aria stood, staring at the wall, shaking her head. *No, this is not real. This is not real. It's just a dream.* She clenched her eyes shut, thinking she would wake up in a matter of seconds when she opened her eyes again. But when she did, she was still standing in the dim corridor. A part of her knew that Luke, Avi, and Mrs. Mckinney were waiting for her on the other side of the wall, so she braced herself. Slowly, she stepped towards it and put her foot through. A drafty air seeped through her jeans, but the magical wall didn't falter. As she quickly stepped through, she clenched her eyes shut and tensed her whole body up.

Luke and Avi had their hands pressed against their lips to hold in laughs at Aria, who had just appeared on the other side. The other side of the wall looked like a brighter continuation of the hallway they had just been in. The walls were the same smooth stone that was in the rest of the school. Oil lamps hung from the walls, illuminating the corridors, unlike the electric lights she had seen in the rest of the school. There was an empty silence, and an odd smell of parchment, ink, and stone.

"A special charm blocks all those who have no knowledge of magic from passing through the wall," Mrs. Mckinney said to Aria.

Aria stared at the wall behind her where a painting of an old, red barn hung. "Are we in the Vezchia Realm? What is this place?" She took a deep breath, trying to calm a shaky feeling inside her.

Part of her didn't want to believe everything she had been told, but another part did. It's like that desperate animal trapped inside of her had been let free and found its place. She had to let herself believe. She had just walked through a solid wall, after all.

"That wall is a veil, and no. We are not in the Vezchia Realm," Mrs. Mckinney answered and began walking down the corridor. "A veil is a camouflaged bridge between realms— a tear in the universe."

"Where are we?" Aria whispered to Luke and Avi as they followed closely behind Mrs. Mckinney.

"It's known as the Side Realm or Space Realm," Luke said. "It co-exists between the Vezchia Realm and the Mundane Realm. It is hard to explain, but essentially, there is no world within the realm. It's like an empty space."

"Mrs. Mckinney said something about it," Aria said. "So, someone built this place in the Space Realm?"

"Many people built it. Nobody but perhaps the great Diviner would be able to build this place by him or herself with magic."

"The Diviner?"

"It's just some old legend," Avi said.

The three of them followed Mrs. Mckinney through the plain, brick, windowless halls and up a set of stone stairs. At the top of the stairs, a hallway stretched out in each direction. Doors lined the walls of the halls, each one only a few feet from the next. Tiny plaques hung on the doors with names on them. Aria, Luke, and Avi followed Mrs. Mckinney down the hallway to the right. They passed door after door, then stopped at a door that's plaque had not been assigned a name. Mrs. Mckinney held her hand up, pointer finger out, level with the plaque. She seemed to be spelling something out in the air with her finger. Aria wondered what on earth she was doing. Only until Aria noticed the plaque did she understand. The plaque, which hadn't borne a name, now read, *Aria Chesler*. She didn't even notice her mouth was hanging open once again.

"Go ahead, this is your room. I am sure that Luke and Avi can help you find your way back to the cafeteria for dinner when you are done up here. I must go write some letters to the Forces of Light regarding your parents' situation." Mrs. Mckinney strutted back the other way.

Aria reached for the doorknob with her shaky hand, twisted it, and stepped over the threshold. The walls of the room were such an eye-burning white that she had to blink a few times. Her eyes landed on the bed sheets with a checkerboard pattern of the school's colors: sky blue and black. She wished she could just fall into unconsciousness on top of them. A black dresser stood next to the bed and a plain wooden desk was next to that. The room smelled like a mix between cleaning sprays and a collection of dust. She walked to the bed and plopped down on it, sinking into the thick, soft blanket that lay on top. Luke and Avi came into the room and let her bags fall to the ground near the bed.

"I remember when our rooms looked like this, too," Avi said, looking around.

"You'll be able to change the color of the walls and decorate as you wish…. You'll have to change the color of the walls with magic though, of course." Luke scratched the back of his neck. "We're not allowed to actually paint the walls."

"I can't believe any of this," Aria said quietly, taking in more of the room around her, which really was not much to look at. With everything she'd just been told and the strange, dim lighting that made everything seem like a dream, it felt like it really was. "Is this where you guys stay, too?"

"Yeah, everyone gets their own room here…" Luke said. "So, about your parents."

"Oh…Well, I got home and found them missing. My mother left me the letter I already showed you guys. Mrs. Mckinney told me about them being the leaders of the Forces of Light or something. She also said some guy named Malus Malamone wants to destroy them…and me," Aria said, and Mrs. Mckinney's words finally sunk in.

Someone out there in the world wanted to destroy her and her family.

It felt as if knives were twisting in her stomach at the thought.

"But you're safe and Mrs. Mckinney is going to help find

your parents and rescue them. I'm sure she will," Luke said, reassuringly. "Mrs. Mckinney is part of the Forces of Light. Every adult here is."

"Shall we head down to dinner?" Avi turned to head back to the door, rubbing his stomach. "Food always makes things better."

"Yeah…" Aria sighed, her eyes gazing at the wooden plank floor, stinging tears forming in them.

The three of them left Aria's new room, went back through the veil, and down to the first floor. The cafeteria was quieter than usual with less students. Aria thought about Malus and her parents. Her head ached at the fact that they had lied to her about magic. As a result, dinner was rather quiet. It was hard for her to wrap her head around magic existing, but even more, was the tightening feeling in her stomach. A powerful man wanted her parents *dead.* She fought the urge to bang her fist on the table because of all the lies she'd been fed yet felt tears gathering in her eyes because her parents were arrested. She could barely understand what she was feeling. One second, she was angry that they had kept such a secret from her, her whole life, the next she was beating herself up inside for being so seething at them. She felt like vomiting from all the information racing through her aching mind. She wanted so badly to go sleep and not have to process anything that happened within the last few hours.

Luke and Avi helped guide Aria back to her room in silence when dinner was done. She stepped into the darkness of the room and fell backward on her bed. Her mind couldn't stop racing for a second as she tried to fall asleep. All she could think about was magic and her parents being arrested as tears began to soak her pillow. She wished they were right there next to her to tell her everything would be okay.

Chapter Six

ARIA WOKE THE next morning, pulling her blankets off her as her eyes slowly opened and adjusted to the dimness. Her heart ached to see her parents after the nightmares she'd had all night. She'd have to tell Luke and Avi about how life-like they had felt. She sat up and climbed out of bed, her smile wiping off her face.

It had not been a dream.

Aria sank back down on her bed very slowly, dread and fear chilling her like ice. She wrapped her arms around her knees, wishing she could just curl up in a ball and not have to think. Then there was a tapping at her door.

"Who is it?" she called.

"Me—Luke…and Avi," Luke's voice answered from the other side of the door.

"Hello!" Avi's happy tone sounded forced.

"Oh…Uh—" Aria glanced down at the clothes she was wearing, taking in the fact that she was still wearing the clothes she'd worn yesterday. "Hold on."

Aria rapidly dumped out her duffle bag on her bed and picked out a new outfit. When she was dressed and had stuffed everything messily back into the duffle bag, she swung open the door. Luke and Avi stood awkwardly in the doorway.

"You wanna come down to breakfast?" Avi asked, evidently forcing a grin onto his face.

"Sure," Aria answered, but that wasn't what she wanted at all. What she wanted was to lay down in bed, throw the covers over her head, and force herself not to think about magic being real, her parents being arrested, or that evil guy who wants them dead.

Still, she followed them down to the cafeteria, which was even less crowded than the previous night. It seemed many people didn't care to eat breakfast, or they were still asleep.

"I thought all of this had been a dream…" Aria said quietly as they sat down with pancakes, a lump gathering in her throat. It felt so strange and wrong to be at the school so early, like she was suddenly put in another universe. She bit down on her lip and looked away, tears gathering in her eyes.

Luke nor Avi said anything in return.

"Celaena was right…This is not an ordinary school," she added. "But was this what Celaena meant? Did she mean that it's not an ordinary school because it's run by the Forces of Light?"

"Of course, that's what she meant," Luke answered and shoved a bite of pancake into his mouth.

"So, she knows about all this?" Aria's fist clenched at the fact that Celaena knew more than she did.

"Why wouldn't she? Her father is Seth Malamone, son of Malus Malamone," Avi said.

Aria choked on a piece of pancake and spat it back out. "What?" Her voice was loud, though nobody but Luke and Avi were paying enough attention to have heard. That day she had met Celaena came back to her suddenly like being splashed with icy water. Luke and Avi had said Celaena's last name: Malamone.

"Didn't Mrs. Mckinney tell you?" Luke asked.

"No. Why does Celaena go to this school then?" Aria set her fork down, unable to eat anymore with the swirling feeling in her stomach.

"Well, she's on vacation with her *mommy* anyway," Avi said. "I doubt the claims that Celaena and her mother make. Celaena's mother has been declared innocent, but me and Luke think she's guilty."

"Guilty of what?"

"Okay, let me put it this way—Celaena's mother was married to Seth Malamone. Seth and Kora, Celaena's mother, got divorced and Kora was found not guilty of being involved with the Dark Forces. Kora, however, had been known to follow her husband's ways, and it has been rumored that she is still involved with the Malamones', which means that she is involved with the Dark Forces. At her trial, she claimed she wanted to quit those ways and even divorced him, so they held nothing against her. But Celaena keeping the Malamone name is proof enough to me and Luke that they're still involved," Avi explained. "That would explain why Celaena hates you so much. Celaena must have recognized your last name. I mean, we did, too. Most enchanters and enchantresses know the last name 'Chesler' because your parents are the last leaders of the Forces of Light."

Aria took a deep breath, trying to calm the rage beginning to boil within her. So that was why Cruel-laena hated her so much—because her parents hated her family. She sat, thinking it through. With information from the night before and the newest information, Aria's head was in a whirlpool of thoughts. It was strange that her last name was well-known, and yet she'd never even known it. She sat quietly for a great many minutes, just slowly lifting more pancakes into her mouth.

"Why don't many of the students know about…uh…magic?" It felt odd to say such a thing.

"Oh…I guess because their parents don't want them to," Luke said. "Many parents think by them not knowing, they're protecting them. If mundanes found out, they would attack us, just like they did in ancient history. Enchanters and enchantresses have been killed just because magic runs in our blood. I can see why parents wouldn't want their kids to know. But these types of schools keep us safe from all of that."

"That's insane," Aria said, her eyes going wide. "That's exactly what my parents did. They lied to me…Maybe they were trying to keep *me* safe."

She thought about that for a minute. How her parents never told her what their jobs were. How they always got distracted and walked away without an explanation. How strange occurrences always happened around her. How horrible it must have been for all those enchanters and enchantresses that died just because they had magic running in their blood. Maybe that was exactly what her parents had wanted to protect her from.

"I want to learn how to…What's it called?" Aria said, finally.

"You want to learn the art of magic?" Luke asked.

"Yeah, so how do you learn?"

"You'll have to talk to Mrs. Mckinney about it so she can make you a schedule. The other side of the veil is the side that teaches the art of magic."

"Okay," Aria said. "I should learn so I'm less vulnerable. Mrs. Mckinney said I was vulnerable outside of school. I want to be able to protect myself against the Dark Forces if they come after me."

"Well…uh…you should know that Malus is really powerful. Nobody stands a chance against him," Avi murmured.

"At least I'll stand a better chance knowing how to defend myself than knowing nothing at all," she stated firmly.

The boys said nothing in return.

"I'm heading to the office now. I'll see you guys later, maybe after I unpack in my room." Aria stood and swiftly departed.

Aria told Mrs. Mckinney that she wanted to start learning the art of magic, but also asked what the Forces of Light were doing to help her parents' situation. Mrs. Mckinney said that they were working it out and it would take some time. The response made a lump rise in her throat, but at least she would get to start learning magic as soon as Mrs. Mckinney finished making her schedule. Aria managed to make her way back to her room on her own and dumped out her duffle bag to put all her things away. Not being organized made her skin crawl. She pulled one of the dresser drawers open to find it already had clothes, fit to her style, neatly folded inside. Her jaw dropped, but she guessed it was normal in a magical school. Once she had folded up her own clothes and shoved them inside the dresser as well, she put the duffle bag neatly away in one of the drawers.

Aria spent the next hour just lying in bed and staring at the ceiling. This was what she wanted to do most of the day. She wanted to try as hard as she could not to think and just feel numb, but it wasn't working. She could still feel the sweat beaded up on her forehead, the lump in her throat, the hot tears welling in her eyes, and the uncontrollable helplessness residing inside of her. Luke and Avi came wandering into the room and the three of them spent the rest of the day sitting, pointlessly talking, and staring at the blank ceiling.

"That charm is called the Farbara Charm," Luke told her as he laid his hand against her walls, changing the color of them to sage green.

"It looks a lot better." Aria laid on her stomach on the bed. "I wish I could decorate this room more. It's so plain... If I could just go to my house—"

"No! Mrs. Mckinney specifically told you not to leave the school," Luke objected.

Then it was as if the many thoughts Aria had been sitting on all day fell out of her mouth and she sat straight up. "How can I just sit here and ignore the fact that my parents have been arrested? Or that some crazy old evil guy wants to kill me and my parents...None of this is normal...I can't believe any of this is happening! I feel like my life has been turned upside down...I have been locked up in this school for just twenty-four hours and I'm already going insane! I need to get out. I need to go into town or something." Aria couldn't keep her voice from rising.

Luke and Avi just stared, struggling for words.

Finally, Luke said, "Well, maybe...maybe Avi and I could teleport you into the town tomorrow—to Forest's Edge. W-we could just walk around, check out some shops, and then come back. We can't risk going to your house though...Malus or his Dark Forces could be snooping it out."

"Really?" Aria exclaimed, her stomach tightening from yelling at them; none of this was their fault. "Oh, thank you! I think I should head to bed." She feigned a yawn.

They exchanged goodbyes and the door thudded shut behind Luke and Avi. Aria changed into something more comfortable, turned off the oil lamps, and climbed into bed. As her eyes fell shut, a tingly pulsing started in her clammy hands, calling to her again.

Aria nearly dove right out of her bed when she sensed morning had arrived, ready to leave the school. She rushed to shower in the girls' bathroom and get dressed, then she headed back to her bedroom. Luke and Avi were waiting for her just outside her room, Avi with his arms crossed.

"So…uh…you ready to teleport?" A frown appeared on Avi's face.

"Yeah," Aria said, her fingers wrapping around her sunflower necklace.

"Okay, we'll have to go outside because there is an Anti-teleportation Charm on the school." Luke motioned for them to follow him, and they started for the veil.

When they reached the cracking stone steps leading up to the school, Aria shielded her eyes from the overly bright sun.

"I don't think this is a good idea," Avi whispered to Luke.

"Shh," Luke shot at him under his breath.

Aria bit her lip and pretended not to hear them.

They walked around to the shadowed side of the school, where the trees grew close and hid them from view.

"All right, Aria, you will have to hold both my hands," Luke said, nervously running his fingers through his hair.

Aria couldn't tell why, but her heart seemed to leap and sink at the same time when he said that. Heat flushed her face.

"Oh…uh…o-okay." She took Luke's outreached hands and a shiver ran down her spine.

"Now, make an *X* over your chest with your arms."

Aria let go of his hands and did as he said.

Luke gave a little laugh that revealed his perfect white teeth and said, "No, no, you hold my hands at the same time."

His laugh was the kind that made Aria's heart stutter a beat as she tried to follow along.

She took his hands again and, while holding her hands, Luke managed to make an *X* over his chest. Aria did the same. They were inches away from each other now and she felt an odd tingle in the pit of her stomach; butterflies were coming back again. She'd never been this close to Luke. A scent came off him: mint and a dash of strong pine. He was taller than her, but not by much. They gazed at each other momentarily…*Oh, his beautiful blue eyes.*

"Okay, we're going to teleport now," Luke said abruptly, bringing Aria back to her senses.

She watched Avi hold his arms to make an *X* over his chest. He had his eyes closed and then, *poof,* he was gone in an instant. Aria clenched her eyes shut, not quite able to believe what she was about to do. A strange sensation came over her as if a cold wind was blowing all around. The air smelled sweet. Her body jolted, and it felt like she had been sent ten feet into the air. Then she was lightly set back down. All the while, she'd held tight onto Luke's hands.

Luke's hands slipped from hers and her eyes flew open. Her whole body shook from the teleportation, and it felt as if she might fall over. Shadows from a long strip mall were cast over them. A black door stood out from the back wall of the building, a sign on it reading: *Sweets and Treats Bakery.* Aria stepped out around the corner of the shop and saw the tiny, empty dirt parking lot that she and her parents had parked in about a month ago to get donuts. That seemed like forever ago.

"I wish we had money." Aria peered through the large glass windows of the bakery.

The sight of such delicacies made her mouth water. Remembering that day in the bakery with her parents made her eyes begin to tear up and she grasped her necklace.

"Avi and I used to love coming here. They have the best chocolate cupcakes," Luke said. "We would always sneak out after school was over."

They drew their eyes away from the sweets and walked across the street to another row of little shops. A pizza place, a small grocery market, and a pet shop—though they only had a cat adoption center—were bustling with people going in and out. Walking along the sidewalk, Aria soaked in fresh air and the sounds of people going about their everyday business. The boys didn't talk much; they just followed after Aria.

Relief washed through Aria the further they continued, glad to be in a new environment. Being cooped up anywhere for too long made her feel as if the air might suddenly disappear. She needed the sun and breeze. Outside, children were playing in their yards. For a moment she thought she saw the bushy, blond hair of Willow, but maybe she was just imagining it. They turned the corner, walking past the entrance to a little park.

"Should we uh…maybe go back?" Avi asked when he saw they were approaching the police station.

"My parents are in there…" Aria's voice was soft, but Luke and Avi still managed to hear her.

Her heart started to race as she thought about her parents being locked away within the walls of the police station. She knew her parents couldn't have committed whatever crime the police thought they did; they were too kind for that. They'd always told her that they helped people, and now she knew they were the leaders of the Forces of Light. They weren't criminals. She grabbed her sunflower necklace, traced the petals, and chewed on her bottom lip.

"W-we should g-go. I-I'm sure Mrs. Mckinney will notice we are gone," Avi pressed, then whispered under his breath to Luke, "I told you this was a bad idea."

A group of people stood around a section of the station, so Aria proceeded. The station was made of dark gray and white bricks with large, clear windows in the front. Well-kept gardens grew under the windows and the smell of the flowers wafted through the air. Several pointing cops and detectives surrounded a taped-off area, their inaudible voices meeting Aria's ears. Aria walked past a couple of police officers and stared beyond them to see why everyone was pointing at the side of the building.

On the side of the police station, the wall was crumbling away. A giant hole had been gouged out of the wall like something was blasted through it. Through the hole, Aria could see an empty jail cell. Her heart stuttered a beat, immediately thinking of her parents. Without registering what she was doing, and before Luke or Avi could stop her, she walked up to a policeman.

"Excuse me?" Aria asked in the most respectful tone.

"Not now, young lady." The policeman glanced at her and went back to talking to another cop.

"All I want to know is what criminals were in that cell." Aria pointed to the wall.

"Miranda and Oliver Chesler, husband and wife. Now, will you please excuse me? I'm trying to do my job," the policeman answered gruffly, only glancing at Aria.

Aria stumbled backward, a knot tightening in her chest, and her breath came in quickly. Her mind froze, blocking out everything else, as she thought one thing: *my parents escaped.* Luke and Avi caught her just in time or she would have stumbled out onto the road.

"Wait, excuse me, young lady. What is your name?" The policeman had turned back around and was looking at Aria with a great amount of suspicion.

She didn't answer, her eyes still trained on the hole in the wall.

"Young lady, I asked you what your name is and I expect an answer."

He knows! I'm sure they've been looking for me everywhere. Aria's mind spun. *How could I have been so stupid? Why did I make Luke and Avi bring me out here?*

Luke poked her on the shoulder and whispered close to her ear, "Aria, we should go now."

Even though Luke had spoken in a hushed voice, the cop had heard most of it; Luke was terrible at whispering.

"Your name is Aria?"

Luke grabbed Aria by the wrist, who remained glued to the spot still, and began running. It knocked Aria back to her senses and the three of them ran back the way they had come. Aria pulled her sweaty hand from Luke's as she ran, her face flushed.

"C'mon, we just want to talk!" the policeman yelled from behind them.

They dashed past small businesses, houses, and a strip mall. They were coming up to the grocery market, where a bald man outside was passing out free newspapers. Aria skidded to an abrupt stop in front of him, her hand held out.

"I would like one, please," she said, her other hand anxiously tapping on her leg.

Luke and Avi stared at the cops running towards them and then back at Aria, shifting their weight from foot to foot. The man handed her a newspaper and they bolted down the sidewalk again.

They only looked back when they heard the man yell,

"Wait, you look like Aria Chesler!" The man looked back and forth between his newspapers and Aria.

From behind, the police repeatedly yelled, "STOP!"

"We just need to get behind the building, then we can teleport back to school," Luke managed to get out.

The three of them raced down the sidewalk, passed the bakery, and hurried through the once again empty parking lot. They stopped behind the bakery, coughing and trying to catch their breaths. It felt like there was a fire in Aria's throat as they took their positions. Avi had his arms crossed and his eyes closed and then he was gone. Aria quickly grabbed Luke's hands, a shiver going up her spine, and they both made an *X* across their chests. She was so caught up in everything else that she forgot to close her eyes. She felt the cool sensation of a gust of wind and felt as if she was flying. The world faded away and all around her became a dizzying blur of colors as places, space, and the other realms rushed by. Aria instantly felt nauseous and forced herself to close her eyes, squeezing Luke's hands like they were her lifeline.

CHAPTER SEVEN

HER FEET HIT solid ground and she fell over onto her hands and knees in the dirt. She felt her stomach lurch and began retching up nothingness since she hadn't eaten anything since dinner the night before. She continued to keep her eyes closed, feeling like the world around her was still rushing past.

"You didn't close your eyes, did you?" Luke asked.

Aria shook her head as she gagged. Once the heaving stopped, she turned back to them. Luke reached out his hand. She took it and rose to her feet.

"So, did you have fun getting out today?" Avi asked sarcastically as they started for the front of the school.

"You know very well that I didn't… But I did get to find out about my parents escaping their holding cell," Aria said. "I don't know how they managed it. I grabbed the newspaper to see if it says anything about the breakout."

"Yeah, well, you almost got us caught!" Avi's tone was loud and agitated.

"I almost got *myself* caught. The police wouldn't have taken you. They only want me because of what they think my parents did."

"Aria, who knows what they think! They might have taken us in for questioning, too!" Avi crossed his arms and stormed inside.

She looked at the ground, a twisting feeling in her stomach, and bit her lip.

"Ignore what he says. He'll come around." Luke stopped in front of Aria and took her hands in his.

Her eyebrows shot up, staring at her hands clasped in his, but her heart rate picked up.

"What matters is that we are all back safe," he said.

Luke noticed her expression and awkwardly pulled his hands from hers. They continued on inside. Avi waited at the top of the stairs for them, a scowl etched into his face and his arms crossed. Luke and Aria led the way down the hall, then down the dim corridor, and through the veil. The sound of Avi's footfalls echoed behind them all the way to Aria's room.

Staring at the front page of the newspaper, Aria plopped down on the edge of her bed. Luke sat down next to her, and Avi dragged the desk chair over to sit near them. A colored photo of the hole in the wall of the police station took up a big section of the front page. Aria began to read aloud.

"On April 22 of this year, the Forest Edge Police Department reported a criminal breakout. The criminals, Miranda and Oliver Chesler, were to have a hearing this coming Monday, suspected of attempted robbery. These two criminals, however, broke out of the side of the building. How they did it, nobody, not even the Police Department, can clarify. The security guard who was watching the prisoners says, 'Miranda and Oliver Chesler were asleep, so I have no idea how it happened. It was just past midnight and then all of a sudden, the wall exploded. I don't think they were breaking out. I think someone was breaking in!' Police and detectives are still trying to solve the case. Please be careful as you go about your days until these suspected criminals are caught."

"This is insane!" Avi finally said something. His grumpiness seemed to have left him.

"Yeah…That was the night they were taken…" Aria trailed off, captured in thoughts. "My parents wouldn't ever try to rob anything though."

"They probably weren't trying to. Mundanes often arrest innocent enchanters and enchantresses for using magic," Luke said. "They find a reason behind it and put the blame on someone."

"Yeah, that is what Mrs. Mckinney told me." All the strange occurrences that had happened around Aria ran through her mind. She'd been the blame for all of it.

"I've heard that using magic can make alarms go off," Avi said. "Or when something strange happens on a security camera, it doesn't pick up the full scene, and it looks like someone's trying to steal instead. But what does the guard mean someone broke in? Do you think someone saved them?"

"Oh! Maybe the Forces of Light!" Aria exclaimed, excitement welling up inside her. "I'm sure that is exactly what happened. I bet my parents will be coming here any time now and I can go back home!"

Luke stared at his fidgeting hands and Avi's eyes wandered off to the walls.

"Guys, what's wrong?" Aria looked between the two of them.

They both stared back at her with their faces looking somewhat glum.

Luke spoke first, "Well, it's just we—well I know I do—but I like you living here at the school. I don't want you to leave…"

"I don't want you to leave either. We want you to get your parents back, but we really don't want you to leave the school," Avi said.

"I won't leave the school. What would make you think that? I might stay here, but I guess that is up to what my parents say. I like being here, too." That last part was sort of a lie, but she wanted to make them both feel better. Honestly, she liked her home more than her cramped dorm. "I'm just really excited about my parents breaking out… But I do wonder what they are going to do about the police trying to arrest them again."

She looked at the front page of the newspaper. There was an old-colored photo of her from about a year ago that had been taken at her old school. Underneath the photo read: *Missing* with some information about her. She didn't bother reading the information they'd managed to collect.

"I also have the police on my tail. Who knows where they would send me if they caught me. They might send me to an orphanage. I would never see my parents or you guys again!" Aria added as she stared down at the horrible, cringy photo of herself.

"Well, that won't happen. The school is going to protect you until you have your parents with you again," Luke reassured her in a calming tone.

"I know, I just can't help but worry." Aria stared up from the paper into his beautiful eyes… No, that was creepy, so she looked away.

Luke, Avi, and Aria spent the rest of the day as usual. Dinner came and dinner left, and still Aria's mother and father hadn't come like she thought they would. She went to bed early, thinking and hoping maybe they would make an appearance in the morning. Tears soaked her pillow as she drifted into sleep, wishing she knew where her parents were and what they were doing.

"Aria! Aria! HELP!" her mother's voice called from somewhere.

All around was endless darkness. There was a high-pitched scream and Aria could feel sweat beading up on her forehead.

A deep voice, her father's, said distantly, "We need you, Aria."

She couldn't see her feet, her hands, or anyone to which the voices belonged to. She stepped forward and tried to call out for her parents, but no sound came. There was a heinous cackle that belonged to a deep man's voice, but it wasn't her father's. It was like the floor slipped from beneath her feet and she was falling, down, down, down. She screamed, but her voice was silenced, and her feet hit the ground painfully. Her heart hammered in her ears as she tried to call for her parents, but still, she couldn't hear her own voice.

"Aria, you can't escape this. They can't escape this… It is fate," the dark, mysterious voice said.

Just as the room was beginning to brighten, Aria's stomach jolted, and she sat up out of bed. She was still in her room at school, panting, trying to figure out where she was and what was going on. She was in her bed, wrapped up in her blanket, drenched in sweat. Her hand immediately went to her head to wipe off the moisture. Her heart pounded rapidly. Hastily, she got up out of bed, dressed, and went down to the cafeteria as fast as her feet could carry her.

Luke and Avi were eating eggs and bacon at the table they usually sat at. Aria plopped down in a seat in front of them, trying to catch her breath from racing down the halls and steps.

"Whoa…wha's go' you in a 'urry?" Avi asked, his mouth stuffed with eggs.

"What?" She looked at him, clenching her tingling hands.

Avi swallowed and repeated, "Sorry. What's got you in such a hurry?"

"Oh…uh…I just had a weird dream last night and… uh…I'm starving." She avoided eye contact, blinking rapidly, and wiped her sweaty palms on her jeans.

"Well, good thing I grabbed you a tray of food, then!" Luke pushed a tray of eggs and bacon to her.

"Oh, thanks." Aria picked up the fork and started to shove food into her mouth, her feet tapping against the floor. She couldn't wait to get outside and wait to see if her parents would arrive.

"So, what was the dream?" Avi asked.

Aria honestly didn't feel like telling them about it. It was just a dream, even though it had completely freaked her out. She didn't want to make a big deal about it, but she said, "Oh…I was in total darkness…My parents were calling for help…and some man's voice was saying, *'You can't escape this. They can't escape this. It is fate.'*" She wanted to smack herself in the head; that seemed like *way* too much information.

"That *is* a weird dream." Avi shot a face at Luke.

"Yeah…" Aria sighed.

"So, what do you two want to do today?" Luke asked.

"Well, I'm going to keep a lookout for my parents." Aria peered out the window. "It looks like a nice day, so we could be outside and keep a lookout for them."

Luke and Avi both looked at each other like there was something they wanted to say, but whatever it was remained a secret.

When they finished eating, they went outside and sat on the steps of the school. A pressing silence fell on them, not knowing what they wanted to say, and Aria stared at Luke while he was tossing a football into the air next to her. She felt like such a creep, but couldn't help it.

"I'm sure that they'll be coming any time now," she kept reminding them, though doubt began to seep into her mind more and more as time passed. After all, it had been days since the breakout. Why weren't her parents coming for her? They wouldn't just abandon her, right? Her parents surely would not want to keep her waiting, guessing if they would ever return.

"Aria, can you come to my office?" Mrs. Mckinney's voice came as she peered out of the wide school doors.

"Yeah." Aria jumped up excitedly and she strode into the building. *Finally, news about my parents!*

She sat down in one of the armchairs in front of Mrs. Mckinney's desk, relaxing against the comfortable cushions.

"I made your schedule, dear." Mrs. Mckinney pushed a piece of paper on her desk toward Aria. "You are to start it when spring break ends next week."

Aria took the paper in her hands and read through it. She still had all the classes she normally had, but the school day started earlier and ended later. She would be doing school from early morning until right before dinner. Her magical classes were to rotate throughout the week. As much as she was excited to learn magic, she really dreaded the long days that were to come.

"Mrs. Mckinney? Do you know anything about my parents?" she asked when she looked up from the paper.

"I don't know what you mean." Mrs. Mckinney furrowed her brows.

"Like, do you know where they are? They broke out of jail a couple of days ago."

"I am afraid not, but the Forces of Light are doing everything we can to locate them."

"Oh," Aria said, heartache filling her back up. This was not the kind of news she was hoping for.

"For the schedule, you'll have to work hard if you want to catch up with your friends. Now, I must get back to work. Good day, dear!"

Aria stood up and gradually walked back to the steps to sit down. Luke and Avi were now running around the empty parking lot, throwing Luke's football around, and shouting football references to each other that Aria didn't understand. She folded the schedule up and slid it into the back pocket of her jeans.

"Oh, Aria, what was that about?" Avi called when he noticed she'd returned.

"Schedule," she yelled to him with a frown as he tossed the ball back to Luke.

Luke nor Avi said anything in return as they continued to play catch. Avi threw the ball so far away from Luke that they had to run into the forest to get it. When they came back, they were talking to each other in hushed voices. She strained her ears to listen in, but she still couldn't make out what they were saying as they approached.

"Hey…Aria, is it cool if Avi and I go to the library?" Luke asked her, giving an all too obvious forced smile.

"Sure."

She remained waiting on the steps even after they had gone, unable to stop staring down the road as if her parents might appear. She wrapped her arms around her knees and rested her chin on them. The chilly spring air blew a breeze through her hair and rustled the leaves high up in the trees. When April rain began to fall from the sky, she went inside. She didn't go looking for Luke and Avi. In fact, she was quite upset with them. She knew she shouldn't be—and she hated that she was—but they had just abandoned her on the steps, probably out of sheer boredom. Friends don't do that.

They support you through every step of the way, Aria thought to herself.

But you weren't really there for Avi when he seemed sad, now were you? The snarky voice crept back into her mind. *Why should they be there for* you?

Her eyes began to drip tears and she rushed back to her room, feeling angry at herself and the universe.

She let herself fall face-first on her bed and the tears soaked her pillows. She fidgeted with her sunflower necklace. It made her feel safe to clutch it and remember that her parents had been the ones to give it to her. Her parents were gone and now she doubted they were ever coming back. The police might have already arrested them again. She would have to be locked up in school for many years to come! She thought nothing in the world, not even magic, could ease the knot in her chest from her parents' absence. She wanted to punch herself in the tightening knot of her stomach because of her feelings and for being so upset at Luke and Avi. If they really were her friends, they would have actually cared to stay there with her and not let these heart-clawing thoughts consume her. She wished that everything was all just a horrifying dream. All she wanted was comfort in knowing her parents were not in prison and not being attacked by the Dark Forces. It all sounded really bad from what Mrs. Mckinney had told her. She stayed in her room all day. When Luke and Avi came up from the library and knocked on Aria's door, she didn't let them in. She just continued to wallow in her sadness, her pillow soaked with tears.

When dinner came around, she skipped it, even though her stomach was growling like a monstrous beast.

"Aria, please let us come in," Luke's voice pleaded from the other side of the door right after dinner ended.

She said nothing and didn't move out of her bed to open the door, sobs racking her body.

"Aria, please, we brought you food."

Lifting her head, she looked at the door, not knowing

whether to open it or ignore them and continue to be hungry. The hunger grew too much for her to resist, so she made herself get out of bed. The delicious oregano and tomato sauce drifted in from the other side of the door. She turned the knob and opened the door just a smidgen so she could see them.

"Can we come in?" Luke asked.

Aria nodded and tried wiping off her tear-stained face with her hand. She opened the door all the way, stepping off to the side so they could come in. Luke set the food tray on her desk and stood awkwardly on the other side of the room. The door shut with a bang behind her as she walked over to the desk to eat the lasagna. It was still warm and so very flavorful, though she might have just been so hungry anything would taste good.

"Why haven't you let us in all day?" Avi asked, sounding hurt.

Aria didn't answer, feeling as though she had gotten a punch to the stomach when she heard his tone. She waited for an explanation from them first.

"Look, we're so sorry we left you earlier on the steps, but we wanted to do some research on something," Luke said, and he sounded like he truly meant it.

Aria wasn't going to buy anything they were saying, though. "*Oh really?* It's spring break! What could you possibly—"

"We weren't researching for school. We were researching for you!" His tone stayed surprisingly calm.

This caught her off guard, but she still didn't look at them. She just stared down at her tray of food, eating.

"And what was it you were researching for me for?" she asked, trying to sound politer, but it may not have come off so.

"That dream you told us about earlier got me and Luke thinking…" Avi said. "There are some dreams that give out warnings. They're called Premonition Dreams. It is a rare thing that happens."

"It's when the universe is trying to give you a warning or tell you something important," Luke explained. "We wanted to do a little research on them, so we took the chance while you were watching for your parents. We sort of thought that maybe your dream was a Premonition Dream. We wanted to tell you sooner, but we didn't want to worry you with anything else."

She spun around in her chair to look at the two of them and apologized, "I'm sorry, guys. I thought that you guys had just given up on my parents coming and got bored."

"Of course, not…But it was something along those lines." Avi turned away and shoved his hands in his pockets.

"What?" she asked loudly, bitterness flickering back into her eyes.

"Please, just hear us out, Aria," Luke pleaded and shot a disapproving look at Avi.

"I'm listening," she bit out and turned back to continue filling her stomach. Her throbbing hands began to shake as she fought to hold back tears.

"Well, we think that maybe your parents didn't break out. Like the guard said in the newspaper, we think someone broke in…but not the Forces of Light," Luke said.

Aria looked at him and his face contorted as though what he was trying to say was painful. She could tell that whatever he was about to say was not going to be good.

"We think that your parents being in jail left them vulnerable, so the Dark Forces broke through the wall and captured them. We can't be sure though…We could be completely wrong," Luke explained. "It's just that it's very possible and makes sense because Malus has been wiping out the main leaders of the Forces of Light for the last several years."

Aria soaked this in and turned back to her food so they couldn't see her emotions flicker across her face. What they were saying did make sense and they were probably right. They must have been moving all the time because of Malus trying to track them down, which was exactly what Mrs. Mckinney had said. Her parents were vulnerable in jail, so the Dark Forces took them then. She couldn't form words. She didn't want to believe it, but she knew that her parents would've come for her if they could. Her fists tightened in her lap at the way she'd treated Luke and Avi when they were trying to help after all. She pushed her food away, unable to eat anymore, and her stomach threatened to vomit up what she'd had.

"Aria?" Luke asked as he slowly walked toward her.

"I—I…You're probably right. I—I have to d-do s-something," she stuttered. Her whole body was shaking, and tears were dripping out of her eyes. It was worse than prison for her parents. For all she knew, Malus wanted her parents dead. "What d-do I—I do?"

"We can't do anything," Avi said. "The Forces of Light will take care of it. The only thing we can do is tell Mrs. Mckinney what we think and let them take care of it."

"H-how can you s-say that? W-what do you m-mean '*we?*' My parents could be being t-t-tortured or k-k-killed at this very moment!" she cried, her voice growing louder as she spoke. Tears trailed down her cheeks, leaving her eyes puffy and her face red.

"Aria, you would only be endangering yourself if you tried to do anything," Luke said, his eyes softening. "Not to mention, we have no clue where they are."

"And I say '*we*' because we're friends and friends help each other," Avi added to that.

"I'm so sorry for getting mad at you guys and not letting you in." She stood up from the desk and turned towards them, trying to wipe the tears away. Guilt was poking at her like a thousand needles. "I really am sorry."

Aria was much more silent the rest of the day and the next. The crying hadn't stopped much either. She thought she was sure to be tearless eventually, but there were always more tears left to cry. Luke and Avi had gone with her to Mrs. Mckinney to explain their suspicions. Aria kept quiet while they explained everything, staring with her puffy eyes at the corner of the desk. Mrs. Mckinney said she would alert the Forces of Light right away to see if they were correct.

Days passed and they heard nothing about Aria's parents whatsoever. She asked Mrs. Mckinney if she had heard anything each and every day. But she never had anything more to tell her, so she took to crying in her room while Luke and Avi tried to keep her company. Eventually, she just wanted to be alone.

Spring break was coming to an end. School was to restart the very next day and Aria was depressed having realized that Celaena would be coming back.

They were gathered at dinner. More students had been dropped off earlier that day for when school restarted in the morning, so the cafeteria was filled up more. Dinner was quiet so far and boring in conversation. Aria looked up from her food when she saw Mrs. Mckinney coming toward her out of the corner of her eye. Mrs. Mckinney had a deep frown on her face and fidgeting hands. At once, Aria could figure out why she was coming toward her.

Her guess was correct when Mrs. Mckinney said in a delicate tone, "The Forces of Light have sent me word that the Dark Forces have captured your parents."

CHAPTER EIGHT

ARIA COULD NOT manage a sound to express the unbearable, twisting ache that followed Mrs. Mckinney's words. Her eyes filled with more shiny glass-like tears again.

"H-how d-d-do you know? Are y-you s-sure?" Aria stuttered after a few minutes, her face flushed and her eyes growing puffy.

"The Forces of Light managed to track them down while they were being transported by the Dark Forces. However, the Dark Forces sensed themselves being followed and attacked our troops," Mrs. Mckinney said with a soft look on her face. She placed her hand gently on Aria's trembling shoulder. "We are doing everything in our power to help your parents. I have to go write some letters and make phone calls to the Forces. I am so very sorry, Aria. *Please*, come see me if you need support." And then she left.

Aria sat, still gazing at the spot where Mrs. Mckinney had been, fiddling with her sunflower necklace. She traced the petals on it as an aching lump formed in her throat. The tray of food in front of her began to rattle slightly as a pain twisted in her chest and Luke held it down on the table. Her breathing quickened and shuddered. Red-hot anger, like knives piercing her chest, coursed through her. Every emotion was confusing. She wanted to weep like she would never be happy again. She wanted to sort everything out and protect her parents from harm. But she also wanted to smash everything in sight and yell at people to help her as if they could. She felt condemned and alone, like she had already lost them forever. How could someone bear this emotional pain?

"Aria…we are so, so sorry," Luke said, his eyes flickering with pity. "If only there was some way we could help."

Aria looked up at Luke and Avi as tears ran down her face and blurred her vision. She figured people were staring at her, confused about why she was crying. Certainly, none of them knew what had happened to her parents yet.

"We understand what you are going through," Avi said.

Aria shook her head. "No, no you don't."

Avi's eyes watered and he gulped, but Aria, not taking notice, got up from the table and slowly made her way back to her room to cry, and maybe even smash some things.

She flopped down onto her bed and let out a long, high-pitched, pain-filled scream. That didn't make anything feel better. She shoved her face into her already damp pillow and cried some more, clutching her sunflower necklace. After a few minutes, she felt rage boiling inside her like a blazing fire, so she got up and started throwing some of her shirts at the walls. She even threw her school bag at the wall with a loud thump. When that got old, she screamed again and curled up under her bed covers to cry. She felt every bone in her body trembling, sweat pooling on her forehead, and her hands were clammy as she balled them into tight, pulsing fists. Soon enough, her head was throbbing. She felt so alone, useless, and helpless in this immense world. What was she but a young teenager? She could do nothing to help the people she loved. She couldn't make the unbearable pain go away, or the anger, or the fear that she was going to lose her parents, the only family she had.

Time slurred together like the tears trailing down her face. Aria wasn't sure how much time had passed before there was a knock on the door. The sounds of her crying and wheezing slipped out into the hall, then the door was thudding closed behind someone. The chair at her desk scraped across the floor, and a familiar scent of pine and mint drifted to Aria's nose. Aria lifted the covers just enough to peer around them. Luke was sitting at her desk, staring at the mound of blankets piled on top of her. She let the covers fall completely over her again; it was embarrassing for him to see her like this. She was a tear-stained, snot-covered, depressed mess.

A few moments of sniffling passed before Luke said gently, "What Avi meant is that we understand why you are feeling the way you are. Avi definitely does a lot more than I do. I thought you ought to know—it's just not up to me to decide…But seeing as you have hurt Avi's feelings more than once now by accident, I thought I should tell you."

Aria turned over, slowly lifting the blanket to reveal her reddened, wet face. "W-what? I—I h-hurt his f-f-feelings?" She felt like a pit had just opened in her stomach at the thought of hurting Avi.

"Yeah, when you said that we don't understand, you made Avi upset. Avi's parents died when he was really young. They were one of the thousands of lives lost in working for the Forces of Light. He barely remembers them. He was then given to his aunt. She works here. Her name is Mrs. Helma. And now he is stuck living at the school with her." Luke scratched the back of his neck. "Anything that reminds him of that upsets him."

She felt guilt and sympathy knot up in her chest, twisting like a knife. How could she have been so selfish?

"I f-f-feel so b-bad! I—I shouldn't h-have s-said what I s-s-said," she sobbed, warm tears dripping down her face as she sat straight up on her bed. "Where is he?"

"It's okay, you didn't know. Just…don't mention to him that I told you. He really doesn't like people knowing," Luke said. "He doesn't even want people to know he's related to Mrs. Helma. He's playing a video game in my room since I sort of snuck a computer into it…" He stood up from the chair and sat down next to her on her bed. "Now, are *you* okay?"

"I—" She hesitated. Should she really tell Luke how she really felt? "Yeah…"

"Aria, you've been crying in here for over an hour. You can tell the truth. Are you really okay?"

"No. I'm tired and I—I lost them…"

"You didn't lose them, Aria. The Forces of Light will get them back. If the Forces of Light helped to stop the Dark Days, then they can get your parents back."

"The Dark Days?" She paused and looked down, tears dripping down her cheeks, and murmured to herself, "There's no way to know they'll get them back for sure."

"The Dark Days were the time when the Dark Forces were at their strongest, taking over huge parts of the Vezchia Realm. And I know the Forces of Light will get your parents back because they're the best, better than Enchanting Control."

Aria was lost in all the different names of things, but she was too tired to figure it out. She yawned and her breath shuddered again.

"I should leave and let you get some rest." He stood up and strode to the door.

As his hand reached for the doorknob, Aria said, "Wait! Will—will you stay with me, actually?"

"You want me to—to stay?" he asked, his hand leaving the doorknob.

"Yes, just for a little bit, please…If you leave, I might break something in here." She gestured to the dresser and all her shirts flung around the room, then wiped fresh tears away. It was embarrassing for him to see her and her room this way.

"I'll stay."

Aria leaned back against the pillows, her head throbbing like a heartbeat. Luke sat down right next to her and nervously ran his fingers through his hair. She breathed in deeply, wiping the tears away. The air felt like it had gotten cooler, so she pulled her blanket up to cover her arms. The awkward silence between the two of them was unnerving, so Aria had to break it.

"I don't think I ever told you, but you and Avi are my first friends," she said.

"Really?"

"Y-yeah. I always moved, so people made fun of me for being the new kid without friends. I would have some friends for all of a week and then they would turn on me. Having powers I couldn't control didn't help either. Sometimes my magic would get out of control, I guess. At least, I think that's what Mrs. Mckinney said. Strange things would happen and they blamed me for it all." Her breath shuddered again.

"Oh, I'm sorry about that, Aria."

"I'm glad I have you guys. My parents always wanted what was best for me, but I didn't want to put even more burdens on their shoulders. So, I never said anything about what happened at my old schools. They were so happy when I finally made friends…but now…they're…" It was too hard to finish the sentence. Fresh tears poured down her face.

Luke wrapped his arms around her and her tears soaked

his shirt. "Everything's going to be okay," he repeated over and over again.

Aria felt her eyes drooping and when Luke pulled away, she closed them. In minutes, the soft sound of her snores filled the room.

Luke stayed with her, listening to her as she murmured about how she didn't want to go to school, how she didn't want to have to see Celaena Malamone again. He continued to whisper that everything would be okay, running his fingers over her hair, until he knew she was in a deep enough sleep. He crept off her bed and across the room as her snores grew louder. The oil lamps were turned off and he snuck out the door to his own room, ruffling his hair as he stepped into the darkness. He shook his head at Avi's sleeping figure rolled up in blankets on his bed, the door thudding behind him.

The walls were a dark red, but they looked more like black in the dark. The blueish glow of Luke's computer screen lit up the rock band posters covering the walls, most of them hung up by Avi because he had too many memes covering his own. Luke stepped around all the dirty clothes, comics, and Avi's school papers strewn across the floor to get to his black dresser. Avi came in there a lot, so many of his own things were in Luke's room, including the dirty laundry he didn't feel like taking down to the washroom. Digging through his dresser, he pulled out a couple of spare blankets and a pillow that he kept for when Avi decided to have a sleepover in his room. He threw the blankets and pillow on the floor and laid down to fall asleep, but he couldn't get his mind to stop running. He felt bad for leaving Aria in her room alone, having to wake up the next morning with the weight of emotional pain on her shoulders, but it was awkward watching her sleep. A deep knot formed in his chest, wishing there was some way he could help her.

The moment Aria woke, reality struck her like a brick, but she forced herself to get out of bed and ready herself for the school day. Breakfast was quiet even with Luke and Avi. It pressed on her, making her wish there was something to distract her from everything that had happened the night before. Aria would never forget last night, especially how she had wanted Luke to stay with her. She didn't want to be alone. She wanted someone to talk to. Remembering it made uncomfortable heat creep into her cheeks and up her neck as she walked down the halls.

Her first-hour class was now Potion Brewing. After that was her usual English class. All the classes she'd had before would still start at their normal times. As she was shuffling through her backpack before breakfast, she'd discovered the other side of the veil, the magic side, had now appeared on her map as well. She hadn't even taken a good look around the magic side of the school. She only knew what was on the way to and from her room. Following the map through the veil, she walked down the stone steps and turned down a hall brightly lit with oil lamps.

The circular classroom had stone walls that seemed to trap the cool air inside as she walked past rows of metal tables. Her eyes roved over the equipment laid on them—metal ladles, tall metal bowls, goggles, and rubber gloves. A bald man with a chestnut complexation, gray suit, glasses, and a scarlet tie embroidered with potion bottles sat behind a metal desk at the back of the class. He seemed to be checking to see that he had collected the right potion ingredients. Behind the man, the wall was lined with floor-to-ceiling bookshelves filled with bottles of weird solutions and potion ingredients. Aria felt eyes trained on her as she moved past the younger students to sit near the green, blank, moveable chalkboard staged next to the teacher's desk. As she took a seat at an empty table, the teacher clapped his hands together, drawing the class' attention, and gave a wide smile that made his eyes light up.

"Hello, students! Welcome!" his deep, cheery voice echoed across the room.

He looked around the classroom, saw Aria, and nodded as if acknowledging her, but not directly calling her out. She appreciated that.

"You all know me as Mr. Felix! Today we will be making a Silencing Potion, otherwise known as the Zippity-Lips Potion. Before we begin today, I would like to review some things first."

A Silencing Potion? Ooo, I would love to give a potion like that to Celaena, Aria smiled at the idea of it.

"What are the safety measures we take when making a potion?" Mr. Felix asked the class.

Many hands went up around the classroom, but Aria was clueless.

"Miss Lila." Mr. Felix pointed to a red-haired girl in the back.

"We must wear goggles and gloves, sir," the girl answered, tucking a strand of hair behind her ear.

"Correct! Now, Lila, why do we wear goggles and gloves?"

"We wear them in case of splashes and explosions."

"Correct again!"

He turned toward the board and wrote something in the air with his pointer finger. Words appeared magically on the chalkboard: *Always remember to put on your goggles and gloves when brewing a potion.*

"So, can anybody tell me why we use metal or concrete bowls instead of plastic, glass, or wood?" Mr. Felix asked, turning back to the class.

More eager hands shot high into the air.

"Ah, yes, Isaac," Mr. Felix said and pointed to a blond-haired boy with glasses in the front of the classroom.

"We use them because some potions, especially if we do it wrong, will melt the plastic, shatter the glass, or burn through the wood," the boy answered with a smile.

"Why don't we just use a cauldron like mundane folk think we do?" a tall boy called out from the back sarcastically.

"Jack, you were not called on nor did you raise your hand," Mr. Felix corrected. "And using cauldrons is utterly preposterous! Anyway, Isaac, you were correct. Now, let's begin the potion. Put on your goggles and gloves. First, you are going to add room temperature water," Mr. Felix instructed as he dumped a modest bowl of water into his empty, tall, metal bowl.

Two dishes, just like Mr. Felix's, appeared on every table, even in the empty spot next to Aria. After putting on her gloves and goggles, she poured the container of water into her empty bowl and waited for further instructions, almost bouncing on her heels.

"Now add in six scoops of fairy dust. You will have to find it on the shelves behind me. Grab your smaller bowls, line up, and take turns grabbing it off the shelf. It is important to be able to find and identify the ingredients you are using. It builds familiarity with them."

Aria stood up with her smaller metal bowl and hurried to the already forming line near the shelves. While she waited, her eyes wandered to the strange ingredients. Up close, the jars looked to be filled with gels, hairs, leaves, flowers, and ground-up powders. Some of it was revolting to stare at, but Aria could only think of it as peculiar. To everyone else, this was another normalcy, but to Aria, it was a brand-new world she was now submerged in.

The line dwindled until there was one person in front of Aria putting the jar of fairy dust back down on the shelf. Aria picked up the jar filled with a metallic, gold, shimmering powder and scooped out her portion. Walking back to her seat and staring into her metal bowl, she thought of how it looked like fallen bits of stars. She plopped the fairy dust into the potion and the water turned to a lavender color, like the soft flowers you would see in a meadow. A gasp slipped from her lips at the oddity of it.

"Now, add the following ingredients on the board," Mr. Felix directed.

The next ingredient was a single troll nose hair.

That's absolutely disgusting! Aria found it hard to believe anyone would actually drink it. She walked over and grabbed one, long, nasty troll hair out of a tube from the shelves. Dropping the hair into the potion, she cringed and directed her gaze back at the board.

-Pheonix tears
-Sphinx mane hair
-Moonstone dust
-Ground Croccota fang

"And now stir it all together," Mr. Felix instructed after everyone had finished adding in the last bits of the potion.

Aria stirred hers and it turned from a deep, plum violet to a transparent liquid. Staring at her reflection on the potion's surface, a faint smile crossed her face.

"When you are finished, I will take a look around at your potions and take samples from your bowls. I will test that they work and grade them tonight," Mr. Felix said.

Miniature bottles appeared from thin air on the tables. Mr. Felix strode down a row of tables to gather samples, giving kind comments that carried across the room. While his back was turned, she grappled to fill both the bottle given to her and the one that appeared in the empty spot next to her. It felt wrong, but a part of her thought it might come in handy. It was only a little bit after all. Then she slipped the extra sample into her school bag.

Mr. Felix snatched up her sample and gave her a grin before calling out, "Okay, have a wonderful day, everyone!"

Aria's next three classes felt as if they were dragging on ten times longer than they were in reality. Her mind kept switching back to Potion Brewing and the need to understand the world she was now a part of. Noise filled the cafeteria when lunch finally came around. Aria spotted Celaena glaring at her from across the cafeteria. She changed her gaze back to the table as she sat down.

"I really don't understand potion brewing. It's easy to follow the directions, but I have no clue what anything but water is. I want to know why ingredients are used in a potion. Do you guys understand what everything is?"

"Yeah, but we started learning all this stuff last year. Maybe it's because you're starting later than everyone else and you know nothing about anything magic," Avi said and stuffed food in his mouth. "You'll catch on."

"You guys started last year?" Aria's jaw dropped slightly. She figured they already knew how to control their abilities, but hadn't realized she was so far behind them. She bit her lip and glanced away for a moment.

"Yeah, it's the law that any magic school can only teach students of age thirteen or older... Parents or guardians are allowed to teach kids at any age though," Luke replied. "It's because magic can be dangerous."

"No wonder all the kids in my class looked just a bit younger than me…"

Luke and Avi's eyes trained on something near the entrance to the cafeteria. Willow was making her way toward them in a soft lavender dress, her staticky blond hair bouncing behind her. Her eyes seemed to twinkle, a bright smile revealing her dimple.

"Hello," Willow said to everyone, then turned to Aria with soft eyes, gently touching her elbow. "I heard what happened to your parents and I am so sorry. I wish there was some way I could help you and them. If you need anything, just ask me and it's done."

"Thank you," Aria responded quietly, grief crushing her again. Her fingers anxiously found her sunflower necklace, tracing the petals of it. "Wait, how do you know?"

"I heard it from Celaena. I quote, 'Did you hear? Aria's parents were taken by the Dark Forces!' Then she laughed like she thought it was hilarious." A deep frown appeared on Willow's face.

"Great, I'll have to deal with Celaena talking about it." Aria rolled her eyes, but deep down, the words stung.

In the same way that Avi and Luke suspected Celaena was involved with the Dark Forces, Aria could tell Celaena knew something more about her parents' capture.

"I also saw it in the newspaper. I was outside and saw cops run past my house, calling your name. Were you in town?"

"Yeah…I was, but it was a horrible idea to have gone." Aria sighed.

"Yep, I knew it would be before we had even left," Avi injected.

They all looked at him in annoyance. The reminder was unnecessary.

"Well, on a high note, I got my cat over spring break. He's

up in my room. His name is Twilight. Since I just started studying astronomy, I thought it was a cool name for him," Willow said, making the conversation sound much more positive.

"He's in your room? Like…here…*at school?*" Aria asked as if she'd misheard what Willow said.

"Yeah, you're allowed to own pets here…but once the school day begins, they must be kept in your room. You're not allowed to have large dogs though, or any animal that takes up too much space. Maybe a small dog?" Willow explained.

"Oh, I didn't know that." There were a lot of things Aria didn't know.

"Yeah. Like, I saw one kid walk in with a snake around his neck yesterday!" Willow pressed her lips together to hold in a giggle.

"You're joking, right?" Luke asked, raising his eyebrows.

"No, seriously! He got yelled at by Mr. Monroy," Willow responded. "Anyway…I really like to sit with all of you… so I was wondering, could we maybe…be friends? We could hang out more now that I'll be staying here for the rest of the semester—my mom is taking a trip with my little brother next month, so I thought it might be a good idea."

Avi blushed so badly that he looked like he had a horrible sunburn.

"Of course," Aria answered and forced a smile. She still felt a heavy weight tugging on her because of her parents' situation, but she felt it might somehow feel worse if she let it show.

Willow had been hanging out with them over the last several weeks anyway, so why would they not be friends? After all, Willow was not acting like a weirdo anymore. Aria was actually surprised that Willow didn't think they were all friends yet. She was kind, gentle, understanding, and everything that makes up a good friend.

"That makes me elated!" Willow smiled, making her eyes seem even brighter.

The next three classes passed slowly, and Aria found that she couldn't stop drumming her fingers on her desk in anticipation of her more exciting, magical classes. Finally, when her regular classes had finished and the halls began to clear out, she headed through the veil, following her map.

The Basic Enchanting classroom was large and open with bright oil lamps hanging from the ceiling. Aria walked inside, striding past students on rows of cushions on the dark, concrete floor, facing a chalkboard hanging on the stone wall. She took a seat on one of the cushions in the back row. A middle-aged woman with long curly blond hair, black leggings, leather boots, and a fuzzy fur vest sat behind the dark mahogany desk in the back of the room. Behind her were bookshelves filled to the brim with textbooks. The teacher stood and walked around the large, propped-open, wooden chest right next to the desk. She walked off to close the door and then stood in front of the class again.

The teacher gave a warm smile. "Today we are going to be working on focusing our energy to knock people backward with a Knockback Enchant. Though, class, can you all just wait a moment? Aria, sweetie, follow me."

She gestured for Aria to follow, and they walked to the back of the classroom. The eyes of the other students drilled into her.

"Aria, have a seat," the teacher said. "My name is Mrs. Helma."

Hmm, so this is Avi's aunt.

Mrs. Helma drew a thin book off one of the shelves and

put it on the desk in front of Aria as she sat down. The book was shiny, and the cover had swirls of magic over the surface, the title being: *Learning to Control Your Gift.*

"Just read as much as you can get through today. I have to go teach the other students, but as soon as you finish reading this book, I'll give you a test to make sure you understand it. After that, I'll start teaching you things," Mrs. Helma said and then strolled back to the rest of the class.

Aria looked longingly at the class as Mrs. Helma began to teach. She didn't want to read; she wanted to learn. How was she supposed to defend herself against the Dark Forces with knowledge from a book? This wasn't what she had in mind. Reluctantly, Aria opened the book and began reading.

So, you are learning to control your magical abilities? The first key is focusing your energy on what you want to do. Some things may be harder to do than others, but once you know how to focus that energy of yours, it will be like an instinct. The second key is to never give up.

Aria glanced up from the book and watched the rest of the class practicing magic. The students were in front of dummies with their hands raised at chest level. The thudding of them falling echoed across the class. Every time a dummy fell over from a Knockback Enchant, a student would run to pick it back up. Where the dummies had even come from, Aria had no clue and so badly wanted to ask. Had they been conjured? Mrs. Helma was strutting around, stopping to help students. Aria made herself stare back down at the book and continued to read.

Hand motions are needed for many enchantments. Once you know what you are going to do, you perform the correct hand motions or say the word, though words are only used with some enchantments. For some enchantments, saying the word can intensify it. You need your energy to perform magic and you have to focus on creating what you want to happen with it. However, always remember that you will always be able to use magic, for energy cannot be created nor destroyed—only blocked in some cases. Practice makes perfect. It may be easy, or it may be hard, but you will get it eventually.

This is worthless information. Aria rolled her eyes, but she continued reading. Every so often she would look up and watch the other students, hoping maybe she could learn something other than *focusing her energy.*

"All right, that is enough. I will see you all tomorrow! Have a great rest of your day!" Mrs. Helma called out when class was over.

At once, students began scurrying out of the classroom noisily, but the sound soon diminished as they all disappeared down the hall.

"Aria, take the book with you. You can keep it," Mrs. Helma said, approaching Aria as she got up from the desk and grabbed her school bag.

"Oh, thanks." Aria put the book in her bag, zipped it back up, and slipped it back on her back. "Have a good day, Mrs. Helma."

History and Legends class was a cramped room with rows of desks and bookshelves lining the walls. She walked past the wooden desk in front of the class, which was covered in papers, notebooks, post-it notes, and textbooks. Somehow the desk looked cluttered yet organized. There was a little golden sign on it that read: *Mr. Monroy.*

As Mr. Monroy came walking into class, his thin hands behind his back, Aria took her seat among the other students in the second row. Mr. Monroy fixed his French beret sitting upon his black, gelled hair. He seemed to tower over the rest of the class. He curled his black, perfectly gelled mustache between his fingers. A frown appeared on his face as he looked at the class and his eyes narrowed.

"'Ello, class, today we will be reviewin' the Divinin' Powers and the legend of the Diviner," Mr. Monroy said in a heavy, unrecognizable accent. He didn't glance at Aria once, as if she wasn't even there. "The Divinin' Powers are rare powers gifted to some enchanters and enchantresses. There are a few different Divinin' Powers. Can anyone list one?"

Though so many hands shot into the air, nobody looked eager to answer. Everyone in the room looked bored out of their minds like this lesson had already been taught a thousand times before. Was this supposed to be a boring lesson? Aria glanced around at the frowns on all the other students' faces, her brows furrowed in confusion.

"Harper…" Mr. Monroy sighed.

"The Divining Powers are Shape-shifters, Mind-readers—" Harper explained, nearly bouncing up and down in her seat.

"I said *one*," Mr. Monroy stated. "But, yes, those are the Divinin' Powers, those and Omni-communication, Nature-manipulation, and Healing. I know most of you probably already know what the Divinin' Powers are and you might even have one…but it is in the curriculum—I mean, it is important to talk about these powers and their history. Now, please, take out your books and read *The Legend of the Diviner* from the legend section."

Aria raised her hand up in the air to say she didn't have a book, but to her surprise, one appeared right in front of her on her desk. Mr. Monroy turned away from the class to sit at his desk, glancing up at Aria with a kind smile. She took a deep breath and when she exhaled, she felt some tension leave her. She took her hand down and flipped the pages of the textbook to get to the legend section at the back. Everyone around her was already reading as she stopped on the page about the Diviner and began.

For hundreds of years, stories have been told about the great Diviner. The Diviner was the most powerful being in the universe who could yield all of the Divining Powers (Shape-shifting, Mind-reading, Healing, Omni-communication, and Nature-manipulation). The last Diviner was said to be named Evangeline Voland, but she died centuries ago of unknown causes. If the Diviner ever really did exist, the last Diviner disappeared without a trace, leaving people to wonder if she is just a story. The Diviner is merely a legend to some but to others, whoever the Diviner is, they are the one who will bring peace and hope.

In the middle of the page was a drawing of some kind, like a symbol. There was a crescent moon with a star at the top and bottom. Aria stared, intrigued by this symbol. Then she realized that it was the school's emblem. What was their emblem doing in a legend about the Diviner?

Alaric Malamone (deceased), was the creator of the Life and Death Stones. The Life Stone has been in the protection of Malus Malamone, leader of the Dark Forces, for centuries. It is unknown how these Stones came to be, but they are what is said to have stopped the Diviner from being born. It is also unknown how to destroy them and bring back the legendary Diviner, but in Viden lies the last remaining copy of The Death Stone Riddle, which supposedly holds the answers in an unknown language.

The Diviner's powers were said to have been passed on to whatever infant was born with a worthy destiny when the Diviner died. And so, the cycle continues on forever. However, there have been no confirmations of people with all the Divining Powers from the Enchanting Control Testers.

Many believe that the Diviner is just a made-up story to ease the minds of the young. Could it be that the legendary Life and

Death Stones are real, but the Diviner is not? The only person that could confirm if the Diviner was ever real or not is Malus Mal- amone. What do you think?

Aria reread it over again a couple of times while the others finished reading. Her stomach clenched as her eyes lingered on the name Malus.

"All right, now we are going to discuss what we think. Do you think the Diviner is real or just a legend?" Mr. Monroy asked, his voice laced with his thick accent.

Not many people raised their hands, obviously too shy to admit whether they believed or not.

One buffer boy in the back shouted, "This is nonsense! The Diviner isn't real! It's just rubbish adults tell kids!"

Everyone turned their heads backward to stare at the boy who had spoken out.

"You are to raise your hand in my classroom!" Mr. Monroy yelled, his cheeks reddening. "Detention, mister!"

The rest of the class was less fun since students didn't want to actually discuss anything. They were assigned to do some research on the Divining Powers. This was great news to Aria because she'd already planned on doing that. She felt a pull of fascination toward the story of the Diviner but couldn't decide for herself whether she believed in it or not.

After the long day of hard work, Aria plopped her bag down on the ground beneath the cafeteria table.

"So, how did you like your first day of *magic school*," Luke asked with his usual bright and handsome smile.

"It was great. I have some homework from History and Legends class. I thought we could all do homework in my room after—" Aria's voice was cut off by a cruel, smug voice from behind.

"How are your parents doing, Aria? Are they—How do I put it?—A little *tied up* at the moment? If you get what I mean…" Celaena laughed.

Aria had been so occupied with getting to classes and working hard to learn magic that the thought of what had happened to her parents had managed to slip her mind. How could she let something like that slide out of her thoughts? She felt guilt twist in her chest like a fire being awoken. Even though Celaena just wanted to be a jerk, the words hurt just the same. It caused fury and heartache to flood her brain. Before she could even think about what she was doing, she reached into her front pocket of her school bag on the floor. A crackling and pulsing of energy lit in her hands again, calling her like an old friend. She felt around and clasped the miniature glass bottle full of the Zippity-Lips potion.

"Leave me alone, Celaena." Aria didn't look at her.

Celaena was yapping about something, but Aria couldn't comprehend a single word. The potion was now just underneath the table. She flicked it open and felt an urge she'd never felt before. It was like an instinct and she didn't know where it was coming from. As she put her hand over the top of the bottle, she felt the pulsing of her palm grow stronger. She lifted the liquid out of the bottle and into the air, feeling a strange sensation coming from her hand. She directed the potion out from underneath the table just as Celaena paused, her mouth gaping open. Before Celaena could react, it went into her mouth. She coughed and sputtered before she tried to keep talking. But she had swallowed the potion and now, no matter how much she tried to flap her mouth, no sound came out. Celaena looked aghast and offended, her eyes bulging. Aria was in a bit of a shock as well. What had she just done? She could barely process what had just happened but didn't care either. Celaena tried to scream and she stomped her feet in rage, like a two-year-old throwing a temper tantrum. When Aria started laughing outrageously, peoples' heads turned in their direction. Celaena glared viciously down on her, but looked defeated and stomped away, her face red with temper.

"What did you do?" Avi asked, his fork stopped in mid-air on its way to his mouth. He looked just as in awe as Celaena had.

Luke and Willow were just staring at her, their jaws dropped.

"I used the Zippity-Lips Potion on her. I don't know what came over me. I just thought I could do it, so I did." Aria took a deep breath to calm down from laughing.

"Wow, you used magic…and on purpose…You might get in trouble though," Avi said and shoved more food in his mouth.

"Well, I don't care anymore. Celaena got what she deserved. Maybe she'll learn not to be such a Cruel-laena." Aria smiled, proud to have used magic without even knowing how. The pulsing was still faintly rushing through her veins like a crackling energy.

None of them could help it; they all smiled, feeling great that Celaena was finally put in her place.

Then Luke asked, "What were you telling us before Celaena interrupted?"

"Oh, right. I was saying that I thought all of us could do our homework in my room tonight. I just have to go to the library and get some books first."

"I'll come with you! I have to take a few books back anyway." Willow jumped up, slinging her bag over her shoulder.

Aria opened the fancy glass doors, the smell of old parchment and ink hitting her in the face. The oblivious librarian didn't look in their direction as they passed by the study tables.

"What kind of books are you looking for?" Willow swung her school bag off her shoulders. She unzipped it and took out several hefty books.

Aria squinted her eyes at Willow's bag, wondering how she'd even managed to fit all of them in there and what she thought *a few* were. Willow set the books on one of the wooden study tables. All of them had weird titles, including the one she'd seen before, *Mystic Beings of the Sea*. Willow slipped her bag on her shoulder again and picked her books back up.

"I need books on the Diviner and the Divining Powers," Aria answered. "And maybe some on controlling powers. Mrs. Helma gave me a stupid book about that, but it doesn't teach me how to do anything."

"Oh, well, those would be found in the magic section. I remember when Mrs. Helma gave us those first books. I like them. Reading is always the best way to learn something and I found a lot of information stored in the pages of that book," Willow said as she began walking down a row of bookshelves, Aria following after her. "When reading, you have to look past the words and find their true meaning, like a hidden message. There are so many things you can learn from a book. You just have to give it a try."

They walked through the rows and rows of bookshelves to the back of the library, where the lighting was dreadful. An old bookcase built into the wall held a Greek-titled book. Willow pulled on it. The wall looked like it was a swirling liquid for a moment, then solidified again—a veil. The bookcase looked entirely the same, but now Willow just waltzed right through it. Aria walked after her and they both appeared on the other side. Everything looked the same as the other side of the library, but instead of electric lights, there were oil lamps. Aria wondered how much electricity could run in the Space Realm while Willow turned around and pulled on a book from the bookshelf they had just emerged from. The veil sealed itself back up and it was a solid bookshelf again.

"Take a look around while I go give these books to Mrs. Pin's doppelganger." Willow smiled.

"Who's Mrs. Pin? And she has a doppelganger?" Aria raised her eyebrows in confusion.

"Mrs. Pin is the librarian. Don't you know that?"

"Oh, yeah," Aria lied.

"Her *doppelganger* is just her identical twin sister, who happens to be the librarian for the magic section of the library." Willow walked away with her soft purple dress ruffling behind her.

Aria browsed the rows and rows of books, looking for anything that would be of use to her. She found *A Divine History, The Full Legend of the Diviner,* and *The Stones that Stopped it All.* She could not help but wonder what all of the books in the magic section were about. There were so many books—books on magical creatures, potions, ancient history, and more. Willow came wandering back with a brand-new stack of books and together they checked them out.

On the way to Aria's room, Willow talked up a storm about all the new books she got and how gorgeous the one was.

"*Finally,* you guys took forever," Avi joked, standing outside of Aria's room with Luke.

Aria simply smiled and opened the door to let them all in. They stepped in, swinging the door shut with a thud. Willow had never been in Aria's room before, so she took a moment to take in all the blandness. The desk chair scraped across the floor and Willow took her seat in it, beginning to read the table of contents in one of her new books. Aria laid out her own books and notebook on her bed and laid down on her stomach.

"What are you guys working on?" Aria asked.

"Math, writing, the usual. We do have a little we have to practice from Basic Enchanting though," Luke said, spreading his papers and books across the floor with Avi.

"Basic Enchanting was *so* boring today. She made me read a book the whole time." Aria sighed.

She took out the book that Mrs. Helma had given her in class and began reading it, sighing impatiently every couple of minutes. There was suddenly a faint scratching at the door and Willow jumped up to see what it was. She opened the door just a tad to peer through the crack.

"Oh! I wonder how he got out of my room," she said. "I left the door unlocked, so maybe he managed to open it. I watched a video that said cats are very smart and can learn to open doors."

She opened the door more and bent down to pick up her cat. The cat was entirely black, with not a single other color penetrating its black fur. It had green eyes, short fur, and wore a collar around its neck. The collar looked simple with an itty-bitty pearlescent crystal hanging from it and a nametag.

"Aria, is it okay if Twilight comes in?" Willow asked, turning to show everyone her adorable cat.

"Of course."

Willow set the cat on the floor and it instantly bolted across the room to jump on Aria's bed. After Willow closed the door, she sat back down at the desk to read her books again. Twilight laid down next to Aria, watching her hands move across the pages of her notebook as she wrote down notes.

"Aw, he likes you," Willow grinned, looking at Aria and Twilight for a moment.

Aria ran her hand over the cat's fur and went back to work. She stopped for a minute, thinking, before asking, "What is Omni-communication?"

Luke looked up from his homework and answered, "It's the understanding of all languages, sometimes even animals."

"Oh, wow." Aria scratched something down in her notebook. "What do you mean *sometimes?*"

"Well, some minds are stronger than others," Willow said. "A cat's mind, for instance, would be harder to penetrate than a beetle's because a cat is smarter. But an animal's mind should be easy to read in general. It's humans that are hardest because they might know how to fight the invasion of their thoughts."

"That sounds more like Mind-reading than Omni-communication," Luke said. "The reason I say sometimes is because you can't exactly hear what an insect says. They're too tiny."

"I think what I said could apply to both." Willow went back to reading.

Aria looked back at her books, but this time she flipped open *The Stones that Stopped it All.*

The Life Stone has the power to take the life of someone and give it to another, however, it cannot revive the dead, for no magic can do that. Malus Malamone, leader of the Dark Forces, has been known to be using the Life Stone to make himself live longer. The Death Stone takes the power and strength from an enchanter or enchantress and gives it to another. This information has been gathered by the Forces of Light—

"Ow!" Aria spat. She eyed the three claw marks scraped into her skin, then eyed Twilight, whose claws were outstretched. "What did he do that for?" she scolded, glaring at the cat.

The cat seemed to glare right back.

"I don't know," Willow walked over and lifted Twilight from the bed. "Maybe he thought you were trying to play since your hands are moving across the paper?"

"Probably."

Twilight laid in the corner of the room, but didn't take his eyes off Aria.

Hours passed and Aria could feel her eyes falling low. Surely, it was past curfew. Luke and Avi were cleaning up their stuff to sneak back to their rooms, meanwhile, Willow had already fallen fast asleep with her face stuck in a book. They stood up, bid Aria good night, and then tip-toed out of the room. Aria wasn't going to bother waking Willow up. She cleared the books off her bed, turned off the oil lamps, and got into bed.

Once she had fallen into a deep enough sleep, the weird dream she'd had less than a week ago crept into her mind.

"Aria, you can't escape this…They can't escape this…It is fate," the mysterious voice echoed.

Then something outside of the dream lunged at her and she was jolted awake.

On her chest was Twilight, his claws out again, and his eyes trained on her. Aria sensed it was early morning as the cat meowed. She pushed the cat off her and he jumped down onto the floor with a thump. Getting out of bed, she looked around. Willow was on the floor, curled up in a ball, but still asleep. Aria picked out her clothes for the day and quickly got dressed in the dark while Willow snored and Twilight hid under the bed, meowing—probably for food. She grabbed her *Learning to Control Your Gift* book off the floor and stuck it in her bag, then slipped her bag over her shoulder, and left the room. Twilight watched her leave, his green eyes and crystal collar glowing faintly in the dark.

The empty corridors were brightly lit, even in the early

hours of the morning. She walked down the deserted corridors and through the veil. The halls on the other side of the veil were just as luminous but completely empty and there was an eerie silence. She went down the steps and into the cafeteria, which was devoid of people as well. After sitting down, she began reading *Learning to Control Your Gift*.

It seemed like forever passed until students were making their way into the cafeteria for breakfast. Willow had gotten ready for the day when she finally came down to eat with Aria, Luke, and Avi. Aria put the book away, having finished it.

After breakfast, Aria proceeded to Complicated Magic. She, of course, didn't understand yet another class; she knew almost nothing about even basic enchanting. During her next magic class, Basic Enchanting, she passed the test about the book. She was surprised she hadn't been reprimanded for giving Celaena the Silencing Potion yet, but luckily Celaena also hadn't spoken to her since.

That night, Aria, Luke, Avi, and Willow were studying again in her room. They'd been reading, writing, and helping each other out for an hour already when there was a polite knock at the door. Aria got up from her bed to open it, having to step around Twilight, who was laying on the floor, licking his paws. She pulled the door open and in the doorway was standing Mrs. Mckinney. Dread pulsated through her like an electric wave of shock at what terrible news she was probably about to tell her.

"Come with me," Mrs. Mckinney said and turned back down the hall.

Aria glanced a worried look back at her friends before closing the door and following.

She sat down in front of Mrs. Mckinney's desk, her fingers rapidly drumming against the seat.

"So, I hear you have taken a potion from class and used it on Celaena Malamone?" Mrs. Mckinney raised her brows.

Aria felt relief that it was not unfortunate news about her parents wash over her…Then heat flushed her face as she realized she was in trouble.

"Yes, I did," Aria admitted softly.

She hated being reprimanded, but she wasn't ashamed of what she did.

"I hate to do this to you, Aria, because of what is happening with your parents right now. But I cannot just let this go," Mrs. Mckinney said, disappointed.

Aria thought she was going to get expelled for a second, then realized that she was not allowed to leave the school and that they had to protect her. She had no clue what magical punishments were like. What if they shoved her in the kitchen freezer? Or turned her into a slimy frog?

"You are going to have detention with Mr. Monroy tomorrow after dinner," Mrs. Mckinney said.

Aria was taken aback by the simplicity of the punishment, but also relieved. Shove her in the freezer? Turn her into a frog? What was she thinking? Her relief faded, however, when she remembered Mr. Monroy's personality. She got the impression that Mr. Monroy didn't like people who broke the rules.

CHAPTER NINE

ARIA WALKED BACK to her room feeling beyond frustrated and annoyed. How come Celaena got to treat her like crap and she, who stood up for herself, had to get punished? It wasn't fair! *None of this is fair*, Aria thought to herself as she pushed open the door to her room. Luke, Avi, and Willow were cleaning up all of their things to head back to their rooms.

"You guys are going already?" Aria came to a stop in the middle of the room.

"Hey, what happened?" Luke asked, standing up with his school bag.

She strode over to her bed and plopped down on it with a sigh. "I got detention with Mr. Monroy."

Twilight, who was laying on her bed, went to swat at her playfully. She pushed him away and he jumped to the floor with a meow.

"Seriously?" Avi said. "I *did* say you would get in trouble though."

Willow shot Avi a reprimanding look, so he picked up his bag and hurried out of the room after saying, "Goodnight."

"Well, I'm sure it won't be that bad," Luke reassured her, but the next day didn't prove to be any better than how Aria imagined.

The next morning, she took a shower in the girls' bathroom and headed down to the cafeteria. Willow was sitting and staring at a book called *The Rare and the Wild: Cats*. Across the table from her were Luke and Avi, discussing their thoughts about the Divining Powers and the legend of the Diviner.

"I would want to be a Shape-shifter," Luke was saying as Aria sat down next to Willow.

"Yeah, but there is only so much you can do with that power. You would not even be able to Shape-shift into another existing person. I would want to be the Diviner if it existed," Avi said.

"You don't believe either?" Willow asked, looking up from her book.

"Nah, just a myth, if you ask me."

"I want to believe, I really do, but there is no proof that there ever was a Diviner…unless you want to go asking the most unmerciful man in the universe if it is true," Willow stated.

"Legends and myths always come from somewhere," Aria said, but nobody paid attention.

It wasn't that Aria believed in the Diviner. The topic was very confusing, but she knew that there was a source for every myth out there. After all, mundanes were said to have killed off witches, which she'd never believed, and then she found out she was an enchantress. Willow was right though; there wasn't much proof.

"You won't believe what I heard! Aria Chesler has *detention*," Celaena jeered from behind.

Aria turned her head and glared at her. "Yeah, but I don't mind, really," she lied. "Plus, I have detention with my *favorite* teacher, and I just happen to be his *favorite* student."

"Mr. Monroy's your favorite teacher? Oh, well, I'll just have to ask him when he decided to like any of the children here," Celaena said with a sly smile. "Because in case you missed it, he doesn't like students much."

"Maybe that's just the impression you get because he doesn't like *you*," Aria retorted, a smirk spreading across her face.

"Oh really, you think? Well…good, because I stole five gold coins from his desk the other day," Celaena stammered, looking irritated and infuriated. She flipped her silky, black hair, stomped away, and left the cafeteria.

"She stole from a teacher!" Willow exclaimed, then she began scrambling all her books back into her arms. "I must go inform the principal."

"Just be glad she didn't try to kill him," Avi said.

Luke, Willow, and Aria looked at him questionably.

"What? She *is* the granddaughter of a killer," Avi responded to their looks.

Willow had somehow managed to read two whole books by lunch, and they were thick books, too. Aria wondered if she had skipped her classes and just read the entire time, but that didn't seem like Willow. She was way too goody-goody for that.

At the end of the school day, having finished all of her classes, she went to dinner. She poked at her food, silence like a blanket over her and her friends. In Basic Enchanting, they'd been learning the Knockback Enchant. Mrs. Helma said it was the easiest of all Enchants, and yet she hadn't been able to perform it. In that moment, as she stood in front of one of the dummies, it was as if the magic in her veins was dormant. *I'll get the hang of it*, she told herself, but she still felt jealous of the fact that everyone else in her class was a year younger and had done it with ease. And Aria now had that tingly feeling of magic coursing through her veins, crackling with nerves. It was as if her own magic was mocking her. Luke and Avi started debating about which Divining Power was better, yet again. She wanted to participate in the conversation so that she could block out Celaena's jeering from across the cafeteria, but her lips stayed sealed. Willow had her head stuck in a book, her eyes skimming across the pages as if the words were the most important thing ever.

"Why do you read so much?" The words tumbled out of Aria's mouth.

"Because it's fun, plus I like to learn new things," Willow answered. "Words are magic and with them, you can see, hear, taste, smell, and touch things you never would in real life. You can learn things that you never would anywhere else."

Then she was back to scanning the words in her thick book about astronomy.

The halls were quiet as Aria made her way down them, her feet moving slowly and reluctantly. She really disliked how there were no windows on the other side of the veil. It felt narrow, tight, and eerie without the natural sunlight, though the sun had already set an hour ago. She opened the door to History and Legends and stepped in, her eyes adjusting to the low lighting.

"You are late," Mr. Monroy's accent seemed to become thicker with his irritation.

Aria felt something furry swish past her ankle. "Only by a minute."

Mr. Monroy was at his desk, writing things down in a large book. He looked up from his work to raise his eyebrows at Aria, creating creases in his forehead.

"Oh, sorry." She quickly looked down.

This was already off to a bad start.

"Sit." He pointed to a desk that had papers piled sky-high on it. Then he muttered, "Rule breakers are the worst kind of people."

Aria walked across the room and sat down.

"Grade the papers," Mr. Monroy said and went back to writing with his feather quill.

Great, I get to do his job. She began grading papers one by one with the answer key that Mr. Monroy had left on top of the mountain-high pile of papers.

It seemed Aria was there for hours on end. Her eyes were drooping low and she was growing exhausted. Her hands were aching from having graded so many papers, her eyes were tired of reading, and her back was cramping from sitting hunched over. Of course, Mr. Monroy paid no attention to Aria and did not acknowledge the fact that she was about to pass out at the desk. Just as Aria wrote a big, fat *F* on Celaena's paper, even though it was correct, Twilight jumped out of the shadows and up onto the desk. The papers, both graded and ungraded, were sent flying everywhere, getting mixed up on the floor.

"WHAT DID YOU DO?" Mr. Monroy screamed, jumping to his feet.

Aria was startled and jumped to her feet, her eyes scanning the room for Twilight. She caught sight of his bright green eyes and crystal collar glimmering in the dimly lit room.

"My—it's my friend's cat," Aria said, trembling as she ran to pick Twilight up.

"GET OUT NOW!" Mr. Monroy snapped his quill and threw it down on his desk. He pointed to the door, his face red as a tomato in the dim lighting.

Aria hurried out of the classroom holding Twilight and the door slammed shut behind her. She was still shaking out of shock, anger, and fear of whatever punishment she might get next because of what Twilight did.

She clenched her teeth down on her tongue in frustration. Twilight struggled to get away from her arms, meowing like he was in pain. He stuck his claws out and swiped them across her arm, creating three shallow cuts. She quickly dropped him to the ground with a thump. He sat for a moment to clean his fur while Aria looked at the scratches.

"You know what? Forget it! I'm not taking you back to Willow. I'm not going to get myself caught outside of my room past curfew while you attack me for no reason."

She sprinted down the halls even though the energy was already drained from her. Twilight ran as fast as he could to keep up with her, meowing as he followed. She got to her room, slammed the door shut right in the cat's face, and locked it. After kicking off her shoes, she laid down on her bed with the lights off and fell asleep in an instant.

When she woke the next morning, she could easily tell that she had slept in late. She felt uptight and wanted nothing more than to be with her friends. Her fist tightened as she sat up from bed, angry with Twilight and annoyed with how Mr. Monroy acted. Most of all, she was sick of waiting for answers. She wanted to know where her parents were and what the Forces of Light were doing to save them. So, at breakfast, Aria explained her plans of talking to Mrs. Mckinney to Luke,

Avi, and Willow. She told them that she was tired of waiting for the Forces of Light to do something, tired of waiting for news, but they told her to wait. It took every bit of self-control she had to listen to them.

A few days later, after trying to be patient, she marched down to Mrs. Mckinney's office. Waiting was like having needles poking at her, demanding she do something. Aria walked in without bothering to say anything to Miss Stax or knock on Mrs. Mckinney's office door. Mrs. Mckinney was on the phone, so Aria sat down to wait, tapping her fingers to the sound of the clock.

When she had finally gotten off the phone, she asked, "What can I do for you, Aria?"

As much as Aria felt furious about not constantly being updated about her parents, she politely asked, "Is there any news about my parents?"

Mrs. Mckinney was silent for a few moments.

"Sadly, no," she said at last. "We haven't sent any troops out since the first one. Many people got injured last time and they're still healing. We have no clue where they're keeping them right now…I'm sorry."

Rage boiled through her. Her parents were captured and the Forces of Light still hadn't done a thing about it? She felt her face contort to show fury and her insides felt like a fire was coming alive.

"You mean nobody has done anything?" Aria yelled.

"No. It's like I said. People got injured and we are still assessing the situation," Mrs. Mckinney answered, remaining calm. "But just in case we don't find them before the end of the school year—"

"Don't find them before the end of the school year?" Aria jumped to her feet.

"Please, Aria, there is a place you can go. Most students go to it if you'll just listen to me. You can go to Camp Enchanted."

Aria didn't want to listen, though. She irritably blew a puff of air and stormed out of the office, leaving Mrs. Mckinney to gape after her. Stinging tears gathered in her eyes, not just because of her parents, but also because of the way she treated Mrs. Mckinney. She wanted to turn around and apologize, but couldn't get her feet to move back in that direction.

Later that day at lunch, she told her friends what Mrs. Mckinney had said.

"To be fair, I see what she's saying…" Avi said, but then immediately regretted it from the look on Aria's face.

"It's been two weeks!" she shouted and many people turned to see what was going on. The burning fury inside her seemed to still not have died down. "If they don't do something faster, I'm going to rescue them myself!"

Lunch was silent after that. Luke, Avi, and Willow avoided looking at Aria. Her heart felt like it cracked into a million pieces. Guilt poked at her like thousands of red-hot needles. Her temper was hot inside her, but it wasn't meant for them.

"I'm sorry," she said after a while, but it was so shamefully quiet that none of them heard.

She sat in the shadowed corner of the Complicated Magic classroom, everyone else's voices distant as guilt burned a brand on her heart. Lunch was still fresh in her mind, her own upset voice replaying over and over again. She couldn't bring herself to be close to anyone else, so she sat away from everyone, freezing and unfreezing a glass of water in front of her.

"Once an object is frozen with a Freezing Curse, it can only be unfrozen with magic. And anything—even a living creature—can be frozen." Mr. Migotchi, a wrinkly, balding man with bags under his eyes, walked around. His wife also taught the Complicated Magic class—accidents happened often.

"Oh, no! Gerold!" Mrs. Migotchi called across the room. Her gray bun bobbed as she shook her head.

Aria looked up from her cup of ice to see who had been frozen now. One tall, skinny boy with sandy blond hair had thick ice covering his skin and holding him there like a statue. That was the third time he had frozen himself and he wasn't doing it on purpose.

"Students, please don't direct your hands at yourselves when you use the Freezing Curse. Once you are frozen, you won't be unfrozen until someone else unfreezes you." Mr. Migotchi pinched the bridge of his nose and shook his head as his wife unfroze Gerold.

What he said made a question pop into Aria's head, so she stood up from the corner and raised her hand.

"Yes, Aria?" Mrs. Migotchi saw her hand up first and walked toward her.

"If someone freezes themself, that will preserve their body then, right? Until someone unfreezes them?"

"Yes, but that person's mind would stay conscious the whole time. It would be very boring for that person, not to mention the fact that their brain would wear away over time. And to be in that state with ice covering your skin would be very cold," Mrs. Migotchi answered, then strolled back the other way to help Gerold again.

Aria sat back down with her cup and placed her hand over

it, spreading warmth through her veins, then into her palm, and down into the cup. The water unfroze, turning back into a chilled liquid. She focused on heat, like the fireplace she and her father would sit in front of several years ago. She loved that old house. She loved the way it smelled like pine, all the trees right outside, and the way the firewood would crackle and pop as her father told her jokes. She would laugh and squeal, and then she would make him chase her around the house, pretending she was a fairy princess. Those days were gone, though. Her parents weren't by her side anymore.

The glass underneath her hand abruptly shattered from the cold. A shock coursed up her arm and she jolted her hand away. When she turned to look at her hand, a painful stinging shot through her skin. Her hand was covered in blood, a small slice right through her palm. Everyone's eyes were pinned on her as Mrs. Migotchi ran to help. Aria hurried to jump up, clutching her palm as her hands shook and hot tears gathered in her eyes.

She wouldn't let herself cry, though, as she was taken down to the office to get her hand wrapped up.

"Hand wounds always bleed a lot. You'll be just fine, dear," the nurse said.

"Thank you." Aria gave a half smile and left to head to dinner since the bell had just rung.

When Aria sat down with her tray of food in the cafeteria, Avi exclaimed, "Oh my, Aria! What did you do to your hand? That isn't paint, right?"

She looked down at her hand. There was dried blood soaked through the bandage. "Oh…uh…I just cut it in Complicated Magic."

"On purpose?" he asked, his brows furrowing.

"No, not on purpose." She gave him a look, raising one eyebrow. "I just cut it. It was an accident."

"How bad is it?" Luke reached his hand forward to take a look, but she pulled it back.

"Guys, I'm fine," she said, forcing a smile onto her face.

"Aria, we all know you're not fine, especially with how you acted earlier," Willow jumped in. She had her astronomy book right next to her but, surprisingly, wasn't reading.

Aria sighed and her stomach clenched. She really hoped that somehow, by a miracle, they would have forgotten about that. "Guys...maybe I'm not fine...but..." What was someone supposed to say in a situation like this? Aria was lost for words. "I'm glad you guys care so much about me, but I'll be okay."

Would she be okay, though?

"Do you want to do homework in your room again? We could be there with you to talk if you need," Willow asked.

"Actually, me and Luke wanted to play baseball behind the school—" Avi was saying, but then Luke elbowed him in the ribs. "Luke! What'd you do that for?"

"Maybe we should stay with Aria," Luke said.

A pit opened up in her stomach; they were pitying her.

"Actually, I don't have much homework. You guys go do what you want to," she said, trying to hide the sadness that was creeping into her voice.

"Okay...but are you sure you want to be alone?"

"Yeah, I just need to clear my head."

"Okay then," Avi said, pulling out a baseball from his bag on the floor.

Aria pushed away her half-eaten burger, not feeling like she could eat anymore. She felt hot tears welling in her eyes, making her stomach feel sick. "I'm gonna head off to my room."

"I'll walk with you," Willow volunteered, jumping up and grabbing her book.

Together, they walked to Aria's room, Willow constantly

talking about several different things. The words were hard to focus on with everything else running through Aria's head, but they were an appreciated distraction. She didn't want to have to focus on anything else but what Willow was saying.

"…and then Twilight started purring! He loves his new mouse stuffed animal so much!" Willow said joyfully as Aria approached the door.

"Well, thank you, Willow, for taking the time to walk with me," Aria said, forcing a smile.

"Yeah, of course. It's not fair to be alone. Are you sure you don't want to hang out? We don't even have to do schoolwork if you don't want to."

"I really appreciate the offer. I really, really do, but I need to clear my head…And probably take a nap." Aria grabbed the doorknob and swung the door open.

"Okay, if you say so, but if you need anything, my room is just down the hall. I'll be writing a paper all night, so just come get me if you want to talk." Willow gave a kind smile and then headed back down the hall.

Aria closed the door, thinking of how terrible the day had been. The oil lamps were already turned off, so she kicked off her shoes and jumped right into her bed. She wished she didn't have to be alone. She wanted to be around her friends. But she felt she deserved the lonely darkness; she had yelled at Mrs. Mckinney and them. A lump rose in her throat, her stomach twisted, and her eyes burned as she let the tears finally come. She winced as she grabbed her pillow with her injured hand and shoved her face into it. Her mind was so confused. Was she supposed to be angry or sad? Did she want to be alone, or did she want to be with her friends? She wasn't sure she knew anymore. All she knew was that she wanted her parents back and the pain to stop. She turned over and stared at the blackened ceiling.

Then out of the darkness, a hand suddenly clamped down on her mouth, preventing her from screaming. Her heart rate suddenly picked up and a tremble racked through her body. She kicked her legs out, but they only made contact with the air, so she punched her arms in all directions. Her fist hit against a soft, black fabric that was thrown over someone, but she couldn't see them. The room was silent except for the muffled sound of her yells for help and her feet kicking the blanket on her bed.

"What do you know?" a mysterious, deep voice said, the tone laced with hostility.

Aria shrieked, trying to call for someone who might be out in the hallways. Maybe Willow was still there. She tried to wiggle away, kicking and punching like a fish caught underneath a bear's claws.

"If you don't tell me, I will hunt you down like prey. I *will* find you, wherever you are," the voice said again—

She sat straight up out of bed, shaking and looking around through the darkness. Feeling around, she realized she was alone, just like Willow had left her. There was no voice, no person next to her bed, and no hand clamped down on her mouth. *A dream*, she concluded, but it felt like it was more than a dream. It felt *real*.

I'm just stressed. I just need to relax. She fell back against the pillows and released a long exhale of relief. *I'm just stressed*, she kept telling herself until she drifted back to sleep.

It turned into weeks of constant headaches for Aria. At some point every day, she would cry, whether that was in her room at the start of the day, or when she looked in the bathroom mirror and saw herself—she looked so much like her mother that it was heart-wrenching now. Nothing her friends said or did made her feel any better. She felt like she would never feel any better, like she was slowly being consumed by grief until there would be none of her left. She was broken and alone.

Even as it grew closer and closer to the end of the school year, Mrs. Mckinney still kept telling her the same thing: the Forces of Light didn't know where her parents were and were not actively doing anything to save them. Every time she asked, she couldn't tame the fire within. Her powers seemed to have gotten more powerful from being used and as a result of that, Mrs. Mckinney's clock was now shattered. Aria didn't mean to break it. All she did was shout and it broke into tiny shards and pieces of wood. She offered to fix it or replace it as tears poured down her face, but Mrs. Mckinney told her it was fine.

The voice in the back of her head kept feeding her corrupt thoughts that made her head hurt. *They're dead. They have to be. Why would Malus keep them alive if he's truly as unmerciful as they say? They're gone and you're never going to get them back.*

But what if I try to get them back myself?

You get them back? This was all your fault in the first place! the voice told her.

She had to ignore the overwhelming thoughts, though, if she was going to use magic in class without breaking more things. However, struggling to get a rein on using magic only made things worse. Mrs. Helma kept saying she needed to calm down, and that maybe being upset was causing the struggles. She'd managed to do a Knockback Enchant, but took a few tries each time. It was such an easy enchant, yet the harder ones came easier. She'd learned a lot, but not nearly as much as she wanted, especially when the school year was about to end.

It was the day before the last day of school. A mix of chaos sounded through the Basic Enchanting classroom—bangs, calls for help, and thuds as students reviewed what they had learned. So far, Aria had been slowly moving around different objects. Using magic was a strange thing to Aria when only months ago she had found out about it. She loved feeling the beat of power like it was calling her and the force push from her hand across the room to move an item. The pure energetic power crackled through her veins. It was like this was her purpose. It made her feel more than alive.

She topped the tall tower she was constructing with heavy, wooden blocks, and Mrs. Helma began walking towards her, watching as Aria started unstacking the blocks.

"I want to see you summon smoke," Mrs. Helma said as she made the blocks fly back to the corner of the room with the swish of her hand.

A few weeks ago, Aria had been taught to summon Black Smoke, but she still didn't understand what use a ton of smoke was. It was not normal smoke, though; it was more of a black fog. No other student had been taught it. It was just her. Everyone else had been learning how to direct air currents while Mrs. Helma showed her how to manipulate the smoke. At first, she'd hesitated, unsure she'd be able to do such a thing when no one else knew it. It had taken multiple tries, but when she finally had succeeded, she could feel the air around her shift, like she was one with the element.

"Mrs. Helma, what am I supposed to use Black Smoke for?" Aria dared ask.

"Mrs. Mckinney told me to teach it to you. I don't know why, but I bet she has her reasons…The Dark Forces use Black Smoke often. It may be good for you to know how to bend it at your will as well. Now, summon it, please."

Aria summoned the smoke easily. It was like separating the different types of air from each other. It faded into the room around them, shocking some of the other students in the room when the Black Smoke caught their eye. The black fog stayed close to the floor at Aria's command.

"Change its color," Mrs. Helma instructed.

"What?" Aria looked at her, her eyes widening and flickering with confusion.

Mrs. Helma glanced around the room at all the students who had stopped practicing to watch Aria. "Get back to work, please!" She called before turning back to her. "You summoned it, now change it. You can change any aspect of it. It is at your command. You can change its thickness, its color, its toxicity, anything."

"But I don't know how to."

"You may not, but your gift does. I heard about Mrs. Mckinney's clock."

Aria's stomach clenched shamefully. "I promise, I didn't mean to break it."

"Aria, nobody is mad at you. At that moment, your power did what it wanted to, but you have to control that. See, you may not have known how to shatter that clock, but your gift did, which means you are capable. Believe in yourself."

Aria sighed and imagined best she could that the smoke was another color. It immediately turned dark, amethyst purple before the school bell rang.

—✶—☾—✶—

Later that evening, Aria plopped down on her bed while Luke, Avi, and Willow arranged their things for their last study session. Twilight was there, too, which Aria was not very happy about. Scratches littered her skin from him always trying to play like a kitten. She wanted to tell Willow to keep her cat out. But after how kind Willow had been to Aria and how hot-tempered Aria had been about the Forces of Light, she didn't want to make her kick her cat out. Now, Aria drummed her fingers rapidly on her notebook, biting down on her lip. All day she had been stressed to the core, but she balled up the feeling and tucked it away. She hated putting burdens on people. She could figure things out herself, right?

Willow was at her desk with her eyes planted in a book as usual. On the floor, Luke and Avi were talking about a basketball game they had watched last night, unable to focus on their homework, but also not caring to turn it in. Aria willed her mind to finish her work, but all she could train her mind on was the mound of ever-growing thoughts in her head and the tapping of her fingers on her books.

Tomorrow was the last day of school. How could that be possible? And after all that time the Forces of Light still hadn't succeeded in bringing her parents back. So now, she could only wonder where she would go. The stress about it was like a heavy weight pulling her under. This school was built to protect children and teach them magic, but when the school year ends, that would mean she would have to leave, right? If she was being honest with herself, she hadn't thought much about the end of the school year because she thought she would have her parents back by then. She knew she should ask Mrs. Mckinney, but she was tired of speaking to her and being told that nothing was being done to help her parents. She wondered where Avi would go. He had his aunt, Mrs. Helma, but would he be stuck at school with her over the summer or would they go somewhere else? She was contemplating this and whether she would ask Mrs. Mckinney where she would go or not while she laid on her bed, staring at the blank ceiling. She had the idea that maybe she could ask where Avi was going, but there was the possibility that that could upset him. It was an ongoing war inside her mind.

Aria was pulled from her train of thought when Twilight jumped onto her bed and laid down next to her to rub his head on her knee, purring.

"No, no, no, I have had enough scratches from you," Aria said irritably and pushed the cat away from her.

Twilight quickly sank his sharp teeth into her hand and jumped back down to the floor, meowing like Aria had hurt *him*.

"Ugh!" Aria shouted as blood began to drip down her hand. "I can't take this anymore!"

Luke, Avi, and Willow probably would have thought she was yelling about the cat if they hadn't known better.

She ignored the fresh bite from Twilight and started shouting all the things that had been on her mind all day. "The stupid Forces of Light still haven't tried to get my parents back! Like, do they even care? They say that they are the leaders of the Forces of Light! They say they know how to destroy Malus and his stupid Dark Forces! Yet, they don't want to rescue them? Why are my parents the only ones that know how to destroy the Dark Forces? What even is it that will destroy them? And where am I even going to go when school ends since they haven't gotten my parent's back?"

Aria's eyes flooded with tears, and she shoved her face into her pillow, letting out a muffled scream.

Luke, Avi, and Willow's eyes went wide, and they stared at each other for a moment before Willow stood up with soft eyes, and strode over to Aria, sinking into the bed.

She put her hand on Aria's, and said in her calming, light

voice, "You should really talk to Mrs. Mckinney. I know you don't want to, but she is the only one who can answer all your questions. And aren't you coming to Camp Enchanted with us?"

Aria turned back around to face Willow with her shiny, glass-like eyes.

"Camp Enchanted?" she asked, wiping tears with her hands, and completely ignoring the fact that Willow thought she should talk to Mrs. Mckinney.

"Yeah, you know, the magic camp almost everyone goes to over the summer. Everyone has been talking about it…Well, of course not everyone, because there are the people that don't even know about magic, but you know what I mean."

Aria really hadn't been paying much attention to what was going on around her, but she vaguely could recall the name of it from somewhere. Had Mrs. Mckinney said something about it? She probably should have listened to what Mrs. Mckinney had to say.

"I *might* have heard of it…" Aria said. "But not anything about it."

Luke and Avi jumped to their feet, both with bright smiles on their faces.

"It's the best!" Luke's eyes lit up. "There are fun games and events all throughout the summer. You would learn way more magic than you do here! I thought you had already been signed up, weren't you?"

"I don't know," Aria replied.

"Well, if you don't know, you should ask Mrs. Mckinney to make sure you are," Avi said.

"Fine, I'll ask her tomorrow." Aria dreaded the thought of it.

"Tomorrow? Tomorrow is when you pack. You'll have to ask her tonight," Avi urged.

"What? But it's getting late!"

They all stared at her with looks that read: *well, you gotta do what you gotta do.*

"Fine." Aria sighed. "But then you guys have to go back to your rooms."

Luke and Avi bent down to gather up their unfinished homework and Willow picked up her stack of books.

"Well, see you tomorrow," Avi said.

"Goodnight, Aria." Luke left the room with a smile twitching at his lips.

Avi swiftly followed behind him.

"Sweet dreams," Willow wished to her, leaving the room with Twilight scurrying past her feet.

Aria gathered up her courage and tried desperately to push that fury down deep inside her so that she wouldn't make an outburst again. Then, when she was ready, she marched through the corridor, through the veil, and down to Mrs. Mckinney's office.

The office was dark inside, with no staff sitting at their desks. The creepy silence made the hairs on Aria's arms stand up. She saw a light slipping its way under Mrs. Mckinney's door. Without knocking, she pushed it open.

"Oh, hello, dear. I was not expecting to see you at this time," Mrs. Mckinney said, looking up from a paper she was holding.

She didn't look like the cheerful Mrs. Mckinney she always was. Maybe she was expecting Aria to shout at her again. Guilt and shame knotted up in Aria's chest, and she had to swallow a lump in her throat. She walked to one of the cushioned armchairs and sat down.

"Hi," Aria said politely. "I was just wondering if I was signed up for Camp Enchanted…You know, because the Forces of Light have still not rescued my parents and are doing nothing about it."

The ball of temper inside her made her say that last part—made her feel the *need* to.

"Aria, I have told you many times already that the Forces of Light are still assessing the situation, but yes. You are signed up for Camp Enchanted. The bus will take everyone there after dinner tomorrow, so make sure to pack." Mrs. Mckinney folded her hands on the desk, her tone sounding slightly annoyed.

"Okay," Aria said and quickly got up to leave before her temper made her say something she would regret.

She wanted nothing to do with Mrs. Mckinney or the Forces of Light anymore. She just wanted her parents back, and she was about done waiting. Maybe her parents would actually be safe if *she* did something about it. Mrs. Mckinney was a nice person, but Aria wished she would finally tell her that the Forces of Light had saved her parents, not that they were doing nothing at all.

CHAPTER TEN

THE LAST DAY of school went rather smoothly. The teachers were much more relaxed and let the students do whatever they wanted within reason, that is, except for Mr. Monroy. Celaena was now ignoring Aria, which made Aria just a little happier. Dinner time could not possibly come any sooner, though. She hadn't even been able to pack her bags yet. Right after she'd talked with Mrs. Mckinney she had plopped down in her bed and fallen asleep.

After a hasty and nearly silent dinner, Aria hurried off to pack her duffle bag. She threw her clothes in there, even jammed the clothes she had originally found in the dresser, and tossed in some other things of hers—not bothering to fold anything. She tossed the duffle bag over one shoulder and her school bag over the other. She rushed back down to the main floor of the school, coming to a stop as she came to the crowd gathering outside the school doors. Teens of ages thirteen to eighteen were gathered on the steps, just inside the school doors, and out in the parking lot. They all had bags in their hands and slung over their shoulders. Of course, Celaena had a fancy black leather suitcase that her friends were admiring for some unknown reason. A bus drew

Aria's glare away from Celaena and she watched as it drove to a stop in the parking lot. The doors propped open and everyone ran toward them, shrieking with joy. Luke, Avi, and Willow found Aria in the chaotic crowd so they could sit together, and they pushed through to the doors.

Aria shoved her bags next to Luke's on the floor and sat down next to him on the leather seat. Across the aisle, Willow sat next to Avi, who was blushing a little more than usual. Twilight laid between them, purring as she rubbed his soft head. Willow smiled at Avi for a few seconds then changed her gaze to the front of the bus. Avi blushed an even deeper shade of red and looked out the window to hide it. Aria noticed and couldn't help but smirk.

A mix of conversations rose throughout the bus as it lurched forward and drove away from the school.

"How long is the ride?" she asked, looking from Luke, then across the aisle to Willow and Avi.

"Usually only threeish hours." Luke shrugged.

"*'Only?'*"

"Yeah, it's not that long."

Aria was used to driving long distances to get to each new house she moved to, but it had been a while since she had gone anywhere at all. She was going to get bored fast.

"Well, what are we going to do on the way?"

"Nothing." Avi leaned back against his seat.

Aria sighed and slumped back against her and Luke's seat, too. Luke's gaze pinned to her and she turned her head towards him. She couldn't resist the urge to look at his eyes. A pinkish tint spread across his cheeks.

"So…" he said.

"So…" Aria repeated, but the conversation didn't go any further.

Willow whipped out a thick book and began reading while Avi kept his eyes planted on the back of the seat in front of him. Meanwhile, Aria had a lot of things on her mind because no matter how many times she vented to her friends, she never felt better and probably never would. While Luke was staring out the window, Aria kept glancing at him. She had to knock it off. What was wrong with her? Normal people didn't keep staring at someone. She sat there, still continuing to stare, thinking through everything on her mind.

"Wanna play a game of Go Fish?" Luke asked after an hour, snapping Aria out of her train of thought.

"Sure." She was glad to have something to do.

Luke pulled a deck of cards out of the duffle bag at his feet and they began playing.

A few rounds of the game passed, a smile plastered on Aria's face as time flew by like the trees outside the bus window.

"Go Fish!" Luke exclaimed with a grin, his eye meeting Aria's.

A half smile twitched at her lips.

"Do you have a—" Aria was saying, but then the bus lurched forward and came to a stop, causing all of their cards to fall out of their hands and onto the floor.

Twilight slid off Willow and Avi's seat, then he bolted down the aisle. He was out of sight before Willow had time to go into a frenzy about him leaving her.

"Nobody panic! Everyone remain seated!" the woman driving the bus shouted over the speakers, but there was alarm in her own voice.

Avi pushed Willow back down into her seat, preventing her from going after Twilight.

"But Twilight!"

"He's on the bus. He's fine," Avi reassured her.

Aria, along with others, peered out to the front of the bus to see what had stopped it, her eyes widening as she took in the sight. A dark hooded figure stood in the middle of the dirt road with their hand raised up at chest level, forcing the vehicle to come to a stop. The figure was cloaked in all black, their face unable to be seen underneath the hood. The sight of the figure made Aria's skin crawl. She could sense a tense, vile feeling in the air. Panic spread rapidly throughout the bus and it grew loud with frightened whispers. Aria couldn't tell what the bus driver was doing, but it looked like she was trying to call for backup from the Forces of Light. The figure slowly let its hand down, then dashed to the right of the bus, disappearing into the dense trees that were on both sides of the vehicle. The bus driver instantly hit the gas pedal and the vehicle sped down the road.

After a few minutes of the bus moving at an alarming speed, something struck the side of the bus and it wobbled back and forth. Everyone screamed as they tumbled out of their seats and into the aisle. Aria hit her head on the metal part beneath Willow and Avi's seat, struggling to right herself. Pain immediately began to spread through her skull. The vehicle came toppling the other way and Willow slid into the aisle. Aria grabbed the seat behind her and pulled herself out of the way before Willow could crush her. Willow clung to the seat, but her legs dangled out into the aisleway. Windows shattered around them as Luke and Avi hung to their seats for dear life. More teens fell out into the aisle, screaming.

"Duck away from the glass!" the bus driver screamed, hanging from the driver's seat and trying desperately not to fall through the glass windows.

The bus abruptly stopped tipping, so Aria scrambled back into her seat, shaking. Luke looked her up and down with concern etched on his face and grabbed her elbow lightly.

"Are you okay?" He had to speak louder over all the yells of everyone else.

"Yeah. What's going on?" Aria half-shouted.

"I don't know but look!" Luke pointed out the window as something caught his attention outside.

The figure was standing on the side of the road now. It made an *X* over its chest, vanishing from thin air. Voices rose in panic throughout the bus as others witnessed it as well, but Willow was more concerned about her cat.

"Where's Twilight? Has anybody seen a black cat?" Willow yelled across the bus.

Nobody made a response. They were all staring out the window at where the cloaked figure had just been.

"Everybody back in your seats!" the bus driver shrieked over the speakers. "I have to activate the Invisibility Charm!"

"An Invisibility Charm?" Aria asked Luke.

"It will turn the bus invisible so we aren't followed. Charms can be put on anything, even this bus." His eyes searched out the window.

The bus gave a slight shake and then zoomed down the road at an extremely fast speed, everything passing by in a blur.

Aria followed Luke's gaze as her heart hammered against her ribs. "Followed? Who was that? What do they want?"

"That was someone from the Dark Forces, no doubt. They all wear black cloaks like that… I have no idea why they would attack the bus, though." Luke glanced across the aisle at Willow and Avi.

Willow was sobbing, thinking she'd lost Twilight in the attack and Avi was comforting her, telling her everything was going to be okay. Luke looked back at Aria, who was trembling terribly. With her head throbbing painfully, the realization hit like a bucket of ice being dumped over her head. She didn't look up at him. Instead, she stared at her shaky hands as tears welled up in her eyes.

"They attacked…because of me…" she said, her voice a whisper as she thought of the dreams she'd had. "I'm putting everyone in danger."

It was obvious that she was right, but Luke was unwilling to say so.

"You aren't putting everyone in danger." He laid his hand on her shoulder and looked at her face with soft eyes.

Tears dripped down onto Aria's hands and he wiped them off. She felt her heart stutter a beat and she looked at him, his face turning to a light shade of pink. He quickly moved his hands away.

"I *am* putting them in danger. I don't want to be the reason people get hurt," Aria said, staring back down at her hands.

"But nobody got hurt and once we're at camp, everyone will be safe. The Dark Forces don't know where it is."

Aria didn't respond, her lips trembling, so Luke left it at that.

Dark shadows were cast in the woods, the sky turning to bright orange and pink with the setting of the sun.

The bus pulled down a long winding road that led into a deep forest of tall, bushy, varied trees. It drove on for a while longer before driving under a tall wooden arch across the road with a sign hanging from it that read: *Camp Detnahcne.*

"It says Camp Det-na —" She tried to spell it out, but then they were too far away for her to see it.

"It's *'Enchanted'* spelled backward. It discourages anyone from entering, but there are hardly any houses for hundreds of miles," he said.

Off in the distance of the forest, lights shone from log cabin windows. A building—half made of stone, half of logs—stood just outside the parking lot filled with many other buses. The doors propped open and everyone rushed to get off the bus, their arms filled with bags. Sweet, fresh air filled Aria's lungs and a shiver ran up her spine.

People were everywhere, filing inside the building and making their way up the campground paths, or just standing around. Aria didn't recognize any of the people there from the school, other than the people getting out of the vehicle behind her.

A loud woman's voice broke over speakers somewhere, "Welcome newcomers! If you are new to the camp, please make your way into the camp office building in front of you. If you are not new, please make your way to last year's cabin unless you would like to make a change this year. After tonight, all cabin members are permanent. Schedules and maps of the camp will be found in your cabins. Thank you!"

The massive crowd of people began breaking up.

"See you later, I guess," Luke said and he walked off with Avi.

Willow still had tears in her eyes from losing Twilight. She gave a light wave to Aria and headed through the crowd of campers as well, leaving Aria alone.

Aria weaseled her way through the campers to get to the office building. Wooden benches lined the log walls inside, many of them filled with teenagers waiting to get checked in for the first time. She walked past a propped open door on her left and sat down to wait. All around her, people were going in and out of different doors, the noise echoing off the bland walls.

A woman holding a clipboard stepped out from the open doorway that Aria had previously passed. It was Miss Stax. Aria's lips parted and questions filled her head.

Why is she there? How *is she there? She didn't come on the bus.*

Then Aria realized that she could have just teleported. *What if Mrs. Mckinney is here, too?* She didn't like the idea of it.

"Aria," Miss Stax called as she spotted her on the bench.

She got up and followed Miss Stax through the door she'd come through. Miss Stax led her past rows of desks, all covered in computers, papers, and pencils. Men and women were seated at the desks, helping teen after teen.

"So..." Miss Stax sat down at her desk, making clicking noises with her mouth. Aria stood there awkwardly as Miss Stax flipped through a stack of papers for a few minutes, wrote something on a piece of paper, then said, "Okay, so you are in cabin number thirteen. You can meet your cabin members before heading off to bed. Have fun!"

Miss Stax offered her a smile, handing her a map so she could find her cabin.

"Thank you very much," Aria said, forcing a grin onto her face before leaving the room.

She made her way past the dissipating crowd and up a path that led away from the office building. Lights dotted the sides of the dirt trail and the glow from cabins illuminated the distance. The late evening air was cool on her skin with the smell of pine, fresh grass, and something sweet thick in the air. Even in the darkness, it was peaceful walking through the campgrounds. Laughter and cheer filled the air, radiating off every joyful person in the camp. In the moment, it was easy to forget everything that had happened within the last few hours—easy to forget that her parents were in the hands of the people who had stopped the bus. Her heart tightened and that feeling of contentment left her as quickly as it had come. She heaved her heavy bags down the path, following the dimly lit map.

The cabin had a wooden sign over the door with the number thirteen engraved into it. When she opened the door, a sweet flower fragrance drifted to her nose. Three wooden bunk beds with burgundy blankets were up against the walls, one on each side of the square cabin, and one at the back. Matching cubbyhole shelves filled with fabric bins stood next to the bunk bed at the back, one on each side of it. A large burgundy carpet was laid out in the middle of the floor. Off to the left was a door that led to the bathroom. On the bottom bunk, Willow was unpacking her things and Twilight was curled up against the pillows.

"You found him!" Aria shut the door behind her.

"Yeah, turns out he was somewhere on the bus after all. He followed me through the crowd. I thought he had flown out a window or something…"

"Where is everyone else?"

"I guess they're just not here yet. Oh, shoot! They forgot to give me a schedule!"

Willow looked around on her bed, eagerly trying to find her schedule. She gave a sigh, then picked up her laundry, and put it away in a cubbyhole.

"I'll have to go back down to the office to get one." Willow strode to the door.

"Okay, well, I'll be here," Aria said, but Willow had already left.

Setting her bags down next to Willow's bed, she blew out a puff of air. She climbed up the ladder to the top bunk above Willow's, claiming it as hers, and snatched her schedule before climbing back down. She stood in the middle of the room with her back to the door, her eyes scanning the schedule.

Suddenly, an arm wrapped around her neck, putting her in a headlock. Her arms pinned against someone's body and her schedule flew to the floor. A strong lavender and sage perfume drifted from the person.

"It's payback time, Aria. Maybe you'll learn not to mess with me, not to shove a potion down my throat," Celaena's cruel voice shouted in her ear. Her tone was like metal scraping across metal.

Aria felt her lungs being closed off from oxygen, Celaena's arm tightening around her throat.

"Let…go…of…me," Aria tried to say, but it was barely audible.

With a thud, Twilight jumped from Willow's bed and strutted over, claws out. Aria's head began to pound and she couldn't determine whether Twilight was going to try to protect her or play like always. She struggled to pull away from Celaena's tight grasp.

"Not so strong, are you now? And there's *nobody* around to save you," Celaena cackled in her ear.

Aria's eyes darted around until they landed on the burgundy blankets on the beds. Her hand moved around as if it were trying to grab the blanket, and then she pointed it at Celaena's face. The blanket, which had been so neat on the unclaimed bed, soared through the air and wrapped around Celaena's head. Celaena immediately let go of Aria and stepped back, gasping for air. Twilight lunged for Aria playfully, but she stepped out of the way.

"You could have killed me!" Aria's face was bright red and heated.

"That's what I was—" Celaena began after she pulled the blanket from her head, but the door swung open.

Willow and two other girls stepped into the room. One of the girl's thin, bronze-toned hands went to her mouth in shock, looking between Aria and Celaena with her chocolate brown eyes. Her shiny black hair framed her face in thick curls. The other girl walked into the room with purpose in her step as she tied her blond hair into a pony. Her green eyes widened and her hands fell beside her plump figure.

"What happened here?" Willow asked, looking from Celaena, whose hair was messed up and was holding someone's blanket, to Aria, whose face was red as hot iron from fury and air deprivation.

"She tried to kill me!" Aria yelled, pointing at Celaena.

"She tried strangling me with a blanket!" Celaena pointed her finger at Aria. Her tone seemed to mock the one Aria was using.

"No! I tried to defend myself from being strangled by you! And—and Twilight tried to attack me, too!" Aria shouted, her mind in a whirlpool of thoughts.

Celaena rolled her eyes and walked to the back of the cabin.

"Do not blame my cat for anything!" Willow crossed her arms, narrowing her eyes.

"I'm not—It's just—" Aria stuttered, but Willow wasn't listening anymore.

Celaena plopped down on the bottom bunk in the back of the cabin, then laid down as if nothing had just happened.

The two other girls claimed the bunk bed on the left of the cabin and began looking over their schedules, all the while Aria stood in the middle of the room with her mouth hanging open. How could Willow act this way? How could she just brush off the fact that Celaena tried to strangle her to death?

"Willow?" Aria stared at her, hurt twisting through her like knives.

"We can talk about this tomorrow. It's been a long day. Let's just try to get some shut-eye." Willow's voice sounded tight and her eyes avoided Aria.

"Shut-eye? I don't want to sleep in the same room as Celaena! Did you miss the part where she tried to kill me?"

Willow didn't reply to her and she noticed Celaena was smirking because of it.

"Fine, but if I die…" Aria trailed off, unsure of what she was even going to say. Without getting changed for bed, she climbed up her ladder.

Celaena giggled to herself with malice.

Despite there still being an empty bed left, the blond-haired girl stopped reading her schedule and turned off the light.

Through the darkness, Celaena said, "Don't be scared…I mean, don't let the bed bugs *bite*." Then she laughed a vicious, though quiet, laugh.

Aria had a hard time falling asleep that night because, though she hated to admit it, she was petrified that Celaena would kill her in her sleep. She knew she could just go down to the office and ask to switch cabins, but she had an idea.

She was relieved to wake the next morning, still breathing in that sweet, pine-scented air. Celaena was already long gone, and Twilight was missing from the cabin when Aria sat up, rubbing her eyes. Willow was searching every crevice for him like crazy. Across the room, the two other girls were sitting on their beds, watching Aria with curious eyes.

The girl on the bottom—the dark, curly-haired one— asked, "Were you telling the truth last night? Did she really try to kill you?"

"Of course, I was telling the truth!" Aria didn't mean to, but her voice rose, and she jumped down from her bed with a thump.

"Okay…Well, my name is Elaine. What's yours?" She didn't look like she believed Aria in the slightest.

"Aria."

"I'm Natalie," the blond-haired girl said from the top bunk.

Aria nodded in acknowledgment and bent down to go

through her duffle bag that still sat at the bottom of her ladder. She picked out a pair of jean shorts and a plain tank top, then hastily dressed in the bathroom. After she was dressed, she was outside in the hot summer air, a slight breeze wrestling with the branches of the trees. The bright morning sun was held high in the sky, causing the trees and buildings to cast slim shadows on the trails that wound throughout the campgrounds. She had no idea where breakfast took place or what direction she was even going, but she knew it was likely to have started already. Because of the boiling, rage-filled fumes running through her, she'd forgotten her map back in the cabin. The grumble of her stomach told her she should have brought it with her. Storming down the trails, she wished she could go down to the camp office and tell them what Celaena had done, but that would get Celaena booted off the camp, which Aria didn't want. She knew Celaena must have something to do with the Dark Forces and that she could lead her to her parents, she just didn't know how yet. Her mind was trying to form a plan.

She walked down a winding path for a while before coming to a log building much larger than the office. Hanging from the roof of the wooden porch was a sign that read: *Mess Hall.* A face peered out of the door, which stood to the side of the porch. It was Luke.

He called out to Aria, "Hey! There you are! Come in and eat. We're all waiting for you! We made sure to get you some pancakes!"

"Great!" Aria said, feigning enthusiasm.

She stepped up the porch stairs and through the door after Luke. When she walked into the mess hall filled with polished, wooden, rectangular tables and matching benches, the smell of the buffet hit her in the face. A short line of campers stood at the back of the massive room, filling up their plates with food that made Aria's mouth water; eggs, bacon, pancakes, maple syrup, hash browns…Most of the campers were gathered around at the tables, stuffing their hungry faces with food. The loud noise of constant talking reverberated off the walls and high ceiling. Luke led her across the wooden planked floor and past the clear, yellow-curtained windows overlooking the porch. They sat down where Willow and Avi were already eating. Aria wondered how Willow had gotten there faster than she had. *Maybe because she knows this place better*, she thought. As Aria picked up her fork, she noticed Luke, Avi, and Willow suddenly looked rather serious.

Before Aria could even get a bite of food into her mouth, Luke asked, "What happened?"

Aria's hand holding her fork stopped mid-air.

"I told them," Willow said.

"I thought you didn't want to talk." Aria dropped her fork down with a clang and looked away from the table.

"I said that last night! Did you really want to discuss this in front of Celaena and those other girls?" Willow's voice rose to a frustrated octave.

Aria's eyes went wide and she glanced at Luke and Avi to see theirs did, too. They had never seen Willow get a temper with anyone before.

"Sorry," Willow mumbled.

"Well, you got so angry that I said something rude about your cat, and then—" Aria said, dropping her temper a bit.

"It's called acting. But seriously, if you ever say another word against my cat again—"

"So, what happened?" Luke repeated, breaking the tension.

"I thought she told you." Aria resumed eating.

"All she said was that Celaena tried to kill you," Avi said.

"Yeah, she did." Aria then had to explain everything that

had happened. "And you guys told me she was just a harm-less bully."

"Well, that was before. This is now. You need to tell the office," Avi stated.

"No, I need her to stay at camp. If I told the office, they would kick her off the grounds or have her arrested or something."

"Why do you need her?" Luke asked.

"Because she knows something about the Dark Forces. I just know it. I'm done waiting for the Forces of Light to save my parents. I'm going to do it on my own," Aria answered, surprised by her own words. She'd never actually admitted aloud—even to herself—that she was going to try to save her parents.

"What?" the three of them exclaimed in unison, looking like they'd just been hit in the face unexpectedly.

"You could get hurt!" Luke smacked his hand down on the table and shook his head.

Twilight reappeared, jumping up to sit on the bench beside Aria, and snatching a piece of her bacon.

"No, no, no, get that *thing* away from me," Aria said, look-ing at Twilight with disgust.

Nobody made a move to get Twilight.

"He's not a *thing*," Willow stated. "I'm glad he's here because I couldn't find him anywhere earlier. I bet he's been exploring the campgrounds like a good little kitty."

Aria could tell she was biting back something else, probably about her speaking a word against her precious cat.

"Back on topic, please," Luke said, turning to Aria. "So, you're going to rescue your parents on your own?"

"Yeah, I'm done waiting for people to do *nothing*."

"Well, do you have a plan?" Avi asked.

"Um…uh…well…not exactly…" Aria bit her lip, tapping her fingers on the table.

"Great. That's *real* helpful," Avi said sarcastically.

"We'll have to come up with it later. The first event starts soon," Willow said, her voice now laced with excitement.

"What do you mean '*we*?'" Aria asked.

"Look, Aria, if you think any of us are going to stand by and watch you walk into dangerous situations, you're wrong," Luke said. "We're friends, so we're going to help you whether you like it or not." Before she could object, they were grabbing their things and leaving.

The first event was down by the lake, so Aria had to cautiously go back to cabin number thirteen to retrieve her map. After leaving the empty cabin, she strolled down the long paths, past all the cabins, through a part of the forest, and finally found the lake. She wondered how it could even be considered a lake. Yes, it was huge, but not nearly the size that an average lake was. It was a gorgeous, deep blue, and the trees and clouds reflecting on the surface. She could clearly see the land and forest all the way on the other side. It was big enough to not be a pond but small enough to not be a lake.

A group of campers was already gathered on the sandy shore. Mrs. Helma was at the lakeside in a swimsuit, her cheerful voice rising above everyone else's. Only a few others were wearing swimsuits, including Avi. Aria was not entirely shocked that Mrs. Helma was there because Miss Stax was also. She could take a guess that the camp was run by the Forces of Light, too.

"Today we will be swimming in the lake and learning how to bend water. Water can be hard to control because it wishes to take the form of what it is in. When we bring water into the air, it will wish to contort and separate to take up the space around it, which can be hard to handle," Mrs. Helma called around to everyone gathered at the shore.

Most people sighed as if the lesson was pathetic.

The group of campers started descending into the water. When Aria reached the water, it soaked through her clothing, refreshing on her hot, dry skin, and cooling her off instantly. The further she went, the higher it rose until it was at her waist, and Luke, Avi, and Willow joined her side. Willow reached out to touch Aria's hand for a second, then stepped away as if she hadn't done anything. She always thought it was odd that Willow did that.

All around them, water was shooting up into the air, then plopping back down with a splash, causing drops of cool water to splatter their skin.

"I won't let you guys help me save my parents," Aria stated as she tried to make the water move at her command.

"That's not your decision to make," Willow told her.

"I don't want you guys in danger." Aria smacked her hands down on the water, inhaling deeply.

"And we don't want you in danger either!" they half-shouted in unison.

"We're going to help you," Luke said as he splashed water into the air.

"Yes. And you know we are good friends when we are willing to put our lives and everything we love in danger for you," Avi added in a high, almost sarcastic tone.

Luke and Willow looked at him like he'd said too much. Aria blew out a puff of air, knowing there was no way she could convince them not to help her.

Finally, the water formed into a ball, and she made it come up a few feet in the air, but it plopped back down, sprinkling them with water. For the first time in a while, Aria laughed.

Luke spun his hands around a ball of water and flung it in Aria's direction, making her brown hair look almost black with water. Then Avi and Willow joined in, turning it into a game of splashing and showering each other.

By the time lunch rolled around, the four of them were soaked, but feeling more upbeat than before. Dripping with water, they walked back to the mess hall.

"I had an idea," Luke said as they sat down with food. "A Tracking Potion."

"A what?" Aria asked through a mouthful of food.

"A Tracking Potion," he repeated. "We can give it to Celaena. Then we can track her and see if she is in touch with the Dark Forces. It might lead us to your parents. I don't know if it will work, but we can try."

"Okay…But how does it work and how are we going to get her to take it?"

"Well, I'll have to get the recipe from my brother—"

"You have a brother?" Aria exclaimed, her eyebrows shooting up and her jaw dropping slightly.

"Yeah, I have an older brother named Christopher. He's not very social…He's not the nicest to be around either…Anyway, I can get the recipe from him. We give it to Celaena and through what is left over from the batch, we can see wherever she goes, and it doesn't wear off until the potion goes bad…which I don't know when that is. But then we run into the problem of her not taking it. She can't know we gave it to her, or she would stay far away from anything to do with the Dark Forces. We have to make sure she doesn't remember. But how?"

"I think I can help with that." Willow's face flushed red, and she looked down, her breaths coming in shaky.

"How?" Avi asked.

"Well…uh." Willow hesitated. "I'm a Mind-reader."

Chapter Eleven

"WHAT?" LUKE, AVI, and Aria exclaimed in unison. Their eyebrows raised as their eyes went wide, jaws dropping.

Aria could barely comprehend the words that had just come out of Willow's mouth. They had been friends with her for a while and they were finding out such news *now*?

"Yeah, I'm a Mind-reader. I can remove the memory of you guys giving the potion to Celaena," Willow whispered, trembling. Fear flickered in her eyes.

"Why are you shaking so badly? Are you okay?" Aria asked, laying her hands on the table.

"Well, it's just—it's just, I've never told anyone before. My mother told me never to let anyone know. I even told weird stories to people so they would leave me alone and it would be easier to keep my secret."

"Oh," Luke and Avi whispered under their breaths.

"Why couldn't anybody know?" Luke asked her.

"To many people, Mind-readers are considered creeps, and I didn't want people to make fun of me for that." Willow still remained very quiet, her eyes unable to meet theirs.

Well, the way you acted still made you seem creepy, Aria thought.

"I can feel your emotions radiating off of you. If I touch your hand, I can hear your thoughts and feel your emotions on an even deeper level. If I touch your forehead, I can see your memories and even alter them. People find that creepy and an invasion of their privacy, even if I can't see and know everything about them. It would take hours of looking through memories to know certain things," Willow explained. "The worst part about it, though, is me being a Mind-reader makes me a weapon. People could use me to find out what someone isn't telling them. When I look through their memories, it forces them to relive it…They see it all…They hear it all… They feel it all…For some, it's torture." Her tone had grown even softer, forcing Aria, Luke, and Avi to strain their ears to be able to hear her.

Aria's eyes went wider and she blinked a couple times. She didn't know much about the Divining Powers other than what the basics were of each one, but Mind-reading seemed so complicated that her own mind seemed blown away. She realized her mouth was hanging open a bit and she quickly closed it. They all stared at Willow in an awkward silence, plunging her into a deeper look of distress.

"It's okay, we won't tell anyone," Avi said before picking up his sandwich. "Your secret's safe with us."

"So, you can remove the memory of us forcing Celaena to drink the potion?" Aria asked, just to clarify.

Willow nodded, her bushy hair bouncing around her head.

Aria looked at Luke and Avi for a moment. Avi was blushing severely and looked like he might faint. Then it dawned on her why Willow was always so touchy. Willow would have known Avi liked her all along. *If I touch your hand, I can hear your thoughts and feel your emotions on an even deeper level.'* It must have occurred to him as well. Willow had been reading their emotions since the day they met.

"Okay, well then that's settled," Aria said, trying to bring everyone back on topic, even though she really didn't want her friends to get involved.

It was hard to imagine that Willow was telling the truth about being a Mind-reader, but Aria knew Willow would never lie, especially about such a serious thing.

Willow stared down at her plate without saying another word, breathing in deeply. Luke, Avi, and Aria kept assuring her that nobody had heard and that nobody would find out about her secret, but she still sat quietly staring at the corner of the table.

The first day of camp couldn't have gone quicker than it did. Soon enough, Aria was back in the cabin, the sky painted a dark pink outside. Willow was lying on her bed, face down in her pillow, still trembling because of revealing her deep, dark secret. She'd climbed right in bed and pretended to fall asleep; the faking was obvious. Aria ignored Celaena, who was sitting on her bed, drawing on her hand with a pen. She grabbed a book about enchantments, charms, and curses from Willow's cubbyhole.

Maybe reading could be a little helpful, Aria told herself as she climbed up into her bed.

"What's that blubbering buffoon crying about?" Celaena asked, hostility lacing her voice, and the bed shook. She looked down to see Celaena kicking the side of the bed harshly.

"She's not crying," Aria said and rolled her eyes back to the words in the book.

"Oh, really, huh? What about you? Are you crying after what happened last night?" Celaena amused herself. "You know, when you tried to strangle me last night and I had to defend myself."

Aria tried as hard as she could not to let Celaena get to her. She couldn't react and let Celaena get what she wanted.

"Do not ignore me! Be respectful!" Celaena shouted up at her. "Give people answers and you won't wind up somewhere you don't want to be…I mean, just look at what happened to your parents."

"Leave me alone," Aria hissed through clenched teeth.

She tried desperately to sound like she didn't care, but Celaena knew how to get under her skin. She couldn't believe that Celaena would hint at such things when Elaine and Natalie were in the room. Though the two of them were in such a deep conversation, planning what to gossip about to someone, that they were missing the biggest scoop.

"I wasn't actually trying to kill you yesterday, just so you know. I'm just a small wave in a raging sea," Celaena remarked and walked back to her bed.

What's that supposed to mean? Aria's eyebrows furrowed and she blew a puff of air as she began reading.

She was left wondering many things that night when the lights went out. One thing for sure, though, was that Celaena definitely knew something about her parents. What on earth did she mean *'I wasn't actually trying to kill you yesterday?'* Aria had been suffocating in a headlock! As for this new plan to rescue her parents, she couldn't stop contemplating ways to leave her friends behind. Late into the night, she tried to come up with ways to sneak away without them, but she couldn't come up with a stable plan.

Morning came slowly and restlessly. She got up before Celaena was even up, which was quite surprising to her. Willow and Twilight were already long gone out of the cabin. Hurriedly, she got ready in the bathroom before stepping outside, the sun spreading warmth over her skin.

She didn't care about the schedule anymore. In fact, she didn't care about much anymore. The cool summer breeze swept through the trees, rustling all the plant life, and carrying the smell of the forest. The sun was shining radiantly on the campgrounds, waiting for the perfect moment to make the day hot. As Aria walked down the campground paths, she thought to herself. All she wanted now was her parents. That was one of the many things planted in her head, the one big goal she knew, the one thing she truly cared about at the moment. She also knew her friends were going to try to help her, but she had to find a way to stop them. The only thing she could come up with, though, was to let them help with the potion, then she would run away, and they would be left there, safely at camp. It was not a great plan.

The mess hall was mostly empty and quiet since breakfast had just begun. Luke, Avi, and Willow were sitting at an otherwise empty table in a back corner of the hall. Twilight sat next to Willow as she rubbed his head and he purred. Aria strode over and sat down next to Luke without bothering to get any food. She didn't feel very hungry at the moment.

"I got the book," Luke said.

"Book?" Aria asked, squinting in confusion.

"The book that has the recipe for the Tracking Potion. I stole it from Christopher this morning."

"Oh, great." *Right, the potion book.* She felt her hands start to shake and clenched them into fists, nervous about what she was getting herself into.

Luke pulled the book from a tan leather bag next to him and put it on the table. It had an indigo cover with gold words imprinted on the front: *Complicated Potions for Experts*.

"Don't show that here," Aria told him off, glancing around.

Luke hurried to put the book back under the table. "Why?"

"Because people will think we're up to something. Nobody can know."

The rest of them looked around. The mess hall was still pretty empty.

"Fine, then we need to go somewhere else so we can talk about it."

"Where?"

"Maybe the forest? Nobody goes in there much," Willow suggested.

"Yeah, that sounds good," Avi agreed.

"Okay." Aria nodded.

They threw out their food and hurried out of the mess hall, Twilight scurrying after them. When nobody was around, they disappeared behind cabin number eighteen. Creeping through the forest, over all the sticks and stones, and through the under-growth, they came to a massive oak tree with a wide trunk. They plopped down in a circle behind the tree to be hidden from view. Luke took the book out again from his leather bag.

"Even though I got the book, there are still some problems…" Luke said. "We need all of the ingredients." He began flipping through the pages while everyone peered over his shoulders.

Twilight scratched at the roots of the tree that came up from the ground as Luke found the page and began reading it aloud.

"Water boiled with blue flame, one singular troll nose hair, ground up Siren scales, alpaca spit, Nevidit Slime, three leaves from Stranger's Vine, and moonstone dust."

"That is disgusting!" Willow exclaimed when Luke had finished.

"I refuse to go anywhere near a Nevidit for its slime!" Avi crossed his arms.

"What's a Nevidit? What's Stranger's Vine?" Aria asked.

"Nevidits have a slime that covers their whole body, which allows them to turn invisible if they wish to. They are horrible, gross, mischievous thieves!" Willow explained. "I would never want to come across one of those greedy creatures!"

"I wouldn't want to come across one of those either then," Aria said.

"And Stranger's Vine is a vine that attacks strangers. It recognizes people that have been around it and people that haven't. It's honestly the weirdest plant ever," Avi added.

"Wow." Aria raised her eyebrows, shocked that something like that could even exist. "Well, how are we going to get this stuff?"

"Stranger's Vine might be found here in the forest, but we'll have to break into the potion pantry for the rest of the stuff," Luke said.

Aria took a deep breath and replied, "Okay."

"But what about all the camp events?" Willow asked. "Are we still going to do them?"

"I don't care about doing them anymore." Aria shrugged.

"We will have to show up to them or *people will think we're up to something,*" Willow quoted her.

"Fine, but then after they are over, we'll meet back here after the events to work on the potion, okay?" Aria asked.

"Yeah," they all agreed.

They hid Luke's leather bag under tons of leaves, sticks, and pine needles, the book tucked safely inside. Then they left the forest to head to a camp event that was already in progress. As soon as they emerged from behind cabin number eighteen, Twilight ran down the path in the opposite direction of them.

"You're not afraid he'll get lost?" Aria asked Willow.

"Not really. He always turns up eventually. Plus, he seems to really like being outside with all the trees and other animals."

In a patch of grass surrounded by cabins and other long buildings, Mr. Monroy was teaching how to produce an enchanted fire. Piles of sticks lay around on the ground with campers sitting next to them, constantly snapping their fingers, but nothing happened. He shot all four of them nasty glares as they walked over to the class late and sat down next to their own piles. The sun was so hot on Aria's skin that sweat was beading up on her forehead.

"Hold your hand near the wood and snap your fingers. Think of creating fire on the wood—Yes, Natalie, I am aware that you cannot snap your fingers, so how 'bout you practice that," Mr. Monroy said in his thick accent and curled his mustache between his fingers.

Natalie slowly put her hand down, her face flushed.

Aria put her hand over her pile of wood, trying to picture that there was a fire there, and she snapped her fingers. Nothing happened. She snapped again and looked up to see others had already lit sparks on their piles of sticks. Sighing, she willed energy to flow through her veins and into her fingertips. She focused harder, imagining that flames were flickering on the wood, dancing across it. She snapped again and a small flame appeared on the twigs. A grin spread across her lips.

❉─☾─❉

"When are we going to break into the potion pantry?" Willow asked as they plopped back down behind the large oak tree, a light breeze blowing through the trees.

Birds chirped above them.

"Tonight?" Aria suggested.

"Yeah, me and Willow can get the stuff from the potion pantry and you and Luke could…maybe go into the woods to search for Stranger's Vine?" Avi asked.

"You are just afraid of that plant!" Luke said.

"No…uh…I just know how to get into the office without getting caught!" Redness rose into Avi's cheeks.

"Fine by me," Aria agreed. "But what is blue flame?"

"Blue flame is fire that is ignited by fairy dust," Willow said. "We can get the fairy dust from the potion pantry as well."

"Then that is settled. Luke and I will meet you guys here tonight just after curfew."

"Okay," Willow said. "But let's get to the next event."

The four of them left the forest, talking amongst themselves as they walked down the campground paths. Luke and Avi were whispering in hushed voices, and as much as Aria strained her ears to hear, all she got was—

"Dude, be quiet!" Avi jabbed Luke in the side and they laughed.

"What do you think they're talking about?" Willow asked as they started down a path shadowed by trees.

Aria shrugged. "I don't know. *Man* stuff?" She looked to Willow with a smirk on her face. Willow snorted and the two of them laughed. Willow continued to grin as they arrived.

In a large field where the grass grew tall and poked at everyone's legs, there was an event. Massive blocks, tanks of water, piles of wood, dummies, and other obstacles had been placed around the field to help campers practice their magic. Teachers walked back and forth, directing campers with what they needed help on and instructing them on new things. Magical sparks flew this way and that from teens practicing enchantments, and other campers were raising blocks high into the air. Aria, Luke, Willow, and Avi created a tall tower of blocks by levitating them beside one of the large tanks. The tower began to wobble, and in an effort to stop it from toppling, Aria tried to use a Knockback Enchant to push it back the other way. But it backfired, pushing her away from the tower and into one of the tanks. She sank to the bottom, then came up coughing and sputtering as everyone's heads turned to her.

Aria marched down the paths toward cabin number thirteen drenched in water. With a pounding in her head, she walked into the cabin, dripping water on the doorstep.

She stopped dead when she saw that Celaena was sitting alone on her bed, fidgeting with something. Aria felt a jolt in the pit of her stomach, having not expected her to be there. She took a step backwards and her hand found the doorknob again. For a moment, she stared at Celaena, as if expecting something. Celaena looked up at her with her evil green eyes.

"Scared, Aria?" she teased, a brutal grin crossing her face.

"No. Why would I be?" Aria said.

"Well, I can see you're holding the doorknob. Are you going somewhere? You only just got here," Celaena sneered. "What happened to you? You're dripping water all over the carpet."

Celaena stood up from her bed, trying to be nosy.

"I—that's none of your business," Aria retorted.

"Hmm…" Celaena approached her. "Isn't there an event going on right now?"

"Yeah." She let her hand leave the doorknob, every hair on her arms standing on end.

She walked right past Celaena, toward her cubbyhole,

grabbed new clothes, and hurried into the bathroom to get changed. When she opened the bathroom door, she expected Celaena to attack her, but the cabin was now empty. Relieved, she threw her wet clothes in the hamper by the door for the cleaners to collect and left the cabin. The sun made her wet hair shine as it framed her face with curls. She walked down the path that led to the mess hall, her stomach rumbling with hunger. She wondered if lunch had even been an option today, or had her and her friends just been too busy to even bother?

For a while, she sat on the shaded stairs of the mess hall with her head in her hands. The air was getting cooler and the humidity was lacking, which made Aria sense dinner approaching. A sizable group of people walked towards the mess hall. They were noisily chattering with one another. Aria stood up from the porch when she saw Luke, Avi, and Willow strolling towards her. Without saying another word, she followed them into the hall.

"So, how are we going to get out of our cabins tonight?" Aria asked, as this had just now occurred to her as she sat down with her food.

"Oh, it will be easy for us. This guy, Charlie, snores like a freight train," Avi laughed.

"It won't be easy for us. Celaena is watching me and if she sees both of us out, she'll know something's up." Aria dared a glance at the door as Celaena entered the hall.

"Just don't go back to your cabin. Hide in the forest until nightfall, then say you got lost or something if she says anything," Avi suggested.

"I don't know…" She seemed skeptical.

"That's all I can think of."

"I think it could work," Willow agreed.

"Okay then…Let's hope it works."

After dinner, Willow and Aria snuck off to the oak tree and waited while the sun slowly set, leaving them under the brightening stars and twilight sky.

"They'll be here any minute," Aria kept saying.

Lights from cabins were slowly turning off in the distance, the sky fading into a deep indigo. The crunching of leaves and sticks crackled through the air and two silhouettes approached them through the trees.

"We're here," Avi said. "Ready?"

Aria stood up from the moist ground, feeling a sinking, nervous feeling in the pit of her stomach. She knew they were breaking camp rules but didn't care. She just hoped they wouldn't get caught and wished her friends weren't in this mess with her. Her hands shook at the thought that they might get in trouble...or worse.

"All right." Aria clenched her hands tight.

"Here's the bag to put the ingredients in." Luke found his buried bag and handed it to Avi.

"Thanks." Avi took it from him and slung it over his shoulder.

"We'll sneak through the back door," Willow told him.

"See you guys later, I guess," Avi said, giving a wave of his hand. "And good luck."

Luke patted Avi on the back and they exchanged their good lucks before Willow and Avi headed back down to the campgrounds.

"So..." Luke said, staring off into the distance like he was expecting a conversation to pick up.

"Let's go." Aria looked at his face through the darkness.

"Right. It will likely be deep within the forest."

"You're the leader." She started after him.

Soon the camp was no longer visible. All lights were out of

sight except the moonlight peeking through the treetops. The stars were bright and visible through the trees like a gorgeous cosmos painting. Aria tilted her head to stare at the night sky as she walked, everything reflecting in her wide blue eyes. When the trees blocked her view of the stars, she held her palm face up and a flame appeared to float right above it, illuminating the ground.

"Whoa! When did you learn to do that?" Luke pointed at the fire, its glow casting upon his shocked face.

"While Willow and I were waiting for you and Avi. I taught myself."

"Does it hurt?"

"No, it's just warm."

They walked farther through the forest and Aria began to shake, goosebumps rising on her arms. The night air made a shiver run up her spine. She'd forgotten her jacket back in the cabin because it was summer, so she didn't think she would need it. With the fire in her palm, she still thought she didn't. But what really was causing the shaking was fear of being deep in the dark forest, where all sorts of animals were hiding in the bushes and behind tree trunks.

"Are you cold?" Luke asked.

"No, not really." Aria tensed, trying to hide the slight tremble.

"Here, take my sweatshirt." Luke pulled his hoodie off himself.

As she took it, a half-smile spread across her face. "Thank you."

She extinguished the fire in her palm and pulled Luke's sweatshirt on. It smelled like him—like mint and a hint of pine. She couldn't tell what color it was through the darkness, but it was either black or indigo, and a bit oversized. When it was on completely, she lit the flames back up in her hand.

"Is that better?" he asked.

"Yes." In truth, she was still trembling.

She felt somehow better, though—somehow more comforted by wearing Luke's sweatshirt.

They walked on for a while longer in silence before Aria asked, "If Stranger's Vine can be found in the Mundane Realm, why have I never heard of it? Why can't we just get the leaves from the potion pantry?"

"We can't get it from the potion pantry because Stranger's Vine always has to be relatively fresh or it won't work in potions. And it usually only grows in areas where magic is used more often. It rarely grows were mundanes can see it...and if they do, they usually don't survive..." Luke trailed off.

"Don't survive? Luke, we are looking for this thing right now and you are telling me that people don't usually survive its attacks?" Aria shrieked, her heart beginning to thump strikingly against her ribs.

"Mundanes don't usually survive because they don't have magic to fight it off and they don't know one of its weaknesses is fire...I'm sure we'll be fine."

Despite what Luke had said, fear still coursed through her. She looked through the forest, using the little bit of light she was able to produce, for anything that could resemble a Stranger's Vine.

"Let's pick up the pace. It must be around here somewhere." She passed Luke up, who was walking rather slowly, as if carefully.

"NO! ARIA! DON'T STEP THERE!" he screamed, but it was already too late.

A vine wrapped around one of Aria's ankles, pulling her feet from under her, and she fell backwards to the ground, her head banging off of a tree root. Something sharp jabbed into her ankle and she let out a cry as the plant pulled her toward a tree covered with dark green leaves. The fire in the palm of her hand had gone out and she could barely make out anything around her. Luke stood far back, using a Knockback Enchant, which was pointless towards all the vines that were flying this way and that.

Dark vines speckled in tiny, sharp, jagged thorns and leaves covered a large tree and the ground around it. The vines were flying into the air and creeping across the ground toward Aria. She screamed in pain and horror as the plant wrapped itself around her and crept up her body. Thorns stabbed in her legs as they tied them tightly together. She tried to create a fire in her hand to burn the plant away, but a vine sprouted from the forest floor, wrapped around her wrist, and pulled it firmly to the ground. Poisonous spikes pierced her wrist and more screams tore from her throat.

"Luke! Help me!" Aria screamed with tears in her eyes.

The sharp, thorn-covered vines were up to her waist now, starting to constrict her. In her other hand, she attempted to produce a fire, but another vine pulled it to the ground as well.

"I can't! I don't know how!" Luke shouted back in panic.

He stared at his shaky hands now, as if expecting something to appear in them. A tiny flicker of light appeared in his palms, but it quickly vanished.

Several more thorns jabbed into Aria's skin as they crept up her arms and body. The thorns were easily cutting their way through Luke's sweater, staining it with blood. Her arms and legs began to feel odd like there was a toxin running through them. She screamed and screamed as the vines constricted her, digging the thorns deeper into her skin. A flame suddenly appeared in the palms of Luke's hands, but then it was gone again.

"I am so sorry, Aria! I'm trying!"

The plant swung one of its vines at Luke, nearly hitting his leg.

"Luke! Watch out!" Aria yelled as loud as the constricting plant would allow.

The vines were almost at her neck. She was going to die. She found she could already barely breathe as the plant grew tighter around her stomach.

"H-help…me," she gasped.

Luke managed to make a large fire in his hands and hurried to throw it at the vines before it could vanish again. The Stranger's Vine caught fire on the tree and the flames burnt down the vines. Immediately, the plants shriveled up and retreated from Aria's damaged body before they could completely burn up. She just lay there, gasping for air, and crying at the agonizing pain.

Luke rushed to the plant to snatch three leaves before the whole thing was covered in flames. Then he ran to her, falling to his knees. "Can you stand?"

"I- I think s-s-so."

Luke grabbed her arm carefully, watching out for her wounds, and helped her to her feet.

"Ah," she cried.

He put his arm around her back to support her. She leaned into him, resting her head on his strong shoulder, and wrapping an arm around his neck. They watched the Stranger's Vine burn against the tree before Aria raised her hand slowly and unsteadily to put the flames out. The vines were now nothing more than a pile of ash on the forest floor.

Aria leaned against him as he half-carried her back through the woods. She limped on her bleeding legs, wincing with every step. They didn't talk on their way back to the massive oak tree, but Aria whined and cried in Luke's ear. When they reached it,

Aria sank onto the ground, back up against the tree, and tried to look at her wounds. He helped her pull off the sweatshirt and the cool night air suddenly brushed her skin. Luke made a fire in the palm of his hand to help her examine them. Blood was oozing out of jagged cuts all over her legs and arms. In her arm, a thorn remained stuck, so Luke went to pull it out.

Aria stuck out her hand to stop him.

"No, no," she panted.

"It has to come out. Stranger's Vine's thorns release poison if they're left in too long."

Aria removed her hand and Luke quickly ripped it out. She groaned, but then bit her lip to prevent herself from crying out so close to the campgrounds. Footsteps grew close and she scooted herself more behind the tree, thinking maybe someone had heard her screams from deeper in the forest.

"We got some of the ingredients. Luckily, they had Nevidit slime," Avi's voice said as he approached.

"But they didn't have fairy dust. Fairy dust is the most needed ingredient for all potions! Why would they not have it?" Willow rhetorically voiced, sitting down next to Aria in the darkness. "Oh my! Aria! What in the name of Viden happened?" She stared wide-eyed at Aria through the light from the fire in Luke's hand.

"Keep it down," Luke told her. "Stranger's Vine attacked her."

Avi sat down next to Luke. "She needs to see a Healer," he urged.

"No, no, they'll ask questions," Aria objected.

"So, what? The poison from the thorns might already be in your blood. The poison will slow down the healing process and you will bleed to death," Avi said. "You have to go to a Healer! We'll take you right now."

Avi grabbed Aria's arm to pry her up from the ground, but Willow pushed him back.

"No, not now," Aria said.

"What do you mean '*not now?*'" Avi's brows furrowed. "You mean in the morning?"

"Yeah, sure. The morning," Aria said softly, her breathing getting slower.

"No, no, you can't go to sleep now." Luke's warm hands grabbed the sides of her face lightly, pushing her tangled brown hair out of her face. "Aria, stay with me."

She sank all the way to the ground, laying down. Everything she heard seemed so distant. She could hear Luke, Avi, and Willow's voices trying to keep her awake, but she was slipping. Yawning, she closed her eyes and was left in total darkness.

Chapter Twelve

ARIA GRADUALLY OPENED her eyes to the glaring lights above her. All the pain came back to her in a rush like a hard slap in the face. She groaned and bit down on her lip. It felt as if a heavy weight had settled into her bones and poison rushed through her veins.

The room came into focus; the eye-blinding white walls and curtains separating several beds in a row, the shaded window overlooking the camp's front parking lot, and the monitors and fluids resting beside the bed she laid on. Aria lifted her head up a bit to see Luke sitting next to her in a cushioned chair.

He looked up from his nervously fidgeting hands and into her face. "Aria, you worried me—I mean, us. We knew you were still breathing, but you just gave us a scare. We brought you here—to the camp's infirmary—as soon as you passed out. Willow and Avi went to go get you some breakfast."

She gradually sat up fully, her breath shuddering at the pain that ran just beneath her skin. Leaves and dirt were caked in her hair. Now she could see her bloodstained arms, legs, and clothes more clearly. The cuts, however, were gone, leaving behind smooth, scarless skin.

"Here, keep it," Luke handed Aria his sweatshirt, which was ripped and stained with her blood.

"Oh, thanks." She set it beside her on the bed.

"The Healer who healed you said the poison from Stranger's Vine is still in your system. They've been giving you medicine through that tube, but it hasn't cleared it out yet." Luke pointed to the needle stuck in her arm.

She glanced down at the needle, her heart sinking at the thought of the Healers possibly knowing *why* they had been in the woods in the first place. "What did you tell them? About us going in the woods?"

"I just said we were going on a walk. They didn't ask too many questions after I told them you'd been attacked by Stranger's Vine. They were more concerned with stopping the bleeding and getting the poison out of your system."

Aria blew out a sigh of relief. *Then they don't know about the potion.*

The door swung open and a wrinkling, blond-haired woman walked in, wearing a badge that read: *Cassandra Ruff—Healer*.

"Good morning, dear. It's good to see you're up now." Cassandra, the Healer, walked around Aria's bed to check the medicine flowing into Aria's bloodstream and the monitors. "Do you feel any pain?"

"Yes," Aria admitted. "But it's dulling."

"Good. That's the medicine doing its job. In an hour or two, the medicine will have cleared the poison out and you should be ready to leave. It's a good thing your friends brought you here when they did." She took one of the empty bags of fluids down, switching it for a new one. "I'll be back. Call for anything that you need." Then she strode away, clicking the door shut behind her.

Willow and Avi came into the room a few minutes later with heaps of food on two trays.

"Aria! You're awake!" Willow exclaimed as she and Avi sat down on the edge of one of the other beds. "We brought lots of food so you and Luke can eat. Avi and I already did, but Luke refused to leave."

Willow handed her one of the trays and she forced herself to eat despite the dull ache in her bones that made her not want to. As the next two hours passed, the pain drifted away as if it had never been there at all. Aria tried to keep her mouth shut as much as possible, her head the last to stop aching. The medicine rushed through her veins, leaving behind a refreshed feeling and wiping away the poison.

"Thanks for bringing me here," Aria said into the silence of the room once her head had cleared of pain. She turned to Luke. "And thanks for saving my life last night."

"Of course," Luke said just as Cassandra, the Healer, walked back into the room.

"How do you feel, dear?" Cassandra stepped up to Aria's bedside and carefully pulled the needle from her arm.

"Better."

"The pain is all gone?"

Aria nodded.

"Then the poison is gone. It's a wonder what some magically enhanced medicine can do." Cassandra grinned. "You are free to go now. I do have a question before you go, though. Why did you go in the woods for a stroll? It's banned to all campers unless there is an event in there."

"I didn't know it was banned. We just wanted fresh air," Aria lied, glancing at Luke, Willow, and Avi for help.

"Fresh air? At a camp…that's outside?"

"I like the smell of trees," Aria answered a little too quickly.

"The camp is surrounded by trees, dear." Cassandra raised her eyebrows skeptically.

"Well, I…uh…I like to sniff them up close," Aria responded but then regretted it. That was not at all what she'd meant to say. That just made her sound utterly ridiculous.

But that being said, Cassandra just replied awkwardly, "Okay…Well, no more going in the woods. And I suggest taking a shower." She gestured to Aria's bloodstained limbs.

Aria nodded in agreement. She grabbed Luke's sweatshirt and hopped off the bed. Luke, Willow, and Avi followed after her as she started for the door.

A breeze blew past them when they stepped outside, enveloping Aria in the fresh smell of pine, maple, flowers, and grass.

"You like to sniff trees up close?" Avi asked, quirking an eyebrow up and smirking.

"Don't judge me," Aria said, but a grin pulled at her lips.

The sun was hot on the trails, making sweat bead up on her forehead. They followed after her down the empty trails toward cabin number thirteen. Luke ran his hand through his disheveled hair when she stopped at her cabin door to stare back at him.

"We'll see you later," he said with a smile twitching on his lips.

"Yeah, tree? After lunch?" Aria asked vaguely in case there happened to be someone, somewhere, listening.

"Yeah." He let the smile escape his lips and darted back down the path.

Aria smiled back, his face imprinted in her brain.

Willow and Avi waved before following after him, exchanging whispers with each other.

She opened the door to the cabin and walked in, caught off guard when, once again, Celaena was there. Aria quickly bolted into the bathroom without shutting the door before Celaena could see her covered in dry blood.

"Who's there?" Celaena asked. "Has Aria finally shown up? Or is it the weird little Willow? They were gone all night. Hmm…I wonder where they were."

She heard Celaena's footsteps nearing the bathroom and her heart sank. Celaena stopped in front of Aria before she could close the door, looking her up and down and raising her eyebrows.

"What on earth happened to you?" She wrinkled her nose.

"That's none of your business," Aria said and pushed Celaena out of her way.

Celaena caught her arm and looked at the blood staining it.

"Where were you last night?" She let go of her arm, her face twisting with disgust.

"Again, *none of your business*," Aria stated.

She strode over to her cubbyhole, shoved Luke's sweatshirt in it, and picked out a new outfit. Shooting a glare at Celaena, she walked back to the bathroom and the door thudded in Celaena's face.

"I know you're up to something, Chesler, and I'm going to find out what!" Celaena screeched through the door.

Great, way to not be suspicious, Aria told herself and blew out a frustrated puff of air.

She rinsed the dried blood, dirt, and leaves from herself in the shower, then got dressed and brushed through her horribly tangled, wet hair. The breeze blew over her smooth skin as she stepped outside and she took a deep breath, feeling mentally tired, but physically energetic. She wanted to lay down in her bed and fall asleep. She didn't want to have to deal with Celaena or focus on anything. But at the same time, she wanted to get started on the potion.

After wandering down the paths for a while, she made her way behind cabin number eighteen, up to the massive oak tree. She hoped by some chance that time had flown quicker than she thought it had and that it was somehow lunchtime now. Her stomach growled with hunger. Moving pine needles, leaves, and sticks around, she managed to find Luke's leather bag hidden on the forest floor. As she sat down on the ground, she took a big inhale, taking in the fresh, pine-filled air. Inside the bag was the potion book and the potion ingredients that Avi and Willow had gathered. She flipped through the pages of the book until she found the Tracking Potion recipe and skimmed the page, just to have something to do, but then her eyes landed on the part that said: *Let the potion sit for two hundred and forty hours with access to the sun.*

She did the math in her head. *That's ten days!* She blew a puff of air, slammed the book shut with temper, and shoved it back into the bag. She didn't want to wait any longer to save her parents. She wanted them back now! But, nope, she would have to wait ten days for the potion to cure, not to mention the fact that they didn't even have the fairy dust yet. Just as she leaned back against the oak tree with her arms crossed, Luke, Avi, and Willow came creeping into the forest.

"How are you feeling?" Willow asked.

"Fine, I suppose," Aria replied. In all honesty, she didn't feel very fine after what happened the night before even though she'd been healed. "But why—"

"How long have you been here?" Avi interrupted.

"For a while. But why did nobody bother to tell me that the potion is going to take ten days to *cure*?"

"Oh, I meant to tell you, I just forgot. What's the problem though?" Luke sat down next to her.

"*The problem* is my parents have been missing for two

months and now I have to wait even longer because of the time the potion takes to make!" Aria's tone was tempered, but her stomach clenched. She didn't mean to get so loud. She pinched the bridge of her nose.

"Aria, please calm down. We are trying to help, but this is the best we can do," Willow said, remaining calm.

"Sorry." Aria rubbed her eyes. "I didn't mean to be so rude."

"We have to go see the fairies for the fairy dust and then we can begin the potion," Willow told her.

"How are we going to do that? Where are they?"

"They're here on the campgrounds. Nobody sees them since they're skittish. Their colony resides in the field where Aria fell in that water tank," Willow said and Aria's lips pressed into an embarrassed line. "Sadly, someone took them from the Vezchia Realm and put them here, then they populated, and now they call this camp home. It's sad how people mess with creatures who wish to be left alone. We could go see them now...but they don't just give away their fairy dust."

"We have to give them something they want," Avi answered the question that Aria had formed in her head.

"Well, what do they want?" Aria asked.

"Don't know, we'll have to ask them." Luke rose and offered her his hand.

"What?" Aria gently grabbed his hand and stood. "How in the world do we do that? Don't they speak a different language or something?"

"Yeah, they speak Fairish, and they speak softer than a whisper..." Luke responded. "But, Willow, Avi, and I discussed that issue on our way up here. Willow can just read their minds and communicate through some telepathy thing to see what they want."

"You have telepathy, too?" Aria turned to Willow, her jaw dropping a bit.

"I may be a Mind-reader, but there are many properties to that power."

"Well, then let's go." Aria jumped up from the ground, dusting all the dirt off of her.

Without any hesitation, the rest of them followed her out of the forest. They walked down the paths, through a part of the forest, and to the huge field surrounded by trees, which was now cleared of blocks, dummies, piles of wood, and tanks. The grass grew very tall around the edges of the field, whereas other spots of grass were dry and dead.

"Where are they?" Aria looked around as they stood in the middle of the field.

"You have to sing their song so they know you're trustworthy enough," Willow said. "I told you they're skittish."

"And how do you know their song?" Aria asked skeptically.

"I read it in a book."

Of course, she did.

She stepped forward from their little group and began singing loudly. To Aria, the song just sounded like high-pitched gibberish, but when Willow stopped singing, tons of fairies, the size of a quarter of a pencil, began moving out of the forest's edge. They flew over to her in a flash, wearing little clothes made out of old cloth, leaves, and woven grass. Metallic gold sparkles covered their skin and wings, which looked as if they would break if you touched them. Their wings were so delicate and intricate, fluttering so fast you could barely tell they were there.

A fairy fluttered into the palm of Willow's hand. For a while, there was silence as Willow stared at the fairy and the fairy stared back at her. Aria looked closely, so intrigued by the creature. It was rude to stare, but how could she not? The fairy's mouth was moving, its little, human-like eyes locked on

Willow. Suddenly, the fairy flew away, disappearing back into the forest, and Willow turned back to Luke, Avi, and Aria. Aria tried to wipe the look of awe off her face, but it wasn't easy when she had just seen a *real* fairy.

"They want cloth in exchange for their fairy dust," Willow said with a delighted smile. "That was the queen. She's very kind."

"They want cloth?" Aria asked, just to clarify. It seemed like an odd thing to ask for.

"Yes, to make clothes for themselves. It's not easy for them to get it on the campgrounds unless they steal it. And fairies would never steal—they're fair in everything they do. But she said that we will have to bring a bottle for the fairy dust."

"Where are we going to get the cloth?"

"Well, I already have some. I was going to make a cute outfit for Twilight, but I haven't gotten to it yet…Speaking of Twilight, I wonder where he is. I haven't seen him since yesterday. I bet he's enjoying this nice weather." Willow said, then began walking back toward the trails with her face pointed toward the sky.

"Where do fairies even get their dust from?" Aria followed after her with Avi and Luke right behind her.

"They produce it themselves. They make it magically appear from their hands, and then it allows them to fly and use other forms of magic," Willow explained. "Unique creatures, fairies are."

After dinner, Willow was rummaging around her cubbyhole. They had gone to another water-controlling lesson together after seeing the fairies. Only a few hours ago they had to walk back to their rooms dripping wet. Now that they were dressed in dry clothes, Willow was searching for her cloth but must have misplaced it since she couldn't find it anywhere.

"It was here! I swear!" Willow yelled in frustration.

Elaine and Natalie weren't paying attention. They were, instead, showing each other their water tricks with a cup of water on the ground. Aria tried to ignore Celaena, who sat on her bed, watching them like a hawk waiting for the right moment to prey.

"What are you even looking for?" Celaena narrowed her eyes to slits.

"My fabric that I am going to use to make an outfit for Twilight." Willow didn't dare look at Celaena.

Celaena fell off her bed and onto the floor, bursting into a fit of laughter. Willow turned around and bent down to feel around under her bed for it.

"I found it!" She exclaimed. "Hey, what are you doing here? I've been looking everywhere for you as well."

Willow reached her hand under her bed and pulled out not only different colors of folded fabric but also Twilight. She plopped her fabric on her bed and lifted her cat up into her arms, giving him a hug. The cat didn't look too pleased. Celaena's laughter got louder, tears streaming from her eyes. Aria raised one eyebrow as she stared at Celaena and leaned against the bedpost, wondering what on earth could possibly be so funny. Twilight suddenly hissed at Celaena and she immediately stopped laughing, gulping before climbing back onto her bed. She twiddled a pen and began drawing on her hands again. Willow put Twilight down, then he jumped on her bed, and curled up in a ball. She tucked her fabric away in her cubbyhole, walked over, and sat down next to her cat. Aria tore her gaze away from Celaena and grabbed one of Willow's educational books from her cubbyhole to read the remainder of the night before sleeping. She didn't generally read much, other than the occasional fantasy book, but maybe Willow was right about books. They held a lot of information, and Aria needed to know much, much more about the world of magic.

The bright morning sunlight beamed through the clear windows. Celaena sat on her bed as if waiting for Aria and Willow to wake up, but they ignored her as they got ready. Aria's heart drummed in her ears. Celaena watched Willow grab an outfit from her cubby, but didn't notice her sneak the fabric between her clothes before she hurried into the bathroom. Aria picked out her clothes too, and waited next to Twilight on Willow's bed until she was done. Celaena kept her eyes locked on Aria, making every hair on her arms and head stand up. Finally, the bathroom door opened and Willow came out of it, her bushy blond hair wet and straight for once. She threw her dirty clothes in the hamper near the door and left the cabin with the cloth peeking through her hands.

"Why does she have that fabric?" Celaena asked.

"Probably to go sew it together…Uh…Luke borrowed her sewing kit so he could…uh…repair his pants or something," Aria lied and walked to the bathroom. "What does it matter to you?"

She then slammed the door shut before Celaena could even reply. She was tired of Celaena watching her every move and asking questions she had to make up stories for.

Celaena was waiting right outside the bathroom door like a stalker when she opened it. Aria pushed past her, clenching her mouth shut to keep herself from making a comment that would set her off, and left the cabin, Celaena trailing behind her at a distance.

In the mess hall, Aria slid onto a bench next to Luke and watched over Willow and Avi's shoulders as Celaena sat down with her group of friends. Her eyes were still locked on Aria. Aria changed her gaze to Luke, then down at her hands.

"She's watching us. Don't look," she said, glancing at each of her friends.

"Celaena?" Avi asked.

"Of course. She knows we're up to something and she won't take her eyes off Willow and I. How are we going to be able to sneak away to the fairies?"

"Lose her, I guess," Luke said.

Aria and Willow gave a frustrated sigh.

After breakfast, they headed down the paths that wound throughout the camp. Celaena followed behind them at a distance, her eyes pinned to them. They went to the front of the campgrounds, then back near the forest, split up, and met back at the field in an attempt to lose her. Celaena had followed Aria when they split up. Aria hid behind cabin number twenty-five, watching as Celaena swore and frantically searched for where she had gone. Once her back was turned, she bolted down the trail and disappeared into the forest.

Fairies were gathered around in the field, in much greater numbers than before. The fairy queen fluttered right in front of Willow, who held out the fabric for the fairies. Luke pulled out the little jar and a funnel he had taken from his brother to hand to Willow. Many fairies took hold of the cloth with their teeny tiny hands and helped each other take it into the forest. Willow grabbed the jar and funnel from Luke, then held it out to all the fairies gathered in the field. It was such a stunning, incredible, and breathtaking sight to see as one by one, the fairies released their handfuls of metallic gold fairy dust into the funnel. The dust spun through the funnel and collected into the bottom of the jar, shimmering like gold sparkles. All the fairies dropped their dust into the jar, filling it up halfway, before retreating into the forest again. Willow pulled the funnel out, closed the jar, and handed both back to Luke. The fairy queen's mouth moved in silence and Willow nodded before the fairy queen flew away, and they left back to the oak tree.

"Now we can begin brewing the potion," Aria said as they came to the oak.

"Yeah. We'll leave it behind this tree while we're in the process of making it, that way it will be hidden," Luke said.

"I'll go collect the wood." Avi walked a few feet away and started picking twigs off the forest floor.

"What about camp events?" Willow asked.

"I really don't care about doing any of them other than the lessons anymore. And Celaena already figured out we're up to something, so it's pointless to pretend that we aren't," Aria said.

"Oh…" Willow seemed disappointed. "Well, if you aren't doing them, neither will I."

Luke grabbed a metal bucket that he must have hidden earlier out from under a pile of leaves.

"I'll go down to the lake and fill this with water," he said and then he was off.

Avi's collection of wood plopped to the ground near Aria and Willow. They pushed the pile a few feet away from each tree and made it flat and neat for the bucket to sit on. Avi disappeared through the trees again and came back several minutes later with tons of rocks. He let them all fall to the ground with a thud. Together, the three of them surrounded the twigs with the stones so the fire couldn't spread.

"Now we just have to wait for Luke to come back with the water," Willow said, directing a smile at Avi.

Aria took the jar of fairy dust out of Luke's bag next to her. She sprinkled the wood with the golden, metallic dust and then they waited for Luke. He came back with half a bucket full of water a while later and carefully set it on the pile of timber, water splashing over the sides.

"What took you so long?" Aria asked.

"The lake isn't that close to here and I saw Celaena on my way back. I had to be careful she didn't see me." He pointed to the wood underneath the bucket. "Could you?"

Aria nodded and snapped her fingers near the pile of wood. The sticks caught fire, but not just any fire. It burned a mesmerizing blue.

CHAPTER THIRTEEN

ARIA WATCHED THE gorgeous blue flames flicker and dance under the bucket of now boiling water.

"Aria, could you—" Luke went to ask.

"Yep, got it." With a swipe of her hand, she extinguished the blazing fire.

"It was pretty, wasn't it?" Willow said, still staring at where the flames had been.

"Yeah." Aria nodded.

"It says that we add the alpaca spit now. We should just dump the whole thing in." Luke leaned against the tree next to her, staring down at the potion book.

"I call dibs on *not* doing that." Avi sat on the ground, plucking grass.

"I guess I'll do it," Aria volunteered.

Luke reached into the leather bag and handed the glass bottle of alpaca spit to her. The bottle was filled with a thick, grassy green substance, and she could smell the horrible aroma of it leaking from the bottle—the smell of vomit and rotting flesh. She pulled the cork out and dumped the entire thing into the bucket of steaming hot water, ignoring all potion-making safety protocols. The clear water swirled and changed to a banana yellow.

"How?" Aria gasped at the abrupt change in color. The way it had been clear before made a need for understanding burst into her mind.

"When you boil water with blue flames, it causes the water to contain magical properties," Willow said.

"Now we have to rip apart the troll nose hair." Luke wrinkled his nose.

Nobody volunteered.

Aria sighed, stuck her hand in the bag, and pulled out a thin tube labeled: *Troll nose hairs*. The cap popped off and she pulled out one long troll nose hair while Luke, Avi, and Willow's faces twisted with disgust.

"I can't wait to make Celaena drink this." Aria smirked at the thought of it.

She tossed the tube back to Luke to put in his bag and she ripped up the hair, letting it fall down into the water.

"Now, we let it sit for twenty-four hours before we add the rest of the ingredients," Luke said.

Aria grunted in frustration and stood up, dusting all the dirt off her pants. "Okay, well, let's head back down to camp then. I have a lesson with Mrs. Helma."

They all stood up, Luke making sure to hide his bag and the book back under the leaves again. It was two o'clock in the afternoon when they left the oak tree. Aria's stomach growled for food and water. Not to mention, she was aggravated that the potion would take so long to brew, so she was hangry. She would have to wait till dinner though. Mrs. Helma was inside a stone building, instructing others how to do a Knockback Enchant. Aria was annoyed that she had to keep practicing that over and over again instead of learning something new.

"Oh, Aria, you are late," Mrs. Helma said.

"Sorry, I got lost," Aria lied.

She took her place in front of one of the many dummies that were all over the room. Focusing hard, she managed to block out most of the noise around her: pounding echoing off the walls as dummy after dummy hit the floor and Mrs. Helma's voice as she continued to instruct others on how to produce a Knockback Enchant. Aria raised her hands at chest level and imagined that the dummy in front of her was Celaena. Power crackled through her veins and she willed it to gather in her palms. Breathing deeply, she felt a force push from her hands, across the room, and it blasted the dummy to the ground. After running to pick it back up, she began again. Now, she pictured it was Malus, even though she had no idea what he looked like. The way she pictured him was that he had black, horrendous eyes, a face like a green monster, and wore a black cloak that all the Dark Forces wore. It fell over. Then she pictured it was Twilight being annoying. It fell over again.

About an hour passed of going back and forth over the same enchant. The air inside the small building was dense with heat and seemed to get hotter the harder she worked.

Finally, Mrs. Helma's voice called out, "Okay, okay, the lesson is over."

In the mix of the other campers, Aria burst out of the humid building and out into the even hotter sun, sweat beading up on her skin. As she crossed the grass, targets, a group of campers, and flying arrows caught her eye.

"Oh, hey, Aria!" Avi called, dropping his bow and arrows to the ground, and ran up to her.

"Hey," Aria greeted. "I didn't know you did archery."

"I don't, but they had an extra space open, so I thought I

could use the practice if we're going to go rescue your parents," Avi said. "Where's Luke and Willow?"

"I know that Luke had a lesson, but it's probably over by now."

"And Willow's probably at some book club."

The mention of Avi, Luke, and Willow helping her save her parents made her feel uneasy, but she had to admit, he was funny. She still hadn't quite figured out a way to leave them behind.

They walked past the mess hall now crowded with crafting enchanters and enchantresses. The smell of meats, bread, and spices drifted through the air from the chimney.

"I'm starving," Aria said, grabbing her stomach.

"Yeah, me, too," Avi replied. "Wanna go check on the potion?"

"Yeah, maybe it can take my mind off food."

And with that, they headed up to the oak tree.

The potion was luckily still there and left undiscovered. It had cooled down and now looked like a giant bucket of mucus.

"That is disgusting!" Avi voiced in distaste.

"Yeah, but I can't wait to make Celaena taste it," Aria said, a smirk twisting at her lips. Celaena deserved a lesson.

The next day, Luke, Avi, Willow, and Aria went up to the oak tree to check on the potion just after lunch.

"Now, we add ground-up Siren scales," Luke said, looking at the potion recipe.

"I'll do it." Willow took the glass tube of ground-up Siren scales and poured the ash-like gray powder into the bucket. It smelled foul like rotting fish. The potion instantly turned to a light purple without needing to be stirred.

"Now, add the Nevidit slime," Luke instructed.

Avi scooted as far from the bucket as possible, like being even remotely close to it was revolting.

"Okay." Willow wrinkled her nose as Luke handed the bottle of the vile stuff to her.

She pulled the cork out and dumped the whole glob of gray slime into the potion, sending splatters of the potion into the dirt. After she tossed the bottle back to him, he put it in his bag. Luke's eyes met Aria's, making her face turn a tinge of red and butterflies appear in her stomach. But she still didn't know why. He looked away, taking something out of his bag.

"I'll add the leaves from Stranger's Vine." He knelt next to the potion and tore the three leaves up, letting them fall into the potion.

Aria's heart hurt for a moment. She would never forget the pain from that moment when she thought she was going to be killed by a plant.

"Now, the moonstone dust." He took out a bottle of blue, glowing dust and poured it into the potion. It was like a falling stream of blue glitter with hints of silver. The potion swirled, then turned to a shimmering light blue, like that of the sky. "That's it. In about ten days, the Tracking Potion will be ready, and we can give it to Celaena. Then she can lead us straight to the Dark Forces and your parents." He leaned back against the tree and stared at Aria with his charming smile.

"Great," she said, forcing enthusiasm into her voice.

⁕(⁕

Hours later, crowds of people made their way down the paths to the mess hall, Luke, Avi, Willow, and Aria following suit. The smell of fresh food hit Aria in the face, making her stomach growl as soon as she stepped through the door. She quickly got herself some food, piling it high, then sat down with Luke, Avi, and Willow. She was so hungry that she immediately started shoving bites into her mouth. Luke, Avi, and Willow just stared at her with stunned faces.

"What?" she asked.

"You're…just eating so fast." Avi's fork stopped in mid-air on its way to his mouth.

"I haven't eaten anything since lunch."

"Um, that was only a few hours ago," Avi reminded her.

"Don't judge me," Aria told him and shoved more food into her mouth.

Luke fought to hide his amused smile, but failed, and her face went red.

Aria and Willow walked into their cabin after dinner, Aria feeling stuffed. *Maybe I did eat too much*, she thought. Elaine and Natalie must have still been at dinner because the only other person in the cabin was Celaena, searching their cubbyholes.

"Hey!" Aria shouted.

Celaena quickly spun around and narrowed her eyes. "What?"

"Get out of our stuff!"

"Why?" Celaena cocked her head to the side. "Got something to hide?"

"No, but we don't want you getting into our stuff!" Rage boiled inside Aria.

"Well, I didn't find anything anyway. But I'd watch your backs if I were you…I know something you don't." Celaena flipped her long hair behind her back and crossed her arms.

"What? What do you know that we don't?" Aria demanded.

"Hmm…you know…I've seem to have forgot*ten*." A sly smile spread across Celaena's face.

Aria felt her heart quake inside her chest. *She knows about the potion!* Was she hinting about the ten days it would take for the potion to cure? If she did, wouldn't she tell someone? Wouldn't she destroy it? What was she playing at? Aria's face went red and she could feel Willow shaking a little beside her. Celaena smiled a wider grin as she took in their reaction.

The door opened behind them, so Willow and Aria stepped aside as Elaine and Natalie came into the cabin with their faces alight.

"There's a camp bonfire tonight." Elaine grinned. Then she saw Willow and Aria's faces, a frown fading onto her face. "What's going on here?"

Celaena's cruel voice suddenly changed to sound sweet and innocent when she said, "Nothing. Is it okay if I go to that bonfire with you? It sounds fun!" She forced a fake smile on her face that somehow looked so genuine.

Elaine and Natalie opened the door back up and Celaena followed out after them. When the door closed, Aria let out a long, muted, high-pitched scream she'd been trying to hold in.

"How does she know?"

"Maybe she doesn't. Maybe she's hinting at something else. And, even if she did know, we can still force her to drink it." Willow sat down on her bed, twiddling her thumbs.

"Maybe," Aria said, aggravated. "That is all we have is a bunch of questions and the answers are all maybes." She plopped down on Willow's bed too, sinking into the plush mattress.

Twilight, who had been taking a nap, got up and walked all the way to the other side of the bed to lay back down.

"Celaena is just trying to get on our nerves," Willow said.

"Can't you sense her emotions and read her thoughts?"

"I have to come in contact with her to hear her thoughts. I can feel her emotions, though. They're confusing. She's trying to unnerve us because it is funny to her. She's angry, but not at us. She is afraid of something. She is confused with her own self, not sure what she's supposed to do."

Aria sighed. "I feel so trapped. To be honest, I'm scared. I plan to rescue my parents, but I'm scared to fight the Dark Forces to accomplish that. I know this isn't going to be easy—" She began crying and put her head in her hands. "I couldn't even fight off Stranger's Vine. I just don't know what to do."

"That's why we are helping you. You're not alone, Aria. We're friends and this is what friends are for. To be your support beams that strengthen you. You are strong and brilliant. The Stranger's Vine is hard to fight off. You are lucky to still be alive. You are not weak. In fact, only a few months ago, you didn't even know magic existed."

"Thank you," Aria said, somehow feeling slightly better.

Willow sat down next to Aria and rubbed her back, suddenly making Aria feel calmer and more tired. Aria cried more, remembering all the times her mother had rubbed her back to make her feel better when she'd been upset.

"I know you guys all want to help me, but it will be my fault when one of you gets hurt. I don't want you guys to get hurt," Aria told her.

Willow didn't respond.

The sun hung low on the horizon, making the sky outside a dark, blended pink and purple, and the day turned to night.

—✦—☾—✦—

Morning came and morning went. Luke, Avi, Willow and Aria went to check on the potion right after breakfast. It was still curing, and luckily unmoved by anyone or anything. After that, they had to split up until lunch to go to their magic lessons.

At the end of the slow day, Willow and Aria studied books about magic in their beds. Aria knew she needed to know much more than what she did if she was going to save her parents. Celaena was finding it hard to insult them about things now since they were not running off and showing up late to classes as much.

On day five of the potion curing, it started to pour rain, causing the dirt paths to become muddy. The sky became a dark gray and the air became chilly with a breeze blowing through the treetops. Most of the camp huddled up in the cabins playing games and such while Aria, Luke, Willow, and Avi hurried to the oak tree and tried to cover the potion before the rain could ruin it. They'd have covered it before if it didn't need hours of sunlight to cure. The potion now looked like swampy water with bits of Stranger's Vine leaves floating around in it. Avi had to raid the camp kitchen for a pot lid, so when he returned, he was covered in mud splashes from running through puddles.

"Got it!" Avi yelled as he hurried up to the oak tree with the lid. He held it high into the air and then smacked it down on the potion to cover it.

"Good, I was getting tired of covering it with my body," Luke said, flashing a smile at Aria.

Luke's dark brown hair was drenched in water, looking almost black. He ran his hand through it, water dripping onto his face. The strangest urge to run her own hand through it came over Aria, but she shoved her hands in her back pockets and simply smiled back at him.

The next five days passed, two of them consisting of rain

and boredom. Willow and Aria were stuck in the cabin while it rained with Celaena watching them like a hawk. It left the two of them on edge. Luke and Avi were in their own cabin, playing board games with their cabin members—Christopher, Charlie, and Stefan. Aria was relieved when the rain stopped, and the mud dried up so she could leave cabin number thirteen. She hurried out of the cabin with Willow right behind her. Celaena had been too busy gossiping with Elaine and Natalie to notice them sneaking away. At the large oak tree, they lifted the lid to look at the murky, swamp-looking liquid.

"That is disgusting," Avi said, his face twisting in repulsion.

Luke unburied his leather bag from underneath all the dead leaves, the potion book safely wrapped inside, and took out a little empty glass bottle. He dipped the bottle into the potion to fill it up, leaving the rest of it in the bucket. After wiping some of the excess potion off on his pants, he put it in his bag.

Suddenly, sirens started blaring loudly from the campgrounds. The abrupt loud noises of alarms startled all four of them and they looked through the trees down into the camp. People were flinging open doors to see what the commotion was. Then, there were high-pitched screams and yells reverberating off every building and tree. People were yelling inaudible warnings to one another, running around frantically like bothered ants. The smell of smoke floated through the air, starting to cloud the sky above. They looked at each other with uneasiness and dread in their eyes. Luke swung his bag over his shoulder, and they hurried out of the forest.

Campers were fleeing into the woods, running past them without looking back. Nobody seemed to care that that was where Luke, Avi, Willow, and Aria were coming from.

"RUN!" Everyone screamed over and over again at the top of their lungs.

Luke, Avi, Aria, and Willow rushed down the paths and ran into Miss Truffle, who Aria was surprised to see since she hadn't seen her at all since the school year had ended.

"Aria! There you are!" Miss Truffle shouted with relief over the blaring sirens. "You and your friends need to run! Get far away from here!"

"Why? What's going on?" Aria's hands began to shake.

"Just do as I say!"

Alarm spread through Aria like ice, causing her to stare shockingly and freeze in place.

A ball of fire flew from somewhere behind Miss Truffle and hit a nearby building, setting it to flames.

Someone could be in there!

"There is nobody in there! Everyone is evacuating to the forest! You need to go, too," Miss Truffle yelled as if she knew what Aria might be thinking.

Aria trembled from head to foot, every hair on her arms standing up, and Avi grabbed her wrist to pull her toward the woods.

"Let's go, Aria!" Terror filled his voice.

"JUST GO!" Miss Truffle pleaded as she ran to help a younger girl in crutches evacuate.

Aria just needed to see what was wrong, though, so she ran down the path, toward the front of the camp. Luke, Avi, and Willow followed after her, urging her to come with them to the forest, but she wouldn't listen. She stopped in her tracks when she saw exactly what all the sirens, screaming, and warnings were about. Down the path was a dark, hooded figure whose face was hidden. On the shoulder of the cloak was a gold embroidered dagger. At that moment, Aria realized what Celaena had been hinting at.

Chapter Fourteen

S HE STOOD MOTIONLESS, staring at the member of the Dark Forces before her. She should run yet she remained in her place. All the screams seemed miles away from her as her heart thumped in her ears. Luke, Avi, and Willow begged her to follow them into the forest, but all Aria could manage was one step backward.

"Aria, let's go!" Luke shouted, panic setting in his voice. "We need to go!"

"No, you guys go. These people…they took my parents. They will lead me to them." Aria stood her ground.

"I have to find Twilight! I haven't seen him since earlier this morning! He ran off to play with Harper's cat," Willow cried.

"OVER HERE!" the figure ahead of them yelled in a deep voice. "I FOUND HER!"

"Run!" Aria shouted back at her friends.

"We won't leave you!" Luke stated.

Five more cloaked people appeared from around a long log building.

"Follow me!" Aria said through her clenched teeth.

She ran to her left, into a small, shadowed alleyway between two buildings. On one side was a tall concrete building and on the other was a log cabin. Sweat ran down her back as she ran; Luke, Avi, and Willow following in haste behind her. She was trembling with horror, her own head in a confusion of thoughts. She wanted to fight the Dark Forces with all her might, make them show her where her parents were. If they didn't show her where they were, she would use them to find them herself. But how? She was nothing more than a teenager, who had barely learned how to fight with magic. They would easily be able to take her down if they wanted to. She was petrified at the thought.

Suddenly, something struck the building to the right and the chunk of the wall and roof came plummeting down, separating her from her friends. Dust was everywhere, getting into her eyes and nose, causing her to cough. Debris fell to the ground, causing a massive pile up of wood, concrete, tile, and plaster. She fell backward and groaned at the impact as the air was knocked out of her lungs.

A gasp caught in her lungs and she batted all the dust out of her sight. "LUKE! AVI! WILLOW!"

"We're okay!" Luke's voice shouted back from the other side. "Are you okay?"

Aria stood up, dusting the little splinters of wood off her. "I'm okay!"

"Good, RUN!" Luke yelled. "They want you, not us!"

"I can't just leave you!"

"Just get out of here, Aria," Avi told her through a crack in the rubble.

"Go, Aria. Save yourself!" Willow's shaky voice called out.

Aria stood there for a minute, debating with herself. They were right, of course. The Dark Forces wanted *her*, not them.

"Just promise me, that you'll save yourselves, too," Aria

shouted over the sirens, then continued running down the alleyway before they could respond.

Guilt created a knot in her chest. She didn't want to leave them, especially when it was her fault they were there in the first place.

The dust was settling on the ground now. As she rounded the corner, she was enveloped in fresh air and the hot sun on her head. She turned to head toward the back of the camp to go to the forest like everyone else. Then something caught her ankle and she tripped, slamming her face into the dirt path. She heard a painful crack and felt something snap in her face, but she couldn't place where it was because the pain spread so rapidly like sharp needles stabbing into her skin. Her scream of agony echoed off the cabin a few feet away from her. Something warm ran down out of her nose and down her lips as whatever had her ankle dragged her backwards on her stomach, the path scratching her skin. She subconsciously licked her lips and tasted metal.

The pulling stopped and she immediately turned over to sit straight up. A hooded figure towered over her. The figure removed their hood, revealing a beautiful woman, her pale complexion highlighted by the sunshine. Her dark brown eyes sparkled with triumph under thick lashes and she tossed her wavy chocolate brown hair behind her.

The woman gave a pleased smile before calling out, "I HAVE HER!" to the other Dark Forces members. Her grin and posture gave the resemblance of a predator having captured its prey.

Aria looked at her ankle to see that there was a thick vine wrapped around it, rooted to the ground to keep her trapped there. Her heart dropped to her stomach as memories of Stranger's Vine flooded her brain. Shaking, she grabbed the vine and pulled, trying to tear it off.

"Uh-uh-uh, missy," the woman shouted and kicked Aria backwards.

She fell back to the ground, but she bounced back quickly, raised her hands, and blasted the woman into the air with a Knockback Enchant. The woman landed several feet away from her, groaning in pain.

Aria grabbed at the vine again, trying to somehow break it. It was so thick and strong, though, that no matter what she did, she couldn't free it from her ankle. She could hear Dark Forces members shouting from nearby. They were coming close. She had to think fast…But the only other idea she had would be agonizingly painful. She could use fire to burn through the plant, but it would burn her as well. It was her only option at that moment. It was that or be captured…or worse.

She stuck out her palm and made a fire in it, then pressed it against the vine. She couldn't help but scream as the flames licked at her skin, eating away at the vine and her own flesh. The vine fell away and she could clearly see the wound. It was horrible, shiny, red, blistering, and excruciating. Tears dripped down her face, mixing with the blood from her nose, as she tried to stand up. Several more hooded people came around the corner of a building, yelling as they saw her flee.

Aria started to run away from the hooded figures, limping as her heart raced in her ears. She ran and ran, her throat feeling like there was a fire in it. She lifted her fingers to her nose and pulled them away to see them slick with blood. The silver-smelling blood was running down her jaw and neck, staining her shirt. She hid behind the mess hall to catch her breath and used her shirt to wipe away the blood that was flowing out of her nose, but it was useless since it was still bleeding.

Not too far away, she could hear the hooded members shouting, "I think she went this way!" They seemed undecided of where to check, though, as their footsteps faded away in different directions.

Aria peeked out from behind the mess hall, and seeing that the coast was now clear, she took off down the path. If she could just find Luke, Avi, and Willow, then she would know they're safe.

This is all my fault, she thought angrily. *I should have just listened to them!*

If she'd run into the woods like everyone else, maybe she wouldn't have been in this situation. Why did she have to be so stubborn and determined?

I just thought I could save my parents if I stayed.

She crept over a path and then behind another log building, peeking around the corner. Sneakily, she made her way back to where the wall had collapsed. She turned down the alleyway, expecting to see Luke, Avi, and Willow still there, but nobody was at all. Worry set in, but not for herself. What if they were taken by the Dark Forces? What if they were hurt? She had to make sure they were safe, but she didn't know where they even were. Helplessness took over, causing one hand to find her sunflower necklace slick with blood, and the other to find her hair. Wishing she was out of this mess, she tugged on her hair like she was going to pull it out.

She turned on her heel and decided she would search the entire camp and forest top to bottom to find her friends. Making haste, she headed toward where a line of cabins stood. Just as she was about to turn behind one, something cold struck her back. Every muscle in her body slowly went numb and she stumbled against the hard log cabin. She struggled to move and stand up straight, but she couldn't. Her whole body went limp, her muscles loosening, and she fell to the ground, immobile. Everything but her eyes were useless to her, with her fingers being the last thing to go still. Her eyes darted around, but she was unable to see the person who had hit her with the enchantment.

A face peeked out from behind cabin number twenty to her right. It was Luke. They locked their tormented eyes on each other as footsteps grew closer from behind Aria.

"Silly little girl, you think you can outrun the Dark Forces?" a woman's cruel voice sneered from behind her.

The voice sounded so very similar to Celaena's that Aria thought maybe it was. She reconsidered that, though, because Celaena would never call her a '*little girl*,' they were the same age. That would be like Celaena calling herself a little girl as well.

Luke jumped out from behind the cabin with his hands raised and blasted the woman off her feet. Aria heard the woman slam into the side of the cabin and fall unconscious right behind her. Luke hurried to Aria, looking around for where to pick her up at. She just stared back at him, unable to do anything. He chose to grab her arms and lift her to a sitting position, then grabbed her lightly around her stomach to drag her behind the cabin.

Willow, who had a large bruise on her arm, and Avi, who had a cut running down his leg, were sitting behind the cabin. Willow's hands were clenched together under her chin as she shook with fear.

"Aria, it will wear off soon. It's an Immobile Enchantment," Luke whispered as he set Aria down gently.

He saved my life again, she thought. *I need to repay him.* Then the little sarcastic voice in the back of her head said, *well, getting someone into situations like this is a terrible way to thank them.*

Luke walked back out from behind the cabin, carefully

watching for any other hooded figures. A minute later, he came back roughly dragging the unconscious woman behind the cabin. The woman looked almost like a copy and paste of Celaena, except for being an adult and having wavy, shiny, black hair, and gray eyes instead of straight hair and green eyes. She was also wearing the same cloak that all the Dark Forces members wore—black with a gold dagger embroidered on the shoulder. Aria found she was able to move her mouth, having made her jaw drop slightly.

"Who is that? What are you doing with her?"

"This is Kora Blanc, Celaena's mother," Luke answered and Aria's eyebrows shot up. "I'm hiding her back here so we can give her the potion instead." He opened his bag and pulled out the bottle of swamp-water-looking potion.

"So, this is Celaena's mom?" She just had to clarify she had heard that right. *No wonder the woman and Celaena look so alike.*

"Yeah, Celaena's mother," Avi said. "I was right. I knew it. She *is* still working for the Dark Forces!"

"*We* knew it," Luke corrected.

"Yeah, right."

Luke opened Kora's mouth and poured the potion down her throat.

"Aria, what happened to you?" Willow asked.

"Some lady wrapped a vine around my ankle. I fell and I think I broke my nose." Aria winced at the pain.

"You need to see a Healer," Avi urged.

"Well, I can't do that while the camp is under attack, now can I?" Sarcasm laced her voice.

"I suppose not..."

"A vine? She must be a Nature-manipulator," Willow said.

"Okay, she has the potion. We have to get out of here before she wakes up." Luke drew their attention back to Kora.

"Here let me remove her memory," Willow said.

"Is that really necessary? I mean, she's unconscious." Avi pointed at Kora's limp figure.

"I can disorientate her, giving us more time to get away from here before she remembers what she was doing."

"Okay, do that then," Luke said.

Willow crawled over to Kora, pressing her hand to her forehead. She was quiet for a while as she scanned through Kora's memories. When her face looked a little disturbed, she said, "Okay, it's done."

"Aria, can you feel anything?" Luke asked.

"Other than pain, no."

"I don't think I can carry you…I mean, I could try."

"Just leave me."

"What? Are you insane? Do you not understand?" Luke half-shouted. "We will never just leave you. Ever."

"Be quiet! You'll give away our location!" Willow told him off.

Twilight came running through the trees and leapt into Willow's lap, taking a seat.

"Twilight!" Relief filled Willow's voice.

Kora started to stir, coming out of her unconscious state. Luke, Avi, and Willow looked at her with wide, frightened eyes. They had missed their window to flee. Luke grabbed Aria's arms to try to pick her up, but Kora's eyes flew open. Kora sat up so quickly that it was freaky, like something you would see in a horror movie. She looked confused for a moment before turning around to face Luke, Avi, Willow, and Aria. Luke let go of Aria and raised his hands to protect her, blocking her from Kora as he knelt on his knees. Avi and Willow followed suit. Twilight jumped from Willow's lap and stood in front of her, baring his fangs and swiping towards Kora with his claws protectively.

"What happened?" Kora wondered to herself aloud. "Oh, yes." Her cruel eyes landed on Luke. "You think you can protect her? You *children* don't stand a chance against me! Move aside or face the same fate as her!"

None of them moved a muscle, except Twilight, who angrily hissed at Kora, drawing her attention to him. A look of what might have been fear flickered in her eyes and her intake of breath was quick.

"Fine…but mark my words, children, we'll be back," Kora said, narrowing her eyes to slits, but a wicked smile swept her face. She crossed her arms over her chest and then vanished from thin air.

They fell back, releasing long breaths, and Twilight laid back down in Willow's lap. Aria's brows furrowed at the cat, confusion dawning in her eyes. *Did he just scare her off?* She shook the thought from her mind to focus on the problem at hand.

"I'm a weakling," Aria said softly, not meaning to say it aloud.

"No, you are not!" Willow stated. "Aria, you need to stop saying that. After all you've been through, you are not weak."

"The only reason I'm alive is because Luke keeps saving my life," she reminded her.

"You're welcome." Luke looked bashfully down at the ground.

"Thank you," Aria said. "I need to repay you somehow."

"No, you don't." He looked the other way to hide his reddening face.

She went quiet for a while as she laid there, her whole body hurting, and her muscles feeling cold and numb. She felt tragically defeated…and petrified.

"Are they all gone?" she asked at last.

"I don't know…I'll go see." Luke stood up from next to Aria to have a look around and Avi followed him from out of hiding, leaving Aria and Willow.

The time seemed to pass so lazily in those couple minutes they were gone.

"Yeah, I think they're all gone," Luke said as he and Avi sat back down on the ground near Aria.

"They turned off the sirens," Avi said, even though it was obvious that the blaring had stopped.

"Can you move yet?" Luke asked.

"I think I'll be able to soon." Aria managed to lift a finger. "I have a few things I need to say to Celaena," she added through gritted teeth.

"Like what?" Avi asked.

"That was her mom, wasn't it? Obviously, Celaena told her where the camp was!" Aria replied.

"Wouldn't her mom already know where it is?" Avi asked, raising his eyebrows.

"Not necessarily," Willow piped in. "Parents don't have to know where the camp is if campers take the school buses to get here. The camp is supposed to keep all outsiders out, even parents. It is one of the camp policies, meant to keep us all safe from parents that might be ambling in dark magic…like in the Dark Days."

"Even if Celaena's mom did know, Celaena was hinting at something the day we started the potion. This was what she was hinting at. I know it is!" Aria lifted her hand off the ground unsteadily just as the clacking of heels grew close.

Luke, Avi, and Willow hurried to gather back around her, ready to defend her from whoever was coming toward them.

"There you guys are!" Miss Truffle exclaimed, clutching her chest in surprise.

Miss Truffle's nose was bleeding slightly and she had a small cut on her arm, but other than that, she looked unharmed. The three of them relaxed and settled back down to reveal Aria, who was now slowly opening and closing her hands.

"Oh dear!" Miss Truffle's eyes went wide at the sight of her. "What happened to her?"

"Attacked, obviously," Aria answered, annoyed. What was it with people always asking questions they knew the answers to?

"Can you get up?" Miss Truffle asked.

"She was hit by an Immobile Enchantment by Celaena's mother," Luke said.

"Kora Blanc?" Her eyes grew wide.

"Yeah," they answered in unison.

"Oh dear. We will get you a Healer," Miss Truffle said, hurrying to Aria's side.

"No, no, leave me," Aria said.

"What in the world do you mean? You are hurt!" Miss Truffle said.

"I'm well aware." Aria picked up her arm, feeling all her muscles gaining strength again. Gradually, she pulled herself into a sitting position. "Just go find the others in the forest. Make sure everyone else is okay. I'm fine, really," she said, though that last part was a lie.

Miss Truffle got up slowly and followed her instructions, which was quite shocking that she was so obedient even when a teenager was telling her what to do.

"You need to see a Healer," Avi demanded once Miss Truffle was out of sight.

"First, I want to see Celaena." Aria pushed herself to her shaky feet. She stumbled to the side, but Luke caught her in his arms before she could fall. A shiver went up her spine and heat rose into her face.

"Thanks," she said awkwardly. When he didn't let go, she added, "You can let me go now."

Luke listened and Aria found her feet walking toward cabin number thirteen, her friends following behind her with Twilight at their feet.

Many of the buildings had been demolished, left as nothing but ash and smoke. All around was chaos as teens made their way back into the camp, where buildings were up in flames and others were knocked down. Many cabins had been left destroyed completely, leaving nothing but debris. The dust and smoke from all the ruin clouded the sky, the breeze taking it away from camp. People were crying all over the place, staring at the fire and rubble as adults tried to put out the flames with water from the lake. They passed the mess hall, which still stood, but they could see a massive fire in the front of the camp. Aria guessed that the office had been taken up in a blaze. Adults were gathering teens in groups, trying to organize the chaos and get people to Healers. Almost everyone was unharmed, but shaken to the core.

All this damage and for what? Aria Chesler? She was just an ordinary girl, aside from the fact that she could produce magic from her hands. Yeah, she was the daughter of the last remaining leaders of the Forces of Light, but that didn't make her special.

Cabin number thirteen stood completely left alone, undamaged. Aria bounded up the path, limping on one leg, and busted open the door, rage filling her whole body. Celaena was alone, standing in the middle of the room, arms crossed, facing the door with a smug face as if she expected this.

"YOU SENT THEM!" Aria screamed. Her throat felt like it was being clawed at.

"Sent who?" Celaena asked innocently, but a vile smile crossed her face.

"THE DARK FORCES! DON'T PLAY INNOCENT! YOUR MOTHER ATTACKED ME! SHE WAS GOING TO KILL ME!" Aria yelled, spitting blood that had begun to drip down her face again.

"Ew, don't drip blood on the carpet." Celaena flipped her hair and tossed back her head. "My mother, you say? Hmm… Sorry you had the pleasure of meeting her. I didn't send them though. I wouldn't want to endanger my friends and I."

"Aria, let's just go," Avi said from behind her.

Aria shook furiously in the doorway, her heart beating fast and burning with fury. "THEY WOULD NEVER ATTACK YOU!"

She wanted to strangle her, yell at her, and break everything she owned, but Willow must have sensed that because she quickly grabbed Aria and pulled her out the door. The door shut in her face, but before it did, she saw Celaena grinning. Willow grabbed her by the arm and pulled her down the path before Aria could bust back in there and do something irrational.

"You should have let me—" Aria was saying furiously.

"What? Rip her to pieces?" Luke cut her off. "Aria, you're better than that."

She took a deep breath, calm slowly filling her up from hearing him say those words.

They walked down the path to the office, which as Aria had suspected, had been set on fire and was now being drenched in lake water. A small group of Healers were gathered around in the grass, healing a couple of people that had gotten injured in the attack.

"Oh, there she is!" Miss Truffle exclaimed, looking shaky.

Aria approached the group of Healers and they surrounded her in a rush, trying to wipe away every little injury like she was royalty. A Healer bent down to her ankle and swiped her hand over the flesh-eaten burn. She wanted to scream out as the skin regrew, making it feel like it was being burned all over again. Then a Healer slowly waved her hand over Aria's nose. She felt the bone fix back into place and reattach itself, making a painful cracking sound. She cried out, then bit down on her tongue so hard she tasted blood. After they were done, all the major pain was gone and not a single scar was left.

"All fixed," one of the Healers said and they all walked away to help the others that were injured.

She certainly didn't feel '*all fixed.*' Her body still ached and she felt mentally drained, but she had things to do.

"Potion," she whispered as she walked past Luke, Avi, and Willow.

"Okay, let's go," Luke said, and Avi sighed.

They walked through the campgrounds, into the forest, and up to the oak tree. The potion still remained undiscovered, even after everyone had ran into the forest. They lifted the lid to see the murky substance inside, but no magic happened. No image, directions, or location appeared in the potion.

"Shouldn't it be showing us where Celaena's mother is going?" Aria asked, frustrated.

"Yeah...I don't know why it's not working," Avi said. "Maybe we did the potion wrong."

"No. We followed the directions and I double checked that we did, too. It will work eventually," Luke said.

"*Eventually?*" Aria repeated. "I don't have *eventually.*"

"Just take a break, will you?" Avi said. "The camp was just attacked less than an hour ago and you already want to be going after the Dark Forces?"

"Yeah! I want to save my parents!" Aria answered, annoyed. "Wouldn't you?" She immediately regretted saying that when she saw Avi's face. "I didn't mean that—" Her voice broke, hot tears beginning to well in her eyes. "I'm sorry, guys. I—" She wiped the tears and turned away from them, guilt pushing needles through her heart and breaking it to shards.

Every camper whose cabin had been destroyed in the attack was gathered in the mess hall that night. Blankets, pillows, and random bags of belongings were scattered all over the floor. Girls were on one side of the mess hall and the boys were on the other. Aria and Willow laid next to each other that night, surrounded by a bunch of other campers in the pitch-black hall. Their cabin may not have been destroyed, but there was no way they were going to sleep in the same room as Celaena ever again. Aria and her friends were the last to go to sleep in the crowded mess hall that night. Everyone's snores were loud in their ears and they couldn't stop recalling the day in their minds. Aria, when she finally fell asleep, had events of the day replaying in her head.

CHAPTER FIFTEEN

JULY WAS COMING to an end. The hot sun was beating down on the campgrounds, which were in the process of being repaired. Willow and Aria were still sleeping in the mess hall two weeks after the attack and camp was no longer running as it usually was. Many parents and guardians had been allowed to pick their children up from camp after being notified of the attack. This made heartache ball up inside Aria, squeezing her heart so she felt like she couldn't breathe; the Dark Forces were after her and had *her* parents. She was getting more and more frustrated with the Tracking Potion for not doing its job. What if the Dark Forces came back for her like Kora had said they would? She couldn't let the camp go into more ruin. She couldn't let innocent people get hurt just because of her. If the Tracking Potion would just work and show her where Kora had gone, she might be able to find her parents. She was convinced that wherever Kora had gone, her parents would be. All she needed was for the potion to work, then she could sneak away from the camp without her friends following her.

She lay staring at the high, beamed ceiling of the dimly lit mess hall. The rising sun leaking through the yellow curtains was the only light in the enormous room. A smell of different breakfast foods slipped its way out of the kitchen, making her stomach roar. All around her were the loud snores and breathing of the campers squished into the hall. Willow lay awake as well, but she remained still and silent like a corpse. Her unbelievable stillness was creepy, but Aria could see the rise and fall of her chest to know she was breathing.

A million thoughts ran through Aria's head. She didn't have much hope left inside her. She was sinking in the swamp of despair and was slowly being dragged further down. She thought of the Tracking Potion, murky gray, and not a single image to show where Kora had gone.

It's not going to work! I'll never get my parents back! I'm weak and useless.

A single tear shed from her eye and she wiped it away. Willow suddenly turned her face to look at Aria's, reaching out to touch her hand. Aria knew what she was doing but didn't care. It was invading personal privacy, but out of all the people she knew, Willow was the most understanding when it came to feelings. Aria felt comforted knowing that she didn't have to put her emotions into words for Willow. She would just know.

Willow moved her hand and looked away to process Aria's thoughts just as Kora's words echoed throughout her head, *'Silly little girl!'*

Was she just some silly little girl? Aria felt like she was. She thought maybe she was foolish for ever thinking she could be the one to save her parents, but as if that would stop her.

I will try, and I might fail, but at least I tried. And if I can, I'll try again.

The hall was full of waking people now, many rubbing their eyes, yawning, and blinking at the sudden light. A couple chefs brought plates of food out of the kitchen to put them on a metal table at the other end of the hall. One of the cooks pulled the curtains open and light flooded the room, forcing campers to cover their eyes. Campers started getting up in a rush to grab the food once their eyes adjusted. Willow and Aria spotted Luke and Avi getting up on the other side of the hall to get the steaming food. The smell of fresh bread, bacon, and spices wafted through the air. Stepping around all the pillows and blankets, they walked over to get food as well.

Willow and Aria sat back down on their blankets with their eggs and bacon. It was not the cleanest or even easiest way to eat a plate of food, but all the tables had been removed to make room for people to sleep.

"Tree?" Willow asked, though she already knew Aria wanted to go there.

"Yeah," Aria replied. "Maybe we'll finally see something."

"Yeah, hopefully."

Aria sensed the jitters Willow had. The look in Luke, Avi, and Willow's eyes every time they met Aria's flickered with fear, and Aria felt it, too. She hated the thought of having to fight the Dark Forces to save her parents, but she would do it anyway. She had to. In her opinion, they were lucky, though; they would never have to fight the Dark Forces because they wouldn't be going with her. They just didn't know that yet.

Aria ate hastily, then hurried out of the mess hall with Willow, knowing Luke and Avi would follow after them when they finished eating.

And they were right because they caught up to them not far down the dirt path, Avi calling, "Wait up!"

Willow and Aria stopped in their tracks to turn back around.

"You guys heading to the tree?" Luke halted in front of them.

"Yeah," Willow answered.

"Okay…" His eyes locked on something behind Aria.

"What?" Aria turned around to see Celaena walking towards them.

Celaena flipped her long black hair behind her back, a smirk spreading across her smug face, and stopped a few feet away.

"Hello, duds," she said. "Off to go find somewhere quiet to talk? Hmm…I hope I'm interrupting something."

Celaena went around them, smiling a satisfied smile, and they watched as she disappeared behind a building.

"I absolutely despise her!" Aria's fists clenched. "I don't understand how she is still here at this camp. We told Miss Truffle her mother was here with the Dark Forces and had attacked me. Why haven't they kicked her out yet?"

"They probably didn't believe us. After all, we're just children to them. Nobody believes that Kora Blanc is still a part of the Dark Forces," Avi said, annoyed.

"Yeah, and they're all idiots!"

A boy a year younger than them, who was reading on a bench on the side of the path, looked at Aria like she was crazy, raising his eyebrows.

"Oh, what book is that?" Willow's attention was drawn to the book in the boy's hand.

Aria shook her head, giving a sigh.

"Let's just go before she comes back to taunt us some more," Luke suggested.

"Right," Willow mumbled.

They hurried down the trail and disappeared behind cabin

number eighteen, where Twilight jumped out from a bush to follow after them.

Still, there was not a single image floating around in the potion. Aria sat, gazing into it so intently she might have strained her eyes. Luke was next to her, his hand on the forest floor nearly brushing hers. The tapping of a woodpecker echoed through the forest, Willow watching it hit the tree with its little black beak while she rubbed Twilight's head. A few feet away, Avi was apparently trying to make a spear out of a stick.

"Why are you doing that?" Luke asked him.

"If we are going to go after the Dark Forces, aren't we going to need weapons?"

Luke shook his head and stared back into the potion. Still nothing. Aria sighed, exasperated, and got off the forest floor. She stretched her legs, looking into the treetops where a light breeze rustled the leaves. She turned back at the group, as if expecting to see something new.

"We must have made the potion wrong," she said for what had to be the millionth time. "That or it doesn't work how we thought it did."

"It must just take time. Maybe it will show us what we want when she arrives where she's going," Luke said.

"Luke, it's been *two weeks*," she reminded him.

"Yeah, I know, but we didn't make the potion wrong. I have checked it and rechecked it. We did everything right," he said.

She slumped back down on the forest floor next to Luke to stare at the potion again, her hands now clenched in her lap. He gave a sigh, which sounded like it was caused by disappointment, as he watched Avi fail to make a spear. Scratching the back of his neck, he got up to help Avi. The woodpecker flew from the pine tree and off into the sky, so Willow's gaze changed to her cat. Aria continued to stare at the potion in the bucket for another few minutes. The potion abruptly stirred as if a gust of wind had blown by, but the air was completely still now. It swirled, the murky water fading into a blue, then a bright gold, and a foggy mist began to settle around the edges of the bucket.

"Guys!" Aria exclaimed.

"What?" Luke spun around.

"Something's happening!"

They crowded around the substance, peering into the metal bucket. The potion whirled like someone was stirring it, then the color changed to an image. The Tracking Potion was working.

Kora opened her eyes. There was a disgusting taste left in her mouth, but she could not recall eating anything in the last several hours. It tasted like a mix of Siren flesh and Troll, but there was definitely the taste of Stranger's Vine in there. *The brat poisoned me*, was the first thought she could form, but she was not the worried in the least. Disoriented for a moment, she sat up. She expected to see just the Chesler girl lying immobile, but to her surprise, there were three young teenagers. They were guarding the girl, who had apparently been pulled behind a cabin with her. Unmistakable fear flickered in all of their eyes; it was easy to read someone's fear after all the years she had spent working for the Dark Forces.

"What happened?" she asked herself.

She tried to recall what happened: she'd hit the Chesler girl with an Immobile Enchantment and then some brat knocked her unconscious. Her eyes landed on the dark-haired, freckled boy. There was definitely dismay written all over his face, but also a flicker of something else. That something else seemed to be a great amount of care for someone. She recognized him… but from where? Oh yes, he was the one that knocked her out. He would pay for that.

"Oh yes." she said. "You think you can protect her? You *children* don't stand a chance against me! Move aside or face the same fate as her!"

The children didn't move. Brave, but naive children, they were.

A hissing noise rose to Kora's ears, like the sound of a cat, and her stomach jumped. She looked down to see a black cat, blacker than the night sky. It wore a gorgeous collar with a hanging white crystal that glowed faintly. She understood what the cat was saying as it hissed. It wanted her to leave, to go away, to leave the girl and her friends alone. It seemed so protective over the four of them and wouldn't hesitate to attack her. Kora heard the cat's ferocious thoughts float through her mind, the rare gift of Omni-communication flowing through her veins.

"Fine…but mark my words, children, we'll be back."

She made an *X* with her arms on her chest and teleported from the campgrounds to the Master's house in the Vezchia Realm.

It was a dark, eerie, haunted-looking mansion that had belonged to the Master's father, Alaric Malamone. There was a long brick path leading up to the mansion. The bricks that made up the path were chipped, and the paint had been worn away over the centuries. Up the right of the path were wagons, some of them filled with animal traps, and others had cages on wheels that attached to the wagons. These enclosures were meant to escort prisoners from different Dark Forces' hideouts, but the only prisoners the Master had at his home right now were the Chesler girl's parents.

Kora walked down the path, through the broken metal

gate. She could only teleport so close to the mansion, for Master had put a charm around the property to ensure that people could not teleport in and out so close. Master had his reasons for that.

A thick and nearly impenetrable gloom had settled around the countryside of Tungsinn, where the Master's home stood, centuries ago. The fog clouded around everything, including the long stable building in the distance, which housed Master's tall, beastly horses.

At the end of the path sat the old, brick, contemptible mansion. The windows were dark and dirty, making it hard to see through them even if you could see them through the gloom. The marble steps leading up to the wide, elegant, wooden doors with brass handles were cracked. The mansion itself was a very creepy sight that would send anyone running in the opposite direction, but to Kora, it was homey.

She walked past the once-working fountain that stood in the middle of the rounded courtyard. It was cracked, crumbling, and filled with rats, a dark green liquid, and mold. She walked up the marble steps and opened the wooden doors, stepping into the dark, silent mansion. Master Malus was not home, which she knew, but she continued on anyway.

The entrance hall was massive and dark, with many doors leading into different rooms. There was a door to her left and to her right. She walked past the two elegant, curved staircases that led to the second floor, then turned down the hall, where a light spilled from an open room. As she strutted toward the light, shouting and loud talking met her ears. She entered the lounge casually and plopped down in a chair to relax, putting her legs over the arm of it. The room was filled with the ten people who had come along with her to get the Chesler girl. They all had their hoods removed now, some of them relaxing on vintage sofas and chairs. Most of them looked infuriated as they stood up and paced. Silence fell when eyes landed on Kora.

"What took you so long?" a man with spiky blond hair asked, raising his eyebrows.

Kora knew this man was Chad, an annoying thinks-he's-so-amazing sort of guy. She despised him, to be honest, and she knew he didn't like her either. She also knew that the only reason he never voiced his opinions of her was because he was frightened of her. Many people were and Kora took pleasure in it.

"Oh, just that I almost had the girl. If it had not been for her stupid friends, I could have easily captured her myself. Every time we almost have her, the other children get in our way," Kora answered, rage filling her voice.

"I underestimated her once and I won't do it again," a woman with long, brown, wavy hair stated. This woman was Ebony, a spectacular Nature-manipulator. "She's smart."

Ebony was what you might call friends with Kora, but despite that, Kora screamed, "SMART? DO YOU THINK IT IS SMART TO NOT GIVE MALUS WHAT HE WANTS? DO NOT COMPLIMENT THAT CHESLER GIRL!"

"Calm down!" Chad yelled.

"I wasn't complimenting her! I'm saying we need to be smarter next time. We need to be smarter than a few teenagers!"

"Well, what do you suggest we do then, *Ebony*?" Kora asked sarcastically.

Before Ebony could answer, Chad suggested, "We get rid of the girl's friends. Destroy them if we have to."

"We don't need to do that! Malus told me and my ex—" Kora was about to explain.

"Seth?" Chad asked as if he was seriously that clueless.

"Who else do you think?" Kora asked, agitated. "Moron.

Anyway, Malus told me and Seth a second plan if the first was to fall into chaos. The second plan is already underway."

A sly smile crossed her face. It looked just like her daughter's, who she believed was too soft and too weak.

—✳—☾—✳—

They lifted their heads from staring into the bucket of potion, having seen Kora walking up a long, brick path to a rich, eighteenth-century mansion.

"Where do you think that is?" Aria glanced at each of them.

"I don't know," they answered in unison.

"But I bet it's in the Vezchia Realm," Luke said.

"I need to get ready so I can go." Aria's feet began to walk back out of the forest.

"What? Now?" Avi asked.

Luke caught her by the wrist to stop her.

"Yeah." She spun around and stared into his deep blue ocean eyes.

He let go of her awkwardly. "We're coming with you."

"No, you can't!" She argued. "If you come with me, you will get hurt or killed! I don't want that to happen to any of you!"

"And we don't want that to happen to you!" Luke grabbed her by the shoulders lightly and unexpectedly, looking at her with a pleading face.

She didn't understand what he was doing, so she raised one eyebrow slowly in question. He immediately let go and shoved his hands in his pockets.

"We have a better chance together than you by yourself," Avi stated.

"No, no, no," she kept repeating.

"We want to help you get your parents back. They're the leaders of the Forces of Light, *our* leaders," Luke said.

"We are coming with you, Aria, but we cannot go *now*," Willow said. "We need to gather things, then go, but not tonight. How about in the morning after a good night's rest?"

Aria sighed, rubbing her eyes. They were right. She needed them to help her because there was no way she could save her parents on her own. She also had to pack for the journey. Her heart screamed at her for even being about to agree.

"Fine," she agreed through clenched teeth, angry with herself. "We leave at dawn."

Luke, Avi, and Willow gave a sigh.

"What do we need?" Aria asked.

"You don't know what we need?" Avi raised his eyebrows, and the three of them looked at her blankly.

"No."

"We need food, water, clothes, and—and…" Luke said, trying to think of more things.

"And weapons!" Avi piped in.

"And weapons, I guess," Luke repeated.

"I'll leave Twilight here. He'll be safer at camp, and I know he'll be fine," Willow told them.

"Okay, well, let's go gather that stuff then," Aria said, and they backtracked out of the forest.

Aria and Willow snuck into their cabin and luckily found it was empty of people. They grabbed their school bags, dumping them into an empty cubbyhole. Each of them stuffed their bags with a couple of outfits, a light blanket, a small pillow, and a couple of essentials like a toothbrush and hairbrush. Aria made sure to grab her sage green sweatshirt, too. When they were finished, they hustled out of the cabin and dropped their bags off at the oak tree, their stomachs growling.

In the mess hall, campers were gathering around where their beds had been laid out, the noise reverberating through the hall. Luke and Avi came to sit down on the floor with Aria and Willow to stuff their faces.

"We got our bags. They're behind the mess hall. Avi and I are going to break into the kitchen to steal some food tonight," Luke whispered.

"Okay, good idea," Aria said and took another big bite of her sandwich.

A few hours later, the sun had fallen below the horizon, and now outside was darkness. Aria tried to sleep, but she couldn't. She sensed Willow's open eyes staring straight up through the blackness, too, as she thought about different, terrifying things that might happen the next day. Her heart was beating so fast and so loud in her ears that she swore the others could hear it thumping. She clutched her sunflower necklace, tracing the grooves of the petals with her fingers. Tomorrow was the day she would leave the safety of the camp and teleport to the Vezchia Realm. The Vezchia Realm, the most dangerous of them all, and the one that she didn't know much about. She would likely have to fight, which she had almost zero experience at.

Eventually, drowsiness took over and she fell asleep late into the night with nightmares filling her head.

The next morning, Aria carefully crawled out of bed at the crack of dawn and shook Willow awake. With a motion for Willow to follow her, they tiptoed around the sleeping, snoring campers to Luke and Avi. They both were clearly having nightmares of the day that lay ahead of them because they gasped, their eyes wide, when Aria and Willow woke them up. Silently, they stepped out of the hall into the moist air and brightening light. Luke and Avi stopped to grab their bags from behind the mess hall first before they continued to the oak tree.

No one spoke at first, staring at each other. Aria could see the fear flickering in their eyes again.

"You guys don't have to do this. Once we get there, there is no turning back," she told them. She still hoped she could convince them to stay out of harm's way.

"I'm not letting you do this alone." Luke crossed his arms.

"Neither will I," Willow said.

"I won't…either." Avi leaned up against the oak.

"So, how do we get there?" Aria took in a big inhale of the sweet pine air. She still knew nothing of how the Vezchia Realm worked and barely anything about teleportation.

"We have to teleport somewhere we know well enough to imagine ourselves there," Luke said. "We could easily teleport to that house, but we've never been there before, so we could end up getting injured in the process. We have to be able to know what the place feels like or it could be even more dangerous than it already is."

"Where do we go then?" Aria asked.

"Well…my parents used to always take my brother and I to Diamond Falls in the summer to swim. I could teleport you guys with me. Diamond Falls is in the Vezchia Realm, and who knows, maybe it's even close to that house," Luke replied. "If not…well, it will be tricky, but hopefully it will work."

"Hopefully?" the rest of them asked in unison.

"Yeah…" Luke scratched the back of his head, probably thinking they should have worked out the *getting there* part better.

"I read in a book that teleporting in large groups is very—" Willow tried to explain, worry seeping into her voice.

"Whatever, let's just do it." Aria was willing to do whatever it takes to get her parents back.

"Okay, everyone grab hands, close your eyes, and clear your mind," Luke instructed.

They put their bags on their backs and joined hands. Avi's face turned a tinge of red when Willow rushed to grasp his hand. Aria closed her eyes, remembering how last time she didn't. The air around her started to change, stirring up a staticky energy that made the hairs on her head stand up. Warm tingles ran up and down her arms. She tried to clear her mind, but it wasn't working. At first, she thought of Luke's hand in hers, how soft it was.

No! That's creepy! Clear your mind! she yelled to herself in her head.

Then, she couldn't stop thinking about the dangers that lay ahead and the now-known danger of just teleporting. She imagined herself being ripped apart between the different realms.

No, clear your mind!

A few moments passed, Aria growing anxious the longer it took to teleport their whole group. Suddenly, cool air wrapped around her, and her stomach jolted at the feeling of being sent high into the air as they teleported to the Vezchia Realm.

Chapter Sixteen

SUDDENLY, ARIA'S FEET landed in icy water, and her eyes flew open in surprise. She had expected to appear on solid ground, but instead, she was in waist-deep water. It prickled at her skin, raising goosebumps on her arms and legs. Behind her, she heard the loud rushing of water, like that of huge waterfalls crashing into the water below it. The water was so crystal-like and clear. It was a light teal and more beautiful than anything Aria had ever seen. It reminded her of all the gorgeous ocean beaches she had seen in pictures and in movies.

The ocean? she asked herself. She took a look around, taking in the gorgeous view. It wasn't the ocean. Instead, it was a lake with a river running through the woods. All around them was the muddy shore with thick trees—pines, elms, oaks, and birches—and underbrush. Aria let go of Luke's hand and began wading to shore, glancing behind her at the huge, gorgeous, teal waterfalls cascading down a cliff to join the lake. On top of the cliff was more thick forest with a flock of strange birds chilling on a ridge of it.

Once Aria got to shore, she plopped down on the ground to try and assess the situation. She stared at the falls that protruded from the rocky wall and flowed neatly into the water below. It was such a stunning sight that made her wish she could just relax and watch the waterfalls for hours. The river got deeper and darker the further it flowed to the right. Luke leaned up against the tree right behind her as something strange caught her eye. Down the river, about thirty feet away, sat five giant, gnome-looking creatures. They looked like twenty-foot garden gnomes with tall, multicolored, pointed hats. Their mismatched clothes were covered in patches, rips, and dirt. Many of the creatures had long, tangled, bushy, orange hair, beards, and mustaches. Long black hairs stuck out of their large, pointy noses. They slept in the deeper part of the river, blocking its flow and soaking in the morning light.

"W-what?" Aria tried to ask.

"Trolls," Luke answered before she could get the full question out.

"It's best if we don't wake them up. They're generally kind creatures, but also unpredictable," Willow said. "So, I don't think we should go near them and we should be quiet." She stared off at the splattering waterfalls with a smile. "This is such a gorgeous place."

"Yeah," Luke said. "I always loved this place."

"So, this is Diamond Falls?" Aria asked, raising her eyebrows.

"Yeah," Luke answered.

"You said your parents always took you and your brother here, right?" Aria stood up and put her hands on her hips, staring around at the scenery.

"Yeah…" Luke didn't seem to see what she was getting at.

"Then why is it in the middle of a forest?" Aria asked loudly in a high-pitched voice. She didn't mean for it to come out so rude, so she was a little taken aback by her own tone. "Sorry," she mumbled.

"Well, what were you expecting?" He gestured around at the beautiful sight.

"I don't know. Maybe a civilization?" Aria said. "Something like Niagara Falls, perhaps."

"What's that?" Avi asked.

"You don't know what Niagra Falls is?"

"No, I've sort of lived my whole life surrounded by magic and I've never learned about different places in the Mundane Realm so…"

Willow shook her head at him. "Avi, we learned about it years ago in school. Remember?"

"No, I probably wasn't paying attention."

"Anyway, it's just I thought Diamond Falls would be somewhere with…maps…people…places." Aria rubbed her eyes, a little annoyed. How were they supposed to find the place Kora had gone *now*? She wanted to kick a rock in frustration. *This is all the stupid Dark Forces' fault!*

"Look, Aria, this is the only place we could go. Everybody starts somewhere, but no one can start nowhere," Willow said.

"Fine." Aria's gaze changed to the ground and she clutched her sunflower necklace. "Then we should get going."

"Okay," they all agreed.

They started into the forest, not knowing where they would go for shelter, let alone where the creepy house Kora had gone to would be. They walked on for hours, trying to stop as little as possible. The air got more humid as the day went on, making sweat thicken on their foreheads. Aria's stomach growled, but she wouldn't let them stop to eat. She was determined to keep going, even though the hunger was growing unbearable. The smell of pine trees and grass was strong in the air. Birds chirped overhead and little creatures ran around on the forest floor, most of them unrecognizable beings.

After many, many hours of complaints from Avi, Aria let them stop.

She plopped down on a log and sighed. "I am starving. Who has the bag of food?"

Something suddenly seemed to occur to Luke and Avi as they leaned against the same tree. They immediately looked at each other, Avi biting his bottom lip and Luke's eyes wide.

"What?" Aria's brows furrowed with concern.

"We—we forgot the bag of food," Avi said softly, looking ashamed, but Aria heard every word he said.

"YOU WHAT?" She jumped to her feet.

"Keep it down!" Luke told her off, but couldn't meet her eyes.

"You forgot the bag of food? How on earth could you forget something so important?" Her face grew hot and red like molten iron.

Both Aria and Willow looked at Luke and Avi with flaring nostrils and bitter eyes, their stomachs aching. She felt an uneasiness in the pit of her stomach, but not just from hunger, from yelling at them.

"We were waiting in our beds last night for the kitchen to clear out so we could sneak in…but we…uh…fell asleep." Avi's tone grew quiet.

"I honestly cannot believe you two!" Aria exclaimed. "What are we going to eat then? Because I'm not teleporting back to camp after we got this far. We're lucky we were even able to sneak out with Celaena watching us all the time and Mrs. Mckinney so concerned about our safety."

"We could hunt," Luke suggested.

"I don't hunt." She looked down at her hands.

"What do you mean?"

"I don't kill things…I—I just can't bring myself to *kill* something."

"Fine, then we will because we are men." Luke's voice cracked, dipping into a deeper tone, and he placed his hands on his hips.

Despite Aria being furious with the two of them for failing to get the bag of food, she started laughing at Luke. She burst out in uncontrollable laughs with Willow and they had to sit down on the log, clutching their stomachs.

"What?" Luke asked, looking at them.

Once the giggling had subsided, Aria said, "Let's just keep moving. We can find food closer to dinner time, but keep your eyes peeled in case you see some as we move."

They all agreed, though rather reluctantly since they were already so hungry, and they continued deeper into the forest, still without a clue as to where they were going.

They passed a red kitsune, a nine-tailed fox, with three kitsune cubs following behind. The cubs were rolling around in the bushes but quickly hid behind a bush when they heard Aria and her friends approaching from behind them. The mother kitsune hid behind the bush, too, but didn't fit, so she gave away her cubs. Aria let out a small laugh and stared at the fascinating creatures for a moment before continuing on. Of course, Aria didn't know what the creatures were, but she recognized them from old folklore she had seen somewhere.

The late evening neared and Aria couldn't take the hunger any longer. If she kept putting off eating, she would vomit up the nothingness in her stomach. She'd never known the feeling of extreme hunger or thirst before.

"We need to find water." She looked around at their surroundings.

All she could see were trees, undergrowth, and strange birds flying around in the branches.

"We'll split up and look for water and food. Avi and I will find food and you two can find water," Luke said, and then he and Avi disappeared through the trees.

"Let's hope they know what they're doing." Willow sighed, then turned away to look for water.

Aria and Willow stayed within eyesight of each other, not wanting to get lost. Aria got distracted for a moment, watching a red bird high up in a tree. The bird flew onto a branch, then suddenly caught fire, turning into ash. With shock in her eyes, she hurried back to Willow. They plopped back down on the hard, mossy log, having found no water, just as Luke and Avi came back.

Willow and Aria expected to see food in their hands, maybe even something juicy to quench their thirst, when Luke and Avi came back through the trees, but they had nothing.

"Where is the food?" Willow asked, sounding like she was interrogating them.

"We…um…don't know how to hunt." Luke scratched the back of his neck.

"Are you kidding me? You said you were men, so you knew how to hunt!" Aria half-shouted. Then, softer, more so to herself, she added with her eyes wide, "We're gonna die out here."

"Don't worry, we will find something for us to eat," Avi said quickly. "Did you find water?"

"No, none anywhere," Aria answered hopelessly. She put her head in her hands, trying to think of what to do.

Luke and Avi headed back through the trees, disappearing

from sight as they exchanged whispers. The only thing Aria could catch of their quiet talk was the word *'impress.'*

Many minutes later, Aria heard a rustle in a bush and she quickly stood up, afraid an animal was going to jump out. Luke and Avi came through the bush with smiles on their faces, bearing berries in their hands.

"Food!" Aria and Willow exclaimed in unison.

They instantly ran to Luke and Avi and grabbed berries from their hands, the black juices covering their hands. The four of them stuffed their faces with the berries as they sat on the mossy ground, not bothering to check what kind they were. As soon as they bit into them, the disgusting, bitter, tangy, sickening taste filled their mouths. They made faces of disgust but couldn't stop eating; they were so hungry. Even after they had finished their handfuls, their stomachs seemed to growl even more than before.

"Is there more?" Willow asked but looked like she hated the thought of eating anymore.

"No, that was all that was on the berry bush." Luke suddenly clutched his stomach. "I think I'm going to be sick."

He leaned over and vomited all over the forest floor. Avi, Willow, and Aria scooted away from him, but the smell of the wretched stuff lingered. Aria suddenly felt nauseous, like she was going to puke up everything she had just eaten. Willow leaned over and was sick, too, barfing up the berries. Just as Aria got to her knees to choke up everything she had eaten, Avi began puking, too.

When they could finally stop throwing up, Aria shouted, "Those berries were toxic!"

"Sorry…we—" Avi said shamefully.

"Willow and I will do the foraging now!" Aria stood up and stalked off, hungrier than she had been before.

Likely, they would starve and die, or they would die of dehydration. Aria knew she shouldn't be angry at any of them. After all, they were the ones helping *her*. Fury and guilt twisted in her chest like several daggers—daggers that were meant for the Dark Forces, not her friends—but, instead, she was taking that anger out on them. She knew how wrong all of it was, and she wanted to kick herself because of it.

After sulking behind a tree for a while, the sky now painted with stars, she walked back to her friends. Willow, Luke, and Avi sat far away from the vomit-covered area, staring at her.

"I'm sorry I yelled and that I keep getting mad at all of you," she apologized. "I'm not really mad at any of you…I'm just scared and worried…I know you guys are trying to help me, so please forgive me."

She sat down on the darkened, mossy, forest floor next to Willow.

"Of course, we forgive you," Willow said. "We understand."

Having no need to explain her feelings to Willow, Aria knew she would understand more than Luke or Avi.

They laid down on the soft, dirt ground with light blankets thrown over them and small pillows beneath their heads. Luke and Avi were several feet away from Willow and Aria, though Aria could sense someone staring at her from where they were at. She slipped on her sage green jacket, but the chill still managed to get to her skin. She wished she had Luke's hoodie as well, but it was back at camp, covered in blood. The cool night air and wind didn't rest, and neither did the nocturnal animals of the forest. She thought of wolves, which led to the thought of werewolves. She knew werewolves existed and how they were created from a book she'd read at school, but knew they didn't roam the woods like in all the folklore she'd read. Werewolves were bitten humans, infested with a poison that changed them into hungry monsters, just like vampires. She'd read that werewolves often lurked in dark alleyways and places with people for them to prey on, not forests. Staring at the treetops, she hoped they were safe, as she let the nightmares creep into her head.

A bird cawed overhead in the trees. Aria opened her eyes, the morning light blinding her. She blinked, shielding her eyes, and sat up. Dirt was all over her jacket, pants, and tangled up in her hair with leaves and pine needles. Her pillow somehow managed to move several feet away from where she had been sleeping. Luke was a few feet away, staring up at the treetops as the birds sang their early morning song. He looked over at Aria, their eyes meeting, as Willow woke from the sound of the birds, too. Avi was the only one still laying on the ground, sleeping like a rock.

"Avi, wake up!" Aria shouted, clapping her hands together. She opened her backpack that sat next to her and took out a hairbrush to brush out the leaves and clumps of dirt.

Avi stirred a little in his sleep but didn't wake. Luke got up and walked over to him, giving him a little shake and he sat upright, panting.

"Wha—" Avi said, looking around as if something had attacked him. "Oh, hey guys."

"I'll go find food…hopefully," Aria told them as she rubbed her painfully dry throat. She felt lightheaded from not having anything to drink in the last twenty-four hours.

Without another word, she left them, passing through the trees to find food or water. She passed a berry bush, but it was empty of fruit. No doubt, it was the same berries they'd eaten last night.

She walked on for about half an hour, halting many times to stare at the creatures of the forest. Another red bird flew high up in the trees, so she paused for a moment to watch. It caught fire as it flew, but it didn't turn to ashes like the other had. She continued on, stopping again when she saw what looked like a horse off in the distance. Squinting, she tried to determine what the white, four-legged creature was, and then it disappeared. She recalled it having a shimmery tail, and what looked like a mane. As she carried on through the forest, she halted again a few minutes later to stare at two odd fish circling each other in a teal, crystal-like, stream, which was probably coming from Diamond Falls. The fish looked like koi fish, one being black, and one being white, but they both had markings on their scales that looked a lot like old runes. She watched as they leapt out of the water and up the stream that ran over rocks.

Wait, a stream! she suddenly realized.

Hurrying to her knees, she stuck her hands in the warm water and gulped down as much as possible. The water trickled through the cracks between her fingers as she lifted it to her face. Then she drank again, and again, the water relieving the dryness of her throat. She stood up from the water as it dripped down her jaw, staring around for food. There were the two fish, but she didn't even know if they were edible and she couldn't bring herself to kill them. She needed to tell her friends about the water she had found. But first, food. All she could see around were leaf-covered plants, trees, spiky plants, and some mushrooms. Seeing the odd spiky plants, she hoped she wouldn't run into Stranger's Vine. Willow would know if any of the plants were edible, right? After all, she was always reading informational books.

Aria walked back to her friends, taking note in her mind of where the stream was so she could find it again.

"I found water!" she exclaimed to them as she came through the trees.

"Really? Where?" Willow jumped to her feet and pulled her bag onto her shoulders.

Luke and Avi rose quickly, slipping their packed bags onto their backs, and Aria led them to the stream.

"Shouldn't we clean it?" Avi asked as they approached the rushing water. "So we don't get a disease?"

"Yes, don't drink the water yet. I have a water bottle we can put some in," Willow said. She took out a metal water bottle from her backpack and unscrewed the top off. "I'll purify it."

"What about us?" Avi motioned to Luke, Aria, and himself. "We don't have one."

"We'll have to share," Willow answered, then added to the looks on their faces, "Unless you want to dehydrate to death in a couple of days."

"That's disgusting!" Avi's face blushed a smidgen.

Luke looked at Aria in an odd way, their eyes locking, but she hastily turned away. Willow filled up the bottle of water as Aria looked around for the two fish that had been there, which were now long gone over the rocks. Willow put her hand over the top of the water bottle and pulled it back, dirt and bacteria rising into the air. Aria cringed at the fact that she'd drank the water before all of that was removed, but she'd been so thirsty. Willow let the bacteria fall back into the stream and they passed the water bottle around, making sure it didn't touch their lips.

"How did you learn how to do that?" Avi asked Willow before taking a sip.

"My mother taught me survival skills. Now, this water should only be drank when absolutely needed so we can spare it as long as possible." Then Willow spotted the mushrooms at the bottom of a moss-covered tree. "Pleurotus ostreatus!" She rushed to the mushrooms and squatted next to them.

"Um, what?" Avi asked, raising one eyebrow.

"They're oyster mushrooms! Pleurotus ostreatus is their scientific name."

"And?" Avi asked. "I'm not a mushroomologist or something, so I don't understand what you're talking about."

"They're edible!" Willow clarified, plucking a bunch from the bottom of the tree.

"How do you know?"

"I read it in a book," she answered simply, then shoved the mushrooms into her mouth before any of them could stop her. She swallowed, making a very disgusted face. "They taste absolutely dreadful."

"I am *not* eating that." Avi crossed his arms.

"Suit yourself, but it's the only food we have at the moment, and in case you don't remember, that is partly your fault." She began plucking more mushrooms from the oak tree and the forest floor, then shoved them into her bag.

Luke and Aria grabbed a few mushrooms from the base of another tree and reluctantly ate them, almost choking on the dry, dirt taste of them. The mushrooms were covered in dirt and tasted bitter, yet tangy. Avi finally caved, hating the feeling of hunger, and ate several as well, though he looked as if he would barf it all right back up.

They began their trek through the woods again, hoping they would find a village or town of some kind, so they could seek guidance to the creepy mansion Kora had visited.

It turned into almost a week of the same events over and over again. Aria, Luke, Avi, and Willow were growing extremely tired, horribly unkempt, and their bodies ached from lying on the ground each night. Aria could barely believe almost a week ago she had been at camp where there was food, warm beds, showers, and safety.

She saw many strange creatures each day they walked and each night she lay awake—she couldn't stop tossing and turning. The red birds that caught fire seemed to really like the woods and she couldn't stop wondering what they were. Each day, they ate the mushrooms Willow had gathered and then they foraged for some more. They took tiny sips of the water, making sure to not let the bottle touch their mouths. They drank from puddles of water after Willow purified them, which was the result of one rainy day when they had to take shelter in a short pine tree. They had still gotten drenched with the freezing water, but less so under the dense protection of the pine tree's branches.

Aria was left asking herself if they were even doing the right thing and if they were even going in the right direction. Every day she felt she was going to be sick, mostly due to the growing pit in her stomach…and possibly from a diet of only mushrooms and water.

It was the morning of the sixth day in the forest. There was a different smell in the air like some type of meat was roasting in an oven. Of course, there was also still the smell of pine needles and dirt, but Aria could smell a barbecue as they were packing up their things to start their trek again. The air was surprisingly cooler at that moment with the wind blowing, so Aria put on her sweatshirt.

"We're getting low on water," Willow said.

They hadn't drank much of the water Willow had taken

from the stream, so how it was nearly gone, Aria could not guess.

"How? We only drank it a few times, and even then it was just a few sips!" Aria wondered.

"Um…I drank it a few times." Avi twiddled his thumbs.

"You what?" Aria asked, her eyebrows shooting up. "We agreed that the water was for emergencies only and you drank it anyway?"

"I was thirsty," Avi replied quietly.

"I cannot believe you, Avi." She shook her head and slid her bag onto her back.

"We'll just have to find more water," Luke said beside her.

"Then let's get going," Aria said, and she started off further into the forest.

Several hours passed as they walked in silence, then suddenly, Aria heard something rustle. She looked behind her at her friends, but all of them had stopped at the noise, too. It could have been one of the many harmless creatures of the forest. The woods had a great many of those and nothing had been dangerous…*yet*. Then there was an earthshaking thud. Aria's heart rate quickened, her pulse leaping into her throat, and she took in the panicked looks on her friends' faces. A tree moved, but it wasn't actually a tree…or was it?

Many of the trees moved all at once with loud creeks, revealing that some of their branches were really arms and legs. Aria didn't know if they were really to be considered arms and legs, but that was the closest thing she could think of when she saw them. Her eyes went wide with shock and horror, and she took a step backward. These creatures looked like smaller trees, towering over Aria and her friends at a height of thirty to fifty feet. Their skin was made of bark with leaves penetrating their skin. Their faces looked to have been carved by skilled woodcarvers, giving them each a mouth, two black eyes, and ears. From their heads grew branches this way and that, and from those branches grew delicate dark green leaves. They looked like giants made of bark, easily able to blend in with their surroundings. If you looked closely enough, you could tell that each creature had its own distinct features, but Aria wasn't paying attention to that.

Willow gasped. "Timber Giants." She sounded breathless, staring upwards.

"Maybe they can help us," Avi said.

Aria looked at him like he was insane. "What? Are you crazy?"

"Aria, Timber Giants are kind creatures," Willow told her.

The Timber Giants together began to grunt and speak their language in deep voices.

"What are they saying?" Aria asked.

"I have no idea." Willow took a cautious step backwards.

One of the giants stomped its big, toeless feet, which made the ground shake. The Timber Giants began to shout things, which were barely understandable with how their voices echoed and how incoherent the words were. One thing Aria could catch of their loud grunts, though, was "Procotoniski bangiliski!"

"Did they say bang?" Avi asked, sounding afraid.

"I don't want to wait and find out," Willow said with worry edging into her voice.

A Timber Giant swatted its long arm down at Aria, but she jumped out of the way. All of them took off running through the forest as fast as they could, their legs aching as they raced across sticks and stones. The Timber Giants followed after them, catching up easily with their long strides. The smell of tasty meat cooking started to thicken in the air, growing closer. Aria looked backward and tripped, falling sideways into a tree. The rough bark scraped across her skin as she slipped down, hitting the roots twisted over the ground. The giants were so close now, while Willow and Avi were far ahead of her. A bark-covered hand reached down to pick her up, but Luke pulled her out of the way and helped her back to her feet.

"You—you saved—" Aria stuttered, her eyes meeting his.

"Yeah…" Luke trailed off, awkwardly scratching the back of his neck.

"GUYS, LET'S GO!" Avi called from ahead of them.

Aria and Luke raced towards Avi and Willow again just as the Timber Giants shook the forest floor with their steps.

"Why are they attacking us?" Aria panted when they caught up with Willow and Avi.

"They can't understand us. I think that they think we're a threat." Willow suddenly turned around an old elm tree to confuse the giants and Luke, Avi, and Aria followed.

One of the giants stretched out a hand, grasping Avi around his torso. He gave a shriek and Aria, Luke, and Willow spun.

"AVI!" Willow screeched, hurrying forward and looking about for something she could use to help him.

Avi started clawing at the Timber Giant's bark-covered hand to break free just as Willow ran forward and struck the giant in the leg with a tree branch.

Avi screamed kicking out at the giant. "Let go of me you big oof!" The Timber Giant flung him to the side and his back hit a tree. He gasped as the breath was knocked out of him.

Luke ran to him and offered him a hand to help him up. "Are you okay?"

"I'm fine. Let's just get out of here before these things kill us," Avi said, grabbing his side.

The giant swung for Aria and Willow aggressively, but they ducked out of the way as Luke and Avi hurried towards them.

They four of them took off through the forest again, the Timber Giants not far behind.

A long, tall, gray, wooden fence came into view—a clear sign of a village. They hurried to the fence, backing up behind a massive tree and wedging themselves beside it.

"Bola! Bola!" the Timber Giants began to yell to each other. They started to retreat, disappearing back into the deeper parts of the forest.

What does 'Bola' mean? Aria wondered.

Aria, Luke, Avi, and Willow crept down the fence to look through a large, splintered hole in it. The smell of meat roasting was unmistakable, making all four of them clutch their aching stomachs. Having been eating only mushrooms, they were starving.

On the other side of the fence, a mix of English and another unrecognizable language was being spoken. There were shouts and sounds of sizzles, many of the shouts sounding like violent threats. They stared through the fence at the village. It looked very poor and lowly; the houses were made of wood, the paint and stain worn away with the wood graying in decay. There were people, either in rags or in black and gray leather outfits. Almost everyone in the village, from what they could see, was holding knives and clubs, and were covered in dirt, coal dust, and grime. Weird chicken-looking creatures were freely running around everywhere, looking more like a hybrid between a chicken and a peacock. Naked, weird, and very ugly, short, gray creatures with gray slime covering them were digging through all the garbage that scattered the village's dirt streets. The creatures had huge, bulging, ugly eyes and pointy noses that curved downward.

"Ew! Nevidits!" Avi exclaimed. "We have to get out of here!"

"No, hold on." Something caught Aria's eye.

Avi continued to complain about the Nevidits rummaging through the garbage and Willow voiced how the town looked hostile, but Aria wasn't listening. She was staring at the people in hoods—the people who were wearing black cloaks with a golden dagger embroidered on their right shoulder.

CHAPTER SEVENTEEN

PANIC BEGAN TO set into Aria and she could sense it setting into her friends as well. None of the people in the village gave the Dark Forces members two looks, seeming not to care that they were mingling with them.

"I said we need to leave," Avi repeated.

"But we can't head back into the forest," Willow said.

"Yeah, if we do that, we'll be smashed to pieces." Aria could still feel the vibration in the ground from the Timber Giants' footsteps.

"So, we just stay here?" Luke asked her.

"No, we go into the village."

"We what?" He raised his eyebrows. "I must have misheard you."

"No, you didn't. It's the only way. I'm sure they won't recognize me…and if they do…There is no other way. If we head back into the forest, we'll be killed."

"And if we head into the village, we will *also* be killed," Avi piped in sarcastically. "Just look at all those weapons they have! Wait a minute, I forgot to grab weapons, too."

Avi smacked his forehead just as Aria climbed through the

hole in the fence. She hurried across the dirt street and ducked behind an overflowing trash can. The smell was like rotting fish, but luckily there were no Nevidits hiding in it. Luke, Avi, and Willow bolted across the street once a wagon passed. They joined her behind the trash can, sweat running down their backs because of the heat. Aria gestured for them to follow her as she snuck back out of hiding and ran behind a saloon where the shadows could conceal all of them. They followed after her, watching closely to make sure nobody on the streets noticed them.

"What exactly is your plan?" Avi asked, giving her an intense look.

"I don't know. To get out of here, I guess."

"Well, that's a *great* plan, since you got us *in here*," Avi said, then he paused for a moment. "Kidding, it's a horrible plan! Not even a plan!"

Aria ignored him, having noticed two people walking down the side of the road. It was Kora and a wavy chocolate brown-haired woman, the same woman who had tripped Aria with a vine. Her heart stopped for a moment as sweat began to run down her forehead. Now, she knew it was a mistake to have entered the village. What were they doing there? She strained her ears to hear their resounding conversation from across the road.

"Kora, why have we come to Bola again?" the brown-haired woman was saying.

"Ebony, I have already told you what must be a thousand times by now. We have to pick up an ingredient for Ciaus. You know we can only get it through the Black Trade. And Bola's the closest and quickest place to get Black Trade items," Kora answered, annoyed. "How about you actually pay attention next time I tell you something."

So, that is her name: Ebony, Aria thought, continuing to watch Kora and the other woman walk down the street. Her heart rate sped up and she had a headache forming as she tried to think of a safe way out of the village.

"What ya' doin'?" a weird voice asked from behind, startling her.

She stumbled out of hiding with a loud crash as she fell sideways into a trashcan, tipping it over. Many eyes looked around to see what made the clash of metal, many eyes landing on Aria, including Kora and Ebony's.

Luke's voice rose in alarm, "Aria!" She looked up to see him pointing to Kora and Ebony now making their way over with wickedly delighted smiles.

"It's the Chesler girl!" Kora's voice echoed against the buildings.

"A Nevidit!" Avi exclaimed with disgust.

A Nevidit was standing next to where Aria had been moments before, a sly smile spread across its face. "Hello." The creature smirked. "Why you hiding behind my favorite garbage can? It's mine. Only mine. Everyone knows that."

Aria quickly got to her feet and Willow grabbed her hand.

"Come on," Willow said, her voice sounding panicky, as she began to pull her down the alleyway.

They ran as fast as they could, trying not to trip on all the garbage that lingered in the shadows.

"STOP THEM!" Kora's voice boomed.

Many weapons were pulled and shouts echoed off the buildings as people called after them.

"DO NOT INJURE HER!" Kora shouted and the weapons were slowly put away in confusion.

Did these people not know how to stop someone without attacking them?

Aria's sweaty hand had slipped from Willow's. She was in the front now, leading them down a narrow side street. The mainly empty street was overshadowed by tall, feeble houses and buildings. A ginger cat was laying in the dark shadows as they ran past and Nevidits were rummaging around in the garbage cans, flinging rotten food and random pieces of trash. They looked up as they saw Aria and her friends race past and they started climbing out of the trash to run after them. Word sure does travel fast, especially when Kora is screeching at the top of her lungs.

Aria's heart thumped against her ribs aggressively. She blocked Kora and Ebony's shouts from her head, trying to figure out where to go. They ran past a group of people in black leather and grime who looked a lot like thieves.

"WHOEVER BRINGS ME THE CHESLER GIRL WILL WIN A SACK OF GOLD!" Kora's voice could be heard over all the houses and buildings.

The group of thieves started after them, determined to obtain a sack of gold.

As Aria ran, she panted to the others, "Drop the bags! They're weighing us down!"

They pulled off their bags but didn't stop running, letting their bags fall to the ground. A thief immediately picked them up to take, not that there was anything of value in them.

Aria turned the corner where there was a little pen filled with some pigs. Next to the pig pen was a chicken coop and a house. She hurried to hide behind the coop filled with those hybrid chickens. Luke, Avi, and Willow ducked behind the chicken coop as well, falling to their knees and panting for air. Aria breathed in deeply on her knees, fidgeting with her sunflower necklace.

"I told you this was a bad idea," Avi said.

"Now, Avi, really?" Aria rolled her eyes. "I was not expecting them to be here."

She stared down at her sunflower necklace, tears filling her eyes. All of her thoughts ran to her parents, wishing she was in their arms and out of this situation. Memories of the day her mother had given her the necklace flooded her mind. It was on her birthday about a year ago that she had received the necklace…*About a year ago*…She tried to recall what day it was when they had left camp. It had been July 27, which meant that it was now August 2nd. Tears and sweat poured down her face as she remembered it's been exactly a year.

"Well, they *are* here," Avi was saying. "And we are trapped in a village of thieves."

"It's my birthday," Aria said suddenly and unexpectedly.

"What?" Luke's mouth fell open, his eyes softening.

"Oh, Aria, I'm so sorry," Willow sympathized, resting her hand on Aria's.

Aria knew exactly what she meant because in those words was the hidden message: *Sorry your birthday is the absolute worst because you're being chased by the Dark Forces and your parents are being held hostage by them.*

"Happy fifteenth birthday," Avi said quietly, almost shamefully.

"Thanks." Aria's voice was even softer.

She wasn't sure how to respond or what to even say and guessed they didn't either.

"Gold, gold, gold. I like gold," a high-pitched voice chanted from somewhere.

Out from the side of the coop, an appalling Nevidit jumped out, causing Aria's stomach to launch into her throat.

"Are you the Chesler girl?" the Nevidit asked, pointing to Willow.

"No."

Avi cringed away at the sight of the creature and the proximity he was to it.

"Are *you* Aria Chesler?" The Nevidit pointed to Aria.

"What's your name?" Aria asked, trying to stall as she looked at Luke, Avi, and Willow for help. She knew she could blast the creature away from them, but that would give away their location and make a scene.

"I am Ody. Now, what is *your* name?"

"I—I" Aria stuttered.

"Tell me or I cut your hair!" Ody cackled, pulling out a small, razor-sharp dagger from behind his back like a maniac.

"Whoa, put that thing away!" Aria told him.

Luke got to his feet and jumped in front of Aria.

"Maybe I'll cut his hair, too!" Ody laughed, waving his dagger.

"Why would you cut our hair?" Aria backed away from the Nevidit, her eyes locked on the sharp blade.

"Hair sells for gold! Now, tell me your name *or else*."

"I don't have one," Aria replied before she could even think it through. Immediately, she wanted to shove the words back into her mouth because of how suspicious they sounded.

Ody ran around Luke and grabbed a fistful of Aria's hair, pulling her head toward the ground. She winced and tried to pull back as he was about to bring the dagger down through her hair.

"Hey!" Luke yelled at the creature, using a Knockback Enchant to blast it far away from her.

Ody flew out from behind the coop, screaming when he hit the ground. Almost instantly, shouts rang out in the streets. They had given away their location.

Ody was up on his feet as soon as Aria, Willow, and Avi

were. They quickly ran out from behind the coop as the little Nevidit ran after them, brandishing his dagger. Luke grabbed hold of Aria's hand, seeming determined to protect her. Kora and Ebony raced after them, surrounded by a group of thieves who wanted gold. Aria and her friends swerved to the left to get away, but they were being cut off from all directions by more and more thieves. They circled around, trying to find a gap in the thieves who had them surrounded. Kora and Ebony closed the circle, blocking off the last remaining exit. Kora grabbed Luke by his short, mocha brown hair and pulled him away, his hand slipping from Aria's. Luke grunted and reached for where Kora had a fistful of his hair, trying to break away from her. Around Ebony's arms and shoulders draped a vine like a normal, fashionable accessory. The vines shot from her arms toward Aria, wrapping around her, while Kora put Luke in a headlock. Her arms and legs were pinned together, slowly constricting her until it was too tight for her to move. It reminded her of Stranger's Vine…How weak and useless she had been. The thick, strong vines held Aria a few inches above the ground as she tried to break free of them, letting out a loud, angry shout. Avi and Willow were in headlocks now as well, thieves holding them back as they tried to get away.

"Well, well, well," Kora began, a satisfied smile playing on her lips. "That's four captures all in one day, including the Chesler girl. Master Malus will be very pleased. Take them to the wagon."

Kora started to pull Luke down the street as most of the village's residents cleared away from the scene.

"No, wait! Let them go! Just take me!" Aria pleaded.

"That's not how it works." Ebony tutted.

"Please! They didn't do anything! Take just me! Malus just wants me, right?"

"Actually, I believe this boy here *did* do something," Kora said, harshly pulling Luke's head back by his hair. He ground his teeth to stop himself from wincing and reached backward to tear Kora's hands off his head. "You knocked me unconscious, didn't you, boy? You'll pay for that," Kora spat and grabbed Luke's hands, too.

"Leave him alone," Aria begged, trying to break free of her restraints.

Kora ignored her and began jostling Luke down the street again. The two thieves did the same with Avi and Willow as they tried to wiggle free.

"To the wagon," Kora repeated with authority as Ebony walked after them.

Aria floated inches above the ground, following after Ebony, and trying to think. What was going to happen to her friends? What was going to happen to her? She had to get them out of this mess. The vines were so tight on her that it was painful, nearly squashing the breath right out of her. She tried to make a fire in the palm of her hand, but the vines were so tight around her wrists that the magic wasn't coming.

Why isn't it working?

They were taken through the hideous Village of Bola. Ody followed behind carrying a huge sack of gold and chanting a song about how happy he was:

Gold, gold, gold.
I love me some gold.
Some richie gaves it to me.
Now I am rich as I can be.
Don't need to cut no hair,
'cause now I have got me some…
Gold, gold, gold.

Aria couldn't even recall where or when he had gotten the gold, but that didn't matter.

The forest was now far behind them and a hilly countryside was just outside the tall, black, metal, village gates. A wagon pulled by two horses with a huge cage attached to the back of it was on the side of the road. The cage was made entirely of metal, with the scolding sun beating down on it. She knew that was the wagon they would be tossed into. They were prisoners now.

Ebony opened the metal cage door and threw Aria in first. The vines released her as she fell onto the sweltering metal bottom of the cage. She quickly sat on her feet, trying not to burn herself on the metal. Luke was thrown in second, then Willow and Avi at the same time. They all hurried to the door, but it shut and locked before they could even attempt to get out.

The two thieves walked away carrying tiny sacks of gold as Kora smiled cruelly into the cage.

"I'll go get that ingredient now." She narrowed her eyes at Aria before walking away.

Ebony climbed into the wagon where a spiky-haired man was in the front holding the horses' reins.

"So, that was what took you two so long," the man said, sounding annoyed and looking straight ahead.

"Well, *I'm sorry* Chad. Didn't know you were in such a rush," Ebony replied sarcastically.

"When Malus appointed me as the head messenger, I didn't think this was what it meant," Chad voiced.

"Whether you like it or not, you'll have to do it or have life drained out of you." She looked back at Aria and her friends, smiling with satisfaction.

Chad made a grunt.

It felt like forever sitting in that humid, burning cage. Aria felt like an animal in a zoo where everyone was looking at her— or a hamster trapped in a small cage, shaking the bars to get out.

Everyone *was* looking at her at that moment, too. People had stopped their thieving and selling of illegal products to watch the young teenagers. They probably were curious, wondering why four teenagers were locked up by the Dark Forces. Aria's thoughts strayed to what might happen to her and her friends, mainly thinking of death. She tried to push those thoughts out of her head and focus on how to get out.

I knew this might happen, Aria thought. *And I let my friends get dragged into it. No! Don't think that. They chose to come with me. I will get them out of this mess. I will try and I might fail, but at least I tried. And I will try again.*

When Kora finally came back, she carried a little burlap sack in her hands. She climbed up into the wagon behind Ebony, and commanded, "Take us to the Malamone Mansion, Chad."

Chad snapped the reins and the huge, beastly horses began trotting down the road toward the hilly countryside. Kora turned around to stare down at Aria and her friends. Aria looked straight into Kora's gray eyes, her face scrunched up, not sure what to do or say. Nothing she said or did would have any point.

"Now you'll join your *dreadful* parents," Kora said, a cruel smile spreading across her face. The last word she said had a strange lullaby-like hum to it that made shivers run down Aria's spine. "*Sleep.*"

A drowsiness washed over Aria, making her eyes suddenly fall low. She slipped against the cage bars. Luke, Avi, and Willow's eyes drooped and yawns escaped their lips. Avi fell sideways next to Willow and into a sleeping state. Aria's eyelids fell closed, feeling so heavy, and she sunk into a deep, dreamless sleep against Luke.

CHAPTER EIGHTEEN

THE WAGON'S WHEELS turned gears, causing Aria's eyes to fly open. The wagon shifted back and forth as the wheels rolled down the road. She looked around, trying to figure out where they were. Willow and Avi were sitting across from her, their hands bound by ropes. They were awake, staring at her with terror in their eyes. Aria noticed she was leaning on something soft, but strong, so she lifted her head and turned it to see that it was Luke's shoulder she was snuggled up against. She didn't fall asleep like that, did she? Her face turned a tinge of red when she met his depressed eyes. She looked away and quickly pulled herself up straight. Their hands were both tied as well, the rope scratching and burning at her skin. She tried to pull her hands apart, but the knots were too tight. All she did was made the rope cut at her skin more.

"Where are we?" Aria asked softly, trying not to let Kora, Ebony, or Chad hear.

"Don't know," Luke answered just as quietly. "They stopped to tie us not that long ago."

Aria stared through the metal cage bars above Avi and Willow to see they were going up a brick road. The road looked like it could have once been lovely, well kept by the rich, but the bricks were chipped and the paint gone to reveal the gray stone. The wagon dragged forward past a broken, black, metal fence gate that looked like it could have been centuries old. There was a thick, foggy gloom settling everywhere. It was hard to see just ten feet in front of herself with how thick the fog was. The air was suddenly cold and everything got darker. There was an odd feeling in the air, she could sense it: a feeling of distinct malice lingering throughout the mist.

"I don't like this," Willow said, watching the gloom settle in the bottom of the cage.

It was hard to even see out of the cage now, but Aria could definitely see that they were approaching a massive house. The Malamone Mansion.

"We need to get out of here," Aria said quietly, trying hard to keep the panic out of her voice. "Any ideas?"

"I don't get how you can be so strong and brave in a situation like this," Luke told her, sounding almost admiring. His eyes met hers and his face flushed pink.

Was her worry not showing? Aria certainly didn't feel brave or strong. She felt weak and petrified.

"I'm strong because I have to be and brave because if I'm not, fear will overtake me and make me quit. I can't quit when people need me," Aria said.

The words were out before she even knew what they meant.

Kora abruptly turned. "We are here," she said, a twisted smile playing on her lips.

The wagon went around the circular courtyard, past a disgusting fountain, and stopped in front of the giant, elegant mansion doors. The doors burst open and out came a young-looking woman. Through the gloom, Aria could see the woman had black, unkempt, straggly black hair pulled up into an extremely messy bun. She wore the same black cloak that all the Dark Forces wore, but also short black boots and black leggings with purple lace crisscrossing down them. Her hood was down, so Aria could see her face, which was so pale it looked almost white, and her eyes were a menacing gold with beady pupils. The creepy but beautiful girl strutted up to the cage, grinning in a way that made her eyes look like a panther's.

"Hmm…new prisoners," she said, taking a whiff of the air. Her voice was light and eerie like a ghost's, raising goosebumps on Aria's arms. "They smell…different…"

"Let's go, I am sure Malus is waiting," Kora said, jumping out of the wagon.

"Yes, he is." The girl clasped her hands together. Aria's eyes went wide when she noticed the girl's long, black, dagger-like nails. "He is in his office."

"Okay, Viola, you grab the Chesler girl," Kora instructed. "Chad, you grab blondie. Ebony, you grab that one—" she pointed to Avi. "—And I'll grab the other boy."

Kora opened the cage door and grabbed Luke harshly by the arm while Chad and Ebony climbed out of the wagon.

"Luke!" Aria shouted, trying to wiggle towards him in an attempt to save him.

"Is that his name, huh?" A wicked smile spread across her face. "Let's go then, *Luke*." She started pushing him toward the mansion.

The creepy girl, Viola, grabbed Aria by her arm and dragged her out of the cage. Viola's skin was cold, like air inside a refrigerator. Aria balanced herself on her feet as Viola sniffed the air creepily, then shoved her forward toward the marble stairs leading up to the front doors. She clasped her hands around Aria's arms, forcing her to move. Aria tried to pull away from her, but she dug her nails into Aria's skin through her light jacket as if that was exactly what they were meant for. Tears escaped Aria's eyes and she screeched in pain.

"Aria!" Luke yelled from inside the mansion.

"Let them go!" Aria screamed at every Dark Forces member in the vicinity.

"Stop squirming!" Viola stopped digging her fingernails deeper, a cruel smile playing at her sickly-colored lips. "I *will* attack!"

Aria tried pulling her arms away from Viola again, but her grip was so tight the ropes were cutting at her wrists. A small amount of blood trickled down her arms and her wrists. Viola dug her nails into her skin again, causing Aria to scream. It felt like tiny knives were puncturing her skin.

"Knock it off, girl!" Viola shouted and came to a halt with Aria in the entrance hall.

Willow and Avi were jostled up the steps now by Chad and Ebony. They stopped in the entryway where Luke and Aria were trying to pry away from Kora and Viola. Kora lowered her head, being a little taller than Luke, and whispered something into his ear. With a look of fear in his eyes, he fought harder to get away.

"Leave him alone!" Aria yelled.

"Shut up, stupid girl!" Kora shrieked. "I can do whatever I want to him."

"Let's go. Malus wants them now." Viola pushed Aria up one of the two curved staircases.

Once up the stairs, they were shoved to the left down a darkened hallway where the only light came from under a wooden door. Two muscular hooded men stood outside the door to guard it, their faces hidden beneath the hoods.

Viola stopped in front of the men, her chin raised with authority, and said, "We have brought the Chesler girl for Master Malus." She shoved Aria forward an inch.

The man to the right of the door flung it wide open. Viola pushed Aria harshly through the door and into the square room. Aria gulped at what her eyes saw. Weapons, mostly knives, hung on the walls, and chains sat in a pile in the corner of the room. It smelled musty, and dust danced in the light from the oil lamps hanging in the walls' empty spaces. A dark oak desk sat in front of a closed window with drab curtains, and in front of it, a heavy, bulky, metal chair had shackles attached to the arms and legs. Aria's hands began to shake, sweat running down her forehead. Behind the desk sat a hooded man who was, no doubt, Malus. His face was concealed under the hood, but Aria could tell he was observing them as they were pushed into the room. Around his neck was a long necklace with a gorgeous, white, medium-sized stone, which glowed very faintly. The Life Stone. She knew that was what it had to be from all the books she had read.

"Here they are, Master," Viola said.

"Hmm…" Malus tapped his fingers on his desk.

Aria sensed him staring at her specifically.

"What happened to her?" Malus asked. His voice was deep, mysterious, and terrifying, like the one from her nightmares.

"She fought me, Master." Viola let her go.

More blood dripped from the punctures Viola had made and Aria had to fight back tears, biting her lip. Terrified and shaking, she looked at Viola for a second, who eyed her cuts hungrily.

Malus was quiet for a few moments before saying, "I see. Lock the others in the cellar. I want to have a *little chat* with Aria."

"Yes, Master," Kora, Ebony, and Chad replied in unison as if they had rehearsed it.

Luke, Avi, and Willow were dragged out the door, kicking

and screaming. Aria turned toward the door, calling after them, but Viola was in front of the door in a literal flash of black, shutting it in her face. Viola stared down at her with a malicious smile, then she turned to Malus, one hand still on the door.

"Malus, what should I do?"

"Cut her loose."

Viola extended her thumb, firmly grabbed Aria's wrist, and sliced through the rope with her fingernail. She let go and leaned against the door, making sure Aria couldn't leave. Aria tore the ropes from her hands and let them fall to the floor. She rubbed at her aching wrists covered in tiny cuts and blood.

"Viola, leave us," Malus commanded. "Aria, sit."

Viola nodded and left the room, clicking the lock in place from outside.

Aria didn't listen to him. Instead, she watched him closely, unsure of what to do, and expected him to attack her.

"Cutting me loose was a mistake," she bluffed.

"Really? Well, I'm not afraid of a young girl, so I suppose it wasn't," Malus said. "I said to take a seat."

She remained where she was and demanded, "Where are my parents?"

"I said to take a seat!" Malus swished his hand through the air.

The metal chair in front of his desk was dragged from its place. Before she could even react, the chair swept her off her feet and she landed in it. She put her hands on the side of the chair to get up, but the cuffs latched her wrists and ankles in place. The metal was cold on her skin. She tried to pry her hands away from the shackles, but they were strong iron. Shaking her hands wildly, she tried to call her magic, but it wouldn't come.

"Now, let's start over," he said, pulling his hood off.

Aria's eyes went wide when she saw how young he looked. She expected him to be an old, decrepit monster from being centuries old, but instead, he looked like he was only in his thirties. His face was very scarred from the many centuries of fighting and his eyes were a bright, malicious green. Studs of hair stuck out from his shiny scalp from his head being shaven. He looked just as powerful, menacing, evil, and merciless as the books she had read said.

"It's nice to finally meet you *in person.*" A villainous smile crossed his face.

Aria thought that was a weird statement since, number one, they had never met at all, and number two, he likely wanted to kill her.

"Where are my parents?" she pressed, staring straight into his wicked eyes as she pulled at the restraints again.

"*Actually*, I do the questioning around here. As my prisoner, you answer. I believe you might know things your parents… have not told us. I am aware that you have just come to know of magic only months ago, but is there anything you have heard your parents speak of before then? Something about magic? Maybe something about destroying the Dark Forces?"

"Where are they?"

"You will answer me! We can do it the easy way or I get to use my…*tools.*" He lifted a sharpened knife onto the desk, its hilt made of rubies.

"Please! I don't know anything!" Aria shouted, shaking her hands in an attempt to free them from the shackles and absent-mindedly looking at all the weapons that hung on the walls. Her head throbbed, her heart pounded against her ribs, and sweat poured down her back.

Malus stood from his desk and walked around it to squat down next to Aria like she was a five-year-old.

He spoke in a phony calm tone when he said, "Aria, you are young, naïve, and you do not understand what is going on in this world. Just tell me what you know."

"Naïve? I don't understand that you are a cruel monster who has caused me pain, misery, and wants to kill me?"

"There is where you are wrong," Malus said, standing up. "I do not want to kill you, but I will have no problem in doing so. I thought you would know things, so I wanted you to tell me that information. You were tough to get, though, I'll admit. If you stay out of my way and tell me what you know, then I *might* let you and your friends go."

"But you admit you are a monster?"

"Different people see a person in different ways. Good and evil are just two sides of the same coin. It's all about perspective. I, for one, see myself as a benefactor."

"To who, exactly?"

"Myself."

Aria shook her head, wrinkling her nose, and shouted with rage and bluff, "After all the misery you have caused me, I *will* destroy you! I *will* get my parents back no matter what it takes!"

"Maybe you will learn what it is like to be a prisoner and you will change your mind. But first, I must test you."

She wondered what he could have possibly meant. Was he about to test her magical skills or something? Malus turned around, walked back to his desk, and opened a drawer. He had to search around in it for a second before pulling out an odd device. It looked like an ancient metal compass with a needle sticking out from the end of it. The device had the words *None, Shape-shifting, Mind-reading, Omni-communication, Healing,* and *Nature-manipulation* instead of *North, South, East, and West.* A red needle pointed to *None* as he walked back to Aria.

It was a test to see if she had a Divining Power, but why would he care? She already knew she didn't have one.

"Give me your finger," he demanded. "I like to check if people have a Divining Power…or *powers*. I suppose you could call it a hobby."

Aria clenched her hand shut in defiance.

"You are a foolish girl!" He bent down and grabbed her hand to pull out her pointer finger.

"No!" Aria shouted, trying to pull her finger back into her fist.

He pulled the testing device to her fingertip and shoved the tip of the needle in more brutally than necessary. Aria screamed out at the shock of it, but it definitely didn't hurt as bad as when she had broken her nose or been attacked by Stranger's Vine. Blood beaded up around the needle's point and her lip quivered, but she didn't cry. She hid the tears threatening to escape her eyes. Noticing Malus' stunned face, looking like he had gotten the shock of a lifetime, she looked down at the testing device. The needle flicked back and forth between the different powers wildly. Then it stopped at *None* for a second before continuing its strange charade and going back to *None* again. It repeated its cycle like that a few times. It seemed broken, unable to choose anything. Aria waited for it to pick *None* and stay there, desperate for the needle to be removed from her finger, but it didn't. Clearly, it was broken.

"I don't have a Divining Power!" Aria shouted at him, her eyes unable to leave the flicking red needle.

"VIOLA!" Malus hollered, pulling the needle from Aria's finger, and stood up.

His loud voice made all the knives on the walls rattle. He stared down at her while she put pressure on her pointer finger with her thumb, trying to get the bleeding to stop.

The door was thrown open only seconds later and Viola rushed in with a face of evil glee. "Yes, Malus?"

"Throw her in the cellar with the others. Tell the decoders to hurry on solving my father's riddle to the Death Stone as well. I found what I've been looking for," Malus said, staring at Aria.

"Her?" Viola gasped.

"Yes. She is."

"No wonder she smelled so different," Viola said, her inhuman eyes wide. "Should I tie her up?"

"Yes."

Viola walked over to the wall of weapons and took down a short cord of rope.

"No! Where are my parents?" Aria demanded. "I told you I don't know anything! You said I'd be free! You said my friends and I could leave!"

"Plans have changed," Malus replied, now smiling cruelly at her. "There are two options in life: rule or be ruled. I can see your parents never taught you that and that is why you have lost. *I* am the ruler now."

He waved for Viola to take Aria away and the shackles simultaneously released her. Viola grabbed her by her arms, tearing her out of the chair. Aria quickly pulled out of her grasp and bolted for the door, but Viola was in front of her in a literal flash. How was that possible? Aria stopped abruptly and Viola grabbed her arms, pinning them harshly behind her back. The rope looped around her wrists, biting into her skin as Viola tied it tightly. Viola shuffled her out the door and down the dark hall, leaving Malus to his work. Aria tried to pull away, but Viola was being crueler than before.

"Oh, Malus is so glad to have finally found you," Viola cackled in Aria's ear.

"Stop digging your nails into my wrists!"

She tried to get away again and Viola just cackled like a witch.

"What does he want with me? I told him I knew nothing!"

"You cannot *possibly* be that stupid." She started to push Aria down the staircase.

Aria stumbled down the last step and ripped away from Viola's vicious grip, her sharp fingernails cutting across her wrists. The rope fell to the floor in pieces.

What she was going to do and where she was going to go, she didn't know. She had no idea where her parents or friends were being kept. She knew her friends were in the cellar, but where was that? She needed to find all of them and escape.

She ran away from the steps and turned back toward Viola, who stood on the bottom step as if patiently waiting. Aria raised her hands up at chest level, blasting Viola with a Knockback Enchant. Viola flew into the air a few feet and then smashed down onto the marble steps. Without any indication that she had been hurt, she stood up with ease. The enchantment hadn't been enough. She stepped toward Aria very slowly with a delighted smile.

"For once, I will have to disagree with Malus on something. You are not a *complete* weakling, but no one ever dares mess with me because *no one* ever wins." Viola laughed wickedly, showing perfectly white and perfectly pointed vampire fangs. "This is going to be fun."

CHAPTER NINETEEN

ARIA FELT LIKE her heart was going to lunge out of her chest with how hard it was beating. Now it was no wonder to her why Viola was sniffing the air; Viola had been smelling her blood, which made every hair on Aria's arms and the back of her neck stand up. She thought she was done for, but Malus wanted her alive.

"You can't hurt me!" Aria backed away as her voice shook, seeing the hostility in Viola's eyes. "Malus wants me alive."

"*Oh no! I can't hurt you?*" Viola said in a mock-baby voice before flashing her fangs and letting out a growl. "Actually, I can't *kill* you. That doesn't mean I can't harm you."

Aria took off running past the staircases and down a hallway with her heart pounding in her ears, hoping she would find her friends. She turned the corner, only glancing behind her to see if Viola was following, which she didn't appear to be. Suddenly, something struck her from the side and she was pinned against the wall. A rancid stench, like metal and sewage, breathed down on her. Viola somehow had gotten ahead of her and now had Aria's arms pinned to the wall, leaning into her to keep her there. Aria tried to move, but Viola was too strong.

She thought her bones might snap from her intense grasp. Viola had her fangs exposed, her face just inches from Aria's.

"Foolish, that's what you are," Viola said, her breath lingering in the air like the smell of decomposing flesh.

"Get off of me!" Aria spat in her face. "Your breath reeks—"

She was cut off when a high-pitched scream erupted from her throat as Viola's black fingernails dug deep into her skin. It felt like each nail was a tiny knife cutting into her forearms, Viola smiling in satisfaction. Aria aimed her hand the best she could, then blasted her into the opposite wall. She immediately clutched her arms, trying to stop the bleeding, as she ran back to the entrance hall. The only plan she had in her head was to find her friends and get them to safety, but where were they? As she looked around for a moment, panic confused her thoughts. She needed to hurry and think before Viola came after her again.

Before she could even realize someone was there, a vine caught her foot and she slipped. She managed to catch herself with her hands before her stomach slammed into the marble floor, knocking the wind out of her. As soon as she felt the vine release her ankle, she was back on her feet just as Viola zoomed into the room agilely. She ignored the injuries on her arms and her sweatshirt that was torn all over. Now, she was face to face with both Viola and Ebony, who stared at her with what appeared to be interest and curiosity. Ebony wore her vines around both her arms like a fancy fur coat, the vine that had caught Aria shrinking back onto her arms.

"I'm surprised, Viola. I have never seen you struggle with a prisoner before," Ebony said, casually coming to a stop at the bottom of the staircase.

"She's foolish, but a fighter." A smirk returned to her face. "And I thought it would be fun to let her try to fight me."

Aria raised her hands to defend herself.

"So, I see," Ebony said, swishing her hand.

The vines on her arms sped toward Aria. She dove out of the way and threw a Knockback Enchant at Ebony, but it missed, and instead, put a tiny crack in the already worn-down marble stairs. Another vine shot at Aria, but this time she hurried to grab it, lighting it on fire. The fire spread from Aria's palm and up the vine rapidly. Ebony hastily made her vines vanish as if they were never even there before the flames could get to her. She narrowed her eyes and scrunched up her nose.

"I'm done playing games, girl!" Viola bolted after Aria with her fangs exposed.

Aria veered out of the way, but a vine caught her foot and she slammed into the ground. She groaned in pain from the impact but hastily turned over to see Chad and two other hooded members of the Dark Forces coming from around the stairs.

"What is going on here?" he asked.

"The girl is trying to escape." Viola's tone was razor-sharp as she towered over Aria.

Aria's eyes darted around, trying to find something to use against them. Her eyes locked on the paintings hanging on the walls. She directed her hands at them, feeling a pulse in her palm, and forced one from the wall, then at Chad. The painting broke apart when it hit his head and the two people next to him. The splinters of wood and the ripped canvas fell to the floor, leaving Chad infuriated and swearing.

Aria started to sneakily slip out from where Viola was towering over her while she was distracted, but something cold hit her side. An icy limping sensation spread through her muscles, and she became motionless.

"You couldn't do that sooner?" Viola turned to Ebony.

"I like to play with my victims, like you," Ebony said simply and walked back up the stairs.

Chad stalked off down the hall, cursing, and the two people with him followed.

Viola grabbed Aria and lifted her over her shoulder with ease. Aria wondered how such a small person like Viola could effortlessly carry her with just one arm. She dizzily watched the dark halls go by and heard Viola sniffing the air. The air got colder the deeper they descended a rough stone staircase, relieving a bit of pain from her wounds like an ice pack would. They came to a hallway below the mansion where there were a couple of metal doors, one being at the end. After pulling a rusted key from somewhere in her cloak, Viola unlocked the door at the end of the hall. Inside, Luke, Avi, and Willow were sitting, trying desperately to keep warm. Viola dropped Aria onto the raw stone floor without care and left, the door shutting and locking behind her. Aria let out a whine as she trembled, black speckles edging into her vision.

"Oh my gosh! Aria!" Willow exclaimed in horror.

Waves of pain rolled over her as Aria laid on the floor, unable to move.

Luke ran to her side, pulling off her jacket carefully so he could see her wounds. "What happened to you? They didn't torture you, did they?"

"I tried to escape and they attacked me." The draft chilled Aria's bones and she shivered.

"Who?" Luke asked, acting as if keen to avenge her.

"Viola and Ebony." Her voice grew softer, her eyes falling shut for a moment. "Turns out Viola's a vampire."

"She didn't bite you, right?" Avi asked urgently, looking her up and down.

"No."

"Can you tell us what happened?" Willow asked.

Aria explained what had happened to them softly, forcing them to strain their ears to hear her. Everything started to blur together and she felt herself slipping into a half-sleep.

"He wants to imprison you because his tester is broken?" Avi asked, squinting his eyes in confusion.

"Yeah," Aria replied, but she felt it was for a different reason, one she could not put her finger on.

"Sounds like a *him* problem." Avi threw his hands up in the air.

She was drifting away into darkness, her eyes drooping low and their voices becoming distant.

"Aria, no, you have to stay awake," Willow said.

Luke gave a light shake of her shoulder, but her eyes fell shut.

Her eyes flickered open and closed after a dreamless sleep. The pain suddenly came back to her like being hit with a brick. She groaned and heard Luke, Avi, and Willow shuffling closer to her. Her head was resting on the hard ground, throbbing with a monstrous headache. Now she actually took a look around the room, which was small and crammed with empty wine shelves. Sharp, broken wine bottles lay piled in one corner. Gradually, she sat up to face her friends. Her jacket had been ripped to pieces and the fabric tied to her wounds, now soaked through with blood.

"Thanks." She gestured to her arms.

"Luke was the one that did it," Willow told her.

"We need to get out of here." Avi stood abruptly and started pacing.

"*Dude*, she just woke up," Luke said, shaking his head.

"Yeah, I know, but you weren't saying it, so I did."

"*Dude.*" Luke's arm wrapped around Aria caringly.

"Um…" Aria looked at him and his arm immediately went to his side. "Anyway, I know, Avi. Have they fed us yet?"

"No, why would they?" Luke asked.

"Malus wants me alive for some reason. I told you, he needs me and the Death Stone for something."

"What if he's going to drain power from all of us! I mean, Willow has a Divining Power, so she's worth something—" Avi said.

"Hey—" Willow interrupted.

"And then he might drain the life out of all of us with his Life Stone!" Avi continued, looking like he might pass out at the thought of it. "Hold on—" Avi gagged for a second, leaning over like he was going to vomit, but there was nothing to puke up.

"They'll have to feed us if they're going to keep me alive, whatever their reason for it is," Aria said, clutching her roaring stomach. "When they do, they'll have to come through that door. When they open the door, we can attack and make our escape."

"That sounds like a good plan, but what about your parents?" Willow asked.

"You guys will get out of here and teleport back to camp. I will search every room in this mansion until I find them."

"You know very well we will not leave you," Luke stated.

She sighed, knowing she wouldn't win an argument on the subject.

Only a half an hour went by before the door opened, but they were already starving. Luke and Avi stood next to the door, ready so that when it opened, they would be hidden. Willow was hiding behind one of the wine shelves and Aria was standing in front of the door. As soon as Chad opened the metal door, they launched all sorts of enchantments at him. Blue, purple, green, and yellow glows bounced off the walls in a blur of color. Chad flew to the ceiling, hit his head, and then fell unconscious to the floor. The metal tray of rotten food scraps he had been holding fell to the floor with a clang. Aria, Luke, Avi, and Willow rushed through the door and up the stone steps, ignoring the food Chad had brought so they could make their escape. The chilly air was gone as soon as they reached the main floor. They turned down a darkened corridor, up a winding path, and into the entrance hall where Viola, Ebony, Kora, and a few other members of the Dark Forces were waiting. It was like they had expected them to escape.

Aria felt a jolt in the pit of her stomach and came to a halt. Her and her friends instantly raised their hands to defend themselves. It was four against six.

"Trying to escape?" A hateful look appeared on Kora's face. "As soon as I heard that *moron*, Chad, was the one giving you four food, I knew you would escape."

"Let's take them to Malus," Ebony said. "Apparently, he underestimated them. A simple wine cellar is not enough to hold them."

Viola, who was in the front, eyeballed Aria with her golden inhuman eyes. The Dark Forces members were blocking the door, but as if Aria would leave. She wouldn't leave the place without her parents.

"Let's just get this over with." Kora raised her hands at chest level.

But Aria was quicker than she was. It was like a strong instinct, buried so deep inside of her that she didn't even know it existed. With all the might she could gather, she used a

Knockback Enchant against them. The force spread across the room, flinging every single one of the Dark Forces members off their feet, and they crashed to the floor. Her eyes widened and she looked down at her hands. A gasp caught in her throat at what she'd just managed to do, energy crackling through her veins. She snapped her attention back to the sight before her.

"Upstairs," she hurried to tell her friends before anyone could get back on their feet.

Together, they bounded up the steps two at a time.

"After them!" Kora shrieked furiously.

Aria reached the top of the stairs first and ran to the right, her friends following after her. Feet pounded up the stairs, the sound echoing off the old, dusty walls. She thought maybe she could lose the Dark Forces in the huge mansion and come back around to find her parents. She just hoped she wouldn't lose herself and her friends in the process. They turned the corner to head down a long hallway that grew pitch black at the end. A high-pitched scream rang out and Aria immediately spun around. One of Ebony's vines had caught Willow's leg and dragged her down to the ground. The Dark Forces members were crowding into the hallway, a fight breaking out between them and her friends.

Black flashed in the edges of Aria's vision. Something wrapped around her neck and tightened, putting her in a headlock.

"Stop fighting us and they won't get hurt," Kora's voice whispered in her ear. Her hushed voice sounded distant, soft, and evil like a ghost's, causing Aria's breath to shudder.

Her arms were pinned against Kora's body, just like Celaena had done. Aria knew better than to think what she was saying was true, but what if she did actually let them go? Kora's grip tightened as she thought about her options. Aria wished she would have just run away from her friends back at camp so they wouldn't be in danger. The thought of them getting hurt was like a knife wound to the heart. As she attempted to yank out of Kora's restraint, Luke was blown up against the wall and he fell to his knees. She tried to shout his name, but Kora's arm was too tight around her neck. Avi ran to help Luke while Willow fought Ebony, and Viola was nowhere to be seen. In the shadows several feet away, Kora had hidden her from her friends, so no one knew what was happening with her.

Aria was going to cave. She was going to break. She was going to listen to Kora.

No! You can't trust Kora, just like you can't trust Celaena, her conscience told her.

She didn't have to wonder where Celaena had learned it all from.

Just as Avi fell to the ground, Aria's eyes landed on an oversized, fancy painting of a forest to the right of the hall. She moved her hands around and directed them at the painting, feeling her heartbeat in her palms. The frame soared from the wall and hit Kora right in the face with a crack. Kora instantly let go and the massive painting fell on top of Aria. Quickly, she lifted it off of her, shoving it on top of Kora, whose nose was bleeding heavily. She threw Knockback Enchants left and right, causing one hooded member of the Dark Forces to fly up to the ceiling, then fall to the floor, unconscious. One of Ebony's vines caught her arm, harshly slamming her into the white wall. She tried to pull free of it, shaking her arm wildly, but it wouldn't budge. Grabbing the vine again, power surged up her veins and out through her palm came fire. Flames shot up the vine, turning to ash before it could sear her arm.

Luke was up against the wall ten feet away, fighting a Dark Forces member. He shot random enchantments left and right, but they kept dodging them. Aria jumped in front of him, putting her hands up to protect him from an oncoming enchantment. The blue ball of sparks flew right at Aria's chest, and she rapidly put up her hands to shield her face and torso, tightly closing her eyes. She expected some sort of pain or odd feeling, but all she felt was a rhythmical beat in her hands. Opening her eyes, she saw the ball of sparks hovering in front of her, as if blocked by an invisible shield. She moved her hands around the magic, holding it in her own, then threw it at the attacker. The hooded Dark Forces member fell to the ground and stayed motionless.

"How?" Luke asked, his eyes wide.

All Aria could do was shrug before something came out of the darkness and swept her off her feet in a flash. She hit the marble floor with a painful thud, her spine feeling bruised. Something sharp grabbed her ankle, pulling her on her back into the dark end of the corridor. She screamed as she disappeared into the pitch-blackness, the light getting farther and farther away.

"ARIA!" Luke's feet pounded against the marble as he sped after her.

Avi and Willow bolted after her, too, abandoning the fight. Kora pushed the painting off her, wiping blood from her nose before following them with hostility burning in her eyes, Ebony bringing up the rear.

Aria was in complete darkness, a stinging at her ankle as something cut into it. She flailed about on the slippery marble floor, her back sliding across it. Whatever had her foot released and she came to a halt. She jumped to her feet, only to be pushed back down by a strong, icy hand.

"Haven't you ever fought in the dark, Aria?" Viola's voice echoed off the walls. "I do it *all* the time."

Aria hastily stood back up, noticing a light coming from down the hall. The light was just a sliver slipping out from under a door. Pounding feet came toward Aria and the sound of chains jangling somewhere drifted to her ears. Someone ran right into her, grabbing her arm.

"Aria, is that you?" Luke's shaky voice asked.

"Yeah, but watch out—"

Two hands shoved her into the wall with a great amount of force, pinning her there for a moment.

Viola took in an inhale of the air before saying, "You know, Aria, vampires do not need to breathe, nor do our hearts beat… But that does not mean we do not smell what runs in…veins."

She let go and Aria fell to the ground, coughing. Luke's arms were around her in seconds, pulling her back onto her feet.

"Aria?" Willow and Avi's voices echoed off the empty walls.

"I'm here."

Viola's twisted laughs reverberated off the walls, sending shivers up Aria's spine.

"I heard chains clanging. I—I think my parents are in that room down there," Aria whispered, pointing to the sliver of light, but as if any of them could see in the dark.

"Um, which one?" Avi whispered.

"Follow me," Aria replied and grabbed Luke's soft hand.

She crept through the darkness, toward the light. Willow and Avi kept close behind to not get lost. Aria knew Viola was still there, probably watching and waiting for the perfect moment to strike. She shook from head to foot, her heart thumping extremely fast, as she stopped in front of the door.

She felt the door for the doorknob, clasped it, and turned it. Viola's laughs had faded away, leaving them in eerie silence. Aria opened the door and quickly pulled her friends in, then shut and locked the door just as Viola lunged at it. She turned around, tears swelling up in her eyes at the sight of them.

Her parents were both in metal chairs next to each other, just like the one Malus had trapped her in, but theirs were bolted to the floor and chains hung from them. Their eyes had dark bags, and tears, dirt, and dried blood covered their clothes. Their skin clung to their bones and their untidy hair was caked with grime. The shackles at their ankles and wrists had been cutting at their skin, leaving irritated, bloody flesh around it. They tried desperately to talk, but not a sound could escape their lips. It immediately made Aria think of the Zippity-Lips potion.

Around the room, which was very small, lay broken potion bottles and more chains. The walls and the wooden floor were cracking and the wallpaper was hanging off.

"Mom! Dad!" Aria exclaimed, tears pouring down her face. She ran the short distance to them, grabbing both of their cuffed hands. "I'm going to get you out of here."

She started looking for a lock on the shackles, not letting go of their hands as if they might disappear any second.

"Oh, darling, what have they done to you?" her mother asked, tears dripping down her face as she eyed Aria's wounds.

Aria's gaze snapped to her mother's, her eyes widening at the sound of her voice. More tears spilled down her cheeks; she hadn't heard her mother's voice in months. She opened her mouth to ask how she could hear her now, but her mother continued.

"I'm so sorry this is happening to you. I wish we could explain everything, but there is no time."

Behind Aria, Luke, Avi, and Willow looked at each other. Avi's eyebrow quirked up in a question and he opened his mouth to speak, but Willow put a finger to her mouth as if to say *"shh."*

"You won't be able to get us out of here." Her father's lips trembled and tears welled in his eyes. "Malus put a curse on the shackles so that only he could unlock them."

"Darling, you must take your friends and leave. Get to safety. Find the Death Stone and destroy it."

"What? How—" Aria interrupted, tears trailing down her rosy cheeks.

"And then you must destroy the Life Stone, which will destroy Malus—eventually," her mother continued. "You are what will truly destroy the Dark Forces, Aria. I wish it wasn't you and I wish you didn't have to find out like this, but you are the Diviner."

CHAPTER TWENTY

S HE WOULD HAVE been standing stiller than a brick wall had it not been for her trembling. Her, the Diviner? She couldn't be. After all, Avi and Willow agreed it was just a legend. She didn't understand. Her mind was spinning out of control. What had they done to her parents for them to think up such preposterous things? A part of Aria actually wanted to believe such a claim, but it was illogical.

"Me? No, I—I c-can't be," Aria stuttered. "I'm not. Enchanting Control, they said that—"

"I'm afraid you are. The Enchanting Control Testers never knew of you being the Diviner because we were the ones who tested you…And then we lied on the legal papers," her mother explained. "Now, Aria, you must listen to me. You must destroy the Death Stone. Destroying the Death Stone will allow you to use the Divining Powers. Only after you have destroyed the Death Stone can you do the same to the Life Stone. Malus is sure to have tested you by now, so he will know you are the Diviner. You are in mortal danger. He will want to use you."

"No, no—" Aria cried.

"Aria, listen," her mother said. "Once Malus finds a

way—and he will—to break the curse we put on ourselves, he will know that you are the one thing that can destroy the Life Stone, and with it, him. He will know that you are the only one powerful enough to destroy all of the Dark Forces."

"No, I'm not powerful," Aria stated. "I'm weak. I'm still new to magic."

"Please, Aria, please understand." Her father's voice sounded hoarse now as he pleaded. "You have to get out of here before he figures out how to break the curse."

"What curse?"

"We put many complex curses on ourselves so that nobody but you could hear us or read our minds—but you can only hear us when you are touching us," her mother told her. "It was the best we could do to protect the fact that you are the Diviner and what Malus wants most of all. Applying the curses to ourselves weakened us at first, so we were unable to fight back when the Dark Forces captured us."

"You have to go now," her father cut in, his eyes welling with tears.

"I—I—I c-can't leave you." Aria's face was flushed. "This isn't right! I'm not—That's all just a m-myth."

Luke, Avi, and Willow looked between Aria and her parents with confusion etched on each of their faces. Aria glanced at them, nearly having forgotten they were there.

"No, you are very much real," her mother said. "We wanted to tell you when you turned eighteen, hoping to keep you safe from the truth, but we were wrong. We had to keep moving to keep you safe from the Dark Forces. They were tracking us, wanting your father and I for that information. We should have told you a long time ago. Now save yourselves."

"I w-won't leave y-you." Tears poured down her face,

blurring her vision and making her eyes puffy. She wished she could wrap her arms around her parents and never let them go.

"You must," her father said.

"What if I n-never s-see you a-again?"

"You may not, but love endures. In your heart is where we will always be, and by your side, always watching over you." Her father forced a smile onto his face, his eyes soft. "We love you, and happy birthday."

Aria wiped her face of her tears and let go of their hands, slowly backing away toward the door. She could no longer hear what her parents were saying.

Avi raised his eyebrows at her. "Could you hear them?"

"Yeah, couldn't you?" Aria's voice broke on the words.

"No, what did they say?" Luke said.

Willow went to touch Aria's hands just as there was a pounding from the other side of the door. She moved her hands away. She didn't want any of them to know, not now. She would tell them her secret later.

"We have to go," Aria said, her body trembling. "We can't take them."

She looked back at her parents one last time with her teary eyes as if it would be the last she saw of them, before opening the door. Vines instantly shot out from the darkness, wrapping around their limbs and waists, and pulled them into the dark. They all let out a high-pitched screech.

The door slammed shut and the lights within the room went out, leaving them in the pitch-black. They slid on their backs down the marble, struggling against the vines. Aria heard shuffling and shouting, but it all seemed distant and inaudible. She couldn't stop hearing her mother's words repeating in her head. *'You are the Diviner.'* She felt a giant, twisting knot of guilt in her heart. It felt so wrong to be leaving them behind, now being dragged through a dark hallway wrapped in thick vines. She tried to fight against it, but she couldn't even see where anything was. There were loud grunts and shouts as Luke, Avi, and Willow tried to free themselves as well.

Light was approaching down the hall. She could now see the dark green vines that wound around her body, tying her legs together and her arms to her side. Ebony was ahead of them, strutting down the hall as her precious vines dragged them across the marble floor. Viola walked next to Aria, between her and Willow, staring at her and licking her lips hungrily. Aria glared at Viola, her stomach churning. Kora's heeled boots clacked on the marble floor behind them as she went on about something.

All Aria heard of Kora's ranting was, "Let's take them to Malus."

They were dragged down the hall, into the light coming through huge windows in the entrance hall, past the staircases leading downstairs, and down the corridor that led to Malus' office. The dark oak door was swiftly opened by the two hooded guards. Aria tried to break free of the vines again, but they just constricted tighter as she was pulled into the room. Malus stood from his desk at the sight of them, his hood on now.

"What is the meaning of this?" he asked, striding fleetly in front of his desk.

"They tried to escape, Master!" Kora said loudly, her voice ricocheting off the walls and causing the knives on them to rattle.

Despite Malus' face unseen under his hood, Aria could tell he was staring at her.

"What happened to her?" Malus asked, pointing his gloved finger at her.

"THAT BLOOD-SUCKING MONSTER ATTACKED

ME!" Aria shrieked, trying to tear away from the vines. Rage built up inside her like fire running through her veins.

Viola laughed maliciously, a wide, satisfied smile spreading across her face.

"Lock them back away where they can't escape," Malus commanded, waving them away.

"But, Master, they broke out so easily," Kora said. "What if, instead, we got the cursed chains?"

"Send my son to go fetch them then."

Kora rushed out of the room, looking annoyed.

"So, you tried leaving, Diviner?" Malus asked, taking off his hood.

Ebony gasped, her eyes wide.

Luke, Avi, and Willow's shocked eyes locked on Aria. She looked back at them, but only for a moment before glaring at Malus.

"What? Cat's got your tongue?" He laughed.

"Aria?" Luke asked, his eyes wide. "What's he talking about?"

When Aria didn't answer, Avi asked, "What does he mean 'Diviner?'"

"I'll explain later," Aria replied, looking at Malus with narrowed eyes. Her breathing came in rapidly and her fists tightened against the boiling fury.

Kora came running back into the room, panting. "What if we just took them there? To the underground mountain base in Hora? It would be a secure place to store her until you had the Death Stone."

Aria hated how they spoke about her like she was some object and not a human being.

"Fine, but I know very well that you just refuse to speak to my son," Malus said, taking a seat at his desk again. "Load them in the wagon and take them to the base in Hora."

Ebony's vines rose them into the air and they were pulled out of the room. Aria moved her hand around, trying to get enough space between her body and her hand so she could burn the vines, but they were too tight. Ebony, Kora, and Viola walked down the stairs. Aria's head hit the banister and she clanged into Luke.

"You're the Diviner?" Avi whispered. "Why didn't you tell us?"

"Not right now, Avi," Aria said softly through clenched teeth. "Try to burn your way out."

"I can't. I don't know how," he replied as they came to the wide front doors.

"Just focus. If I can do it, so can you."

"Easy for you to say—you're the Diviner."

The door opened and they were taken out into the gloomy, hidden sunlight. Aria guessed it was late evening by where the light shone brightest through the fog. The wagon was exactly where they had left it yesterday…or the day before. She had no idea what day it was exactly. It seemed like it had been forever in the Malamone Mansion.

Ebony brought them closer to the ground as her hand reached for the cage doors and the vines loosened a bit. Aria immediately was able to make a fire in the palm of her hand. She pressed the fire to the vines, burning a hole through them. Before the fire could burn her skin, she slipped out onto the brick courtyard. She quickly stood up, brushing off the pain, and shooting fire at the other vines restraining her friends. Luke, Avi, and Willow were released and fell to the ground with soft groans of pain when they made impact.

"YOU!" Viola shrieked, spinning around.

Aria took off running toward the fountain with wide, afraid eyes as Viola bolted after her. She stopped behind the crumbling fountain, hoping it could block her from Viola. Directly on the other side, Viola stood, staring at her with her white fangs exposed.

"You really are a clever girl, but obviously not clever enough," Viola said. She leapt over the huge fountain with one jump and pushed Aria to the ground.

Aria rolled and rolled before coming to a stop several feet from the wagon. Her head felt like one more blow would make it crack open. She was surprised it hadn't already. Her vision was foggy, little black specks crowding it, and everything moved in a dizzying blur. As she slowly turned over and got to her feet, almost tumbling over, she heard yells and sickening laughs from near the wagon. Viola grabbed her shoulder, starting to push her forward, and Aria kicked backwards into Viola's shin. She didn't budge. Aria made an abrupt turn and slid out of her grasp. Her nails sliced through Aria's t-shirt sleeve and scratched across her skin.

"You can try to, but you will never escape," Viola said.

"Actually, if we get into the technicalities, I already have twice now," Aria remarked.

Behind them, a battle was breaking out between her friends and the Dark Forces. A few other members of the Dark Forces had come through the mansion doors. Luke blasted Kora and Ebony off their feet, but then someone else hit him with a Knockback Enchant. Willow threw small cages, the size of pet carriers, out of wagons, directing them at the Dark Forces. Avi redirected an Immobile Enchantment at a hooded member of the Dark Forces, but they seemed to know how to counter them.

"What is it with you? Why do you want to attack me so much?"

Viola's attachment to Aria, her refusal to fight anyone else, was something Aria had noticed.

"You smell delectable. You humans like things like cake, don't you? Your blood kind of smells like that to me," Viola answered with hostility, making Aria gulp. "It's different. Something I've never smelled before…or tasted. I can smell the great amount of power that runs in your veins. I also hate you, for you are the Diviner. If you had never existed in the first place, my best friend would not have nearly died!"

"What are you talking about?" Aria asked with furrowed brows and backed into a wagon.

"It may not have been you, but if it was not for the Diviner, my friend would have never been betrayed!" Viola screeched.

"You're insane!" Aria slid against the wagon.

Viola went to grab her again, but Aria hastily ducked and dove out of the way. Crawling away from her and getting back on her feet, random questions began to roll into her head. What on earth was Viola talking about? Betrayal? What friend? Aria shook the unimportant questions from her mind and ran across the courtyard to help her friends fight back. Viola leapt at her like a nimble cat again, but fell onto the hard brick ground.

Aria blasted Kora away from Willow, who was leaning up against a wooden wagon full of small cages and bleeding from an arm wound. Kora fell with powerful force near the steps leading up to the mansion doors, grumbling in pain. As Aria hurried to Willow, she redirected an oncoming Immobile Enchantment of blue sparks back at Ebony. When Ebony fell motionless to the ground, her vines shriveled dead and turned a grayish green.

A wagon suddenly went up in a blaze several feet away, sending smoke up through the thick gloom and casting an orange glow on the area. Avi stared down at his hands with shock, a faint smirk on his face. Flames flickered in the palms of his hands, but then they were gone. Luke pushed the wagon with force and it went barreling toward a couple Dark Forces members.

There was a hissing noise coming from somewhere in all the commotion and fog. Everyone stopped to listen, the air becoming still. A black cat approached the broken fountain, hissing fiercely as it went. The cat was darker than the night sky, without a single other color protruding its coat except for its bright green eyes. It wore a fancy collar with a glowing white crystal hanging from it. Aria squinted, noticing how similar the crystal looked to the Life Stone.

"Twilight?" Willow asked with confusion, squinting at the cat as well.

It was like someone hit Aria in the head with a brick. How had she not figured it out sooner? How had she been so blind to it? Everything clicked in place in her head.

Her hands began to tremble, every moment in the past several months rushing back to her in a blur. Her voice shook with horror when she said, "No, Willow, it seems we've met the *real* Twilight. That's Malus."

CHAPTER TWENTY-ONE

I T WAS THE end of March, and Malus was sitting in his office, peering over his father's riddle to the Death Stone again. You would think after centuries of him looking at it, he would have given up, but he was determined to get what he wanted. Suddenly, the door burst open and his son, Seth Malamone, came rushing in.

Seth resembled his father in a way with the taper fade of blond hair and green eyes. His eyes were a more deluded green, though, which reminded Malus of his mother. Strange zigzags and runes shaved on the sides and back of his head gave him a bizarre appearance. Of course, he wore the same cloak all the Dark Forces wore, but his hood was down to reveal his outraged face.

"They are gone!" he shouted in irritation. "We went to their house, but they moved again!"

Malus let out a frustrated shout and pounded his fist on his desk.

"Find them again!" he demanded, grabbing at the Stone around his neck. "They know how to destroy the Life Stone!

This little thing keeps me from dying of natural causes, so I need to destroy what will destroy *it*!"

He waved his son away and Seth left. He was furious. For years, he had searched for the Cheslers, but they were always one step ahead of him. He had destroyed all the other leaders of the Forces of Light, but fifteen years ago, they appointed new ones. If he got the Cheslers and the information they had, the Forces of Light just might fall.

For several more days, Malus sat in his office reading and rereading the same lines of the riddle over and over again. It made no sense. It had never made any sense. There were parts of it that he felt like he had heard at some point in his long life, but he didn't know what any of it meant.

The door opened and Kora, Seth's ex-wife, came running into the room. He smiled a delighted smile when he looked up and saw her. Surely, she would have some better news on finding the Cheslers. She was better at her job than his own son, after all, which is why they had gotten divorced. Seth had been jealous—and still was—of how Malus thought of her over him, so Seth had turned on her, abandoning his five-year-old daughter at the time. Malus thought it was the worst decision his worthless son had ever made. He should have been in Celaena's life.

"Yes, Kora?" Malus asked, setting aside the riddle.

"Celaena has told me that there is a Chesler girl at her school," Kora informed. "The Cheslers must live close to the school then, because she isn't staying there."

"Very well, very well. Anything else?"

"She told me to mention that a girl named Willow, who happens to be friends with the Chesler girl, is adopting a cat over spring break. She thought that might be useful information because you like cats…She said she had an idea—"

"That is useless information!" Malus yelled. "Why would she think that is of any use? Leave me to think."

Kora left the room, leaving the mansion eerily silent, but that was exactly what Malus wanted. He tried to think up a plan, but the cat information kept interrupting his thoughts. He thought very highly of his granddaughter, Celaena, but what was she thinking sending him such ridiculousness? She was a smart girl with so much potential, who always saw the possibilities in things. She knew how to blend in with a crowd—if she wanted to—and get what she wanted. She was a quick thinker and could effortlessly come up with something out of almost nothing…

Wait…blend in with the crowd…Is that what the information was for? How very clever of her.

A heinous grin played at his lips as he understood why Celaena thought the information was useful. She thought he could become a cat so he could spy on the Chesler girl, find out her weaknesses, her abilities, and what she knew about the thing that would bring down him and his Dark Forces. If this Willow girl was such great friends with the Chesler girl, she would lead him straight to her, right? He could follow the Chesler girl home and easily get to her parents. How could the plan possibly fail?

Malus set out for the little pet shop in the town of Forest's Edge, which just so happened to be close to the school and the Willow girl's home. The shop didn't sell pets, but they had a small cat adoption filled with strays, adult cats, and kittens of all breeds and colors. He turned into a cat, just like he had when he was a young boy all those centuries ago, and hid behind a flowerpot, waiting for someone to open the door. The Life Stone around his neck shrunk and reformed into a fashionable collar.

Once he was in, he hurried to sneak into the cat adoption cages before someone could spot him. He had to wait for several days, eating cat food and sitting in a tiny cage. He grabbed at the bars with his paws many times, just to shake them out of frustration. He hated being locked in a cage, having to bow down to every human who was taller than him, but this was part of his and Celaena's plan, and he wouldn't mess it up.

Outside, the air grew cooler as the clock on the wall struck four o'clock. The bell above the glass door rang and a young, pretty, bushy fair-haired girl came into the store, looking at all the cats. The girl wore a gray backpack, so she had evidently just come from school. She grinned as she started talking to her mother about all the things she would do over the spring break.

"Willow," the girl's mother said, pointing to a black, white, and brown spotted cat. "What about this one? You could name it S'more."

"No, I want to name my cat after something to do with the night sky since I'm studying astronomy," the girl replied.

"Right, well maybe you'll be an astronaut."

"No, studying is just a hobby."

Oh, great, the kid's a smarty pants, Malus thought, sighing. The sound came out more of a hiss though. He needed to get the girl's attention before she picked a different cat and left without him. Sticking his paws through the bars, he meowed and instantly caught attention from several people in the small shop.

"Aw, mom, I want that one." The girl pointed at Malus. "He looks like a starless sky."

That was the moment he took on the identity of Twilight.

Malus had to spend only a few minutes at the girl's house being a pampered cat before he saw Miranda and Oliver Chesler being escorted past the house in a police vehicle. He disappeared for several hours while he sent Kora, Ebony, and Chad, his best of the best, to capture Miranda and Oliver Chesler. That night, they had blasted through a hole in the police station and taken them with ease.

For the next day, he watched the girl study, practice magic, and talk endlessly about how she liked this guy named Avi, and how she can't wait until spring break was over so she can see her friends again. He knew he could leave, but he wanted their daughter as well, so he stayed.

With the Cheslers locked away in his mansion, he snuck away from the girl's house to interrogate them. When he returned to the Willow girl's home, he was beyond furious. The Cheslers had cursed themselves, so he was unable to get the information he needed. Outside the girl's window, he heard cops shouting someone's name as they bolted down the sidewalk, but from inside it was inaudible.

Finally, after several days, Willow got dropped off at school to stay there for the rest of the semester because of her mother and brother going on an important health trip, and she took him with her. He was able to see the Chesler girl for the first time and found out her name was Aria. Of course, he'd known the Cheslers had a daughter the whole time he'd been hunting them down, but never knew anything about her. He also found out that she had known nothing about magic all her life, which to him was very peculiar.

What a fool! How can someone not know of the gift they were born with?

As the weeks passed, he kept attacking her, acting like he was just being playful, since being a cat was boring. He snuck away many times to his mansion, where still no enchantment or potion could make her parents talk. Ciaus, a skilled potion master and Mind-reader, could not even penetrate their thoughts.

So, Malus continued to spy on Aria Chesler for the next couple of months. She had gotten detention for using a potion on Celaena, so he devised a plan to kidnap her while she was alone in the corridors. He got her kicked out of detention by a grumpy teacher named Mr. Monroy and tried to take her then. The girl, however, ran off to her room before he got the chance to smuggle her out.

It was a terrible plan, anyway, he told himself when the Chesler girl shut her bedroom door in his face.

He didn't want to create a commotion, so he left it at that and went back to Willow's room.

The school year came to an end and still he hadn't gotten an ounce of information out of any of the Cheslers. The camp bus would pick the teens up soon, and Malus had a brand-new plan. He sat next to Willow on the bus seat while she rubbed his head, which was strangely enjoyable. Several slow hours passed before the plan fell into place. Just as he'd intended, his son stopped the bus and mysteriously disappeared into the woods. Ebony, the best Nature-manipulator he knew, tossed a giant boulder at the bus, and several members of his Dark Forces kept it rocking back and forth. Malus snuck out a window, landing on the ground with a wave of shock through his feline legs, and ran into the forest where his son was hiding. He knew he could easily take the Chesler girl and go, but that would be all too obvious, and the Forces of Light would be sent after him.

"Stop! We lost our chance. They won't stop the bus to make sure everyone is all right like I thought they would. It was a horrible plan, but I have a better one," Malus said to Seth in his human form.

The bus stopped tipping back and forth, and Malus teleported to the camp, risking the serious injuries he could get from teleporting to an unknown place. Later that night, the bus arrived, and Willow took him to her cabin, overjoyed that he was okay. What she did not know, though, was he'd stolen her schedule and was waiting patiently for her to realize it was gone. Another part of his grand plan. This one would work; he was sure of it. Aria stepped into the cabin just as Willow had to hurry off to get a new schedule, leaving her alone, far away from everyone. Earlier, when Celaena had gotten off the bus, Malus had told her the plan and what she would do to help.

"I would be delighted," she'd said, a nasty grin sweeping across her face.

Celaena's arm wrapped around Aria's neck tightly, putting her in a headlock and pinning her arms. Malus jumped from Willow's bed, ready to smuggle the girl out of the camp with Celaena's help. He was just about to change into human form when the girl made a blanket fly from one of the beds up at Celaena's head and she immediately let go. He hadn't anticipated the girl would know how to defend herself at all with how little she knew of magic. He lunged at her, but she stepped out of the way and the door opened. His chance was over.

The next day, he heard the girl and her friends talking about brewing a Tracking Potion for Celaena to take. Celaena wouldn't be leaving the camp, though, so why not let them use it on someone else? And so, he snuck away to his mansion to tell the Dark Forces to attack the camp in eleven days and told Celaena to stay out of the way when it happened. With so many children at camp, he knew the Forces of Light would worry more about protecting them than stopping the Dark Forces. This plan would be the one to work, for he had a plan B.

Ten days passed, and the fight broke out in the camp with screams and booming sirens. He watched from the shadows as his own Forces failed to capture a fourteen-year-old. He could tell they were barely trying. Kora almost had the girl, but then Luke blasted her off her feet, and she fell unconscious.

Meddling children! Malus thought heatedly.

However, what he'd hoped would happen did happen. Luke had given her the potion, which would lead the children right into his clutches.

As soon as Kora woke, he jumped out and hissed. "Go! You lost your chance to get her. You know plan B. The girl and her friends will follow."

And so, they did.

CHAPTER TWENTY-TWO

EVERYONE IN THE courtyard remained still, Kora nodding at the Dark Forces members as if having a silent conversation. Meanwhile, Aria was confused, looking left and right to figure out what was happening. Luke and Avi were standing next to a wagon, watching the black cat in awe and squinting their eyes at it.

"It can't be!" Willow exclaimed.

"Yes, Willow, it is," Aria said, grabbing Willow's wrist and dragging her over to Luke and Avi. "Guys!" She glanced back at the distracted Dark Forces. "That's Malus."

"What?" Avi's eyes grew wide with terror. "You mean the cat?"

"It can't be because that's my cat!" Willow stated in a high-pitched voice, stomping her foot. She looked on the verge of tears.

"That cat isn't Twilight, it's Malus," Aria said. "He must be a Shape-shifter. Think about it. It all makes sense."

"I knew the saying was true! Never let a black cat cross your path," Avi muttered.

They watched as the cat leapt from the fountain and ran back inside the mansion, ending his hissing charade. At that moment, an amazing, but risky, dangerous idea suddenly occurred to Aria. One that would benefit all of the realms.

"I have an idea!" Aria whispered to her friends. "Don't follow me."

She turned around and grabbed one of the small pet carrier size cages that were piled up in the wagon behind her. Then she took off toward the mansion doors, up the cracking marble steps two at a time to catch up to the cat.

"Aria, why are we going back into the mansion?" Luke asked urgently as he hurried behind her.

"What? I said not to follow me!" Aria raced through the entrance hall.

"As if that's gonna stop us."

Strangely enough, the Dark Forces outside didn't follow them.

"Shouldn't we be leaving instead of following a murderous psycho?" Avi asked, pointing back through the doors.

"Avi, just trust her," Willow said as she sprinted after Aria as well.

They ran past the staircases and turned down a corridor that faded into darkness. Aria saw Malus, still in cat form, disappear into the dark just as the lighting started to dissipate. She knew how unsafe it would be to step into the pitch-blackness, but she did it anyway. A pit opened in her stomach and her hands grew clammy. If she could just get Malus alone in cat form…

"Aria, have you ever watched those movies where people idiotically step into dark hallways to follow after an evil person?" Avi asked softly as they followed behind her.

"What?" Aria whispered back. "What does that have to do with *anything*?"

"Because that's what we're doing right now!" Avi said. "And the people in those movies usually *die*!"

"Shh!" Aria told him and he kept quiet.

A faint hissing came from down the hall, so she hurried up, feeling the wall to her left. Soft footsteps hit the marble floor as her friends followed behind her. A white luster rose into the air and turned around the corner. She ran after it, turning down another hallway, having to shield her eyes at the sudden glow. Light poured through a window, illuminating a section of the hallway. Malus was waiting next to the window, the curtains swinging from being flung open. He was in human form, his hood on, and his arms crossed, as if waiting for the four of them.

At first, she was petrified, but then an instinct came naturally into the palm of her hands like the pulse of her heart. There was a feeling inside her, begging for her to use it to her advantage. Focusing her strength with ease, she effortlessly created a ball of blue sparks in her hands. She shot the Immobile Enchantment at Malus, but he stepped out of the way and it missed.

Aria eyeballed the glowing white Life Stone around his neck. She had to grab it and destroy it, just like her parents had said. Closing her eyes and focusing, a strong force pushed from her hand toward Malus. He fell to his feet and Luke quickly grabbed his arms, stepping on them. Swearing, Malus pushed Luke off of him and he slammed into the ground. Aria leapt forward, wrapping her fingers around the Life Stone, and ripped it from his neck. The Stone was frigid, pulsing like an evil, twisted heart, and oddly made her feel lightheaded. Aria pulled her gaze away from the Stone. As Malus jumped back to his feet, he stumbled backward, hitting the wall, and clutched where his heart was. His eyes went wide and he reached for the Stone in Aria's hand, but then lost his footing and hit the opposite wall. A gasp escaped his lips and he twisted his hands in front of him, his sharp jaw clenched tight. The feel of the air suddenly shifted and the dim lighting faded away. Malus' bright green eyes stood out through the fog that was filling the hall and surrounding him. The Black Smoke put the hallway in complete darkness and it shot toward Aria.

Aria's heart raced as the darkness surrounded her, wrapping around her ankles and tightening like a rope. She stuck her hands out and grasped the fog, separating it and shooting it back at Malus. It wrapped around him like a coil as he fought to get a grasp on it again. There was a thud and a grunt. Light shot through the hallway again as the smoke blinded Malus. He shrunk back into cat form, disoriented, and ran, his black fur getting lost in the darkness.

"Are you okay?" Aria asked Luke as he got back to his feet, tossing the cage to him.

"Yeah."

"You have the Life Stone…You're the Diviner," Avi said breathlessly, looking like he might faint. "None of this makes any sense."

"Yeah, I know." Aria shoved the Stone in the back pocket of her jean shorts. "But we're going to trap Malus as a cat…At least, that's my plan."

"How? He can just teleport out of this little cage," Luke said.

"No, he can't," Willow replied. "He has to cross his arms to teleport."

"And…he can't do that if he's a cat," Avi caught on.

"Let's do it," Luke said.

They crept back down the corridor, disappearing back into the dark and feeling the walls as they went. Malus was nowhere to be heard or seen, not even when they turned the corner and oil lamps were turned on. Aria and her friends stayed quiet just in case Malus was somewhere, waiting to jump out when he heard them approaching. They walked sneakily into the entrance hall where Malus laid lazily in cat form at the foot of one of the staircases.

Aria motioned for Luke, Avi, and Willow to slink up to him with her. The cat promptly stood up and bolted up the stairs, meowing. They jumped over every other step as they sprinted after him. The cat ran down the hall to the left, looking like a petrified little kitty. Following him, they raced across the slippery marble floor and almost slipped as they did. As they ran past his office, he disappeared into an opened room. Aria, Luke, Avi, and Willow gathered in the room, but it was empty except for two other doors, one of them cracked open. Aria wrenched open the cracked door and dashed into the bedroom.

There was a velvet carpet and a rich-looking four-poster bed with intricate designs carved into it. Everything was covered in a thick layer of dust and the air smelled rusty, like everything in the room was slowly decaying. Aria ran to the closet door at the back of the room and tore it open. Inside was nothing but bunches of spiders and old, unsent letters. Luke opened the door that stood several feet in front of the bed.

"It's another hallway." He pointed through the door.

"Wow, this place is like a maze. How could someone possibly live here?" Avi asked. "Can we go now?"

"No." Aria peered out into the discovered hallway. "We have to trap Malus first, so he can't hurt anyone anymore."

She jogged down the corridor, her heart pounding fiercely. At the end of the hall, Malus rounded the corner in cat form. They raced after him all the way back down the hall and down the stairs. In the entrance hall, Willow dove to grab him, but he rolled out of the way and through the open doors. They rushed down the marble steps, into the gloom, to discover the Dark Forces were all gone. The courtyard was empty except for

Malus and the many, many wagons. Where had the Dark Forces gone? It was a mystery that would have to wait.

They ran to the fountain, where Malus cowered inside. Rats screeched and hissed at him as they feasted on the rancid solution sitting in the fountain.

"Open the cage!" Aria told Luke.

He pulled it open as Aria quickly grabbed Malus up in her hands and shoved him into the cramped cage. Malus hissed and meowed continuously, looking defeated as Luke shut and locked it.

"Not so tough now, are you?" Aria jeered.

Malus only meowed again.

"That's what I thought." She crossed her arms against the chill of the fog.

They were all alone outside, the air quiet and moist with mist. They could run. They could escape and be free. It felt too easy to her, but as if she wanted to go looking for more trouble. She had to leave and listen to what her parents had said.

"Let's go…We'll take him to…uh…Mrs. Mckinney. She'll know what to do with him," Aria said. "Teleport?"

They grabbed each other's hands as Malus attacked the bars with his feline fangs. Luke held the cage with one hand as he gripped Aria's with the other. She closed her eyes, expecting to feel herself launch across the space between the realms, but her feet remained on the brick ground.

Her eyes flew open to see that she was still at the Malamone Mansion, her friends right next to her.

"Why's it not working?" Fear flickered in her eyes, her brows furrowed.

"I don't know. Willow?" Avi looked to Willow for an explanation.

They released each other's hands.

"It's clearly because of an Anti-teleportation Charm," Willow said as she shook her head. "We need to get off the property quickly before they realize we're getting away."

"Where do you think the property ends?" Luke asked.

"Remember that tall, black gate when we arrived?" Willow pointed down the road. "I bet it ends there."

"Then let's go!" Avi said and began sprinting through the fog.

Luke, Aria, and Willow rushed after him, calling his name, and telling him to stop, but he was already unable to be seen through the thick gloom. They passed the rusty metal gate, which creepily creaked as a breeze blew past it. Luke ran right into Avi, nearly knocking him to the ground.

"Ouch," Avi murmured.

"Dude, don't go running off like that!" Luke half-shouted. "The Dark Forces could be anywhere!"

"Sorry," he muttered.

Luke shot him a glare.

"Now, let's go," Aria cut in, taking Luke's hand in hers, which instantly made him pay attention.

Malus hissed savagely from inside the cage as they clasped hands again. Moments after Aria closed her eyes, she lurched upward and felt herself being lightly set back down on softer ground. Guilt knotted up in her chest again when she opened her eyes to see the camp she'd left about a week ago. She wished she hadn't left her parents back at the mansion, but she had no idea how to make Malus free them. She hoped with all her heart that Mrs. Mckinney would know how.

People's eyes locked on them just outside the camp office, which was still a pile of demolished walls and roof. Mrs. Mckinney's mouth moved, but she seemed unable to get the words out until she came to stand right in front of them.

"We have been searching for you children for a week!" Mrs. Mckinney shrieked, then pointed to Willow and Luke. "We had to call your parents! Where have you been? What happened to you? Why on earth are you carrying a caged cat?" She waved over a group of Healers who were watching from a tent. "Healers, fix them up, please."

Several Healers gathered around them, inspecting their wounds and sliding their hands over every single one. One at a time, the ripped-up pieces of Aria's jacket were taken off, showing the gruesome punctures beneath. Tears formed in her eyes while the skin burned and itched as it regrew, leaving not a single scar behind. She bit her lip and took the cage out of Luke's hands to hand to Mrs. Mckinney.

"This is Malus Malamone," Aria said. "He's a Shape-shifter. He kidnapped us, but we caught him."

"W-what?" Mrs. Mckinney looked like she might faint.

"This is Malus Malamone," she repeated, sighing. "He has been spying on us all these months as a cat. We captured him."

Mrs. Mckinney stared at the caged cat hissing and displaying its fangs. "Are you one hundred percent sure? He's a powerful enchanter. No one has ever caught him."

"We chased him down ourselves," Aria assured.

"Okay then…I will take him to Enchanting Control. You four get fed and hydrated, but when I get back, I want you to tell me *everything*. Dinner was just finished being served, but the cooking staff will feed you," Mrs. Mckinney told them.

She stepped away from them, forcing a slight smile onto her face, before setting the cage down on the ground. As soon as she tapped the cage twice with her fingers, it disappeared from thin air. With her arms crossed, she vanished as well, leaving Aria and her friends near the office.

CHAPTER TWENTY-THREE

FOR TWO HOURS, they sat in the otherwise empty mess hall with platefuls of food, explaining to Mrs. Mckinney all they had done and what had happened to them…except that Aria had the Life Stone and that she was the Diviner. By the end, Mrs. Mckinney was crying, hugging them, and saying how sorry she was that they had been traumatized like that. Aria could tell she was being genuine. Then Willow burst into tears.

They walked away from the mess hall to get some fresh air and talk in private soon after. People had started to gather in the mess hall for bedtime and they didn't want to be heard. They wandered down the lonely paths, subconsciously walking in the direction of the large oak tree behind cabin number eighteen.

"Why didn't you tell Mrs. Mckinney, you know—" Avi asked Aria, then made his voice softer. "—That you're the Diviner and that you have the Life Stone?"

Aria felt in the back pocket of her jean shorts just to make sure it was still there.

"Because I'm the Diviner and I'm supposed to destroy that

thing. She would confiscate it, deem it unsafe for me to have. I can't let it fall into the wrong hands."

They sat down behind the oak tree, relaxing and taking in the fresh air for a moment. The potion must have been discovered since it was missing. The wind rustled through the dark treetops and blew over Aria's sticky, sweating skin. The cool breeze felt nice after such a long day of battling and torture. She lifted her chin, soaking in the feeling and trying not to think.

"Did you know you were the Diviner?" Luke asked abruptly.

Willow, of course, already knew the answer to that having read Aria's mind so many times without permission.

"No, that's what my parents told me back at the mansion," Aria answered, looking off into the distance. Her mother and father's words echoed through her head, and tears began to stream down her cheeks again. The image of them in chains was stained on her mind, pulling on her heart. "I am the one thing that can destroy the Life and Death Stones, and with them, the Dark Forces will fall. At least, that's what my mom and dad said. I am the only one who is powerful enough to take them down."

"Wait, what?" Avi's jaw dropped.

"Yeah…And speaking of the Life Stone, I shouldn't be the one to have it." She pulled the Stone out from her back pocket. It was still cold and pulsing. She could feel the evil that lurked inside it as if it was calling her to use it. It was an easy call to ignore though.

"What are you talking about?" Willow asked. "You have to destroy it!"

"I may be the Diviner because the magic runs in my veins, but I don't have the powers to destroy it yet," Aria replied. "I can't be the true Diviner until I destroy the Death Stone."

"But it's lost," Avi reminded her. "Nobody has ever found it."

"I'll have to find it then. My parents depend on me doing so, which means I won't give up no matter what. Then I'll break it to smithereens. But before I can do that, I need to ask you guys to do something I would never ask someone to do."

"What?" they asked in unison.

"I need one of you to take the Stone. Keep it. Hide it. I just can't know where it is until the right moment." She turned the Stone over in her hands, her mind feeling dizzy.

"Why?" Avi asked.

"Because I'm the one they want. Once they find out I took the Life Stone and captured Malus, they will have three reasons to come after me—and they will. I can't let them get the Stone," Aria explained. "When and if they get me, they can read my mind or torture it out of me to find out where it is. I can't have it on me and I can't know where it is…But whoever takes it will be in danger."

"I'll take it," Luke volunteered.

She handed it to him, tears swelling up in her eyes as she said, "I can't thank you enough." She leaned into him, giving him a hug and resting her head on his shoulder. For several minutes, she didn't move, her arms wrapped around his well-built figure as tears dripped onto his shirt. He didn't pull away, but instead wrapped his arms around her in a comforting way. When she straightened herself back up and let go, she looked around at all of them. "I can't thank any of you enough."

The next couple minutes were spent in silence, no one sure of what to say, so they just stared at each other. In the silence, everything that had happened played over in Aria's mind like knives to the heart.

"I can't believe you're the Diviner," Avi said in awe, breaking the peace. "I thought you were just a myth."

"Well…I wish I was a myth," Aria said, wiping tears from

her eyes. "But I was obviously put in this world for a reason and I must embrace that. This battle isn't over yet."

The next day, Mrs. Mckinney woke them up early in the mess hall. Aria looked forward to more water and food; it did not seem like enough anymore. She refused to get up, cuddling against all the pillows and blankets she could ask for. Her wounds may have been healed, but she felt as if her mind would never be healed fully. Mrs. Mckinney had to carefully drag her to her feet and bring her food so that she would wake up enough to get ready. They were to attend a court meeting about Malus at the Enchanting Control Office at about noon, which was considered of utmost importance.

After they ate, Aria and Willow got ready in their cabin, where Celaena luckily was not. In fact, she hadn't seen Celaena at all since their return the night before.

All four of them met Mrs. Mckinney in front of the demolished office after getting showered and dressed. She was dressed formally in a gray pantsuit, whereas the rest of them wore casual clothes.

"Everyone hold hands," Mrs. Mckinney instructed.

Aria yawned, still extremely tired, but she grabbed hands with them without complaint. Seconds later, they were whisked away and their feet landed on a wood plank floor.

She opened her eyes, taking in the stunning marble walls with gold flecks embedded in them. Large windows with blue curtains looked out to a massive, beautiful city of marble and white stone. A massive, tall tower of marble and gold rose above all the other buildings in the center of the city. Flowerpots hung from the buildings outside with people in rich-looking but unusual clothing bustling around everywhere. Aria gasped in awe at the gorgeous, breathtaking sight.

"Welcome to Viden, children," Mrs. Mckinney said with a smile. "It's the biggest, richest city in all of the Vezchia Realm."

In front of them was a lengthy, grand desk with many people in blue cloaks and a golden pegasus embroidered on their breasts. They followed Mrs. Mckinney up to the desk and she began talking to someone, but Aria wasn't looking or paying attention. She watched all the people that were hurrying about the massive room, carrying stacks of important papers. She stared up at the towering dome ceiling where rows of filing cabinets floated in the air. People in blue cloaks pulled a filing cabinet down with magic, put some papers away, and sent them back up.

Well, that's an odd way of organizing, Aria thought, and her eyes met Luke's.

Heat rose into her face and she rapidly turned back to the desk. Without even realizing it, her feet followed Mrs. Mckinney down a brightly lit hall to a rectangular room full of people.

In the middle of the marble-walled room, behind a tall, raised podium of smooth white stone, a man stood. The thin man towered over the podium, a creepy smirk spread across his shiny, bald head. His lavender eyes met Aria's briefly before turning to look at the rows of people on benches. Behind and to the sides of the podium, people in suits and dresses whispered anxiously to each other. In front of the podium, a heavy, bulky, metal chair was bolted to the ground. Chains hung from the chair, reminding Aria of the chairs her parents were shackled to. She blinked away the tears that threatened to spill out of her eyes and took in a big inhale. Instead of a person in the chair, however, there was a cage, and in that cage was Malus still in cat form. Aria's eyes pinned to him as Mrs. Mckinney led them to the front row of dark, wooden benches to sit.

A wooden fence made of dark oak closed off the rest of the room from Malus and the judge, the bald man. Aria's heart rate quickened as she watched Malus relaxing in the cage as if this trial meant nothing. It was great to see Malus behind bars, but it was hard to believe a man that powerful, a man that had caused her all that pain, a man that still had her parents locked away, was incapable of breaking free. What if he broke out now? Aria couldn't take her eyes off him no matter how much she assured herself in her head that she was safe. She tuned out the noise as the judge began to talk, putting all her focus on Malus and on trying to calm herself down. *I'm being crazy*, she told herself. *He can't break out. We're safe.*

"Defendant, Malus Malamone is found guilty of murder, child abuse, child endangerment, theft, kidnapping, um… arson…" the judge listed, drawing Aria's attention to him. "Use of the black market, also known as the black trade…Um, I'm going to stop there because the list goes on, but Malus is found guilty and that is what matters. He is to be sent to Hot Rock Top Security Prison."

"Excuse me, Your Honor, but this supposed Malus has not even said a word in his defense and you want to send him to a volcano?" a short sandy-haired woman piped in. The dress she was wearing was so black it looked like obsidian.

"This is Malus we're talking about!" Aria shouted unexpectedly, then immediately wanted to shove every word back into her mouth.

Luke looked at her like she'd made a huge mistake.

"Young lady, there is no proof that this is Malus Malamone," the woman said, standing up as if to make herself seem superior.

Aria stood up, too, not caring anymore. "No proof? My friends and I were at his mansion and managed to capture him!"

"As if I would believe the words of some fourteen-year-old," the woman scoffed.

"I'm fifteen, actually," Aria said, but so quietly that no one but the people next to her heard.

"Your Honor, Aria, Luke, Avi, and Willow have all been there. They speak the truth. This is indeed Malus Malamone." Mrs. Mckinney rose to her feet.

Aria sat down, shifting in her seat and tracing the petals of her sunflower necklace.

"Yes, I know," the judge said. "I believe this to be Malus. We ran DNA tests. We do not wish to make him transform, however, because it is much easier to deal with a cat than a full-grown, many centuries old man."

"Thank you, Your Honor." Mrs. Mckinney sat back down, dusting her pantsuit off.

People seemed to be gathering their things up to leave now and whispers began to spread through the room.

"Wait, Mrs. Mckinney," Aria asked. "What about my parents? They're going to rescue them, aren't they?"

"Did you not hear? The judge said Enchanting Control will be in contact with the Forces of Light to arrange a rescue mission," Mrs. Mckinney replied.

"When? Soon? How?"

"Aria, relax. They will figure it out," Mrs. Mckinney said.

Aria felt quite defeated and insignificant leaving the Enchanting Control building ten minutes later. Not only that, but she felt she'd just witnessed the most pointless thing in history. Why would they need to hold a trial for Malus Malamone of all people? She looked out the windows to the gorgeous city beyond as they were led back into the massive, domed lobby. She wished she could enter the city to look around but didn't want to say a word, feeling she was now incapable of speaking up for herself. Even though she was fifteen and telling the truth, that woman made her feel like a silly, dishonest '*fourteen-year-old girl.*'

They held each other's hands, and before they were dragged through the space between realms and places, Aria's eyes met Luke's again. She felt butterflies mix with the weird sensation of teleporting, but this time she knew the butterflies had a reason. She finally understood the reason for that feeling as she studied Luke's gorgeous ocean-blue eyes. A question arose in her head and she thought maybe they could be more than friends. As she was teleported, she kept her eyes open by accident, thinking, *I can't believe it. I like Luke.*

A Letter to the Reader

Words alone cannot capture how grateful I am that you decided to pick up my debut novel, and words are said to be one of the most powerful things out there. Since I was nine, I wanted to write stories set in a fantasy world, where the characters had to find hope, light, and friendship despite being surrounded by darkness and evil. I was a child with a big imagination, so big that I am quite surprised all the worlds I made managed to fit in my head. I wrote story after story for years, dreaming that one day I'd become an author. And because of readers like you, I now get to share my stories. I'm so thankful for your commitment to the characters of The Great Diviner Series and their adventures, and I hope you'll stick around for the rest of it. Now before you go…Can I ask a favor? As I said, words are one of the most powerful things out there, so would you do me the kindness of reviewing my book on Amazon and/or Goodreads? Word of mouth, reviews, and shares on social media are three powerful ways to get my book in the hands of new readers who will love it.

And while you're at it, make sure to join the newsletter so you don't miss Aria's next adventure!

aaralynnkarman.com

Have a great day!
Aaralynn K.

ACKNOWLEDGEMENTS

Wait, is this even real?! I've dreamed of this for so long, but almost every story I've written got shelved and forgotten. When I finally thought my writing was good enough, I would ditch the idea. I would believe in myself…and then I wouldn't. Meeting Twilight *wasn't the first book I thought could be published, but it was the first one that was. And in a way, all the others before it are now published, too, because* Meeting Twilight *has aspects of each one. Dreams are a scary thing to chase, but in the end, it's all worth it. Without the amazing people who kept me going, I wouldn't have reached this book's publication. So, without further ado…*

Firstly, thanks be to the wonderful Lord—for helping me through this whole scary, amazing process. He put writing and story-telling in my heart before I was even born. He helped me push through all the tough times where Imposter Syndrome got me down, and gave me the fantastic people who lifted me up. In fact, during the process of editing, my Google Drive crashed and I lost my entire manuscript. Luckily, I had printed it out, but I had to type it all back up again. I was really depressed and thought I should just quit, but the wonderful Lord brought me out of that. He helped me realize this dream is worth fighting for. Whether it was strength, hope, or faith that I needed, He provided it to help me push through to the finish line. He never failed me and helped me through the process of creating this story of love and hope.

*To my amazing parents, Heather and Jason—for always supporting me and believing in me. This book would not be here without all your help and support. You both helped me to market, create my website, give constructive criticism, help me figure out what I needed to do, and listen to me when I needed someone to. I am so very grateful for everything you have done for me. I would have given up on my dreams if I didn't have you guys. If it wasn't for you, Dad, chasing me around the house, pretending I was a "Starlit" when I was little, my imagination may have disappeared. If it wasn't for you, Mom, I would not have thought I could do this. I wouldn't even know how to do this. I am beyond grateful for both of you and everything you've done to bring me to where I am today. *Cue the emotional tears* You guys are the ones who taught me to be strong and reach for the stars.*

To my siblings: Piper, Lorelei, Eloise, Hudson, and Quinn—for listening to me talk on and on about writing this book, even though most of you didn't understand much because you were so young. Piper, I am so grateful that you helped me build this story from the ground up. You sat there on the floor of our bedroom, helping me to create characters before the story had truly formed in my head. You listened to me the most when I was writing or editing and in need of someone to talk to about my book (and I bet I got pretty annoying at times LOL.) And thank you, Piper, so much for being the first person to ever read this book and for managing to get through the crazy first draft of it. Without you telling me I needed to publish this and stop giving up, I probably wouldn't have. Hudson, Eloise, and Lorelei, thank you for showing interest and asking me to read this book to you—or as you guys called it, the "Applesauce Book" LOL. All your love gave me the strength to keep pushing on. Thank you for loving all the stories I've written

*over the years. I write for you guys, to give you stories that will
teach you to stay strong, keep going, and have hope.*

*To my Meme and Pap: Marianne and Ronald Chambers—for
always supporting me through every new idea and for reading my
stories. The times we shared talking together on the balcony are
some of my favorites. I love sharing my stories with you guys and I
am so grateful you have been supportive of every single one—even*
Cowgirl and Majesty *(and yes, it does say Willow wrote that in
this book LOL.) That book is what sparked this dream of mine.
Pap, even though you are not here today to see all my hard work
come together, I know you are looking down on me. You always
wanted me to reach for the stars and make my dreams come true,
and it hurts that you're not here to see it happen. XOXO.*

*To my Grandma, Papa, and Grandpa: Susan and Patrick Hen-
nesey, and Russell Karman—for all the love and care you showed
throughout this crazy process. The reminders that I'm doing great, I
just got to keep going, helped fuel me. In the times where I doubted
myself, your words of encouragement and questions about* Meeting
Twilight *helped to keep me going. My necklace of* Meeting Twilight *is one I'll cherish forever. I'm so thankful for each one of you.*

*To my dear friends—for being such great friends and for believing
I could be an author. Thank you for listening to me talk on and
on about this book, my plans for it, and for always telling me how
amazing that is. I loved our little book club and the meetings we
got to have. It really lifts me up to have such great friends supporting me every step of the way.*

*To my beta readers: Emily, Marie, Jacie, and Piper—for being so
encouraging, kind, and giving feedback during that early, scary*

stage of writing. I was so nervous sharing this book with people, but you guys made this journey feel even more worth it. The book was pretty rough at the time, but you guys enjoyed it and gave me amazing feedback to help me make it even better. Who knew people would show so much love for this book! Thank you so much for playing such a big role in helping me get here!

To Cheyenne Nielsen—for all the encouragement, sweet words, and for editing my book to bring it to where it is now. All of the support and kind words helped me to finish the book in those last stages. Without your help, this wouldn't have been possible. I'm so excited to dive into book two with you!

To my author/bookstagram friends—for all the excitement and encouragement, every like, share, comment, and save. Y'all are the best! I am so grateful for every one of you. I am glad I found this amazing community that cheers me on, and that I can cheer on as well.

About the Author

All of Aaralynn's life, she's had a strong passion for music, but at nine years old, writing entered her life, and a new dream was born. Ever since then, she has been writing stories, and obsessing about the ones she reads, too. Inspired by the imaginative world she created as a small child, Aaralynn often writes of magic, adventure, friendship, and finding the light in a world of darkness. When not typing away on her laptop, you can find her juggling a bajillion art projects (like painting, drawing, and illustrating children's books), taking care of her hamsters and bunnies, or hanging out with her large family in Southeastern Michigan.

Aaralynn wrote *Meeting Twilight* at fourteen years old and published it at fifteen, making it her debut novel.

aaralynnkarman.com

IG: aaralynnkarman.writes